For Harriette an
Best wish

Hilda R. Grun—
Queensbury, NY
Nov. 7, 2006

MW01602998

Saint-Boniface and Its Jews

A Novel By

Nathalie and Ladislas Gara

Translated by Jacques and Hilda R. Grunblatt
copr. 1990 Hilda R. Grunblatt

Translated from Saint-Boniface et ses Juifs published
by Editions du Bateau Ivre 1947

Published by

MELROSE BOOKS

An Imprint of Melrose Press Limited
St Thomas Place, Ely
Cambridgeshire
CB7 4GG, UK
www.melrosebooks.com

FIRST EDITION

Cover designed by Sophie Fitzjohn

ISBN 1 905226 57 8

Printed and bound in Great Britain by:
CPI Antony Rowe, Bumpers Farm, Chippenham,
Wiltshire, SN14 6LH, UK

Table of Contents

Introduction

Vichy France in May of 1942 was certainly a difficult place and time for friends, and it was an almost impossible setting for strangers. In the midst of this alien situation, mingle two groups of people – the rural French farmer and the displaced Jewish urbanite, each of whom, at one time in their lives, might have believed that the other represented a curious species.

However, let us now step back to May of 1940. It was then that Nazi Germany invaded France and, in a dominant victory, forced the French to sign a truce which divided the country. Three-fifths of France was occupied by the German army, while the southern two-fifths was able to maintain self-rule. This so-called "self-governing regime" operated from a resort town called Vichy; thus, we have the geographic and political entity known as Vichy France.

Now let us go back even further in time – between 1933, when Hitler first assumed power in Germany, and December 1939. During this period, over 55,000 Jews had emigrated to France – most, of course, settling in Paris – in order to escape the oppressive anti-Semitic activities they encountered in their home countries. France, in this respect, ranked fourth in the number of Jews it received, behind the United States, Palestine and England, respectively.

With the Nazi occupation of France in May of 1940, the Jewish émigrés had the choice of either remaining in the Paris metropolitan area where, eventually, they were sure to be persecuted, tortured, or killed by the Nazis; or, instead, going to Vichy France where the oppressive measures taken against them might not be so harsh. Given these two choices, most of the Jewish émigrés opted for the latter in the hope that they could make a better life for themselves under the blatantly anti-Semitic, but hopefully not murderous leadership of Vichy France.

It is within this political and geographic framework that *Saint-Boniface and Its Jews* becomes a valuable contribution to the literature

1

of the war years, because what we are offered is a careful work of ethnographical fiction. One could call this book ethnographical fiction because, even though the characters and setting are not real, the work itself is a comprehensive study of two cultures – namely, the dispossessed Jews and the rural French farmers. Indeed, the book was written by a married couple who actually lived the experience about which they wrote.

Nathalie and Ladislas Gara moved to Vichy France from Paris in 1940 when the German troops invaded their country. They found refuge in a small village called Ardèche. Even though they had managed to escape direct contact with the Nazis, their lives were still fraught with anxiety and distress because of the anti-Semitic attitudes of their neighbours. The difficulties of their awkward, and often bleak situation inspired the Garas to write an account of their observations which eventually became the ethnographical novel, *Saint-Boniface and Its Jews*.

Ladislas Gara was born in Budapest in 1904. Early in his life he became fascinated with French culture. As a result, when he was a young man he moved to Paris. There he made his living as a journalist and a translator. With the invasion and subsequent occupation by the Nazis in 1940, he and his family retreated to the countryside in Vichy France. When France was liberated, he returned to Paris with his family. However, he found life there very difficult because his apartment and all his possessions had been destroyed by the Nazis.

Gara's economic situation improved somewhat with the publication of *Saint-Boniface and Its Jews*. This work enjoyed immediate success when it was first published in 1947. A literary critic, attempting to explain the book's success, stated that this work was " a bird in the cuckoo clock of the Occupation, a bird with whom one laughed with frank merriment, ...mixed with a bitter, satiric wit."

Even though Gara's book on the indignities suffered by the Jews during the war years sold well, his translations of Hungarian poetry did not find an audience and were not nearly the financial success he hoped they might be.

Eventually, this lack of success in his translations bankrupted him and, according to some of his relatives, his financial ruin could very well have been the motive behind his tragic suicide in 1966.

Nathalie Gara, Ladislas' wife, was born in Warsaw in 1905. When her Zionist family emigrated to Palestine in the 1920s, she decided, instead, to move to Paris. Since she was well-versed in many different languages, she earned a living by translating into French works written in Polish, Hebrew, German, English, and Hungarian.

Just like her husband, Nathalie suffered great indignities and hardships during the Nazi invasion. Like her husband, she, too, had to recover from a life of impoverishment and bitterness after the war.

To help improve her family's financial situation, Nathalie Gara continued her work as a translator. In addition, she started to write travel books. One of her works which focussed on her journeys to Israel, was considered a very important book and was widely read throughout France. She also translated from English into French the American bestseller, *Ring of Bright Water* by Gavin Maxwell. This translated work enjoyed a great deal of success just like her book on Israel.

Nathalie Gara died in 1984. A friend, mourning her death, noted that, in the end, the only event capable of interrupting her long literary career was her funeral.

The Translators

Jacques Grunblatt was born in 1910 in Galicia, a part of the Austro – Hungarian Empire that was annexed to Poland following World War I. After graduating from a Polish gymnasium, he left to study medicine in Marseilles, France. Upon completion of his medical studies, he served as a physician in the International Brigades. His last post was with the Abraham Lincoln Brigade during the Spanish Civil War. When the war ended, he was incarcerated in Gurs, a French concentration camp.

Dr. Grunblatt eventually found his way to Mexico City where he practised medicine for almost five years before emigrating to the United States in 1946.

Shortly after coming to America, Dr. Grunblatt opened a private medical practice in North Creek, a rural community in upstate New York. Here he served as a family physician for the next twenty-five years. In addition to his practice, Jacques Grunblatt served, with great dedication, on many community committees and medical organisations.

Upon his retirement in 1975, Dr. Grunblatt, with his wife Hilda, wrote five chapters for *Our Fight: Writings by Veterans of the Abraham Lincoln Brigade, 1936–1939*. With Hilda's help he also translated into English three books written by European writers. Two translations from the Polish were published – *The Shattered Dream* (1989) is a look at the turbulence in the first sixty years of the Twentieth Century, and *Seven Hells* (1990) deals with the horrors of the Holocaust. In 1989, just three years after working on the translation of Saint Boniface and Its Jews, Jacques Grunblatt passed away.

Hilda Grunblatt was born in Brooklyn, New York in 1922. After graduating from Brooklyn College in 1943, she turned to a career in education. She was a teacher in the New York City public school system until 1949, when she moved with her husband, Jacques, to upstate New York.

For the next twenty-five years, Hilda handled the billing, bookkeeping, and payroll activities for her husband; and when he was short-handed, she assisted in his office. During this time, Hilda and Jacques raised three children.

In the mid-1960s, Hilda was instrumental in bringing a Head Start programme to her community. She helped establish the Town of Johnsburg (NewYork) Library, and served as one of its first trustees. Because of her interest in the arts, she served on the Board of Directors of the Adirondack Centre for the Arts. She was also on the boards of directors for various county organisations.

After Jacques retired in 1975, Hilda worked with him on many translation projects he was undertaking. Hilda also wrote poetry at this time, and some of her work was published in the anthologies of The World of Poetry and The National Library of Poetry.

Saint-Boniface and Its Jews is a remarkable book filled with the most crucial elements of the human condition – laughter and sorrow, anxiety and pleasure, fear and equanimity. All these psychological phenomena are to be found in this work. The authors and translators of *Saint-Boniface and Its Jews* are to be congratulated for taking on the daunting task of a personal exploration into the most desperate and sorrowful time in our modern history, and maybe all history. Indeed, it is my belief that the writers faced head-on the highly challenging task they set for themselves, and that they have done so with great integrity and candour. I hope that you, the reader, will enjoy the abundant rewards of this book as much as I have. I also hope that everyone who reads this work will come away having learned something about the rural French farmer and the dispossessed Jew, each of whom, in the end, had to find some way to get beyond the reality and tragedy of Vichy France.

Martin Wasserman, Ph.D.
Distinguished Professor of Psychology
and Anthropology
Adirondack Community College
State University of New York
Queensbury, New York 12804
(July 2006)

Chapter One

A Tour of Saint-Boniface in Twenty-four Minutes

I

Mrs. Hermelin searches for noon at two o'clock in the afternoon[1] and for two hundred kilos of potatoes

In Vichy France this sixteenth day of May, 1942, Mrs. Hermelin, the wife of the former tax collector, hurried across the hillside meadow with small, quick steps. The bunch of keys she always carried jangled at her side. More than sixty years of age, she ran over heaps of stones, jumped over tufts of golden gorse and the narrow channels cut in the meadow as the noonday sun beat down. Her wizened, angular figure seemed part of the landscape.

Stopping suddenly, she pulled a man's large handkerchief from her purse, cleaned her pince-nez, and blew her nose vigorously. Having replaced her glasses on her narrow, pointed nose, she glanced toward Rochefontaine Castle towering over the village and noted that the shadow of the sundial's hand on its cracked face showed noon. Nevertheless, for economic and strategic reasons incomprehensible to the inhabitants, the government had decreed that all clocks throughout France were to be set according to the time at the Kiev meridian, and so showed two o'clock. Mrs. Hermelin hurried on her way, as if she wanted to regain the two hours that the administration had stolen.

She was wearing a brand-new dress made from a remnant of cloth ordinarily used for mattresses. The cloth had lain on a shelf and had been completely ignored during the three years of the war. In a creative moment, she discovered that the blue and grey striped cotton produced a brilliant effect. With the spirit of decision so characteristic of her, she immediately had this dress made. The result certainly was new and original and quite becoming for a person in her position.

Despite her new attire, the good lady looked worried and irritated. Since yesterday morning she had been combing the neighbourhood,

---

1 Searches for noon at two o'clock in the afternoon (idiom) – looks for trouble where none exists – HRG

hoping to find a supply of potatoes. She needed at least two hundred kilos for the season because she was reopening her boardinghouse at Tilleuls, her family estate, with the approval of her 'poor-man-of-a-husband', the former tax collector, who was afflicted with partial paralysis and progressive senility. Let it be understood that we are not talking about one of those establishments that admitted anyone, nor one that rented rooms to transient couples who might cause Mrs. Hermelin to shiver with horror and unsatisfied curiosity. No, thank God! Nothing of the sort! Tilleuls would be open only during the nice season of the year, to well-educated, well-behaved, and not too demanding guests who, on departing, would reimburse their hostess. This arrangement satisfied Mrs. Hermelin who was the sister and mother of a minister. She knew that even the grave of Christ himself, entrusted to mercenaries, was not guarded without pay. Thus, at the beginning of every season a small announcement in the *Nouvelliste* assured Tilleuls of newly-recruited boarders.

For a long time families, never the same each year, had, by turns, tasted Mrs. Hermelin's edifying conversation and her nettle soup, the speciality of the house. In 1940, a horde of agitated, demanding refugees had replaced the tourists. Several homes in Saint-Boniface had been requisitioned. The beautiful white school house had been put at the disposal of a group of refugee children from Paris, and Mr. Longeaud, the teacher, had to suspend his lessons. Vulgar, middle-class people had even invaded the palatial Rochefontaine Castle. Tilleuls, that distinguished house, also had been unable to escape this invasion. Its main rooms had been assigned to a professor from the University of Nancy. The unlucky wife of the former tax collector had been forced to live in the attic rooms which, once upon a time, were the very ones she had praised so highly to her prospective tenants. Since Mrs. Hermelin haughtily refused to share the kitchen, she had been sentenced to prepare her meals on an alcohol burner in the corner of her attic retreat. Thus, as she drank the dregs from the chalice, she could appear as a martyr and pose as a victim of the underhanded, vengeful plot of the mayor, that notorious atheist and creature of the Popular Front.

"Look at me," she had said to her fellow parishioners of the Protestant Temple. "I'm a refugee in my own home!"

Finally the professor left with his wife, their five children, his assistant, his servant, and his secretary who, according to Mrs. Hermelin, was his concubine. Upon his departure, he had given Tilleuls's owner an envelope containing a sum for the inconvenience. Although everyone in Saint-Boniface and even the neighbouring town of Francheville knew about the hardship she incurred, nobody ever knew about the compensation she had received. She never considered that worth mentioning.

The following spring, Mrs. Hermelin's son, Joseph, came home. He was a former career officer who, shortly after his demobilization, had been named chief of supplies for the county.

He had arrived on the eve of Easter to find his parents busy cleaning. Mrs. Hermelin, perched on a ladder, was dusting a painting. Her husband, whose extremities trembled spasmodically while his saliva drooled from his lips, was trying to place a heavy mattress on a bed.

Mrs. Hermelin, who was always in perpetual motion, could not stand to see her disabled husband idle. Every morning, she prepared a schedule for him that did not leave him a minute's rest. He was the one who had to chop the wood, clean and sweep the rooms, all the while trembling and drooling. His most important mission was to pick the nettles and chop them on a board. He began this task around four in the afternoon so that he did not appear when Mrs. Hermelin served camomile tea, generously offering it (without sugar) only to such influential people as the notary's wife, the deacon's wife, the mother of a bureaucrat from Francheville, and the widow of the Justice of the Peace.

When Joseph had asked the reason for all this house cleaning, his mother had declared that she was putting her house in order so that she could reopen her boardinghouse. Joseph protested. After all, she was the mother of the chief of supplies as well as the treasurer of the 'Legion'. She must not lower herself to the role of a soup merchant and compete with Sarzier, the owner of the Hotel Panorama.

In a moment of weakness she had given in, but shortly afterward she had regrets, which had become stronger as the prices in the hotels in Francheville and other nearby places started to climb. She had engaged in an intense letter-writing campaign to her children that became an obsession and had as its single aim: Tilleuls must be reopened. She had tried to drum it into their heads with the tenacity of a publicity agent.

After much correspondence, she had the satisfaction of having her son Jeremy, the minister, come around to her point of view and, by various stratagems, she brought Joseph to agreement.

Now that she had broken down all resistance, this new difficulty, this stupid, irritating problem of potatoes arose. Ignoring the blooming trees perfuming the air, the rolling hills, and the golden gorse, the preoccupied Mrs. Hermelin continued on her way.

Suddenly she stopped, frowned, and looked around. Fifty metres away the road turned. Nobody was to be seen. She would have time. Without hesitating or even looking for cover, she crouched at the edge

7

of the road to relieve her bladder, which she had to do quite often.

She had just finished when she heard a man's footsteps behind her. Standing up quickly, she turned around and saw Mr. Longeaud, the schoolteacher who also was the secretary to Saint-Boniface's mayor.

Not at all embarrassed, and with the air of a society lady, she gracefully raised her head and said, "Excuse me, sir."

"Don't mention it, madam. Be at ease," answered the embarrassed teacher. He was unsure what attitude to adopt when Mrs. Hermelin spoke.

"You came along at the right time, Mr. Longeaud. I wanted to speak with you."

"At your service," said the teacher, without conviction.

He guessed that an administrative question was involved and had no desire to grant consultations on the road, especially to Mrs. Hermelin who belonged to 'the other side'. For Mr. Longeaud, humanity was divided into two camps: those who shared his opinions and the others.

"This is the problem," said Mrs. Hermelin. "I'm reopening my boardinghouse next month and absolutely need at least two hundred kilos of potatoes for my boarders. Coming from the city, they'll certainly have their ration cards. But where will I be able to use these ration cards in Saint-Boniface? You're an experienced, competent man, Mr. Longeaud. Perhaps you can tell me."

She talked quickly, affecting that sweet smile she always exhibited, except when she spoke to her servants and her 'poor-man-of-a-husband'.

Insensitive to her flattery, Mr. Longeaud assumed the official air he reserved for people from "the other side" when they came to the mayor's office to renew their ration cards.

"I'm sorry, madam, but I don't know how I can be of service to you. Since Saint-Boniface is a rural community, we have no right to honour ration cards for potatoes. Your clients' cards will have to be redeemed in Francheville."

"That's all I wanted to know. The problem is solved."

"But to do that," continued Mr. Longeaud impassively, "your clients must be crossed off their usual supplier's list. Then they must ask for a notarized certificate from the mayor's office, apply to register at the mayor's office in Francheville, and finally register with a vegetable merchant in that city. This will raise a few more difficulties because they won't be housed in Francheville but in Saint-Boniface. At best, they'll receive two kilos of potatoes a month. But better still, why don't you register your boardinghouse officially? Then you'll have certain advantages in securing supplies."

"Well," said Mrs. Hermelin, a bit annoyed but still smiling, "I'll think it over. To tell you the truth, my boarders aren't like the usual clients. They're friends who come to keep me company in the summer. It seems unfair for me to pay taxes like a hotel owner."

The teacher's thoughts were already somewhere else. It was his habit to listen to a customer for no more than two minutes. For quite a while the distant noise of a car climbing the hill had absorbed his attention. Before long the car appeared at the turn in the road.

"Excuse me," he said brusquely.

In one leap he reached the side of the road where he jumped into the ditch, pulled some branches over himself for cover, and lay flat on his stomach.

Mrs. Hermelin watched him, dumbfounded. Had the mayor's secretary suddenly gone mad? It was possible; he was a drinker and an atheist. The heavens sometimes punished those heretics quickly.

The next moment the car passed by, sounding like an old jalopy. The driver, the village priest, a fat man with sweat running down his bloated face, greeted the wife of the former tax collector courteously and then drove toward the parsonage.

Branches snapped at the edge of the road as Mr. Longeaud emerged from his hiding place. He was in a piteous state with disheveled hair, scratched cheeks and muddy clothes because there was a little water in the bottom of the ditch.

Looking around and pointing his finger at the dust raised by the car, he asked, "Who was that?"

"The priest," replied Mrs. Hermelin, recovering from her stupefaction.

"Ah! I'm glad it was only him," said the teacher, sighing with relief. "You see, I don't dare meet any inspectors. That's why I preferred... um...to vanish."

Mrs. Hermelin still could not understand.

"I'm coming from Francheville where I attended a district teachers' meeting and was stopped by a friend who refilled my flask. It's prohibited to transport wine on a public highway, you know."

Only then did Mrs. Hermelin notice that the schoolteacher carried a three litre canteen under his arm.

"Do you think they'd annoy you for such a small thing?"

"One never knows!" replied the schoolteacher, mysteriously. "They've been trying to get me for a long time. Would you like to know why? Because I don't want some of our people bullied! They know what I'm made of and want to eliminate me. The other day I received a note asking me if I were Jewish, but I didn't want to honour them with a reply. If I were a Jew, I'd certainly be in trouble."

"The Jews are being punished by the heavens for having denied the Lord," said Mrs. Hermelin emphatically. "But the day is coming when they will return to Him. I, myself, will help one Jew ensure the salvation of his soul. While waiting for the Judgement Day, one must be alert."

Mr. Longeaud felt vulnerable and ashamed, and changed the subject. He detested the Protestants just as much as the Catholics and was pleased to provoke one against the other, which was easy in this part of the country, where the history of religious wars remained alive.

"You Protestants know better than anyone else. Jerraud, the hardware merchant, declared last week in Francheville's market place that we need another Saint Bartholomew to establish justice. For instance, take the priest. He gets gas for his car under the pretext he's serving two parishes and is the secretary of the peasant union, the Corporation. On the other hand, the minister gets no gas whatsoever and must make his calls on a bicycle."

Mr. Longeaud felt more at ease now and was proud of his diplomacy.

However, Mrs. Hermelin had paid no attention to what Mr. Longeaud was saying. The only thing she had on her mind was the two hundred kilos of potatoes she needed. Since he definitely was of no use to her, the only thing she wanted to do was to end his discourse.

"Oh, it's almost two-thirty!" she exclaimed, consulting the watch she carried on a silver chain. "I'm late already. Goodbye, Mr. Longeaud."

She left the teacher and began climbing a hill toward Barbarie, a hamlet in the township of Saint-Boniface consisting of eleven houses, five of which were inhabited. As for the others, their owners had died and their heirs had deserted the region.

She was determined to wring some potatoes from a farmer.

II

Mrs. Hermelin learns that you need butter to nail down a coffin

After wading through an ocean of mud and rubbish that protected the approaches to Barbarie, Mrs. Hermelin arrived ten minutes later in front of the Legras's house.

The Legras family occupied a spacious house some distance from the other houses on the outskirts of Barbarie. Mr. Legras, a peasant by birth, was a carpenter by profession. In the good old days before the war when gas had flowed like milk and honey in France, one could hear his modern machinery a long way off. Now that noise was replaced by the harsh grating of an archaic handsaw and the discordant scraping of a plane.

Passing in front of a huge shed that housed Mr. Legras's shop, Mrs. Hermelin entered the house without knocking. Inside, all was quiet. The visitor had arrived at a solemn moment. With the pride of a young mother bathing her first-born, Mrs. Legras was immersing a big ball of butter in a basin of fresh water.

Frightened at hearing a noise at the door, the peasant woman grabbed the cover of a washbasin that was lying on the floor and quickly covered the butter.

Too late! In less than a second, Mrs. Hermelin's small, squirrel-like eyes had noticed everything.

"You make butter, my good Delphine!" she exclaimed, with an air that was both envious and malicious. Then, with a nonchalant gesture, she removed the cover and delicately scraped the surface of the butter with her index finger and lifted it to her lips.

"My compliments!" she said. "It's delicious!"

Delphine Legras's face turned scarlet. She was a short, dumpy peasant of undeterminable age, prematurely worn-out like all the peasant women of the region. Her disheveled hair was covered with a black kerchief that protected her ears and was tied under her chin. Large beads of sweat rolled off her forehead. She was always pressed for time and, consequently, behind in her chores. In addition, the smallest distraction frightened her terribly, even if it was only a stranger passing through the village, or the arrival of a letter.

This time her fright was justified. The visitor had arrived at a critical time.

"Sit down, madam," she said, although there was no place to sit in the kitchen, where a bench and two chairs were completely covered with rags and utensils of all sorts. "Have you seen the mailman? He's late again."

Disregarding this clumsy attempt to divert her attention, Mrs. Hermelin persevered unremittingly.

"I'm glad to see that the milk collectors aren't so strict. They left you enough to make a nice chunk of butter."

"Oh no!" protested Delphine Legras. "Do you think this is good butter? The cream was too sour. I can never collect enough to make it fresh. With all the work I have on my hands, I barely manage to watch the cows for an hour or two. They don't eat enough and give very little milk, not even a full pail. It's abominable!"

She heaved a deep sigh and lifted her head despairingly. Then, as usual, whenever she found a good listener, she started lamenting: her husband only left his shop to sit at the table, he was liable to let the animals die of hunger rather than watch them for half an hour...

"Of course, of course," interrupted Mrs. Hermelin. "Everyone carries their cross. I hope the butter isn't sold yet."

"Certainly not! It's for my daughter in Saint-Etienne. She isn't too well and is very unhappy in the city. It's abominable! She succeeded in finding two or three nails for her father so that he can make some coffins. If that isn't abominable!"

For a moment, Mrs. Hermelin was tempted to forget the potatoes in order to haggle for the chunk of butter and to talk Mrs. Legras out of taking it to her daughter in Saint-Etienne. However, faced with the argument of nails, she capitulated, realizing that the fight was unequal.

"I came to ask if you could spare two or three potatoes for me."

Mrs. Hermelin did not know the provincial dialect very well and could use only a few expressions pertaining to numbers. The peasants around Francheville would say 'two or three' which meant any amount from a little bit to a sizable amount.

"So you didn't see the mailman? He should have been here already."

Mrs. Hermelin understood that her chances were slim. Tortuous digressions and sudden changes of subject almost always indicated a refusal.

"You had a very good crop last year, didn't you?" continued Mrs. Hermelin, sweetly. "You must have close to fifty kilos. I'm not very demanding, you know."

"Oh, no!" groaned Delphine Legras. "We're very unlucky even in the countryside. It's just like this poor Brandouille, the mailman. He's not a bad man, but he likes to lift his elbow. It's his occupational hazard. When he used to make his rounds, he was 'paid' everywhere with a drink or a small glass of applejack. When he reached home at night, he was in good spirits. And now..."

"Oh, yes," said Mrs. Hermelin, who was seething inside, "times have changed! One can do without wine! That doesn't bother me. But without potatoes it's very annoying."

"But he can't get along without it," insisted Delphine, completely deaf to the allusion. "His mail route is thirty-five kilometres! Since nobody offers him wine anymore, what do you expect? He's got into the habit of stopping at the taverns, and it costs him at least twenty francs a day. At the end of the month he must be in debt."

Mrs. Hermelin was impatient. Delphine was unperturbed and kept on talking as she prepared some fodder for the beasts.

"His wife takes his money away, so he runs up debts. But even with all of these problems, he's an honest fellow. I've known him a long time. But the other day, the money order was too tempting for him."

"The money order?"

"You don't know about it? The twelve hundred franc money order Mrs. Leborgne's nephew in Marseilles sent her. From time to time, she sends him some supplies: a rabbit, a chicken, potatoes..."

"Ah, potatoes!" cut in Mrs. Hermelin. "I just want to tell you..."

"If only he had held the money order for several days, it would have been nothing, but the idiot forged Mrs. Leborgne's signature. Still, I told you, he was an honest man. This has become an abominable story."

"Yes, alcohol clouds one's judgement. You start with petty larceny and before long you steal an egg, and then you steal a bull. He'll surely be dismissed."

"Not at all! His wife repaid the money to the postmaster, and since Brandouille is married to his niece, the affair went no further. Believe me, it was a close call for Brandouille. Did he get drunk that day! Most likely he's in the tavern right now. That's why he's late."

As she talked, she opened her cabinet and began arranging her dishes.

"My word!" she suddenly yelled. "It's almost three o'clock and I haven't let out my cows!"

Her black kerchief fell over her eyes, and she pushed it back with an exasperated gesture.

For the past three days I haven't had time to comb my hair. It's abominable!"

"I'm going to leave," said Mrs. Hermelin. "Now how many potatoes can you give me?"

"Potatoes?" asked Delphine, opening her eyes wide, as if she were hearing the word for the first time. "You have none?"

"Not a single one. And to top it off, I'll have people during the summer..."

"Mr. Vautier expects people, too," Delphine interjected. "A man, his wife and two children. They're renting the little house near the Grange. Vautier's charging them two hundred twenty francs a month. It's abominable! They're coming from Marseilles tonight."

"You don't say!" exclaimed Mrs. Hermelin, with interest. "Tonight, you said? And will they find potatoes?"

"Surely Mr. Vautier promised to sell them whatever they needed."

Preparing to leave, Delphine opened the door connecting the stable to the kitchen. A strong odour of urine permeated the room.

"Can I count on fifty kilos?" asked Mrs. Hermelin, determined to force a decision.

"Fifty kilos of what?"

"Potatoes, of course!"

"You want potatoes?" asked the astonished Delphine. "Go ask Mr. Vautier. He has two or three in his cellar."

"I'll certainly go there, but how much will you give me? Fifty kilos?"

Delphine stood in the doorway and groaned. "Potatoes! So many people want them now! It's very upsetting! My daughter in Saint-Etienne asks me for some also, she hasn't enough to make soup, and my son in Lyons, and my son in Nîmes, and my daughter in Sorgues! It's abominable!"

"Well, you'll give me whatever you can. If it isn't fifty kilos, then forty or thirty will do."

"I'll ask my husband. He doesn't come out of his shop. I must do all the chores myself! What a life!"

Mrs. Hermelin knew that she would get nothing from Delphine Legras. With regret, she threw a last look at the basin of butter and, quite annoyed, left the kitchen shaking her bunch of keys.

III

Lévy Seignos knows the history of the Revolution and Mrs. Hermelin is aghast

After leaving the Legras's house, Mrs. Hermelin hesitated a moment before crossing a small rubbish-strewn square and walking down a narrow path leading to Serre, the home of Lévy Seignos. The owner was considered odd because he had tried to acclimate apricots and asparagus to the region. However, he was famous in all of Saint-Boniface for his beige linen hat which he wore with the brim turned down. His biblical first name was common among Protestants in this neighbourhood. One could find in Lévy Seignos the same courage and enterprising spirit of his ancestors who, persecuted for their religious beliefs, had left three centuries ago to face a lonesome, adventurous existence in the wilds of Louisiana and Canada. Because of his tenacity and willingness to work hard, he was successful in his small sphere. In Saint-Boniface, one said that Seignos 'was not an unhappy man'.

As Mrs. Hermelin approached the house she was greeted by Cadet's furious barking. Pushing open the gate, she passed under a porch archway that bore the inscription: 'Anno Domini 1287'. Unlike the Legras's house, here no chickens came to leave their droppings in the kitchen. Stopping for a second on the terrace, she could see the entire region of undulating hills covered with a green cap of pines and chestnut trees.

Serre was an amazing architectural structure on a solid foundation and was in excellent condition in spite of its age. Its walls had been preserved during successive renovations and still bore the scars of the old religious wars.

Mrs. Hermelin, who always entered the houses of small farmers without knocking, knocked on this door. The Seignoses were wealthy peasants.

The kitchen was a huge oak-panelled room with a high ceiling. In the rear was an immense hearth with a modern kitchen and a radio next to it.

On a shelf above the radio were some history books and war novels. One of the walls was adorned with hunting gear; on another wall was a battery of copper pots and pans.

When Mrs. Hermelin entered, Lévy Seignos was changing his heavy hobnailed shoes for a pair of wooden ones. His wife, Victorine, was folding laundry on a long table against a wall.

"I hope I'm not disturbing you," said Mrs. Hermelin in her soft, sweet voice.

Seignos protested politely and made small talk with the wife of the former tax collector, while Victorine left her laundry to prepare coffee on the hearth.

"Did you know that Vautier is expecting a tenant?" said Mrs. Hermelin, jutting her pointed nose forward as she sought to introduce her problem.

"Oh yes, I know it," said Mr. Seignos. "They won't be too bad off in that little house. Aren't they from Marseilles? But you, Mrs. Hermelin, are going to have people too."

"You know that?" Mrs. Hermelin asked, feigning surprise. She knew that an event of such importance could not escape the curiosity of the inhabitants of Saint-Boniface. "Yes, I rented the small cottage next to Tilleuls to a fine man from the city. He was recommended to my son Jeremy by a minister from Lyons."

Delighted that she had someone who listened to her, Mrs. Hermelin supplied more details.

"He's a Lithuanian, Polish or Serbian architect. I'm not sure which. He's tired of the city and wants to establish himself in the country. I'll

15

let him convert my shed into a stable for the two cows he plans to buy. That will be convenient for me because my farmer doesn't supply me with milk anymore. The government takes all that his cows produce. And as for potatoes..."

"Will this gentleman know how to milk cows?" interrupted Seignos, with a sceptical smile.

"Oh, he's quite resourceful," replied Mrs. Hermelin, "and he won't do the chores alone. He's coming with his fiancée. They'll be married soon; I'll see to it. My son, the minister, will come to bless their union."

"They're Protestants?"

"She, yes; he, not yet. It will come. He's a high-class Israelite."

"Hear, hear!" said Seignos. "Life for the Israelites is very hard now, especially in the Occupied Zone."

"Oh, I'll protect him," said Mrs. Hermelin. "He'll have no difficulties. He already found some potato seeds and planted them when he first came to rent the house."

"He worked and planted them all by himself?" asked Seignos, incredulously.

"When one is educated, one isn't embarrassed. He's an architect. Anyway, Chazelas sold him the seeds and helped him plant them. It won't be he who will be without potatoes, but I. You see, I've nothing with which to make soup. You can well afford to sell me a hundred kilos, can't you?"

The die was cast. Now Serre's owner knew the reason for Mrs. Hermelin's visit. Old Mr. Seignos pulled on his pipe and did not reply. Meanwhile, his wife served the coffee with a small pitcher of cream and some dry biscuits on a saucer. She offered sugar to the visitor who delicately took a piece and put it into her coffee.

"You haven't taken enough sugar," protested Victorine, softly.

This was simply a polite way of speaking and Mrs. Hermelin knew it. But she could not resist the temptation and dipped anew into the proffered sugar bowl.

"Gluttony is my pet weakness," she said, mincingly. "Your coffee is delicious."

"Do you think so? It's very bad."

This, too, was a polite colloquialism of the region. Victorine knew better than anyone else that her coffee was unrivalled in all of Saint-Boniface. It was made from scientifically roasted barley, not rye, and was always perfumed with a few grains of real coffee.

"A little more cream?" asked Victorine.

"Oh, just a drop," said Mrs. Hermelin, raising her little finger as a sign of good breeding. Then, changing the tone of her voice, she added, "for people like you, one hundred kilos of potatoes is not a trifle. I hope I'm not too demanding."

Seignos was about to give in. How can one refuse an embarrassed neighbour who has nothing with which to make soup? On second thought he answered, "One hundred kilos of potatoes, a trifle? Ask your children in town what they think of it."

"Surely people lack everything in the city," said Mrs. Hermelin. "Because I pity these people, I decided to give up my quiet life and open my big house."

She was making allusions to her boarders, but her listeners, who were ignorant of her commercial schemes, believed that she was talking about her tenants, the architect and his fiancée.

"It's May already," said Seignos, his pipe between his teeth. "Fifty kilos will be more than enough for soup. As for the rest, you'll be able to use the young potatoes. In a few days, they'll be ready to be pulled out."

Mrs. Hermelin was startled.

"Potatoes from my boarders?! And then my 'poor-man-of-a- husband' will never be able to dig them up! I would need a woman!"

This time the misunderstanding was cleared up. Lévy and Victorine finally understood. It was no longer a question of soup for the poor, senile former tax collector reduced to slavery by his wife, but for her little enterprise. From now on, the solidarity between neighbours no longer existed.

Diplomatically, Seignos changed sides.

"Ah, you expect other boarders, too! Indeed, you won't have enough with fifty kilos, nor will one hundred kilos be enough. You'll need at least two or three times that much. And lady, it's not I who'll be able to supply them."

"I'll pay you well!" murmured Mrs. Hermelin. Frightened by her indiscretion, she upped her offer by ten sous.

Seignos shrugged his shoulders. He questioned whether she could afford it. A cunning peasant, informed in his own way, he had understood well before the others that lodgings no longer enriched their owners. Had he not read and reread the history of the Revolution and its paper money at least ten times?

"No, Mrs. Hermelin," he said, firmly, "you'll have to look elsewhere for your boardinghouse."

The wife of the former tax collector paled, suddenly realizing the immensity of her blunder. She stood up and, with a constrained smile, took leave of her hosts.

As she bounded along the road that joined Saint-Boniface and Francheville, she mulled over her vexation.

"They're Pharisees!" she murmured, furiously. "Pharisees and atheists! I've always doubted them!"

IV

With the help of a Russian countess and a roaring lion, Mrs. Hermelin discovers the black market

The usual descent to the road was steep, but Mrs. Hermelin's was even steeper, for she took a short cut that followed a path made in the tall grass that was ready for the scythe. Stopping under a cherry tree full of glistening red fruits that made her mouth water, she grabbed a branch, pulled it toward her, and picked a few cherries. Although the cherry juice was still somewhat sour in her mouth, she crunched the cherries gluttonously all the while savouring the delicate feeling of satisfied vengeance. The cherry trees belonged to Seignos.

Another few ditches to jump, a leap across a wide brook, and Mrs. Hermelin reached the paved road.

She soon encountered a group of ten fourteen-year-old little girls walking in a double line and holding hands. Behind them walked a skinny woman with a bird-like profile dressed all in grey with a cape on her shoulders. With her staff in her hand, she looked like a shepherdess guarding her flock. The girls were singing joyously and as loudly as they could. From time to time, a joke burst forth among the songs:

Beside the River Thames
One lovely summer eve,
An Englishman in short sleeves
Amused himself by singing
Biribiribi, biribiribi, tru la la!

Shocked, Mrs. Hermelin frowned. "What an attire! And what a song! In short sleeves! Why not in...drawers? And the private school pretended to give a more decent education than the public one! It was true that this mix–up was due to Miss Martin, the crazy one who replaced Sister Thérèse in the beginning of the year. This blockhead introduced her own teaching methods! The parents complained about the innovations and Mother Superior Félicie, though Catholic, had principles and would not keep this revolutionary teacher with her cape in the parochial[2] school very long."

Mrs. Hermelin's thoughts, like her capricious walk, returned immediately to potatoes. Her disappointment with the Seignoses did not dampen her zeal. She was already devising new strategies when her attention was attracted to an approaching feminine figure. This person appeared to be about thirty years of age, had prominent cheekbones, and possessed an almost childish charm.

She was the Russian Countess Génia Prokoff who, due to complicated circumstances, had become stranded in Francheville and was engaged in the business of 'family packaging'. She maintained contact with a certain number of rich people on the Côte d'Azur for whom she continually explored the farms in the region, looking for butter and sausages. She sent several packages a week, thereby deriving a margin of profit, which permitted her to pay her bill at the Hôtel Panorama.

Mrs. Hermelin felt a mixture of contempt and admiration for Génia. Unquestionably, she was not a respectable woman because she went to the movies – Mrs. Hermelin saw her leaving the Eden Palace after a matinée one day – she smoked on the terrace of her hotel and she wore make-up. Even worse! You could see her walking barefoot in sandals, displaying polished toenails and painted legs[3].

Yet, Mrs. Hermelin secretly admired her. She was jealous of her skill and asked herself by what sorcery this woman was able to extract from strangers the rarest items while she, a native of the country and a member of high society, could not procure anything.

These contrary feelings were tearing at Mrs. Hermelin's soul, but at the moment when the two women were to meet, she suddenly decided to greet her first.

"Good afternoon, madam," answered the Russian in a melodious voice, while contemplating Mrs. Hermelin's dress out of the corner of her eye.

Mrs. Hermelin could have avoided the whole gesture. Until now, their relationship had been limited to the exchange of a few words in the market one day, but an idea passed through the mind of Tilleuls's owner.

"Lovely afternoon," she said, stopping and extending her hand to the foreigner. "Are you going for a walk?" she murmured, sweetly.

---

2 A parochial school is supported and controlled by a church. It hires its own teachers and administrators. It is required to follow curricular guidelines but its religious teachings are left to the governing body of the church.

3 Painted legs – During the war, no stockings were available. Women diluted a thick liquid with water that they painted on their legs, creating the illusion of stockings.

19

"Yes, madam."

"I'm walking also," said Mrs. Hermelin, "but not for pleasure."

"Oh?" said the Russian.

"Here's my problem. I need potatoes. I'm reopening my boardinghouse in a few days and.... By the way, if you have some friends who wish to spend some time in the country, you'd do them a favour if you gave them my address. I have excellent rooms, you know. Come see me when you're in the neighbourhood."

"With pleasure," said Génia absentmindedly.

"Yes, I have no potatoes. It's sad, but that's how it is. Do you know where I can find some?"

"Some potatoes? They're expensive, I believe," said Génia, a slight smile playing about her lips. "Sarzier from the Hotel Panorama finds them, but at twelve francs a kilo."

Mrs. Hermelin was taken aback. Twelve francs! This was the end of the world! According to her calculations, the most she expected to pay was one third of that.

"Are you sure?" she mumbled.

"Oh, he said so the other day. Everything is going up."

"But it's frightening. How can one survive with such prices?"

Génia let her gaze wander to the meadow where the tall grass waved in the breeze. Then, awakening from her reverie, she looked at her watch.

"You're in a hurry!" declared Mrs. Hermelin, without moving an inch. "But tell me, what are you eating at the Hotel Panorama?"

"Oh, it depends on the day!" said Génia, unable to cut the conversation short.

"But truly," insisted Mrs. Hermelin.

"Well, I don't know...vegetables, some meat, goat, rabbit, eggs, and also some country cheese."

"That's something!" Mrs. Hermelin said, biting her lip. "You're not deprived at Sarzier's! I'm sure all of that comes from the black market."

She regretted having said that. It certainly was not the Russian whom she should call to witness the moral decadence and scandalous black market.

But Génia did not consider these allusions to be directed at her. Vaguely, she promised to send clients to Tilleuls when the occasion arose and walked away with her usual long strides.

Mrs. Hermelin was seething with indignation. Goat meat, rabbit, and eggs! And prices at Sarzier's were not much higher than those she intended to ask. This was unfair competition! As for the shameless Russian, it had been quite wrong to ask her for advice. Naturally, she kept her sources for her traffic secret while the French must break their backs vainly knocking on all the doors. This was an intolerable scandal.

Always energetic in grave moments, Mrs. Hermelin made a double decision. First, she would look up the Sobrevins. Surely, with their big family, they never have enough to eat, and, on the other hand, they were always short of money. As good Christians, they would not dare to ask her the full black market price. After that, she would send an anonymous letter, revealing the shameful practices to the chief of supplies in Francheville. She asked herself whom she should denounce first, Sarzier or the Russian, but she did not hesitate for long. The Russian could send her a few clients occasionally so she had to spare her. Yes, Sarzier was the true enemy. She detested this crafty little man with a hoarse voice and an enormous mop of red hair like a lion's mane. The restaurateur Sarzier was indeed the true devil who, according to the Scriptures, "prowls around you like a roaring lion".

V

Mrs. Hermelin admires a sterile rabbit that will have great consequences on the rest of the story

Mottes, the Sobrevin's farm, straddled both sides of a country road which, after much zigzagging among the hills, led to Barbarie.

This sixty-year-old house was a disgrace and defied the most elementary principles of hygiene. Its plan was unique, having been inspired by the need to economize on labour and material. The one room in the attic received light during the day through a skylight, while the kitchen was the only one in the house with a window. All the other rooms looked as though they were a kind of annex where one only slept. The building faced northeast in such a way that the sun penetrated the interior for only two or three days per year, around the summer solstice at about six o'clock in the morning, when it peeked through the kitchen window at an oblique angle just long enough to notice that nothing had changed since last year.

Noémi Sobrevin, a slender, little brunette with a long pointed chin, and whose protruding stomach showed an advanced stage of pregnancy, had not noticed her visitor. She was involved in one of her long tirades that never stopped until her throat was completely dry. She was talking to Brandouille, the mailman. He was listening open-mouthed, stupefied, grunting and nodding in agreement, trying to place a word here and there. But it required more than that to stop Noémi's eloquence.

"A rabbit?" she said, jeeringly. "Look, really, why not a pig? You aren't greedy! Ah, good afternoon, Mrs. Hermelin. Sit down. You have a very nice dress. In Francheville the other day, when I was looking for a pair of pants for my little Elie (the poor child was running around with a bare behind), the lemonade merchant, Pilon, told me I could bring him as many kilos of rabbits as I wanted, and he would pay me twenty-five francs a kilo. How many kilos do you think I brought him? Not a single one! And you dare ask me for a rabbit! You think I don't know why you need one! Doesn't Francheville's postmaster like rabbit stew? Of course not? Oh, come now! You're lucky my little Abel needs clothes. But I want pre-war material, do you hear me? I want sturdy stuff, not rayon! Fortunately, my children don't like meat. For New Year's I made them a rabbit stew. Didine vomited the whole night. Meat doesn't agree with them. They're not used to it."

These last few words she delivered on the threshold to the stable adjoining the kitchen, just before she disappeared for a second, still talking. She returned carrying a rabbit by its ears.

"If this rabbit were able to have little ones, you could offer me your sister's entire store, and I wouldn't take it. But this isn't a rabbit; its a tiger, a lioness! I've tried all the males in the neighbourhood. I even took her as far as Serre. Nothing doing. No male dares approach her. She frightens them. This rabbit makes me so mad! The other day, she found a little hole in her cage, and managed to get out and made a tour all around. Since then, she goes out every morning. She's eaten my cabbages! In any case, all her escapades have been very profitable for her. Look at her thighs! Your postmaster could gorge himself on them!

As she talked, she found a scale and weighed the rabbit.

"What did I tell you? Eleven pounds two ounces! This isn't a rabbit; it's a calf. And I'm selling it to you at the legal price! And I don't want any stories, do you hear me? Today is Saturday. You're going to see your sister next week, and you'll bring me an apron. Wait, I'm lending you a bag to carry the rabbit. And now run! You're already late. You won't finish before nightfall."

During this entire monologue, Brandouille, a little fellow with red hair and a shiny red nose, had said nothing. Finally dismissed, he left, shaking his head and walking unsteadily.

"Excuse me, Mrs. Hermelin," said Noémi, changing her tone of voice and, without further ado, started to saw wood.

Her protruding abdomen interfered with her bending, but, with miraculous agility, she managed to cut the largest branches.

"He makes me lose so much time whenever he comes, that Brandouille! What a blusterer! Of course, he needs a rabbit! Just to help him forget the money order he put into his pocket! What a coward! I'd teach him how to live if I were his wife."

Now that her eyes were accustomed to the darkened kitchen, Mrs. Hermelin looked around in alarm. In her house, the slightest thing had its place and was immovable. Such unbelievable disorder, such utter confusion reigned in this kitchen that it made her dizzy.

Buried under some mud-spattered children's clothes on an oaken sideboard lay some family pictures, their glass broken. Spilling out from among the clothes, were small heaps of bean, pea, and squash seeds, and on top of it all was a broken wooden shoe.

A cluttered shelf nearby had empty bottles, nails, pieces of string, dirty dishes, lettuce leaves, and a wet pair of drawers. The big table that occupied the middle of the kitchen held an accumulation of all kinds of things: dishes, vegetable peelings, innumerable rags, sewing accessories, a doll without a head, a broken alarm clock mechanism, a strainer, and several bundles. The only windowsill in the house was used as a hamper for dirty laundry. A large heap of wet bedding emitted a sour odour. There one found a mixture of potatoes, a handful of roasted chestnuts, a notebook, and an old prayer book.

"Ah, Brandouille's money order! Yes, I heard about it," Mrs. Hermelin said.

But Noémi Sobrevin was not listening. She had left the saw to put shoes on a child who had just entered, his dirty face wet with tears.

"Be quiet. You see those laces are too short," shouted Noémi. "I'll bring you new ones when I go to the market next week if I think of it."

She began drying the dishes that were dripping on the table. Suddenly, she frowned, sniffed, and brought the rag she was using to her nose.

"What a life! I guessed correctly. I picked up a wet pillowcase instead of a rag. My husband always switches things around."

Indeed, her suspicions were confirmed for, above the furnace where she cooked soup in an uncovered pot, some squares of washed linen were drying, or they may simply have been wet by the youngest Sobrevin.

"I would never have sold him the rabbit," Noémi began again, "but he suggested the apron. His sister has a clothing store in Saint-Paul, you understand. If she opened her shop, one would find enough clothes to dress all the children in the county. And my eight little ones are in tatters!"

23

She fell silent, took on a mysterious and solemn expression, threw the rag aside, and went to open the closet.

To see better, Mrs. Hermelin opened her eyes wide. Closets were her passion. Whenever she was left alone in a room, she could never resist the temptation to open the closets halfway and peek inside.

But she was so upset by what she saw that she immediately closed her eyes and put her hand to her heart. During her lifetime, she had seen many closets, but none could be compared to this one.

Even the mess on Noémi's sideboard, table, and windowsill could never compare to the extreme confusion in this piece of furniture, the traditional sanctuary of all honest homes and legitimate pride of every housewife. The piles of white sheets, the pyramids of handkerchiefs, the stacks of napkins and pillowcases were replaced here by a vertical, inextricable, dizzy tangle of multi-coloured cloth, ribbons, shoes, and stockings which no one could ever inventory and which had been provided, for the most part, by numerous families as hand-me-downs. Whenever Noémi needed some clothing, she dipped her hand into the pile and pulled out whatever her hand chanced upon, adapting it to her need at that moment.

With the ease of a deep sea diver, Noémi Sobrevin pulled from its depths an object wrapped in silk paper. She dried her hands and opened the package. It was a large, fringed, open-work tablecloth of fine linen, one of those ornaments favoured by the rich in 1900 and which young girls worked on for six months, preparing it for their trousseau.

Noémi, her eyes shining with pride, unfolded the tablecloth before her visitor.

"Mrs. Hermelin, you understand good things. What do you think of this tablecloth? All handmade! And without a single defect! I couldn't believe one could find such a piece during the war. I was very lucky! I found it at a charity bazaar. How much do you think I paid for it? It was very cheap. A mouthful of bread. Seven hundred francs! Truly, it's worth more."

Mrs. Hermelin, unaffected by the flattery, made a quick mental calculation. At that price, Noémi Sobrevin could have provided her entire brood with socks, without forgetting a pair of booties for the unborn baby. But to please Noémi, she declared that the tablecloth was magnificent and the price very reasonable.

While Noémi, with a ceremonious gesture, carefully folded the tablecloth, which would come out of the closet again to impress some new visitor, Mrs. Hermelin took advantage of a moment of silence to attack.

"I've come to see you, my dear Noémi, because I absolutely need..." She hesitated an instant and then, like a swimmer diving into the water, she said "...fifty kilos of potatoes!"

Those were the last words that Mrs. Hermelin was able to utter in the kitchen at Mottes during this visit. Determined not to give her visitor a chance to open her mouth, Noémi resumed talking as though she were catching up on the time lost admiring the tablecloth.

"My dear Mrs. Hermelin, you couldn't have come at a worse time," she said in a tearful voice, stopping only for a second to test the baby bottle she was warming for the youngest child, aged one, the temporary baby of the family.

"It's too hot. It could burn the child."

She put the bottle on the table and resumed sawing.

"My dear Mrs. Hermelin, not a chance of it. I could have had enough potatoes for both of us this year, only the devil stepped in. In October, the children were in bed with the measles – they had them one after the other. And we needed to harvest the first chestnuts – they had begun to spoil. I couldn't find a moment to help my husband bring in the potatoes. Suddenly, the weather turned cold just after All Saints' Day and froze about eight sacks. Say good day to the lady, Didine." (A little girl, swarthy like her mother, had just come into the house.) "I don't know if we even have thirty kilos today."

She interrupted her work again, opened a small door, lit an oil lamp, and made a sign to Mrs. Hermelin to come closer.

"Go into the cellar and see for yourself. It's terrible! I'll have to make some soups with flour, provided the miller will let me have several kilos because I have none."

In the cellar, which was on the same level as the kitchen because the house was built into the hillside, one glance was enough for Mrs. Hermelin to see that the mistress of the house had not exaggerated.

Noémi went back to the table, tested the baby's bottle and pouted. "Just my luck. Now it's too cold." She put the bottle to warm again.

"The neighbours would surely lend me a little. Don't cry, David. Your milk will be ready soon. Wait, I'll rock you. Yes, they could lend me some; they've done it other years. But today each is for himself. There's no pity anymore. They persecute the Jews and open new cinemas. God has sent us this war to punish us. But this time it's almost the end. On the plateau there was a young girl of fifteen, a new Jeanne d'Arc, who left with a chariot full of men. Where? You ask me too much. All I can tell you is that she had taken two cows from her neighbour. When she left, she said that the war would end on the 26th of June. We've a little less than six weeks to wait! It's about time it was over. My little Abel has no shoes, and the mayor's office only gives ration

25

coupons to Catholics. When I ask for a ration coupon for a maternity dress..."

She stopped abruptly, as though she had a brainstorm.

"Look, Mrs. Hermelin, since you want fifty kilos of potatoes, ask for one hundred, and we'll share it! Now then, I'm giving you good advice. Go find Vautier at the Grange. He has that much and more. He won't dare refuse you. He's up to his neck in the black market, you know, and since your son is in supply..."

"Yes, yes," Mrs. Hermelin said, without conviction as she manoeuvered toward the door.

"It'll be a great help to me and my little ones."

Stepping backward over the doorstep, Mrs. Hermelin was closely followed by Noémi whose flow of words continued to gush forth, while she scrubbed a saucepan.

"Can I count on you? As soon as my Chayou has her calf, I'll put aside a good piece of butter for you. So, goodbye Mrs. Hermelin, and thank you in advance."

Mrs. Hermelin said goodbye and, with her head whirling, resumed her walk down the road to Saint-Boniface.

"What a waste! Eight kilos of potatoes! Eight sacks! And all those nettles growing around here! I bet they don't know how to use them. If people are poor, it's because they want to be! They don't merit the blessings of the Lord..."

VI

The arrival of the first Jew shatters Mrs. Hermelin's last hope in Christian charity

When Mrs. Hermelin reached the county highway via a side road, she saw Philibert Vautier in the distance, kicking one of the two cows hitched to a heavily laden wagon at the fountain midway between Francheville and Saint-Boniface. With him were his wife and some strangers. After a few kicks, the beast mooed and set off at a trot. The people, animals, and wagon formed a caravan that was soon on its way.

At its head walked Vautier, a lean, but strong peasant whose cheeks were covered with a thick black beard that he shaved only on Sundays. Beside him walked a tall, jolly fellow of about thirty whose pale skin, more than his attitude, revealed that he was a city dweller. To protect his eyes, he wore sunglasses in thick, tortoise-shell frames. His trousers were threadbare, and the sleeves of his jacket were frayed at the wrists. On the other hand, his blue necktie was impeccable. He gesticulated vigorously as he spoke animatedly. However, Vautier did not seem to pay attention to what was being said: his thoughts were elsewhere.

The cows followed, dragging the heavily laden cart. Among the farmer's sacks were boxes, shabby-looking valises, a stove polished like new, a painter's easel, and a number of picture frames wrapped in newspapers.

Then came two women: a dried-up peasant woman dressed in black from her straw hat to her shoes, who was as impenetrable as a mummy and, at her side, a big, blond woman in a tweed overcoat pushing a baby in a carriage. Between the men and women, and seeming to tie them together, was a little girl of five or six whose head was a mass of black curls. Mrs. Hermelin followed at a certain distance and appeared to form the rear guard of the caravan.

As Mrs. Hermelin walked, she wondered who this lady in the tweed coat could be. Then she saw the man dressed in city attire, and it dawned on her. "I'm a fool," she thought. It's Vautier bringing his Jew from the station!"

She quickened her step to observe the newcomers better. When she was about twenty paces behind the cart, she took off her pince-nez, cleaned them conscientiously with her handkerchief, and put them back on her nose.

"My goodness! They look proper, at least from the back! There's a stove. An easel? Oh, but then he's a painter! I'd like to know where Vautier fished them from. He has so few connections in the city. Through the newspaper, perhaps. Oh yes, he subscribes to *Le Petit Dauphinoise.*"

Satisfied to have solved this little problem, Mrs. Hermelin thought about potatoes again. Just as the indefatigable speaker stopped talking, Vautier's wife called him to fix the baby carriage, which appeared to have broken down. Taking advantage of this situation, Mrs. Hermelin took four steps and three goat-like leaps and joined the farmer at the front of the caravan.

"Good afternoon, Mr. Vautier. I'm pleased to have met you. I was just on my way to see you. I'd like to speak with you."

Vautier responded with an indistinct groan, glanced suspiciously at the wife of the former tax collector, and asked himself, "What does she want from me?"

"Look," said Mrs. Hermelin, not at all embarrassed, "some friends are coming to visit me for a few days." (Her experience with Seignos had taught her to keep the opening of her boardinghouse a secret.) "I'm also expecting my son Joseph, you know, the one from the Supply

Agency. He'll probably be assigned to Francheville. He longs to be closer to his parents."

She was still somewhat under Noémi's influence and had just invented this story.

"Then," she continued, in a sweeter voice than ever, "I'll have to feed all those people, and I haven't a single potato. Can I count on you for one hundred kilos?"

Philibert Vautier never flinched. It was as though Mrs. Hermelin's question had sunk to the bottom of a well. She renewed her attack.

"When one owns such a beautiful farm as yours and works it as hard as you do, you wouldn't miss one sack of potatoes, would you?"

The bristling, black-bearded, bony face remained impassive. Mrs. Hermelin's flattery slid off Vautier as over ice. However, his brain worked actively. What would he gain by selling anything to Mrs. Hermelin whom he could not charge as he would a stranger? If that lazy son of hers should come to the county to look for lice on the peasants, it would be better if he did not know that he, Vautier, if he wished could spare one or two sacks at this time.

Vautier assumed an annoyed air and lifted his head.

"It would be a pleasure, but I'm all out of potatoes. The potato sets haven't arrived yet, and I'm asking myself how I'll be able to plant my second crop. You're not the only one having people. I've some also," he said, indicating his tenant. "What do you want from me? They must eat. They come from Marseilles."

Mrs. Hermelin's patience was exhausted. Green with rage, she defiantly raised her nose to Vautier and said, "You'll give me fifty kilos at least, won't you?"

A vague groan escaped from under Vautier's moustache.

"It's quite annoying. If you could find them somewhere else, I'd like it. Don't think it's always easy for us."

Vautier's new tenant came closer and seemed impatient to continue his conversation. Suddenly he stepped toward Mrs. Hermelin, bowed ceremoniously, and, with a slight foreign accent, said, "My respects, madam."

To mask her anger, Mrs. Hermelin responded with a friendly grin.

"Good afternoon, sir. I hear you come from Marseilles. The food supply in the big cities is deplorable, isn't it? What misery! Here, in the country at least you'll be spared that worry, especially at Mr. Vautier's. He just told me he reserved all the potatoes you may need."

Then, turning to Vautier, she asked in a tone she hoped was at once joyous and positive, "But you'll have at least twenty kilos for me, won't you"?

Vautier did not reply. He busied himself with the cows and, raising his stick, cursed them in his dialect.

During Mrs. Hermelin's brief speech, the foreigner bowed several times. Could he, perhaps, hope to find another listener for his interrupted conversation? But the wife of the former tax collector was in a hurry to leave.

"I must go now. I'm late already. I hope to see you one of these days and we'll talk about Marseilles. It's a city I know well. Come see me at Tilleuls with your wife."

She walked rapidly down the road without deigning to even give Vautier another look. In the presence of the foreigner, she succeeded, more or less, in hiding her vexation, but now that she was alone, she gave vent to her feelings. She kicked a pebble spitefully, making it fly. She shook her purse several times and grumbled.

"I should have known better than to deal with Papists! He'll have enough for his Jew, but he has nothing for me! He will hear from me! I must speak to Joseph about him. I must speak to Joseph..."

She continued on her way, mumbling some vague threats. Suddenly, a new idea came to her. Why should she not consult Joseph about the problem of potatoes? He would certainly know all the regulations and might bend them to the best advantage.

Then and there she decided to telephone him. So what if it should cost three francs seventy-five? The situation required sacrifices. Mrs. Hermelin began running quickly toward Saint-Boniface, her keys jangling at her side.

VII

Mrs. Hermelin mobilizes the city to help the country

Saint-Boniface was situated atop a large conical hill, surrounded by wooded hillocks. The clock on the village's little church was visible several miles away. Lower down, the school, built to follow the natural incline of the hill, defied all the architectural traditions of the region by having its white walls pierced by large bay windows in the front of the building which faced south, while its rear faced the houses in the village.

As a centre for many hamlets – some as far away as seven or eight kilometres – Saint-Boniface serviced a total of one thousand souls. However, this small head on the big body of the community consisted of only thirty houses. Half of them were deserted and the rest occupied by fifty-four inhabitants.

The village itself was very old. Grouped around its church, it had always been a Catholic stronghold. But, on the surrounding hillocks, a few menacing citadels of Protestantism relating to the times of the religious wars, remained in the form of massive castle-like farmhouses. Even today, and in spite of various innovations, large sections of the walls of the former farm-fortresses still revealed the scars of cannon emplacements and battles.

With its muddy roads, crumbling houses, and mayor's office located in a decrepit building, the village was not elegant. But it had known better times. According to local legend, Saint-Boniface had been the most important livestock market in the region.

Although a small square transformer at the entrance to the village had supplied Saint-Boniface with electricity for several years, oil lamps continued to smoke in half the houses of the community in spite of oil rationing. The existing electric line could be extended easily from house to house, but many peasants were opposed to it. Was it because it would disturb their routine? Were they afraid of the expense? Most often it was for both reasons.

Now the people preferred to forgo staying up late and go to bed as soon as night falls. The stories of the good old days, when they had stayed up late and danced, and sang the country songs, were only a memory, except for some young Protestants from the neighbouring hamlets who, as soon as they were in a group, struck up religious songs.

About the time the songs disappeared from Saint-Boniface, so did the regional costumes. Sometimes on Sundays some elderly women wore little starched, white caps on their heads, but on holidays the staid Parisian fashion prevailed, a fashion several years old which was sold in Belle Jardinière or Samaritaine, the Parisian department stores. During the week, the men, even the more well-to-do, dressed in rags that ended up as clothing for scarecrows. As for the women, winter or summer they wore black aprons.

Instead of a post office, there was a mailbox in front of the school that Brandouille emptied once a day at different times, depending on the number of stops he made for refreshments. The grocery store was the centre of social and political life. Not only was it a grocery store, but it was also the local government registry, record office, and distribution centre for wine and tobacco. It even had a public telephone booth in the rear of the store. In former times when there were still election campaigns, the rear of the store became a meeting place.

At the top of the hill next to the church was a neat little house surrounded by a well-kept garden, the prettiest in the village. This was the parsonage. The room adjoining the garden served as a lay confessional for Father Mignart, the prime spiritual power in the village; the second was Longeaud, the schoolmaster. Father Mignart was also the secretary of the peasant union – the Corporation, a secret agent for the local section of the Legion, and a serious competitor of Longeaud's as a public scribe. Father Mignart regularly gave audiences to his flock, troubled less by their consciences than by the Chinese puzzle of daily orders issued by the administration.

In the spring of 1942, the shelves in Saint-Boniface's grocery were even more depleted than those of similar establishments. Empty packing boxes were used to fill its shelves. Indeed, since the first hour when restrictions were introduced, Hippolyte Tournier, an independent soul, had refused to submit himself to the servitude of a system that he considered too complicated. Whenever an article began to be rationed: coffee, sugar, soap, etc., he simply stopped selling it. This straightforward solution enabled him to escape accounting for ration tickets and to get rich, almost in spite of himself, by hoarding the precious stocks of hard-to-find items in the back of the store. There were only three items that Tournier had not wished to refuse and continued to sell: wine, tobacco, and oil. For good reasons, no doubt.

When Mrs. Hermelin entered the grocery store, she found Tournier busy talking with Gregoire Laffont, a well-to-do landlord in the village. A litre of wine was between them. Mrs. Hermelin entered the telephone booth at the rear of the store and asked for a telephone number. She soon came out to wait more than a quarter of an hour for her connection. This circumstance gave her an occasion to overhear the conversation in the store while pretending not to pay attention.

Speaking in the regional dialect, Tournier and Laffont were talking about tobacco. It was a confusing tale. Although Gregoire Laffont did not smoke, he had failed to register for tobacco because he had feared to open his wallet every ten days. He quickly realized that he had committed a serious mistake, for a package of tobacco that one did not smoke could be exchanged for nails, wine, or shoes. When he tried to register, he discovered that he was too late; the list had been closed. Tournier had said so. After lamenting the lost occasion, the peasant had finally resigned himself to it.

Since then, Laffont had learned strange things: Tournier had entered his, Laffont's, name in the official registry and, at the same time, he had entered the names of sixteen other non-smokers in the community and was collecting their tobacco rations regularly thanks to the goodwill of Mr. Longeaud, who had furnished the necessary number of registration forms and who was thus ingeniously contriving to obtain a small supplement of tobacco for himself.

"...and I repeat," said Gregoire Laffont, "I want my tobacco. Vergnon from Buttes has managed to receive a certificate from his doctor stating that, although he hadn't been entitled to tobacco because of a lung condition, he is now cured. Then they authorized him to register."

Tournier realized perfectly well that Laffont had wind of the false registrations. If news of this affair reached the Tobacco Bureau, it could have serious consequences for him, but he was not a man to give in easily.

"Then take your sixty francs to Dr. Manueli and have him make out a certificate for you. But between you and me, it would be better to wait until the end of the month when I'll be going to the main office of the Tobacco Bureau. I'll try to settle your business there and then."

All Tournier wanted was to gain time. Evidently, Laffont's card would expire by then, and Tournier could escape from him. In the meantime, he could collect a few more packs of tobacco.

Laffont spat on the floor and ground the spittle with the sole of his shoe. "Oh well, never mind. I'll wait two or three days. But I want my tobacco next month."

"At the end of the month," corrected Tournier. "I know the director and will explain the situation to him myself. It will spare you the trouble of swearing on the carrot."

"On what?" asked Gregoire Laffont, blinking his eyes.

"On the carrot of the Tobacco Bureau. That's the cigar that hangs in front of every tobacconist's shop in town. It's supposed to be a cigar, but I assure you, it looks like a carrot. The bureau has decided to make all those who register late swear on the carrot that they are really smokers. Woe to those who are caught! I saw it in Mr. Longeaud's newspaper. There was even a drawing of a carrot and a man with a moustache, his right hand upraised, swearing in front of it."

"It's a caricature," interrupted Mrs. Hermelin.

"A carica...what?" asked Tournier, suspiciously. "Perhaps so. In any case, it really was a good drawing of one. I'll make out a paper for you, stating that you've always been my client for tobacco. Then you'll give me one or two packs from time to time for my father-in-law who never has enough."

"I hope you won't make me pay for them," said Laffont, angrily.

"You're almost a Jew! I'll be forced to bribe the director to settle your affair, and you still find ways to bargain. Do you agree to it?"

The other mumbled indistinctly in agreement and emptied his glass. He was not too happy over the outcome of this discussion. Tournier had tricked him, and he knew it.

Gregoire Laffont left. Tournier went behind the table, which also served as a counter, and began washing and rinsing the glasses. Displayed for sale on the dust-covered shelves behind him were the remnants of what had once been a grocery store: a few boxes of shoe polish, a small sack of salt, packages of detergents without labels, a big glass jar of mixed pickles. The pickles, which were regarded with suspicion by the housewives of Saint-Boniface, had been left by mistake several years ago by a wholesaler and had been there ever since.

In the middle of the room that served simultaneously as a shop and combination kitchen-dining room for the Tournier family, was the table that Laffont had just left. Without a doubt, Laffont's arrival had interrupted the grocer-tobacconist's snack, the proof being the large loaf of bread and the knife that had not been put away.

For quite a while, this loaf seemed to hypnotize Mrs. Hermelin. Her appetite, stimulated by the long walk, became overwhelming. Her mouth watered as Pavlov's dog had done during his famous experiment. She licked her lips with her tongue. She hesitated a while, but instinct was too strong. Alas, the flesh was too weak!

Approaching the table, she seized the knife and rapidly murmured the inadequate expression used *in extremis* by the civilized being in her that had surrendered. "Will you allow me?"

Stunned, the grocer was speechless.

Mrs. Hermelin cut herself a thick slice of bread and sank her teeth into it. "Mmmm...your bread is delicious! Did you bake it yourself? My compliments."

Just then the telephone rang. With a full mouth, Mrs. Hermelin hurried to the booth.

"Hello? Is it you, Joseph?" she shouted, in a shrill voice. "You've made me wait twenty minutes!" This was followed by an account of her adventures.

"My boarders arrive Monday," she continued, "and I haven't a single potato. I counted on my neighbours, but the spirit of charity has left them. Yes! That's why I'm calling you. If this isn't enough reason... Perfectly! You can do something about it."

The reply she received startled her.

"Absolutely not!" she yelped one octave higher. "I've committed myself to those people. I can't back out. I tell you, I count on you. If that is the case, I must look elsewhere. Maybe they'll have some consideration for the wife of a public servant. I'll write to Vichy. To the Maréchal. To the governor. To everyone. Scandalous? Certainly not! What's scandalous is that people like us are sacrificed in such a fashion. No, I want an answer immediately! Operator, don't cut us off! Of course! Very well! What difference does it make if those are seeds?

A little more expensive? I'll make a sacrifice. All right! All right! I understand. I won't anymore. Goodbye my little one."

*****

Two days later at dusk, a gas driven vehicle stopped in front of the home of the former tax collector. After checking the address, the driver climbed down from his seat. From the back of the small truck, he pulled out two big sacks marked:

VARIETY BEAUVAIS -------SEEDS

For once the city came to aid of the country.

Chapter Two

All Roads Lead to Tilleuls

I

Mr. Longeaud lets his thoughts flow in rhythm with the mileposts

Swinging a stout cane that one of his students had spent many hours decorating with arabesques and initials, a very dapper Mr. Longeaud whistled as he crossed the schoolyard with a sprightly step. Upon reaching the county road, he soon overtook Miss Amélie Martin, the parochial schoolteacher whom he greeted unenthusiastically.

This queer, timid old spinster did not merit much respect from him. She had become stranded in France after having been a teacher of French in a foreign country. Her diploma was only good enough to get her a teaching job in the parochial school. Dressed in grey with a grey cape on her shoulders, she reminded him of one of those bats that flew around the church at night. It was rumoured in the village that she was not getting along well with Sister Félicie, the school director, and that the priest picked quarrels with her over the sacristy. Mr. Longeaud was careful not to put his nose into those arguments. To do so would be beneath his dignity.

Impatient to get to Francheville, Mr. Longeaud increased his pace. His cronies, who shared his opinions: three or four officials, a shopkeeper, the plumber, and Manvin's chauffeur who did not have to return to his high-perched village until late in the afternoon, were waiting for him at the Café de la Poste for their usual meeting on Thursdays, Francheville's market day.

After a few drinks, they went to the Hotel Panorama where, during a meal that the hotel owner prepared especially for them, they engaged in heated discussions until about two o'clock in the afternoon when they ended with a few glasses of cognac, thanks to which Mr. Longeaud achieved a happy state of euphoria. In the greyness of his existence, life was not worth living without this ray of sunshine.

After these Thursday meetings, other distractions appeared mediocre to him. Since leaving the teacher's college, he read only newspapers. He had no romantic adventures that might be a source of complications, and after he sold his car, a Citroen, he hardly went anywhere. He had an old radio, but he did not appreciate music. As for the news, he listened absentmindedly. The Germans were done for; Mr. Longeaud knew it, and the details were unimportant to him. Just fishing was left because he had given up hunting quite a while ago, finding it decidedly too fatiguing. But all that was not worth a Pernod or even a glass of wine.

Francheville, 4.2 km. Mr. Longeaud reached the main highway. "No, nothing is more valuable than a Pernod – lost delights! Even a good glass of red wine is becoming rare," he thought. Mr. Longeaud was not one of those skinflints who considered themselves against alcoholics, vegetarians, or Esperantists, an epidemic of a triple syndrome among his colleagues, but it never affected him.

Francheville, 4 km. "Surely no rush, thank God. It isn't more than the official sermon about the great penitence. Evidently, one doesn't have to be an imbecile if one wants to assure himself his daily wine." Mr. Longeaud thought, not without satisfaction, of the daily administrative sleight of hand that he exposed himself to as the mayor's secretary, thus meriting the gratitude of the inhabitants of Saint-Boniface. "This is nothing compared to the good fortune of being a notary public!" This service to all those favour-seekers permitted him to continue to drink his three litres of wine daily, summer and winter, with his bawdy friends, not counting the little nips of liqueur in between.

Francheville, 3.5 km. "Surely you understand, little glasses." Mr. Longeaud was a lover of heavy red wine. On the other hand, he never despised the strong liqueurs that seeped deliciously down the throat and made life seem so rosy. However, do not conclude from this that he was an alcoholic. There is a difference, even a considerable difference. Yes, he drank freely, but he held his liqueur. Everyone might overstep occasionally, yet you should discount those frustrating, exhausting days when it was almost an obligation to get drunk.

Francheville, 3 km. "Yes, the road is definitely too long. Going downhill isn't bad, but climbing these steep hills with a confused head and rubbery legs isn't much fun. I must admit that the fresh air is sobering and saves me from Mrs. Longeaud's screeching. Always quarrelsome by nature, she's become a harpy. If she were only able to have a child, perhaps her disposition would be better, but since she learned that she must give up the idea of motherhood, she's frigid, eating her heart out and losing weight. She's as dry as a broomstick and ridiculously intolerant. Better not think about it." As for the children... Longeaud had got used to them for he had seen too much. And the parents! "Take that dunce Grandjean. I toiled over the little cretin for two years, three years. I pushed him the best I could and was barely able to prepare him for his certificate, which he received thanks to me. What did the parents offer me as compensation for all the trouble I went through? A dozen eggs!" Had Mr. Longeaud counted on the gratitude of his students, he would have been obliged to tighten his belt quite often. "It's true that the Grandjeans are reactionaries. The father is very influential in the Legion, and the mother is a pillar of the Church. What ignorance in our villages! Go preach the ideas of progress and justice to the inhabitants!"

Francheville, 2 km. Mr. Longeaud was the standard bearer for justice and progressive ideas. All his life he had been an apostle. Yes, he had always been an idealist, and he would remain one. Even in these troubled times, he was always straightforward, never deviating an instant. And yet he was proud that he never joined a party, thus permitting him to maintain his own convictions, for he realized that party membership brought all sorts of irksome obligations. However, he never failed to show where his sympathies lay. As a member of the Human Rights League and the local committee of the Front Populaire before the war, he was often seen at meetings, sitting on the dais among the notables in Francheville. When a conciliatory resolution was needed, his suggestions were always appreciated. All that was an old story! It is true that Mr. Longeaud had not said his last word.

Francheville, 1 km. "Ah, if it were entirely up me! If only my wife didn't hinder me, I'd show what I'm capable of! But she complains incessantly, derides my opinions, and for some time now, even goes to mass regularly. She, a schoolmistress in a public school!" When he had married her, Mr. Longeaud had never expected that, but the priest knew how to entangle her as he did the others. With those ideas it was not surprising that she was holding him back. As if he were not big enough to avoid being imprudent himself! "It's not I who'll do such foolish things like that hothead Galtier who was suspended because he spoke without choosing his listeners. Now he must hide. It's not I, Camille Longeaud, who'll give out ration cards in violation of the law as Serray has done in Saint-Paul. All that is pure bravado. It's futile to expose oneself. One must be prudent because, if you are such an imbecile that you get caught and are imprisoned, you endanger your ideals as a worthy defender, especially at this particularly critical time."

Francheville, 0.2 km. "Yes, an honorable defender like myself, and the future will prove it. In the meantime, one must live in the present, in reality...and the most immediate reality right now is meeting the fellows at the Café de la Poste," toward which Mr. Longeaud, in high-spirits and with a dry throat, quickened his steps.

FRANCHEVILLE...

II
The intimate life of a district's administrative centre told in numbers

"Francheville...4,800 inhabitants," according to Larousse. "Paper mills, saw mills. A town that could easily be a regional capital" wrote a correspondent for the daily newspaper.

The town was served by a ridiculously small county train with connections to the bigger lines. At unpredictable times, a few more cars were added every other week. But Francheville was not a workingman's town. It was a big market town encircled by high hills that were interspersed with hamlets and villages whose inhabitants and peasants flocked to the market in Francheville on Thursdays in the same manner as the thousands of rills and gullies in the high hills flowed toward the mountain stream that cut the town in two. Francheville remained as it had through the ages, a regional commercial centre. Its population was composed mostly of shopkeepers and small artisans. The appearance of workers was a new element. Few in number, they were quiet and barely visible. Thanks to them, Francheville was represented in the Chamber by a member of the guild.

Francheville was a quiet town even in the third year of the war. Actually, the war never reached Francheville; it stopped some forty kilometres away. The invader never pushed any nearer and had even retired somewhat farther north after the armistice. Thus, Francheville knew neither destruction nor bombardments. Its inhabitants neither suffered personally, nor lost their possessions. They even became accustomed to the noise of planes flying south at night. In May 1942, Francheville was one of those rare European cities where nightly blackout regulations were only on paper.

Although the list of those killed in the First World War, found at the base of the Monument to the Dead, was impressive for its length, this time only one of Francheville's inhabitants was killed by the enemy. The letter carrier brought only letters and cards from prisoners of war. In this peaceful town, were it not for those letters and cards and almost one hundred refugees in Francheville and its environs, the war could be considered a kind of faraway thunder, like one of those terrible earthquakes in China whose ravages are known only through the newspapers. Only the Legion was here to remind the inhabitants that they were part of a people vanquished on the battleground, a just punishment inflicted by the heavens on a nation that loved its easy life. "We're vanquished... Vanquished... Vanquished..." the speakers from Lyons and Marseilles repeated emphatically.

Ration cards, food rationing, textile rationing, compulsory registrations, cards for suppliers. Triumphantly, the black market marched across Europe and made its appearance in Francheville, but its manifestations were still timid. On the other hand, bartering already had many adept adherents, the principal one being Mr. Chameix, the active young pharmacist's assistant in the White Cross Pharmacy. For instance, he traded his ration of tobacco for a little bit of coffee. Later, he exchanged the coffee for butter, and finally, the butter for a double ration of cigarettes. One must keep up with the times, isn't that so?

Francheville was a complete city. The only thing missing to make it a big city was its size. Like everywhere else, plenty and paucity existed side by side. What did Francheville have in abundance? Taverns. No one knew the exact number because, in addition to the legitimate establishments, there were cafés and hotels, while on the outskirts some grocery stores served small glasses of wine at the counter. Francheville's climate made one thirsty.

Thirteeen, the superstitious number. Of what were there thirteen in Francheville? Thirteen groceries. Even if the old-fashioned groceries had disappeared a long time ago, the tourists sometimes uncovered very rare objects like a coffee grinder, metallic steel wool, a toothbrush, pots and pans if the merchant remembered where he had hidden them. Generally speaking, business was quiet. At the moment when a definite policy was instituted, the occupation of grocer became a sort of government official. Each knew exactly how many customers he had and what they were likely to buy. No surprise was possible.

Seven, the number of chance. Of what were there seven in Francheville? Seven hotels. Francheville had a glorious tradition of culinary fame. The Hotel Farémido was one of eleven in all of France that prided itself on its three-star rating in the gourmet guide, *Guide for the Epicure*. Its dining room had seen many stars of finance, politics, and the arts. Even in the third year of the war, its food and living quarters were excellent. Since 1940, the Hotel Farémido was always full. The others, also.

Of what were there six in Francheville? Six butchers. They were open two days a week, but they led a very active night life. By truck, cart, or on foot they went at night to the farms where, by starlight, they sacrificed the beasts destined for the black market.

Of what were there five in Francheville? Five houses of worship. The Church, of course, then the Protestant Temple, the Evangelical Free Church, the Salvation Army Post, and the Friends Meeting Room. As for the Methodists, they met in each other's homes. Half of the population was Catholic, the other half was divided among the Protestant sects.

Of what were there four in Francheville? Four libraries. Four libraries and hardly any books. The notions shop[4], like an encroaching weed, invaded the shelves everywhere. However, Francheville's intellectuals still had the municipal library where, for ten sous, they could take home one of two hundred volumes, choosing from among the works of Zenaide Fleuriot[5], Gyp[6], and Georges Ohnet[7].

Of what are there three in Francheville? Three lumber companies. Although the hills of Francheville were covered with chestnut, pine, and oak trees, wood for heating was unavailable since it was taxed. Consequently, these merchants specialized in preparing wood for cabinet making and shoes.

Of what were there two in Francheville? Many things. There were two parties, a Right and a Left, just as it should be. There were two news-stands, one for the reactionary, the other for the "progressive" papers. Now all the papers printed the same news with almost identical editorials.

There were also two state controlled stores. Never in man's memory had a leftist ever entered Widow Collet's shop, nor had a right-wing voter ever bought a box of matches from old Matthieu. Now they were less eclectic and bought tobacco from both stores.

La Ménagère, a large food chain with branches in the smallest towns south of the Loire, had two branches in Francheville. In its window, one store exhibited patriotic slogans and photographs of the tricolour. The manager of the other store sometimes made subversive remarks. All that was unimportant; the money went into the same till.

There were also two pharmacies. The older one, the White Cross Pharmacy, belonged to the mayor. With its serious mien, it remained true to tradition. Its shop windows were decorated with colourful jars, placards advertising an honest laxative, and a few bottles of the tonic 'Jouvence de l'abbé Soury'. The other, the Modern Pharmacy, deserved its name. Its neon sign was out of order for quite a while. It offered the passerby beauty products, bottles of toilet water, belts for sportsmen, speciality drugs, and salves containing hormones.

---

4 In the United States, this is a store that sells small, useful products, like ribbons, pins, needles, thread, and other sewing supplies.

5 Zenaide Fleuriot (1829-1890). Woman of French literature, author of many stories and various plays for young people. (HRG)

6 Gyp — pseudonym of Riquette de Mirabeau, Countess Sibylle de Martel (born 1850). Woman of French literature, published many works full of fantasy and wit. (HRG)

7 Georges Ohnet (1848-1918). French novelist. (HRG)

There were also two physicians in Francheville, one Catholic, the other Protestant. The latter treated patients who were leftists without regard to religion. To be frank, nobody had ever seen Dr. Manueli at mass, nor Dr. Colin in church. About five years ago, Dr. Manueli had taken over a Catholic physician's practice. After World War I, Dr. Colin had bought a doctor's practice whose patients were mainly Protestants. The situation had not changed since then. Dr. Colin was better known in the countryside. Dr. Manueli's patients were the merchants; he knew how to explain to them that one of the best investments that they could make was to preserve good health, and that treatment begun in time was a father's obligation for, by neglecting treatment, a man unwisely jeopardized his future well-being.

Lastly, there were two banks in Francheville. The Popular Bank was for the general public. A branch of a large establishment, Crédit Lyonnaise, whose board of directors acting as a veritable investment department, assisted the wealthy to invest their money. Behind padded doors, the bank director contemplated his clients' confidences and, after having felt their pulse, recommended to one an injection of the Suez Canal, to another a massive dose of the Royal Dutch, to a third a hot operation in Péchinay. International stock retained its magic spell. Thus, thanks to the money from Francheville, the region of Reykjavik was able to acquire electricity. It also happened that the Cafro-Boer Company went bankrupt, and the Nicaraguan government prohibited dividends to leave that country. But then everyone knew that there were dangers in being a capitalist.

Of what did Francheville have only one? The mayor's office, naturally. It was brand-new, had a fake antique bell tower, and was painted an administrative brown. There also was one recently-built, nice-looking hospital run by nuns, one modest railway[8] station, and one post office.

The post office was never empty. On market days, the queue in front of the window extended into the street. The window itself was unique, one of a kind in Francheville. To tell the truth, if one looked closely, one could discover that there was another window, but it was always closed. At all hours of the day, one could see five or six employees behind the barred window, busying themselves with mysterious activities. However, to serve the public, there was only one lone employee. It was not her fault that one must wait an hour to buy a stamp. She was not playing; she worked constantly, but the regulations required that, when she finished one sheet of stamps, she must make long calculations while the crowd waited impatiently.

---

8 Railroad.

What could not be found at all in Francheville? One could not find a dentist. Once a week, on market days, a dentist came from a nearby town. One must surmise that the five thousand inhabitants and ten thousand souls in the surrounding villages could not support one dentist. It was true that no one went to this specialist except to have a tooth extracted. One may say that, on the average, two peasants in the Francheville area had a total of thirty-two teeth of which half were decayed.

There was no municipal stadium in Francheville. Nor were there baths, municipal or otherwise. But that was a relatively recent situation. In one suburb of Francheville, there were ancient Gaelic-Roman ruins of thermal baths, and one of the castle fortresses that dominated the town had the preserved remains of an enormous steam room that an important grandee had built when he returned from the Crusades. It was said that the steam room was still in service at the end of the fifteenth century. One might suppose that progress had done away with its use. However, one should not jump to conclusions. The lords of the twentieth century could still take a bath in Francheville if they could afford it. All they had to do was to go to the Hotel Farémido which offered all the modern conveniences.

III

Mrs. Hermelin prefers nettle soup to carp with dry raisins

There was no porter at the railway station when Mr. Frank Rosenfeld, Tilleuls's new tenant, descended from the train with much luggage. This situation embarrassed him very much. His deep distress turned to relief when Mrs. Hermelin unexpectedly appeared on the railway platform.

"It was a good idea to come on Thursday, market day. A neighbour can put your luggage on his cart," said Mrs. Hermelin, as her tenant, with a golden-toothed smile and heavy jowls, bowed ceremoniously over the good lady's bony hand.

He was a short man of about forty years of age. His jacket was threadbare. Doffing his grey felt hat, he uncovered a very bald head save for two locks of greying hair behind his ears. Although he spoke French fluently, his pronunciation sounded harsh with its rolling 'Rs', making his French quite different from the foreigner she had met earlier.

"It's 11:40," said Rosenfeld, after helping a friendly neighbour lift his valises on the cart. "I'm going to have lunch here. Could you show me a restaurant where one can have a decent lunch at a reasonable price?"

Mrs. Hermelin thought for a second. To recommend a competitor was always delicate.

"I'll take you to the Hotel Panorama," she said, hesitatingly. "There you can have a good meal while waiting until your future wife can prepare tasty dishes with the products of your farm. Speaking of her, how is she?"

"Very well, thanks. She'll join me as soon as she gets her travelling permit."

In this year of 1942, foreigners living in the Free Zone could not travel without special authorization from police headquarters.

"Let's hope it doesn't take too long," sighed Mrs. Hermelin, raising her eyes to heaven. "What a joy it will be for you to be united before God! Believe me, there's nothing as good as family life. Meanwhile, if it's convenient for you, you can have your meals at my place. We're having nettle soup tonight. It's a pity city people don't know it. You'll see, it's delicious."

"I accept with pleasure. Nettle soup, did you say? I'll write down your recipe because I cook for myself when time permits."

Tilleuls's new tenant tried to do everything. He had many talents which he liked to show off. Listening to him, one had the impression that no human activity was unfamiliar or beyond his ability.

"Truly?" said Mrs. Hermelin. "How interesting."

"If you'd like it, "he continued, "one day I'll let you taste some of my country's typical dishes, for example, carp with dry raisins and sweet sauce."

Mrs. Hermelin looked perplexed. Was he making fun of her?

No, not at all, for he continued animatedly. "If it's possible to get a leg of veal from the butcher, I'll make a real treat for you, a dish with prunes."

This time Mrs. Hermelin's stomach turned over, but she smiled courageously. They were passing through the big square where Francheville's anaemic market was about to close. One could see neither pork, nor butter, nor piles of goats' cheese, only a few emaciated calves, four or five flat baskets with seeds, some straw hats, wooden shoes, neckties, and trinkets.

"Ah, if only you could have known our markets before the war!" sighed Mrs. Hermelin. "But we'll appear ungrateful to heaven if we were to complain about our fate. Here in the country, life is still bearable. I pity the poor people in the cities who write asking me to admit them to my boardinghouse. Just reading their letters breaks my heart."

"Don't your boarders come from Marseilles?" asked Rosenfeld, with interest. "Aren't they people you know?"

"Not too well. To be honest, I placed a small advertisement in a Lyons restaurant patronized by intellectuals and nice people."

"Intellectuals?" asked the foreigner, with some concern in his voice.

"That's what was suggested. That's how one knows with whom one is dealing, whereas to advertise in a newspaper..."

"And these...intellectuals?" insisted the tenant, suddenly very attentive.

"Of those who have written, I've given preference to a Mr. Fleury, a distinguished musician. He's coming with his wife and young daughter. I think he works for the radio station."

"He's French, isn't he?" asked the stranger, seeming reassured.

"Of course! He's an official, you know! My other boarder, Mr. Murger, is also a nice man."

"Murger?" repeated Rosenfeld, a bit worried. "I know several Bergers who aren't Frenchmen. Murger is somewhat similar. I wonder..."

"Oh, I don't think so," said Mrs. Hermelin, in an apologetic tone. "The man is very French. Mr. Murger is a young engineer on vacation who is recovering from an illness he contracted as a prisoner of war. He needs to recuperate. This season the nettles will be good for him."

"If I'm asking all these questions," he said, a bit embarrassed, "it's because..."

"But I understand very well," interrupted Mrs. Hermelin good-naturedly. "You're afraid you'll feel estranged in our region. But I can assure you, you'll not be isolated. I met a man from Marseilles on the road the other day. A foreigner. He arrived with his family. I've the impression you and he are in similar circumstances. He's truly well-educated."

"A man in the same situation as I?" asked Rosenfeld, almost apoplectic.

"Yes," Mrs. Hermelin replied, as goodheartedly as ever. "Another Israelite, I presume. So you won't be lonesome."

"This is too much!" shouted the new tenant, rolling his 'Rs' even more under the stress of the emotion. "I came to this forlorn hole because your son, the minister, assured me that there would be no Jews in the community, and the first thing I hear is that there's a whole family of them! I can tell you quite plainly, I'm disappointed, very disappointed!"

Nothing was left of his jovial, straightforward manner. He was barely able to control himself. With glaring eyes, he looked defiantly at Mrs. Hermelin as he pushed back his hat and, in a harsh voice, replied, "If I made a decision to retire to the country, it was to find a refuge, a haven where I could live quietly. But, if this region is like the area around Drôme[9] which, as they say, has become a Jewish-drome, it wasn't worth my while."

"Now, now," said Mrs. Hermelin, uneasily. "I'm not so sure this man is an Israelite after all. All I know is that he's an intellectual and a foreigner."

"A foreign intellectual must always be suspected."

"I assure you," repeated Mrs. Hermelin, "you'll be very comfortable in Tilleuls. Nobody would think of discriminating against you because of your beliefs." With a solemn, mysterious air, she added, "...and as far as I know...my son, the minister, has told me...a big event will soon take place in your life."

"Yes, of course," stammered the foreigner. "Excuse me," he said, in a somewhat quieter tone. "My nerves are raw. Anything can upset me lately. For instance, in front of the ticket counter where I changed trains, I saw a man whose features were clearly Semitic. That was enough to scare me. Luckily, I haven't seen him since. However, this encounter has spoiled my entire trip. I'm telling you once and for all, I don't want to see any Jews here!"

"Well," said Mrs. Hermelin, in a conciliatory manner, "you won't see them in Saint-Boniface. But here we are at the Hotel Panorama, so *bon appetit* dear sir...Mr. Rose...excuse me, somehow I can't remember your name. Would you mind repeating it?"

"Rosenfeld," said the foreigner, modestly.

"That's it. That's it... For us French it's somewhat difficult."

"I understand," said Frank Rosenfeld. "Well then, simply call me Mr. Rose. Mr. François Rose. It's the same thing and so much simpler! My respects, madam."

IV

The white Haitian negro poses a delicate problem for the owner of Tilleuls

"Mr. Rosenfeld certainly is a very bizarre person," Mrs. Hermelin said to herself. "With the pressures of his work in the city, the lack of food, and all the troubles his origin gives him, these sudden changes of

---

9 Drôme is a department and a river; drome is a raft. (HRG)

mood are quite excusable."

Plunged in her own thoughts, she crossed the market place in the other direction. Suddenly, she thought that she heard her name spoken, and turned around. Two peasant women, Noémi Sobrevin of Mottes and Sébastienne Latière of Barbarie, were deep in conversation. Since the two women stood with their backs to her, she thought that she had heard incorrectly and continued on her way.

It was indeed she who was the subject of their conversation. Sébastienne was telling Noémi about a sensational event that she had heard from Irma Laffont, who had learned it from Eugénie Vautier, who had heard it from Rosalie Tournier. The other Saturday, Mrs. Hermelin, overcome by a strange frenzy, had entered Tournier's grocery, grabbed a big loaf of bread and fled, "devouring it like a dog".

This was the result of successive embellishments created in the imaginations of the village women, regarding the little initial episode when Mrs. Hermelin unceremoniously cut a slice of bread while she waited for her telephone call in Tournier's grocery.

"Impossible! Impossible!" exclaimed Noémi, her eyes wide with amazement. "Did you say it happened on Saturday? Oh yes, now I remember. She came to see me that day and held me back from my chores, but I can't believe she was capable of such a thing. She was quite nervous."

Meanwhile, Mrs. Hermelin stopped in front of the White Cross Pharmacy, trying to decide whether to enter and buy the bottle of Jouvence de l'abbé Soury that she had wanted for a long time. She could not make up her mind. Naturally, the recommendation of Aunt Annie was a guarantee, but on the other hand, Father Soury was clearly a Catholic, and she wondered if she should ask herself if his medicine worked as well for Protestants as it did for Catholics. She decided to ponder the matter. However, the temptation was strong. As she was about to succumb to it, an unexpected circumstance interfered. A stranger, a short man of about thirty, with disheveled, curly, slightly reddish hair and thick lips, spoke to her.

"You're Mrs. Hermelin, aren't you?"

Astonished, she looked at him.

"The librarian across the street advised me to talk with you. You're supposed to take boarders. I'm here for a few days with my wife and little son."

He spoke like a foreigner, rolling his 'Rs' and imperceptibly running his vowels together.

"Yes," replied Mrs. Hermelin, instantly flashing her commercial smile. "I do run a boardinghouse."

"In Saint-Boniface, isn't it?" asked the stranger.

"Yes, Tilleuls of Saint-Boniface."

No sooner had she pronounced these words than a terrible doubt overcame her. Mr. Rosenfeld's menacing voice rang in her ears. What if the stranger really were an Israelite also? That would make a scene! Mr. Rosenfeld might get angry. Perhaps angry enough to leave. That would be annoying were she to have boarders in the future and for the advantages she expected to obtain from him: milk, butter, eggs...

"So you want to spend some time in Saint-Boniface? For a fresh-air cure? Are you a foreigner, perhaps? I hope I'm not being indiscreet."

"Not at all," said the foreigner, nonchalantly. "We're Haitians."

"Excuse me?" said Mrs. Hermelin, thinking that she heard wrong.

"Haitians...the island of Haiti. Don't you know it?"

The wife of the former tax collector searched her memory. Haiti... Haiti...it was some island among those islands near America...a country inhabited by negroes. But this man could not be a negro! Though, after reflecting...his frizzled hair...his flat nose...his thick lips....Were not those the precise features of the black race?

Suddenly, an idea came to her. Of course! She ought to have thought of it sooner! He was a white negro! How simple! She had seen that expression somewhere. Had she not read in the *Nouvelliste* that a Brazilian scientist had invented a procedure that made negroes white? If this man were not a negro, he must have a good dose of black blood in his veins. There was no doubt whatsoever that he was Haitian.

Mrs. Hermelin was deep in thought when a little lad of about four, with one foot on a scooter, approached the stranger.

"Hey, Papa! Mama is looking for you!"

Except for his jet black hair, the little fellow bore a striking resemblance to his father. His sunburned face, the colour of mahogany, could be taken for that of a child of the tropics.

Mrs. Hermelin congratulated herself for her sagacity and, turning to the stranger, said. "If you're looking for a boardinghouse, I could let you have a room with two beds. You'll be very comfortable. There's a splendid view. You're lucky because, in a few days, everything will be taken."

The spirit of the businesswoman made her forget the Jouvence de l'abbé Soury.

"What are the conditions?" the stranger asked, prudently.

Mrs. Hermelin considered asking him the same price she had quoted by mail to the other clients, but she changed her mind. An American, even a negro, could pay more, and she upped her price by five francs per person per day.

V

The ghetto of Saint-Boniface

When Frank Rosenfeld left the main highway to go down the chestnut tree-lined road leading to Tilleuls, he was in excellent spirits and whistled all the way while musing about the pleasures that awaited him: a healthy life in good fresh air, and the tranquility and quiet that would quickly make him forget the agitated months he had spent in Lyons.

Since 1940, Rosenfeld's existence had not precisely been a featherbed. He had lived in such a state of terror that he sometimes awakened at night, his ear straining, his shirt glued to his body by a cold sweat. It was terror of being taken one day and sent to a concentration camp or even deported.

In his time, he had had some honours bestowed on him. He was an old veteran and had even been decorated. Aside from being stopped a few times to verify his papers, he had not been seriously upset. However, some others had been less fortunate and thought that he should be made to share in their uneasiness. Several times the police had stopped him in the street to inquire if he were a Jew. Twice, after having been asked for his identity card, he had been taken to a selection centre. They had released him at once because of his honors, but who knows if he would be so lucky the next time?

When he was only twenty years old, he had left his native city of Riga at the end of World War I to fight against the Bolsheviks. Then he had gone to Germany where, although penniless, he was able to finish his studies thanks to some lessons he had given, and in other diverse ways, and also to the devoted friendship of a middle-aged widow to whom he had been introduced in the Café Romanisches. Armed with his architect's diploma, he had worked for several years in Germany. In 1931, when his intuition had warned him that the political atmosphere in Berlin was becoming too charged, he had gone to try his luck in Paris. After several attempts, he had managed to find a stable enough situation. Oh, it was not a question of building stadiums or viaducts, but just simply to devise specifications for a construction firm that offered an ideal house in the suburbs: three rooms and a kitchen built with new materials, "a maximum of comfort in a minimum of space". Improved models were exhibited yearly at the Paris Fair.

In Saint-Boniface he felt that his fears would leave him. He was about to start a new life, a completely new life. This would be the first resurrection of the somewhat harrowing existence of Frank Rosenfeld, a new chapter one could call 'Return to the Land'. It was a return without ever having left it since Mr. Rosenfeld did not know the countryside, except for what he saw through train windows. For that, it was not necessary that Saint-Boniface, this refuge, this haven, be transformed into a ghetto. Absolutely not! Two Jews lost among hundreds and hundreds of natives within a radius of several kilometres, was not *numerus clausus*, and the Jews could pass unnoticed. But one must watch for the future and oppose an invasion by all possible means. The sight of the unknown man with a Semitic profile at the ticket counter came back to him. One of his first measures would be to see the mayor and make him promise not to allow every Jew who applied to settle in the community.

As for Mrs. Hermelin, it would be necessary to stop her indiscretion. What right had she to remind him of his promise to convert? Even though he had declared to her son, the minister, that, after looking into himself, he would give himself to Christ, he had not divulged in what precise way, Catholic or Protestant. In Lyons, Father Paroli worked hard to win him over to Catholicism, even giving him a letter to the priest in Saint-Boniface. As a result, Frank Rosenfeld felt that he should not commit himself without having seen him.

To convert! Was it not a little late since the authorities did not consider any recent conversions? However, the priests and ministers were sensitive to conversions. When Rosenfeld had spoken with Father Paroli and the minister Jeremy Hermelin about his conversion, they spoke in unctuous and reassuring terms in order to win over the lost sheep and bring it back to the fold. The sheep did not ask for much more than protection from the wolves. If only his great-great-grandfather had taken such a happy step, he, Frank Rosenfeld, would not be in this predicament today. He would be like Montaigne[10] whom no one, not even Maurras[11], could reproach for his Jewish ancestry. Suddenly he was filled with bitterness toward his distant ancestor who had refused to give up the traditional caftan and earlocks. The old idiot! To be so stubborn and remain different at any price! Rosenfeld's desire was just the opposite: to be lost in the crowd. Ah, to melt with delight into the masses, to be only an anonymous individual who was not singled out for attention! Then when calmer times would come, he could put on a new skin! It was with this intention in mind that

---

10 Michel Eyquem de Montaigne (1533—1592). French philosopher, moralist and essayist. (HRG)

11 Charles Marie Photius Maurras (1868—1952). Born in Martigues; French poet, writer of philosophical and political essays; monarchist; advocated a 'Catholic France'. Nazi collaborator, sentenced to life in prison. (HRG)

Mr. Rosenfeld had come to Saint-Boniface. He planned to plough[12] a small plot of land with his wife, an Aryan, and to wait until the tempest passed.

Suddenly, the oblong building, known as Tilleuls, loomed from behind a grove of trees. This house appeared so hospitable and peaceful! Surrounded by greenery, it seemed more engaging than when he had come to visit for the first time in April with the cold north wind blowing. Yes, it was a haven, the ideal refuge.

He was entering the house when a shout, emitted in a guttural voice, made him tremble all over.

"Ni Rivka, vi bist di? Di kimst?" (Well, Rebecca, where are you? Are you coming?)

Frank Rosenfeld froze, immobilized as though rooted in the soil by magic.

"Also di kimst?" (Are you coming also?)

The vale, the chestnuts, the paths leading through the gorse, everything came tumbling down in a whirlwind and, when the echo of that voice faded, out of the fog rose Riga with its grey walls and the dark lanes of his native ghetto filled with chants of Talmudists who, with the same voice and using the same language, called to their wives who were gossiping in the yard.

The hallucination faded. Once again the radiant sun illuminated the hills and forests. But Rosenfeld had heard clearly. In Yiddish, a man's voice had called a woman who had the biblical name of Rebecca which had been changed into the jargon of the ghetto.

Rage gripped him. He asked himself into what kind of beehive had he fallen? Was this the haven he sought? It was more like a trap! He was overwhelmed by the destruction of all his hopes. Instantly, Rosenfeld was tempted to return to Francheville and take the first train to Lyons.

Why is it that the realization of such heroic decisions is always frustrated by the little unimportant demands of practical living? Rosenfeld's luggage was already at Tilleuls. His hotel room in Lyons was no longer empty. What was more, he had no permit to return. He had no choice but to face the scourge.

As he approached the entrance with a resolute step, the door opened and a stranger came out. At first he could not believe his eyes. It was the man with characteristic features whom he had seen at the ticket counter!

Rosenfeld was seized with a violent urge to jump on this man and strangle him. In one sense, it was a case of legitimate self-defence, but

---

12 In the US, 'plow'.

he restrained this primitive reflex and contented himself by scorning him.

"Are you looking for Mrs. Hermelin?" asked the stranger. "She went to see her farmer. You're the new tenant, aren't you? She wants you to know that she'll be returning in a while."

"It's all right. I'll wait," replied Rosenfeld, biting his lips.

He entered the living room and sank into an armchair. As he tried to put his turbulent thoughts in order, the door opened and the little redhead came in and went over to him.

"I wanted to open my valises, but my wife put the keys in her purse and then went shopping."

The stranger fell silent for an instant while he observed his listener. Suddenly, he took on an air of impertinent familiarity mixed with mysterious complicity that is commonly assumed when conspirators give the password.

"*Yid?*" (Jew?)

This was too much for Frank Rosenfeld. During his long stay in France, he had been called foreigner, *métèque*, Israelite, Jew, *youpin*, and even *youtre*, but never *Yid*!

Assuming a proud air, Rosenfeld replied, "That's not important. What are you doing here?"

"And you?" retorted the *Yid* not at all abashed.

"You know very well. I've rented a house."

"A house? Ah, I understand! But what do you do for a living?"

"And you?" countered Rosenfeld, very annoyed.

"I? I'm a wrecker."

"A trade just made for you, " barked Rosenfeld. "But a demolisher of what?"

"Of cars. I take them apart and recover the usable parts."

"Of course, actually unemployed. You're Polish aren't you?"

"You think so?" asked the other, with a roguish look. "But your guess is wrong."

"You aren't Polish? Impossible!"

"That's how it is. I'm Haitian."

"What?"

"Haitian. You heard correctly," he said, and proudly placed his passport with his picture before the amazed Rosenfeld.

Rosenfeld glanced at it rapidly, then recoiled in horror. This false document would surely attract the police to Tilleuls before long. "Forged papers!" he said in a strangulated voice.

"Never in your life!" retorted the stranger. "Absolutely authentic. These papers are real."

"Come now! Come now!"

"I assure you! Don't you understand? One might say that you fell off the moon. Truly faux."

VI

The first appearance of the seven Isadores

Mrs. Hermelin's white negro was telling the truth. Although he was not a native of Haiti, a country he had never seen even in his wildest dreams, his passport was not a common lie. It had been issued to him with all the formalities in conformity with the Haitian laws by the Haitian consul to Paris at the consular office, and, what was more, it had a seal and an authentic signature.

Several months ago, thirty-one year old Bernard Bloch, nationality Polish, owner of a little shop in Boulogne-sur-Seine, a specialist in demolishing cars whose usable parts he salvaged and the rest he sold as scrap iron, had been moping in a tiny room in a friend's apartment in Noisy-le-Sec. He had gone there after he had received an urgent summons ordering him to present himself at the police station with all his belongings. The purpose of this invitation was not hard to guess. Down-hearted, his courage failing him, Mr. Bernard Bloch, a man who respected authorities, had been ready to present himself, but his wife, a small, energetic, resolute person, had violently opposed it and forced him to flee, in this case, to hide in the small room that the friend had reserved for him.

On the fourth day of his voluntary seclusion, his wife, Rebecca, arrived. He used to call her Renée in the presence of strangers in order not to offend the ears of the misguided French.

"I've big news to announce," she said. "We're leaving for America!"

At first Bernard thought it was a bad joke, but when she explained her plan to him, he was won over. Renée Bloch, who was employed by a famous milliner, had the idea to speak to one of her clients, the wife of the Haitian consul, who immediately took Renée to her husband's office. Officially, his office was closed. Many consulates and legations had received orders to leave Paris quite some time ago, but the Haitian consul had preferred to stay, even if he had to resign his position. He had listened to Renée's story and had offered her and her husband a way to save themselves. According to a law in his country, the consul had the power to offer provisional Haitian nationality to foreigners who would render some service to his country and would like to establish themselves there. In that case, the charge for an official document would cost one hundred thousand francs.

All this was perfectly legal. The consul had added that, as soon as they would arrive in Haiti, they would have to swear allegiance to the constitution, an indispensable formality without which the document would lose all its value. Renée had gladly accepted all the conditions.

The most difficult part would be to pass the Demarcation Line between Free and Occupied France, but once they were in Marseilles, they could take a boat directly to Martinique. From there it would be just a jump to their newly adopted homeland.

The problem was to raise the money. It was not by taking wrecked cars apart that one could save such a considerable sum, even if one did it for eleven years. Besides their modest savings, the Blochs owned a complete set of furniture, a few pieces of old jewellery, a small quantity of spare parts, and some scrap iron. By selling all that, they might be able to raise the money that the Haitian Republic required for the documents. Renée had not hidden from the helpful official that she was not sure that she could raise enough money for the trip. The consul had assured her that there were philanthropic organizations that helped refugees and candidates for immigration, provided that their papers were in order.

Excited by this project, Bernard Bloch came out of hiding and out of his apathy. He busied himself raising the money, and fifteen days later, hidden behind loaves of bread in a baker's truck, he crossed the Demarcation Line. His wife and son were to follow the next day.

Once he arrived in Marseilles, the difficulties began. First, Bloch learned that the line from Marseilles to Martinique had just been discontinued. To go to Haiti, one had to sail from a Spanish port which not only would add considerably to the cost, but would also raise multiple problems. One difficulty seemed insurmountable, namely the Haitian consul had not been officially recognized in Paris at the time he had delivered the passports. He had used a ruse. He had been a consul in a big city in Spain and had kept the seal and papers with the official letterhead. All he had done was to backdate the passports so that it appeared that he had made them out when he was still an official in Spain. This would have been unimportant if the Blochs had not been required to present their passports to the Spanish authorities, but the day that the Blochs were to ask for a transit visa through Spain, their papers would prove useless.

Completely discouraged by this time, Bloch tried one final move. When one of his paternal uncles was very young, he had emigrated to the United States after a pogrom. He had gone into business for himself in New York, but had continued to write to his brother in Poland once a year. Perhaps he would help him leave the Old World.

Unfortunately, Bernard did not know his Uncle Isadore's address, not even the kind of business he was in. One day he went to the United States Consulate, that new Wailing Wall besieged daily by thousands of candidates for immigration. After waiting from five o'clock in the morning until four o'clock in the afternoon and snubbed ten times by angry policemen who behaved like three-headed watchdogs, Bloch obtained the address of a place where he could find a New York City telephone directory. He found three full pages of Blochs. Of these, only twelve had Isadore for a first name, seven of which were businessmen.

He carefully copied the seven addresses. That same night he wrote seven identical letters as if they were for a chain letter. Then, first thing in the morning, he sent them to the seven Blochs by registered mail. The postal clerk believed that she was dealing with a crazy man.

Bloch moved to a modest, furnished room in Cassis near Marseilles. For several months he watched anxiously for the mailman morning and night. In vain. The seven Isadores were playing dead. Bitterly, Bernard Bloch pondered over the fragility of family ties.

Then, when the last vestiges of his fortune melted in the blinking of an eye, he announced to Renée after a sleepless night spent in meditation, "We've exactly eight thousand, seven hundred and twenty-one francs left. If we continue to live here, we'll have enough for four months. If we go to the country, maybe we can produce what we need."

One hour later, Bloch presented himself at the town hall in Cassis and asked the affable secretary, Marie-Ange, for a safe-conduct pass.

VII

How Mr. Bernard Bloch paid six hundred francs to be admitted to forced residence

When Bernard Bloch had told all of his experiences to Frank Rosenfeld, the latter assumed a very reserved air.

"Were I in your place," he said, pityingly, "I wouldn't even open my valises. This countryside, which I know well now, is one of the poorest in all France. I wouldn't advise you to start your apprenticeship as a peasant here."

"It wouldn't be as an apprentice," said Bloch. "I've been raised in the Polish countryside. From the age of fifteen to seventeen, I worked on a farm to study farming because I'd wanted to emigrate to Palestine. It's because the British Protectorate at that time refused to give me a visa to Palestine that I was forced to come to France. Anyway, I'm used to manual work. For two years I was a worker for Renault, and I never worked with my hands in my pockets. Look at them!"

He stretched out two large calloused hands with thick, short fingers.

"Maybe you're right," said Rosenfeld, dubiously. "But then you've more reason to go to a region where your work will be more rewarding."

"Tell me," said Bloch, winking familiarly, "why don't you go somewhere else?"

"I?" said Rosenfeld, with a distant air. "The situation is somewhat different for me. I've strictly personal reasons."

"I have strictly personal reasons also," retorted Bloch.

"Anyway, you don't know a soul here. I'm even asking myself how you had the bizarre idea to choose precisely Saint-Boniface for your agricultural experiments."

"Ah! That's a completely different story! But since you seem interested, I've no reason to hide it from you. What you say is true. I don't know anyone in Saint-Boniface nor anywhere else in the French countryside. Neither my wife nor I have ever lived in the country. When the time came to choose, I decided to trust to chance. I took a Michelin map of the southeast. I closed my eyes and stopped my pencil on a point on the map. When I opened my eyes, I saw that the point of my pencil was on the 'B' of Saint-Boniface. I liked the name. This little corner of France pleases me. Anyway, it's too late to change."

"Why? You could still go somewhere else."

"Oh no! I'm here in forced residence."

"In forced residence?" repeated Rosenfeld, raising his eyebrows. "They don't put anyone in forced residence, except foreigners expelled from other places. Have you been expelled from Bouches-du-Rhône?"

"Not exactly. I caused myself to be expelled and that's not the same thing. The sad part of it is that it even cost me money."

"This is too much!" exploded Rosenfeld. "You're making fun of me! Usually one pays to be permitted to stay where one is and not to be expelled."

"On the contrary. It occurs very often. In Marseilles, I was introduced to someone who, for six hundred francs, could obtain a forced residency for me anywhere I chose, except in the cities. With a good forced residency, one can be assured that he can remain in a place he likes without running the risk of being bounced from one county to another like a tennis ball. I know many wandering Jews who live like that."

Rosenfeld sighed resignedly. He was definitely dealing with a strong opponent. Nonetheless, he tried to get a formal promise from Bloch not to bring other Jews to Saint-Boniface, but the Haitian would not listen to any conditions.

"I'm just as much at home here as you," he concluded, "and I'll do as I please. If you don't like it," he added, winking like a conspirator, "*Rif mich a pscher!*"[13]

---

13 *Rif mich a pscher.* A yiddish expression. Literally: Call me a pisser. Figuratively: If you don't like it, lump it, or call me names if you want. (Author)

Chapter Three

The Invasion of the Civilized

I

A journalist lost among the green beans and the sweet peas decides to reduce his consumption of water

The honeymoon between the Vautiers and the Verèses did not last long. Mutual disappointments arose even before the caravan reached the Vautier farm, the Grange. Eugénie was shocked to hear the 'lady from Marseilles' asking for detailed information about the cost of living in the region and to see her face darken when she heard the price of some articles that seemed too high to her. Were the new tenants not rich?

Her disillusionment was even greater when she learned that the lady was not Jewish as she had thought, but a Protestant which was a completely different thing. The Jews had a reputation for being excellent clients. Would it be the same for a couple where only the man was Jewish? What if she were the one who kept the purse strings? To Eugénie, all this appeared to be quite complicated and much less appealing than at first.

For their part, the Verèses were very distressed and discouraged when they learned that the electricity had not been installed in their new home yet, despite their landlord's express promise. Vautier ended his silence and gave Verès a long, complicated explanation of which Verès grasped very little, except that the 'lectricity' was not being installed for very puzzling reasons: they lacked a special wooden pole and the delivery of electric wire was delayed all because of an obscure case of neglected furunculosis. However, 'in two or three' days all would be arranged which reassured Verès, the optimist, who was not aware of the true meaning of this local expression.

Like most of the houses in Saint-Boniface, the 'chalet' was dark. Mrs. Ellen Verès was disenchanted. The cleaning had been done very superficially. Debris of all sorts was piled up in a corner of the room. Vautier had forgotten to wash the walls as he had promised in his letter. Except for the furniture that he had brought down from the attic, the chalet had not changed very much since its last tenant and successor to Mrs. Vautier's late mother, namely, a superb black male goat that received all the female goats in the neighbourhood in the fall.

"Here we are in our own place," said Verès, delighted to be able to sit down.

As Vautier worked to hook up sections of the furnace with his son's help, Zette ran to whisper a word into her mother's ear. Ellen gave the baby to the father, took the little girl by the hand, and asked Vautier where the toilet was.

"The toilet?" repeated Vautier, scratching his head. "Use the entire yard in the back of the house, and the trees aren't too far away."

Ellen did not dare understand. She was city-bred and a northerner to boot.

"Don't be upset," said Vautier, reassuringly. "In winter, you can come to our stable. It's good for the manure."

This bleak picture was pleasantly interrupted when Eugénie entered with a towel covered basket on her arm. She had changed her dress for an old, patched, Harlequin-patterned one. With a modest smile, she put the basket on the table.

"Here's your supper," she said, as she carefully uncovered the basket and took out several dishes, placing them on the table. There was a piece of sausage, half a dozen eggs, a small bowl of butter, two goat cheeses, and even a slice of slightly rancid lard.

Then Eugénie turned to her daughter who had followed her with a basket. Taking the basket from the girl, she emptied its contents: a litre of milk, a round loaf of bread, and a few kilos of potatoes, and said, "You've enough for two or three days."

Tibor Verès rubbed his hands together at the sight of all these splendors. The good life had begun.

As for Vautier, once he had finished installing the furnace where a fire now crackled, he busied himself with a very mysterious object.

"What's the metallic cylinder for?" asked Verès.

"It's a carbide lamp to give you some light."

"Carbide?" repeated the journalist, a bit perplexed.

"Don't you know what carbide is?" asked Vautier, putting a box of small grey stones under his tenant's nose.

"Ah, I see! It's acetylene," said Verès, identifying the stones by their characteristic odour.

"Carbide and 'cetylene," replied the peasant. "It's the same thing. But take care, I don't have much. You must ask me for another supply each time."

He unscrewed the metallic lamp's wooden base and inserted a few stones, blew twice on the opening, placed the apparatus in an old preserve jar, poured in a little water, and lit it. A white flame burst forth.

"*Fiat lux!*" cried Verès, enchanted.

"Oh, it isn't luxury," said Vautier, modestly, "but it gives off light."

"How simple and practical!" exclaimed Verès, ecstatically.

His wife was more suspicious. She came to examine the 'carbide' lamp.

"Will we know how to light it ourselves?" she dared to ask timidly.

"Look darling, it's child's play," said Verés, with an air of superiority. "It gives off the perfect illusion of electricity."

Left alone, the Verèses unpacked their valises, removing only the objects of prime necessity. They had put a full pot of water on the stove when Mrs. Vautier came in, carrying a steaming pot.

"It's your soup," she said. "It's too late to prepare some tonight."

"We're certainly swimming in plenty!" exclaimed Verès, as the family took their places around the table. "I wonder what they will bring us tomorrow. Anyway, it's the end of all those scanty meals in Marseilles restaurants that fool the hunger pains and trick the eye: those 'timblales of Bresse' that are only carrots and turnips boiled in water and the coarse stews of Jerusalem artichokes that they dubbed 'mixed vegetables à la Pompadour'."

Smoking a cigarette after dinner, Verès continued to praise the advantages of Saint-Boniface and congratulated himself for having left Marseilles.

"These farmers are the personification of kindness," he remarked. "They bend over backward to please us. You were wrong to show your discontent at not having a toilet. We shouldn't forget that we're in the countryside. I've read in serious history books that toilets were the privilege of the rich in France. It's still that way in the villages. Who knows, maybe the expression 'toilet of comfort' is related to the expression 'to live in comfort'. It should be studied. Whatever happens, we need patience. When we're in New York, we'll have a tiled bathroom."

Ellen listened to him with indulgent scepticism. Ever since they had left Paris two years ago, her husband, the former journalist, had wagered everything on the trip. In Marseilles it was difficult not to catch the fever of emigration that raged everywhere. When two refugees met, they did not greet each other, "How are you?", but "Do you have your visa?" Like everyone else, Verès had applied for a visa to the United States and was in touch with a Committee for the Emigration of Intellectuals.

The formalities had become unbearably complicated. Each paper had called for ten others demanding moral, political, financial, and health guarantees followed by *curricula vitae*, each more detailed than the previous one. When Verès's file had reached the required thickness, an immigration official in Washington, a new Torquemada, devised a nightmare one night. It was the ultimate torture for the applicants before they crossed the 'big sea'. From then on, they must furnish absolute guarantees of their moral and political beliefs and also for preceding generations, their offspring and living parents, as well as notarized copies of death certificates for the deceased. For the members of a large family separated because of the war, it was like squaring a circle. Uncle Sam defended himself ferociously against the onslaught of wrecks from the war-torn Old World. In this fight, he imposed arbitrary rules and was, indisputably, the stronger one.

With the help of his committee, Verès had laboriously succeeded in surmounting the principal stages of this obstacle course. All these aggravations, in addition to the food restrictions, had caused him to lose fifteen kilos in the last six months. He did not wait for final confirmation from the Immigration Bureau in Washington which, according to the experts, would take two or three months. Since he had some money after having sold his apartment and his library in Paris, he had decided to spend some of it on a fresh-air cure and in eating well before his big trip.

Tired from the long trip from Marseilles to Francheville and from food excesses, the Verèses went to sleep immediately. Around two o'clock in the morning, Ellen was awakened by a suspicious noise. The ceiling, which was also the floor of the granary, creaked as if under the feet of fairies. Soon the mysterious noises became louder and awakened Tibor. For the rest of the night, they listened to the rats performing a joyous sarabande.

The next day at six-thirty in the morning, Ellen went to the kitchen to prepare the bottle for the baby who, like a true Verès, was energetically demanding his breakfast. A few minutes later, Tibor, who had just fallen asleep again, was awakened by a suffocating odour and an unpleasant sensation in his throat. When he opened his eyes, the room was filled with dense smoke. And what a smoke! Was the house on fire? Frightened, he dashed down the stairs connecting the bedroom with the kitchen.

He found Ellen kneeling in front of the furnace with her bathrobe covered with soot and ashes, her cheeks on fire, her eyes bloodshot. She had opened the kitchen door to let the smoke out, but the smoke came from the furnace twice as fast as it left through the door, and spread through the whole house.

"My little clumsy one," said Verès, with an indulgent smile, "you don't know how to do it. Don't you see you're choking the fire? Come, let me do it!"

He took some twigs, threw them into the firebox with an old newspaper from his open valise and lit the paper with his lighter. He waited for the effect. He did not have long to wait. In no time at all, a cloud of smoke three times thicker than the previous one, billowed from the furnace. Verès began to cough; his throat felt scratchy. He stood up and opened the window in the room. He repeated this performance three times without success. Mentally, he devised a little physics lesson related to the reciprocal action of hot and cold air, soot and carbon dioxide. Then he began again.

After half an hour of persistent effort, a miracle occurred. The smoke from the furnace stopped escaping into the room. The air cleared slowly.

"You see," he said, "with perseverance one surmounts all."

"Undoubtedly," replied Ellen, "but if this is going to happen each time we make a fire..."

After breakfast, during which the rest of the butter disappeared, Verès went to get a pailful of water, taking Zette with him. Vautier was already watering his garden.

"Will you tell me where I can get some water please?" asked Verès politely.

"Water?" repeated Vautier, with a worried expression. "It happens that the well is almost dry. I must water the beans that I planted yesterday. So, go look for water at the spring on the other side of your neighbour's garden."

"I have a neighbour?"

"Oh yes. You haven't seen Bardette yet? Go past your house and through the garden and take the path between the sweet peas and the beans. You'll see the spring a short distance away. But don't take the little one with you. The old woman doesn't like children. Even you must be careful because she isn't very accommodating. You know, old spinsters..."

Tibor Verès thanked him profusely, took Zette back to her mother, and went on tiptoe toward his neighbour's garden. After he had taken a few steps, he actually noticed a closed door.

Holding his breath, he entered the small path that crossed the garden. A few metres away the path formed a Y. The journalist stopped, perplexed.

"Between the sweet peas and the beans," he repeated to himself, dreamily. Naturally, on his plate he could distinguish between the two vegetables, but here in the garden all the leaves were green, and they all seemed very much alike. "Between the sweet peas and the beans? Life is truly full of enigmas!"

Luckily, the slight murmur of running water from the spring reached him, and he quickly discovered the trickle flowing from under a rock. Very elated, he filled his large jug and climbed up the path. As he walked, he computed the number of trips he would have to make each day. He had read in a magazine that the average civilized man's consumption for cooking and hygiene is a minimum of ten litres a day. This jug contained slightly less than five litres! Four times ten is forty; forty divided by five is eight. In other words, he would have to make eight trips there and back every day.

He was immersed in his calculations and had already passed through his neighbour's garden when he noticed that the door was wide open. Standing in the doorway was a wrinkled old woman dressed in rags with a cat on each shoulder. What a horrible sight! So this was Bardette!

At the sight of the intruder, Bardette frowned, then glared icily at him. Verès bowed deeply, spilling a good part of the water from his jug and, with the courtesy of a man from the shores of the Danube, said what is considered very French there, "My respects, madam."

Bardette raised her head slightly in response, but her lips remained ferociously locked.

Verès excused himself for his intrusion and for his existence. Then, with the light step of a ballet dancer whose feet barely touch the ground, he followed the path.

Eight times a day... Passing sixteen times in front of this witch...

He found Ellen busy making an inventory of her supplies for breakfast.

"...I have potatoes," she said, dreamily. "I could open a package of noodles that we brought from Marseilles. There's still half a cheese and a few slices of sausage..."

"It's quite enough. We don't need to harass them. Let's have confidence in their kindness," said the former journalist. "I bet they'll bring us something of their own free will: a chicken, maybe a rabbit..."

He lost his bet. By noontime, not one of the Vautiers had appeared.

"It's Sunday; they probably went to mass," explained Verès. "And then, during the day they're very busy. We can't ask them to neglect their work for us."

Around three o'clock in the afternoon, the whole family, including the baby in his carriage, started toward the village. The sun was low when they entered the chalet at the Grange. They were delighted with the beauty of the landscape and happy with a small jar of mixed pickles that Verès, with a cry of triumph, had discovered in Tournier's grocery store where he went to register for wine and tobacco. He acquired, for a lack of better things, a box of shoe polish and a tube of rat poison to assure his family a tranquil night.

Verès went to Vautier's house to pick up the bottle of milk. He extended his visit a bit, multiplying the forms of politeness, even saying a few words that nobody appreciated. He wanted to give Eugénie Vautier time to replenish last night's basket, but Eugénie continued to prepare her soup as if nothing more was expected of her. Verès did not express any request for food, but contented himself by asking for a cat for the night to get rid of the 'mice'. This was a friendly euphemism that he adopted to avoid vexing the Vautiers. They let him have the cat.

As soon as Verès got to his chalet, he took the animal to the loft and closed the door carefully. The mice would behave tonight. As for the rat poison, it appeared to be of doubtful efficacy since it was three years old. The box of shoe polish was equally unusable, being completely dried out and only good to be thrown on the garbage pile for Vautier's daughters to 'clean up'.

Night was falling and it was time to turn on the light. Verès took the acetylene lamp and scrupulously repeated the operation that Vautier had executed the night before. He put a match close to the opening. No flame burst forth, but a suspicious gurgling was heard in the bottom of the water-filled jar into which the lamp was submerged.

"The water is supposed to rise in the tube and make contact with the stones which then dissolve to produce the gas that burns to give light," explained Verès scientifically. "We must wait a minute and then light another match."

That is what he did. But at that moment, something unexpected and frightening happened. The gurgling increased in violence; a flame burst forth, lighting up the whole kitchen. Then everything went dark, followed by a terrible explosion. The metallic part of the lamp flew up to the ceiling and fell in a corner of the kitchen with a bang, breaking the bottle of milk.

Zette screamed. Ellen ran to the bedroom to see if the baby had suffered. Verès was pale and only slowly regained his composure.

Verès took the lamp to Vautier who examined it and raised his head saying, "Either you haven't tightened the bottom enough or else you put too much water in the jar. Also the opening is plugged. You know, these lamps always require attention."

63

However, in Vautier's hands, the rebellious apparatus became manageable, and the Verès family was not forced to grope around in the dark that night.

The meal was extremely modest, nothing like the night before. What was more, Verès was haunted by the frankly hostile look Bardette threw at him when he returned to the spring to fill his jug. However, his usual optimism soon returned.

"We're still in a period of adaptation," he declared, philosophically. "Once we pass this awkward stage, we'll take to it like ducks to water. I've known more difficult times."

Evidently, it was before the "Cursed Spring".

II

The tale of two saws

The episode of the "Cursed Spring" marked a crucial period in the career of journalist Tibor Verès. For two years this son of a modest bank employee in Szombathely (Hungary) interviewed and reported for a provincial newspaper in his native land while living on a diet of cappuccino coffee in the cafés of Montparnasse. The salary he received from time to time for his work had been barely enough to pay his most urgent debts.

One day he discovered an item in his newspaper that seemed curious to him. In a hotel room in the capital, a Hungarian baron had killed himself for mysterious reasons. The reporter added that the despondent man had spent his last evening in a nightclub and had asked the conductor of the gypsy orchestra to play the new hit song, "Cursed Spring". The journalist concluded that the song's melancholic refrain had suggested the idea of suicide to the baron.

Verès, who had occasionally worked as an errand boy for an editor of a daily from the south, wrote about twenty lines on this suicide and submitted it to his French colleague.

"Your story isn't bad," he said, "although a little short. It needs to be expanded upon. I'll make it my business. Here's twenty-five francs."

The next day, Tibor Verès read an article of one hundred lines on page three entitled, "The Song That Kills". He was surprised to discover that, to expand upon his short news item, his colleague had added two more victims who, supposedly, had been present at the command performance and had chosen to die the same way as the baron.

Several days later, the Sunday edition of the big evening newspaper published a whole page under a triple headline:

<u>When the gypsy's strings call for death...</u>
EPIDEMIC OF SUICIDES IN BUDAPEST
WILL THE HUNGARIAN GOVERNMENT FORBID
"CURSED SPRING"?

This article – copyrighted by Tibor Verès and completely illustrated with photographs – had brought the sum of two thousand five hundred francs and immediate fame. It had cost him one day's work and the twenty-five francs that he had paid a student of French at the Faculté ès Lettres to correct his most obvious errors. The lesson that he had learned from his Parisian colleague had not been lost.

The rights to this sensational report had been bought the same day by an American agency. That night, Verès received a telephone call from a popular female singer who invited him to her dressing room in a big music hall to ask him for the music, lyrics, and the rights to the song.

Three days later, Tibor Verès brought her not only the music which had been sent to him from Budapest via airmail, but also an accurate, though rather stilted translation of the original words whose refrain went:

"Cursed spring, cursed spring,
Where the sun was radiant and my soul sad
Spring accursed,
Spring of sorrow,
Spring of grief!"

The singer had tried the music on the piano and had instantly become lost in reverie.

"It's rather mournful," she said, making a wry face. "As for the words, they're completely idiotic, but that can be arranged."

Indeed, it was soon arranged. Well-orchestrated by an able musician and given new words by the singer to whom the critics awarded the nickname 'Duse[14] of the Music Hall', Tibor Verès could not find a single word of his translation with the exception of the title, "Cursed Spring". The stage setting added to the song's success. Under the lights the star, draped in black crepe, sang her lugubrious notes in front of a hearse.

---

14 Eleanora Duse (1859–1924). Italian tragedienne. (HRG)

So began Tibor Verès's career in Parisian journalism. Later, under his own byline, "the man of the 'Cursed Spring'", he wrote numerous articles: one on the private life of Greta Garbo[15], another time on Al Capone[16] in slippers, and still another about Mayerling's[17] worst drama. Lassitude and disgust overwhelmed him from time to time. He tried to do something else, for example, an authentic report about the hard life of a cod fisherman on the Isles of Lofoten, where he met and married Ellen Myran, a young painter, and had visited his father-in-law, the captain of a small boat plying the Norwegian coast. But the editor had considered that the subject lacked "sex appeal," and Tibor Verès had inevitably fallen back on his Mayerling, Greta Garbo, and his gangsters.

*****

During the night, the cat, tormented by hunger in its prison, scratched and meowed, waking Verès.

"Wait a little while," whispered Verès to the cat. "Apparently, the mice come out of their holes a little later."

But the tomcat seemed impatient. Suddenly he calmed down. Almost immediately, Tibor Verès thought that he heard the slight noise of running water.

With a start, he sat up as a drop fell on his nose. Maybe it was raining? The roof of the house might be in bad shape, and the rain went through the loft and filtered into the room. But more drops came down. They were warm and had an acrid smell.

Verès jumped out of bed, lit a candle, and climbed the ladder to the loft. There he saw the cat not far from a little pool just above his bed. The pool continued to filter through the cracks between the boards.

Furious, he rushed toward the impudent animal, but it took advantage of the open trapdoor and, with a few bounds, was in the bedroom, then the kitchen, and disappeared through a hole in a broken window pane.

---

15 Greta Garbo (1906–1990). Swedish motion picture actress. (HRG)

16 Al Capone (1890–1947). Born in Italy; American gangster and racketeer. (HRG)

17 Mayerling is the hunting lodge of Crown Prince Rudolph of Austria. There his mistress, Baroness Mary Vetsera, and he were found dead on January 30, 1889. This affair has been the theme of many dramas. The cause of their deaths is still being disputed. (HRG)

Verès washed his nose, went back to bed, turned his pillow over, and tried to sleep. Alas, he found no rest because, several minutes later, the sarabande began.

Awakened by the baby's cry the next morning, Tibor got up and washed. His head was heavy, his eyes burned, and he had a pasty tongue as though he had had a night of orgy. A big task awaited him: the wood that Vautier had provided was exhausted, and he had to split and saw several big branches that his landlord had dragged to his 'chalet'.

Verès had never learned to handle any tool other than his pen. "In this age of specialization, each to his own trade! Isn't that so?" he would repeat often. Now there was no turning back. He grabbed a heavy branch, placed it in front of him and raised the axe. Despite Verès's desperate rage, he barely succeeded in scratching off a piece of bark.

"You won't accomplish much like that," said Vautier who watched him with amusement from his garden. "Take my *chèvre*[18] and bring it here. It will make your work easier."

Vautier's remarks interrupted Verès's ability to concentrate on the chore before him. He left his axe. Deep in thought as he walked toward his landlord's house, he wondered how a *chèvre* would help him cut the wood, but he was ashamed to ask.

Arriving at the house, Verès noticed the youngest member of the family, an imp of nine, merrily chopping wood on a block. How precise his movements were! Such ease and efficiency!

"Tell me, my friend," he said, "where is the *chèvre*? I want to cut some wood," he added, being careful not to be too precise.

Astonished, the child opened his eyes wide.

"It's in front of you!"

With his finger, he pointed to an object that Verès had seen many times, but never known its exact use. So, a *chèvre* did not always refer to a mammal! Reassured, he picked it up and carried it, and put it in front of his chalet.

"You put your piece of wood on top of it, then you can saw the wood," said Vautier.

How simple and ingenious! Evidently, the specialists..."

At this exact moment, the door of the chalet opened. A cloud of smoke escaped.

"The furnace smokes a little," said Verès, somewhat embarrassed. "I bet my wife didn't put in a little *eau de cologne* as I told her."

"What?" asked Vautier.

---

18 Chèvre: goat or sawhorse. (HRG)

"Yes, the furnace smokes terribly and, to improve the draft, I told her to put in a little *eau de cologne* because I have no gasoline."

"But you don't need gasoline or alcohol," said the peasant. "Your furnace shouldn't smoke. You must be forgetting to burn some paper in the draft hole."

"Some paper in the draft hole?"

"You must have seen the little opening in the middle of the furnace at the base of the heating chamber. That's what it's for."

Dropping his saw, Verès ran into the kitchen.

"They're amazing, those country folk!" he exclaimed. "Absolutely amazing!"

Then with a mysterious air, Verès took some newspapers, lit them, and introduced them into the draft hole. The paper blazed and the furnace miraculously stopped smoking.

"And there you are!" said he, like a magician after a successful act. "I must write an article about the empirical knowledge of the peasant and submit it to a newspaper."

He went back to sawing the wood. After half an hour, his back hurt, his hands were blistered, and the nail on his left thumb was missing. He even damaged the tip of one of his shoes slightly. After all his efforts, the pile of wood that he so dearly cut was not even enough for one day. He felt humiliated and exceedingly angry. He cursed his lack of practical knowledge. He raged against his basically defective education that left him ignorant of the most essential things. "We study to be future mandarins, that's what they do for us. Of what use are the logarithm tables and the absolute ablative? They stuff our minds with a jumble of things, but they don't teach us how to use an axe. If I had been a Robinson Crusoe on a deserted island, I would have died from cold and hunger after a few days, whereas Philibert Vautier, he..."

Actually, Vautier felt the greatest disdain for his tenant. Not to know how to split wood! To use *eau de cologne* to start a fire!

"If you're annoyed at having to split wood, I could have my son do it for you. He's used to it. And it won't cost you too much."

"Thank you, but I'd like to help you," said Verès, gratefully.

"Well, I'll let you saw the cut branches into smaller pieces. The firebox in the furnace isn't too big."

If the truth were told, according to the conditions set by Vautier himself, the rent for the chalet included furnishing the wood for heating, but since then Vautier had changed his mind. If one had to promise to furnish wood, it did not necessarily mean that he should deliver pre-cut wood. He had already told Verès that he could find all the wood he needed in the forest about two kilometres from the farm.

"But to help you out," he added, "I could do you a favour and bring the wood in my cart and put it in front of your door. It won't cost you too much."

To raise his tenant's rent this way was not new to Philibert Vautier. He had a well-studied technique. It had been during this time of exodus that his vocation as a merchant had revealed itself. He had become an expert at squeezing every penny out of the refugees, and at the same time accepting their thanks for his 'little services'. He had perfected his methods of extracting all that he could on a remnant of a regiment that had camped near Saint-Boniface. A licence to sell wine had brought him quite an appreciable sum without counting the soldiers' help in bringing in the hay or oats. Never was manual labour so cheap in Saint-Boniface!

When the soldiers, and later the refugees, left the region, Philibert Vautier would be able to buy a large tract of forest land and several fields he had been eyeing for a long time. Land was still so cheap in Saint-Boniface and money so scarce!

"Another small detail, Mr. Vautier," continued Verès, after the deal for the wood was concluded. "Maybe you could sell us a few vegetables. We've hardly anything left except a few potatoes. Alas, your generous gift the other night didn't last long!"

His new tenant's flowery language annoyed Vautier. Often he did not understand half of what Verès said. This time, however, he grasped that the Verès family had consumed the sausages, bacon, cheese, and who knows what else. Maybe even the butter!

"You've nothing left? We eat our sausages and cheese with bread and keep the lard to make soup."

"Well," said Verès whose conscience made him lower his eyes, "I must admit that, when we arrived, we were starving and we engaged in gastronomic excesses."

Vautier shrugged his shoulders and thought, "These city people seem to be speaking Chinese, but that's unimportant. It's my tenant who's asking, and I'm free to refuse if I wish."

"Well," he said, aloud, "I'm going to ask my wife if she can give you a small cheese, but don't count on it every day. I still have a few kids that suck their mother's milk. If you don't have anything with which to make soup, I still have two or three leeks in the garden. They may be a little tough, but what do you want?"

"Some leeks? Very well," said Verès, reassured already. "It's a vegetable rich in Vitamin B. As for calories, the addition of a little butter wouldn't be bad."

"Butter?" responded Vautier, with a helpless gesture. "You came to the wrong person. It's to please you that my wife had collected all the cream and worked the whole day to make your mouthful of butter. We must give our milk to the Supply Agency."

"As far as the milk is concerned, my Junior drinks about a litre a day," insinuated Verès shrewdly.

"Oh, his name is Junior?" asked Vautier. "That's not a name we use around here."

Vautier preferred not to dwell on the question of milk. He delivered the least he could to the Supply Agency, and the major part was for the Hotel Panorama for its clients' breakfasts. However, that was nobody's business.

"But I need milk," insisted Verès.

"It would have been all right three months ago," said Vautier, scratching his head, "but now I've a heifer that drinks the milk not taken by the Supply Agency."

"In short," said Verès, with a sigh, "I see we've arrived at a very critical time. I'm in trouble wherever I turn."

"Maybe," said Vautier, evasively. "Well, I must run to dump the manure."

"Victory!" shouted Verès a few minutes later upon entering the chalet where his wife was changing the baby. "I told you that you have to know how to speak to these people. I obtained another small cheese and a few leeks from Vautier. As for the butter, let's not exaggerate. The heifer needs the milk. In time it will be better, but until then I'll go to Francheville to see what can be found."

When he returned in the evening, he was in excellent humour. His bag of provisions was full.

"I haven't wasted my time," he declared. "All of our applications for ration cards are filed. Evidently, the rations we'll get here will be smaller than those we got in Marseilles," he added in a careless tone. "We're in the country. Unfortunately, we've missed the distribution this month, but we're sure to receive all of our rations next month. I've brought some additional vegetables."

Triumphantly, he pulled from his bag turnips, carrots, and Jerusalem artichokes.

"I got all that without waiting in line. Isn't that remarkable? Surely, the prettiest girl in the world..."

"Apropos the girl," said Ellen, sullenly, "one of the Vautier girls came to tell me that they won't be able to supply us with more than half a litre of milk a day."

"Evidently, it's because of the heifer. Vautier told me this morning."

"But that won't be enough. In Marseilles, we got a litre and a half every day with our cards."

For an entire week, the agonizing problem of milk occupied the former journalist. After finishing his chores for water and wood, and editing his work, *The Paradoxes of History*, he used all of his free time running around the countryside looking for a farmer willing to supply him with milk every day. Each one claimed that he had to give all his milk to the Supply Agency and sent him away empty-handed.

Then Verès had an idea. The Vautiers were required to deliver one and a half litres, just the exact quantity his family was entitled to receive. In pleading his case to the Supply Agency, he maintained that he could obtain his ration right on the farm premises.

However, he did not take the regulations into consideration. The milk had to be brought to the collection centre in Francheville. Distribution only took place in the city, but, for a certain number of francs, the collector, Legras's son, agreed to pick up Verès's milk at the distribution centre and bring it back to Saint-Boniface when he returned with the empty containers.

From then on, at five o'clock every evening, the Verès family was assured of the milk that Vautier had shipped in the morning. When the summer season started, the milk did not gain by this double trip in the hot sun. Heated on the stove, it inevitably curdled.

III

Mr. César Fleury exposes the inconveniences of a three room apartment and men's underwear

A week after Rosenfeld's and the Bloch family's arrival, Tilleuls was almost full. In the dining room, the table was set for nine, including the amiable hostess. Mr. Hermelin, deemed unpresentable because of his infirmity, was relegated to the kitchen with the maid.

Lunch would be served at half-past twelve. The grandfather clock in Tilleuls's dining room was already striking noon. From the kitchen came the clatter of dishes, dominated by Mrs. Hermelin's imperious voice.

Since the end of May when Tilleuls was just about full, Mrs. Hermelin had seemed to come alive. With her forehead creased in thought and an anxious expression on her face, she was like the captain of a boat in the middle of stormy seas, shouting orders in all directions to her husband and new maid. Sometimes, she even caught herself addressing her passengers with the harsh tone she reserved only for the crew, but she regained her poise immediately and finished by modulating her voice so that it was coaxing with a tender *allegro furioso*.

Bernard Bloch sat in an armchair in the living room, reading *Le Petit Dauphinois*. Raising his eyes from his newspaper, he noticed the arrival of another lodger to Tilleuls, a tall, stooped, frighteningly skinny woman with an olive-green face, eyes sunken in their orbits, protruding jaws, and dilated nostrils. This was Mrs. Gloria Clips, the 'Hindu Mummy', as Tibor Verés called her. It was thanks to him that the boardinghouse had acquired this ornament.

Verès had met her at the Seahorse Diner on Quay des Belges in Marseilles. A former movie actress, she was a candidate for emigration like many others, but her chances were better than most habitual visitors to the 'Wailing Wall'. Verès was nice to her, secretly hoping that once she was out of the country she would help him.

It seemed that the 'Hindu Mummy' had very precious relatives in the United States; the best of all was her own husband, Mr. Clips. This former star of the silent movies was a native of Prague who, once upon a time, had married a rich American manager of a theatre company. When the couple had separated, Mrs. Clips decided to roam the globe.

Entering the living room with a barely audible step, she looked enviously at Bernard Bloch who was reading his newspaper and smoking. As soon as he raised his eyes, her nostrils quivered like the wings of an injured bird as she asked, "Do you have a cigarette for me?"

Bloch handed her his pack of Gauloises.

"You're lucky," he said. "I just got my ten day ration."

She lit a cigarette, inhaled it with delight, and exhaled such huge puffs of smoke through her nose that they engulfed her in a cloud like an oriental idol. She was simply dressed in a green turban and a loose, oversized white tunic. From a twisted ribbon around her neck dangled her only decoration, a superb, small peacock feather. This was her good-luck charm, her fetish. She never parted with it, and she managed to put it on every one of her costumes.

"How about your trip to America, madam?" asked Bloch. "Will it be soon?"

"I think I'll leave France in three weeks, and believe me, I'm already anticipating the feeling of joy I'll have when I'll light my first Chesterfield before I board the 'Clipper' in Lisbon," said the 'Hindu Mummy' with a sigh.

"I confess I don't understand why you're still in Europe with all your connections. Verès told me you have a visa marked 'in danger'."

After their marriage, Mr. Clips had obtained a special visa, reserved for prominent people, writers and politicians sought by the Gestapo, for his wife who had retained her own nationality. To be frank, Mrs. Clips had never engaged in politics or literature. What was more, she was an Aryan. The only danger she faced in France was to be without cigarettes. Nevertheless, having mobilized several senators, Mr. Clips had been able to have his wife's name put on a list of privileged emigrants.

"Oh yes," said the "Hindu Mummy." "I could have left three months ago, but alas, all my money was in gold bullion. When I arrived in Marseilles, the first thing I did was to sell all my gold and transfer my money to New York. With the remainder, I bought some jewellery. When everything was finally ready, I had some dollars in New York, some pesetas in Spain, some escudos in Portugal, and my American visa had expired. What a mess! My husband had to ask Washington to extend my visa. In a few days, my troubles will be over. I decided to wait here until the final formalities have been concluded. The region is charming, and I'm pleased to have followed the advice of my friend Verès. Alas, the price of cigarettes is sky-high."

Bloch sought refuge in his newspaper, but the 'Hindu Mummy' came back charging.

"What do you find so absorbing in those pages? They bore me to death."

"You can find something of interest every day," said Bloch. "When I was small, I was sent to a school where they taught us how to interpret the text and to read between the lines. Naturally, it was the Bible. What counts is the method. I keep applying it. Just today I found a really interesting item. It's a small announcement. Come read it!"

He passed the newspaper to the 'Hindu Mummy', indicating where an 'urgent offer' was underlined in pencil.

"Artists, painters, writers, intellectuals!
Return to the land in Saint-Boniface (via Francheville)
with its charming atmosphere and be counselled by
a guide who will be your friend. Write or better yet,
come to see Mr. Du Chesne, Rochefontaine Castle."

As the 'Hindu Mummy' glanced at the advertisement, a forty-five to fifty year old man with a magnificent, pointed, black beard entered the room. After greeting the 'Hindu Mummy' and her interlocutor, he sat down in an armchair. Undeniably, he was a handsome man. His shining eyes burned with a sad flame, and his hair was as thick as a lion's mane. His features were angular yet regular, and his beard accentuated his serious, virile face while his white tie and velvet jacket gave him the appearance of an artist. On his bare feet he wore leather-thonged sandals. This was Mr. César Fleury, who was associated with the music department of the National Radio Broadcasting System. His presence decorated and dominated the Hermelin boardinghouse. His wife and daughter were to join him during the second half of June.

With a studied movement, he picked up an old copy of *Illustration* and turned the pages with a certain air of detachment.

The 'Hindu Mummy', who had just put out her cigarette butt, lost all interest in her last benefactor and turned her attention to the newcomer. Although he felt that he was being observed, he pretended to read.

Mrs. Hermelin, standing in the middle of the corridor, banged her ladle on an old pot.

The passageway was filled with the babble of conversation as the lodgers entered the dining room. In addition to Mrs. Renée Bloch and her son, little Jeannot, there was Mr. Murger, a tall, blond young man of about twenty-five, and Mr. Rosenfeld, who came running quickly from his pavilion with his fiancée, Miss Sten, at his heels.

"Is everyone here?" enquired Mrs. Hermelin. "It's 12.32."

"My guest is late," said the 'Hindu Mummy', looking through the window. "But I see someone on the path."

No sooner had the guests taken their usual places around the table than the gaunt figure of Tibor Verès appeared on the threshold.

"Excuse my late arrival," he said, bowing ceremoniously to Mrs. Hermelin. "My walk this morning took me somewhat too far. I went all the way to Barbarie. You've never seen so many tourists on the roads as this Sunday. No doubt they're city people looking for supplies. The world is upside down. Now the civilized invade Barbarie."

He savoured the effect of his words, having prepared them in advance, and sat down at the table.

"What's this delicious dish?" he asked Mrs. Hermelin, as he tasted his hors d'oeuvre.

"Oh, a little invention of mine, a wild cabbage salad," she said, with a satisfied smile. "Isn't it excellent? The people around here waste it. Alas, in our country they don't know how to use nature's resources."

Rosenfeld, who already knew all of Mrs. Hermelin's culinary theories, interrupted her unceremoniously and addressed Bloch. "Do you know what's playing at the movies in Francheville? Miss Sten and I would like to go."

"I've no idea," said Bloch. "Probably an idiotic film. In general, they're all bad."

"And for a good reason," said Mr. Fleury, stroking his beard. "Today's movies are made by imbeciles."

"Rather by non-believers who corrupt our youth and lead them away from their spiritual duties," interjected Mrs. Hermelin, emphatically. "Isn't it written in *Ecclesiastes*, 'I give you joy now, but this, too, is vanity'?"

The boarders pondered her words for a minute, then eyed the steaming dish that the maid had brought in and placed before the mistress of the house. It was the 'Hindu Mummy' who picked up the challenge.

"Moreover, today's young artists are no match for the heroes of the silent movies," she said, as her hand touched the peacock feather that adorned her flat chest. "Without exception, all of them ignore what love is. Compare the escapades of a Don Juan that they show on the screen today with that of Rudolph Valentino[19] – yes, perfectly – or to the splendid actor Gunnar Tolnaes[20], or even to Waldemar Psylander[21], that unforgettable Romeo of the north who made every woman's heart throb. Such great artists, forgotten! Such masterpieces irretrievably lost!"

"As far as I'm concerned," said Fleury, cutting into his portion of soft stewed beef, "I'd like to see a succession of abstract images, a play of charming forms, colours, lights and shadows – in a word, the perfect film. Once upon a time they tried to make something along those lines, but it was abandoned very quickly in favour of the theatre or canned music. What a horror!"

"I also abhor canned goods," interposed Mrs. Hermelin, distractedly. "To think some people like peas from a can..."

"In one sense, you're an innovator, a revolutionary," said the 'Hindu Mummy' in a conciliatory tone.

"Perhaps," acknowledged César Fleury. "The movies aren't the only sphere in life where we need radical innovations. Our houses and even our clothes are in a deplorable mess, appallingly alike. The present concept of housing and furniture defies common sense."

"Nevertheless," interjected Rosenfeld, "we architects have made considerable progress these last few years. Just before the war, our society in Paris perfected a model I consider remarkable: a modern suburban house consisting of three rooms and a kitchen constructed from new materials – a maximum of comfort in a minimum of space. I can add that yours truly played a role in designing the plans," he finished with a modest smile.

---

19 Rudoph Valentino (1895–1926). American movie idol. (HRG)
20 Gunnar Tolnaes (1879-1940). Born in Norway; star of silent movies; acted in many Danish films. (HRG)
21 Waldemar Psylander: Hungarian actor, star of silent films. (HRG)

"Three rooms and a kitchen," sneered Fleury, charging into his opponent. "I can see it already! Three rooms? No, three prison cells in the style of Henry IV, or perhaps faux modern. You're still in a rut! I, you see, have conceived a plan for a real country house which I'll build as soon as the war is over. First of all, no permanently fixed roof! Why should the architects always enclose us in rabbit hutches? What if I want to read, or sing, or play music in my own familiar surroundings, but under an open sky? My roof would be movable and fold away. I'll just turn a small crank and my roof would disappear. I'll have nothing but starry sky overhead."

"I've seen some theatres with movable roofs in the United States," said Miss Sten, "and if I remember correctly, even in southern Russia."

"Have you been to Russia?" asked Murger, suddenly interested.

"Yes, I know the country quite well. At one time I was a physical education professor and organized courses in schools for girls in many places. Because of this work, I was allowed to travel."

Bloch stared at her, stupefied. Two days ago, she had told him that she had travelled to the major countries as a secretary to a famous industrialist. Miss Sten, it seemed, must have many connections and could pull strings.

She was a woman in her forties, neither blonde nor brunette, neither pretty nor ugly, but with a certain artificial air about her. She had rather coarse features and an inscrutable expression. Everything she said was vaguely mysterious.

Mrs. Hermelin stood up, went to the buffet, opened it and took out a dish of faux crystal containing a handful of cherries. Solemnly, she put the dish in the middle of the table. Since there were very few cherries, nobody dared to touch them.

"Help yourself," she said, encouragingly. "Our cherry tree hasn't been very generous this season, but then we must exercise moderation in eating the first cherries. Health comes before everything, doesn't it? I counted them. There are four for each of us."

"Now then," said Fleury, resuming the attack, "you say three rooms with kitchen, Mr. Rosenfeld? What if friends come one day and I discover I need another room? What shall I do? That's another detail you haven't considered. In my design there would be as many rooms as I wished. My walls would be movable."

"I saw something like that in Japan," said Miss Sten in a blasé tone.

"There's no comparison," continued Fleury, resolutely as the 'Hindu Mummy' gazed at him admiringly. "In my design there would be no Far Eastern lack of privacy. My walls would be movable, but built so that they're soundproof. Your floor, Mr. Rosenfeld, I surmise is perfectly level, isn't that so?"

Rosenfeld looked at him astounded.

"In my country house, the floors would be at a slight angle with gutters along the walls at the lower end to facilitate the maintenance problem. The floors would be washed with big buckets, and the water would drain by an ingenious system of camouflaged ducts."

"That's all very interesting," said Rosenfeld, with a touch of irony. "But your sloping floor makes placing the furniture difficult and dangerous."

"Wrong! In a truly well-organized house where everything is subject to rigorous discipline, all the pieces of furniture have definite places and are fixed. Yes, riveted to the floor. But a picture is worth more than words."

From his pocket, he pulled out several photographs of a blueprint and handed them to Mr. Rosenfeld who examined them critically. However, Rosenfeld refrained from commenting. It would not be advisable to contradict a pure Aryan, and an official at that. So he circulated the photographs after he assured Mr. Fleury that his new ideas were very interesting.

Meanwhile, Mrs. Hermelin, with great ceremony, served coffee made from barley.

"Did you notice the shape of the chairs? They're moulded to the exact shape of the body. Furniture must serve the person and should be adapted to his build, like clothes. But just the opposite is done. Tell me frankly, ladies, do you feel comfortable when you put on a new pair of shoes?"

Before the 'Hindu Mummy' could reply, Fleury continued.

"You're subjecting your feet to torture, trying to mould them to fit the stylish footwear. You also jeopardize your health by hermetically enclosing them in a kind of Faraday cage, thus depriving them of the benefits of cosmic rays. A man, who wants to give his body the fullest benefit should not cover his feet completely – that's why you always see me in sandals in the country. Then again, when the weather permits, one should walk barefoot in order to expose them to the sun, the source of health and vigour. In that regard, studies have shown that the natives of certain islands of Sunda have extraordinary virility."

"How very exciting," said the 'Hindu Mummy'.

"What's true for shoes is also true for certain details of underwear. For instance, men's undershirts and shorts," pursued Fleury.

Either the serving had ended, or she had had enough of these worldly vanities, or else she did not want to get involved in this touchy subject, Mrs. Hermelin rose with dignity and went into the kitchen.

"What sort of undershirt is it that the so-called civilized man wears?" Fleury continued. "Some kind of shapeless sack. When it's short, it doesn't stay tucked in trousers. When it's long, it forces us to have a package of laundry between our legs."

"Really?" said the 'Hindu Mummy', her nostrils quivering.

"As for the undershorts," Fleury went on inexorably, "they're worse and have many inconveniences. The gentlemen will understand me."

"What then?" demanded the 'Hindu Mummy'.

"Then all that is necessary is to adopt my shirt design, an undershirt that completely eliminates undershorts. Buttoned at mid-thigh, it moulds exactly to the body in every instance – I emphasize, the shape of the body – while giving complete freedom of movement."

"How curious!" gushed the 'Hindu Mummy'. "I'd like to see the *patron*[22]."

"He's in the kitchen, washing the dishes," blurted Jeannot Bloch.

Renée scolded her son, but it did not help. The interruption by the little Haitian provoked laughter, irremediably destroying the atmosphere. Fleury gave up expounding his ideas. The dinner finished, Mr. Rosenfeld and Miss Sten prepared to go to Francheville, and the Blochs withdrew to put their son to bed for a nap. Murger, who loved to walk through the fields, left with *War and Peace* under his arm. The 'Hindu Mummy' regretted not being able to continue the conversation privately with Fleury, but it was agreed that she would join Ellen Verès.

"My wife is waiting for you on the hill above Barbarie," said the journalist. "She's gone back to sketching."

He pulled his cigarette case from his pocket. The 'Hindu Mummy', who watched his gesture anxiously, heaved a sigh when Verès obligingly stretched out his arm. She took a cigarette and lit it with sensuous gratification.

Of all of Mrs. Hermelin's lodgers, only César Fleury stayed at Tilleuls. He decided to play some music. For the man of radio, designer of male fashion, architect, movie critic, philosopher, hygienist, and inventor of all things, he had found his *violon d'Ingres*[23], the piano.

---

22 Patron: pattern or boss. (HRG)
23 *Le violon d'Ingres* (French idiom): creative hobby of a gifted person. (HRG)

IV

The man from the discotheque causes the feminine heart to throb

The upright piano that Mrs. Hermelin had played in her youth proved to be a quality instrument. Fleury glided his fingers over the keys. He tried a few scales, played a few chords, and then attacked Mozart's "Sonata in A Major".

Fleury had a true musical gift. He could have been a virtuoso if not a great composer, but his great facility together with his limitless self-indulgence hampered his talent. Having decided that his genius was more important than hard work, he trusted his inspiration exclusively. That was how he had mastered a few concertos and one or two symphonies which his critics recognized as having certain merits. Before he obtained his modest position at the radio station, he had earned a living by giving a few piano lessons gleaned here and there.

Right now, the execution of this small, playful work of Mozart's afforded him almost physical joy. At the moment when he attacked the "Turkish March", he became aware of a strange presence in the room where he had believed that he was alone. Génia Prokoff, enchanted by the music, had entered the room several minutes before, and sat listening.

Fleury stopped playing, turned around, and started to get up.

"Excuse me, madam," he said. "I've finished."

"No, no!" protested Génia. "Continue, I beg you. I love Mozart, and you interpret him so beautifully."

"She's charming," said Fleury to himself. "No doubt she's Slavic, judging from her accent." He had a weakness for brunettes with almond eyes and somewhat protruding lips.

"The maid told me that Mrs. Hermelin will return soon. I must talk with her....But I beg you, keep on playing as if I weren't here."

"For me, the wish of a beautiful woman is an order," said Fleury, half-jokingly, half seriously. After another look at the stranger, he began "Alla Turka".

Génia listened with bated breath. She closed her eyes, reliving the time when she was in the little studio on Bréa Street in the Montparnasse sector where she had spent her honeymoon. Friends of hers had given her a phonograph and some records as a wedding present. Among them was "Alla Turka". How long ago that was! Alexander Prokoff, her husband, was a charming companion, catering to her smallest desire. After two years of marriage, had he not offered her a coat of pony skin saying, "On your adorable shoulders, this modest fur shines as though it were an ermine cape."?

As the last chords of music faded, Fleury paused and turned a furtive eye in Génia's direction to assure himself that she was still disposed to listen. What sort of music would be suitable for this dreamy, sentimental woman absorbed in reverie? Mendelssohn, Schubert, Chopin? The smooth, melancholy Chopin, for whom Fleury had only mild admiration, seemed to be best. After hesitating briefly, he chose the "Nocturne in F". It was a bit showy and of easy effect perhaps, but the stranger was probably not an accomplished musician.

From the very first measures, Génia shuddered. While Fleury's agile fingers ran over the keys, she recoiled into the armchair and felt ill, the victim of an uneasy, painful, tingling sensation. The piece reminded her of her past, a past which evoked less sweet memories for Génia, for she had not remained long in the studio on Bréa Street. That happy period had been short.

Génia's sad thoughts dated to the time when her husband and she had lived at the Hotel Terrasses in an outlying section of Paris. There she had heard this piece played several hundred times by a neighbour, a future virtuoso who had repeated each phrase at least thirty times and whose clumsy fingers always stumbled on the same notes and rhythms. Certain rapid staccato passages had remained in the young Russian's memory, never to be forgotten.

Ever since 1920 when the wave of Russian emigration had carried her, at the age of thirteen, to Paris, Génia had tried several jobs. She had sold Russian sandwiches at the Colonial Exposition and posed for art pictures. She had just begun an apprenticeship without a future in a beauty institute when she met Count Prokoff, a former cavalry officer in the Tzar's army. He had miraculously escaped the common fate of his comrades of misfortune. After driving a taxi in Paris for several weeks, he had changed jobs, becoming a salesman for a new brand of aperitif. They had been married shortly thereafter in the Orthodox Church on Daru Street.

But the former cavalry officer liked to live in high style, merrily spending all he earned and even somewhat more. Génia had to sell her pony skin coat, her record player and records, and a few pieces of jewellery. The couple moved to the Hotel Terrasses on Casablanca Street near the Port of Versailles. This modest hotel had the advantage of permitting its guests to cook on an electric kitchen range. For Génia, the time that they had lived in the Hotel Terrasses had been marked by a succession of worries, humiliations, and disenchantments. Young and shapely, she had finally found employment as a model. Her modest salary had constituted a major contribution to the finances of the couple's chronically debt-ridden household. For a time, everything had been all right. Every night, Génia took trolley eighty-nine to Koubok where she munched on Russian delicacies and blintzes. Alexander took up his rounds again. Alas, Count Prokoff, the aperitif salesman, began to drink, and it was not vermouth, a drink he detested, but vodka – especially Zubrovka – without moderation and in the Russian manner. It had been during that period that their neighbour had begun practicing those rapid staccato passages of the "Nocturne".

Génia associated the music with another painful memory. The Hotel Terrasses had been infected with bedbugs. For a model, a room with such an infestation was not simply disagreeable, but catastrophic. Génia had been the object of some rather harsh remarks from her boss for the bites that appeared on the alabaster skin of her neck and shoulders. The unfortunate young woman had considered changing hotels, but they already owed three months' rent, without counting the coffees with cognac ordered through room service.

With time, the director of the fashion house had discovered other, still more abusive marks on Génia's arms. Alexander, soured by his failures, had taken to beating his wife. Every day the model's décolleté exposed new bruises, and she had been told to leave. Unemployed, confined to the Hotel Terrasses, Génia had listened all day long to her neighbour's rendition of Chopin's "Nocturne". At night Prokoff had meted out blows regularly. Married life lost its appeal. Resigned and passive, she had not considered the possibility of a separation.

Not realizing that Chopin's "Nocturne in F" might be an ordeal for Génia, Fleury flamboyantly dashed through its most delicate passages. He sensed the mounting admiration of the beautiful woman who listened with closed eyes, deep in reverie. Of all the joys that Fleury was capable of feeling, the joy of being admired was the sweetest of all. He continued the flood of music at the piano. This piece was superficial and did not have the deep majesty of Bach, nor the mounting emotion of Schumann. It did not even have the gruff sincerity of certain compositions of César Fleury. Yet Chopin knew how to cause the feminine heart to throb. At the end of the long final *ritardando*, Fleury stiffened an instant, letting the last chords vibrate in the room. He raised his eyes toward Génia, expecting her approval.

The young woman moved slightly, as if she were coming out of a dream. "That was Chopin, wasn't it?" she asked. "You play it to perfection. But I really prefer Mozart."

"You prefer Mozart," said Fleury, stroking his beard thoughtfully. "You're right. I also consider Chopin a charming musician, but second-class. That wandering minstrel of Wagner was perfectly right when he said, 'I believe in God, in Mozart, and in Beethoven'. Were he alive today, perhaps he would add one or two names to his list of idols. But," he said, standing up, "permit me to introduce myself. Fleury, from the Musical Service of the National Radio Broadcasting Service."

"Now I understand why you're such a good musician," said Génia, blushing slightly.

Her companion's bold look troubled her. She was certain that, had she not heard him play the piano, she would have guessed that he would have the soul of an artist. Such a radiance emanated from him! She was reminded of the vague feeling she had experienced when, as a young girl of fifteen, she arrived in Paris inexperienced, barely awakening to life, and responding to everything beautiful, noble, and mysterious.

For his part, Fleury felt a certain intimate emotion shaking his very being. He, himself, was astonished because it had been several years since the presence of beautiful women excited him even slightly. His eyes lingered a moment where her supple silk dress covered the curves of her bosom. Her casually crossed legs showed a pair of firm, tanned calves and a little higher, a small amount of clear, delicate skin was exposed. Mr. Fleury felt more and more moved.

"Do you like Beethoven too, madam?" he whispered in a tender voice, as if he were soliciting an intimate confession.

"Passionately," murmured Génia, turning her eyes away.

Without a word, Fleury returned to the piano, and the chords of "Apasssionata" resounded in Tilleuls's parlour where the drawn drapes gave the room an air of intimacy.

V

Two readers of Tolstoy meet on the way to Tilleuls

Sunday the thirty-first of May, 1942, would remain a memorable day for Delphine Legras. Never had she known so many emotions and fears in the space of a few hours.

It had begun at six o'clock in the morning with Latière's dog, Fricou, roaming around her stable. For quite a while now, she had suspected that the dog was up to no good. Yesterday, in order to encourage the chickens to lay their eggs in the stable – they were laying them in the most impossible places! – Delphine Legras had left two eggs in a nest in the stable. She awoke the next morning with a sinister premonition. Running to the corner where the chickens were, she found the nest empty and the culprit running away on his four feet.

She was still quite angry when little Abel Sobrevin brought her a letter that Brandouille had forgotten to give her the day before. Seeing that it was an official notice, Delphine opened it with trembling hands. Her fears had not deceived her. The fiscal authorities were demanding the sum of six francs ninety. Delphine's heart constricted with anxiety. What was the reason for this demand? She had paid all her taxes last month. It must be a mistake. However, the prospect of having to explain it to the tax collector was enough to make her forehead break out in beads of cold sweat.

Still, she had other reasons to be anxious. Some people trying to buy supplies had come to the neighbouring farms in the morning. No one knew who they were or where they came from. In every case, they were foreigners, although they spoke French. Since they were insistent, old Crouzet became angry, spoke to them in patois, and ended up brandishing his pitchfork. That was easy for Crouzet, a solid fellow in spite of his fifty-five years. But were they to invade her house, what could she do, a poor old woman without any defences?

Then there was the Evangelical meeting. Saint-Paul's minister, who sometimes came to Barbarie to conduct prayer meetings, had sent her a message in the morning, telling her that he would arrive that same evening instead of next Sunday as he had previously announced. She was in charge of notifying everyone. That was easy to say, but what would she do if her son Emile did not return in time to make rounds? It would be abominable. If only her older son, Marc, were here! He had hired himself out for the entire week to plant potatoes on a big farm on the plateau. As for herself, she must make cheese and watch the goats and cows.

All these worries distressed Delphine greatly. While she prepared her dishes and curdled milk, she asked herself by what miracle could she escape all these horrible complications.

Suddenly the door opened. Delphine shrieked.

Standing before her was a cadaverous apparition with an olive-green face wearing brick-red trousers and a man's shirt open to the chest. Its head was wrapped in a green rag decorated in front with a bird's feather. The creature was swinging a whip.

With an instinctive, defensive gesture, Delphine placed herself in front of the table to protect her cheeses and utensils.

"Excuse me, madam," said the intruder who had a woman's voice despite the man's trousers. "I'm looking for someone who should be nearby. Maybe you've seen her pass by. She's a rather large, blonde, young lady with a *chevalet*[24]."

---

24 Chevalet: an easel or a small horse. (HRG)

"A woman with a *chevalet*?" repeated the flabbergasted Delphine, stammering in a barely audible voice. "No, I haven't seen anyone like that go by. Of that I can assure you, especially one with a *chevalet*. There's no horse here, only at Serre, but it isn't a mare and has no colt. I've only seen Magnon's daughter passing with her goats, but she's a brunette and not big."

All the while, the terrified Delphine wondered where this infernal being could have come from. Yet, taking everything into consideration, it was a woman and not a man. But why did she wear trousers? None of the peasant women in Barbarie wore trousers, not even under their skirts as women in town did. Her daughter, who lived in Saint Etienne, accepted the fashion. Whenever she washed her laundry at her mother's during her vacation, she shocked the neighbours. At least she had the modesty to hide her trousers under her skirt. And that cock's feather, what did that mean? And the whip in her hand? Maybe it's for the *chevalet*.

"That's not her," said the phantom, resignedly. "I see you haven't seen my friend. She must have taken another route. I'll try to find her, but before I leave, I'd like to ask a little favour of you."

"A little favour?" stuttered Delphine, distrustfully. This apparition had come to ask for some butter or sausages! This entire story of a little horse and a young person was only a pretext to enter her home. For an instant she asked herself where her son Marc could have put the pitchfork. The spectre with the whip could become aggressive.

"Yes," said Mrs. Clips, with a smile from the other world and, passing the tip of her tongue over her lips, added, "I'm dying of thirst. Perhaps you could sell me a glass of milk."

Delphine sighed with relief. Colour returned to her cheeks. She arranged her kerchief on her head and, with the back of her hand, wiped the sweat from her forehead. She would gladly give the visitor two glasses of milk to make her leave immediately.

"I'm going to warm some for you in a little pot," said Delphine, her voice trembling.

She went toward the stove, but the 'Hindu Mummy' touched her shoulder with her bony finger to stop her. Delphine jumped as though an electric current had struck her.

"Don't bother, madam," said the visitor. "I love cold milk."

"Cold milk?" repeated Delphine, taken aback. "Very cold milk? But it will make you sick. I'm ashamed to give it to you."

"I'm used to it that way," said the 'Hindu Mummy'. "You've boiled it, haven't you?"

"Oh yes....otherwise it's impossible to keep in this heat, but I could milk you a bowlful so it would be warm."

"No, no. I prefer it boiled and cold."

With trembling hands, Delphine extended the bowl of milk, and the 'Hindu Mummy' drank avidly. Then, thanking the peasant woman, she nodded her head in farewell which shook the peacock feather. She left some coins on the table, struck her trousers with her whip, and departed.

Dephine stood immobilized in the middle of the kitchen with her mouth wide open for a long time before she could recover her senses. What a day! She could not bear the weight all alone. Picking up the change, she ran, panting, to Crouzet's house to share the sensational news with him.

Latière's dog had already lapped up the last egg a long time ago while Delphine described, in detail, the incredible tale in which the peacock feather, the green turban, the red trousers, the whip, the small horse, and the cold boiled milk were so mixed up that they created a horror story.

*****

Sitting in the shade of a chestnut tree on a hill that dominated the path to Tilleuls, André Murger looked skyward. The chapter of *War and Peace* that he had read that day had new meaning for him. It was the famous description of the Battle of Borodino, memorable for the stubborn resistance of its defenders. "This is how to fight an invader," he thought. He, too, had participated in a battle, and only one battle during the entire war, but his recollection of it did not compare to the Battle of Borodino.

It had been sometime in the middle of June 1940, in Brittany where André, a sergeant in the infantry, had spent long boring months of physical and moral indolence during the 'funny war'[25]. Suddenly, the enemy had advanced. Fright, spreading through André's garrison, had been heightened by the influx of refugees and two bloody bombardments. Amid the general confusion, the soldiers had tried to prepare for an imminent battle. André's battalion held its position. They had heard cannon-fire and explosions, but had not known where the fighting was. There had been turmoil for a while, and then they had received an order to lay down arms. Treason. Not even that. Their positions had been overcome by an enemy superior in arms and manpower. The commander had considered it futile to continue the fight. The armistice had followed shortly thereafter. Truth be told, the

---

25 Funny war: French name for the period of WWII (1939-1940) when the French were defeated by the Germans. (HRG)

commander had given strict orders intended to prevent the men from saving themselves individually. Taken prisoner like the others, Murger had heard some of his comrades express satisfaction at getting out of the fight so easily. They had thought that the worst that could happen to them would be to spend several weeks in a camp. Afterward, each would quietly return home. Two years passed and they still languished in the stalags. When Murger was freed, it was due to severe bronchitis which he had welcomed as a prisoner, but now it was curing quickly. The memory of this aborted battle had left him with a bitter aftertaste. Without being a hero, he had the distinct impression of having been duped. He had often thought of it while he decorated the public urinals in Lyons with Gaullist posters.

Hearing the slight noise of footsteps on the path below, he noticed a young girl coming from Francheville, a traveller no doubt. She carried a big rucksack on her back and a big bundle in her hand. She stopped, scrutinized the neighbourhood, then noticed André, who had stood up at her approach.

"Excuse me, sir," she said. "Am I on the road to Tilleuls?"

In two bounds André joined her.

"Yes, miss. Tilleuls is about five hundred metres from here. It's the first house on the left."

As he spoke, he stared intently at the stranger. Was she twenty? Not much more than that in any event. She was somewhat small and delicate in appearance, which contrasted sharply with her resolute air and the ease with which she seemed to carry her rucksack. Her sweet face was animated by sparkling brown eyes. Her fine pointed nose was rounded about the nostrils. "A spiritual nose," he said to himself. She had no trace of make-up on her face, although she was a 'modern' girl. "Does she have dimples when she smiles?" André asked himself. This childish idea came to him with such force that he tried to find words to make her smile. He regretted the poor little sentence as soon as he said it, but it was too late to retract.

"I know Tilleuls. I live there myself."

The brown eyes regarded him with surprise, but no smile appeared on the young girl's lips.

Furious at himself, Murger tried to rectify his error.

"You carry a heavy burden, miss. Let me carry it for you."

Dressed in a white sport blouse and a blue cloth skirt that reached to her knees, she carried a transparent raincoat over her arm. André was surprised to find himself interested in all these details, he who was incapable of describing the clothes of someone with whom he had spent several hours.

A book stuck out slightly from the pocket of her raincoat. The blue coloured cover indicated that she was reading a classical masterpiece in a cheap edition. What could she be reading? Added to the mystery of her dimples was the mystery of her choice of reading material.

"No, thank you," she replied in a firm voice. "I'm not tired and it isn't far. But I'd like to tighten my rucksack. If you don't mind holding my bundle and raincoat..."

André took the objects. Since he felt a certain curiosity, he manoeuvered them so that the book fell on the ground. He glanced at it. It was volume three of *War and Peace*, the same one he was reading, but in a different edition.

"Thank you," said the young girl, with a distant air as she reclaimed her things.

"I...allow me..." murmured Murger, not knowing how to ask the young girl for permission to accompany her. But she was already ten metres away and walking at a steady pace without concerning herself with him. André stayed on the road, watching her slim figure walking away. For an instant, he lost her from view, but the bright white of her blouse reappeared through the bushes only to disappear again around the curve.

Absorbed in thought, André returned slowly to the chestnut tree under which he had left his book. He picked it up and began to turn the pages, looking at them with new interest. "What a singular coincidence!" he thought. "What interest could this young girl, who smiles so seldom, have in this book? Is it the sentimental adventures of Natasha? The fate of Prince André? The study of mores? Or maybe Tolstoy's concept of history? Who is she? Mrs. Hermelin didn't expect any more guests this week. Then again, she must have come from some place farther away than Francheville."

André hoped to solve this mystery. After all, she would be staying at Tilleuls. He leaned back against the tree as he searched for possible answers to the enigmas surrounding this unsmiling young girl.

VI

The founder of mailman worship assists in a new phase in the quarrel over the rabbit

Noémi Sobrevin was preparing to go to the mayor's office in the village to renew her ration cards. It was the fourth time that she had decided to go on this errand, but she had never managed to get there before Longeaud and his volunteer aides put the keys under the door and went for a drink at Tournier's.

Even this time she was not too early, although she had already combed her hair and put on her Sunday dress with much difficulty because it was not meant to cover a protuberant abdomen. She had to hurry. She had just enough time to fix a snack for the children who were due home from school soon.

She had taken out a loaf of bread, cut some slices and had only two more slices to cut when she noticed that she had left the cupboard door open.

"What a life! I bet Griffon is eating my cheeses again!"

Leaving the bread and knife on the table, she ran to the cupboard. The cat was not there, but she found the leftover potatoes from dinner that she had forgotten to give to the chickens.

She snatched the dish and ran outside, calling, "You chickens! Ti... t...ti..."

At the sound of the familiar cry, the chickens came running. The last was Bonne, the mother hen, sauntering majestically with her brood. Each time she fed them, Noémi counted the chicks.

"One...two...three...four...eleven"

And the twelfth? Noémi began searching and soon discovered the missing chick under a bush. It was in a pitiable state, probably mistreated by the rooster or the dog.

"What a life!" murmured Noémi.

It was a little hen, one of three in the entire brood.

She took the little chick in her hand, saw it was still alive, and hurried to carry it to its mother. But when she passed in front of the chicken coop, she noticed a pair of dirty trousers lying on the stone sink.

"What a shame! I'd completely forgotten about them! If I leave them here, Lion will tear them to shreds."

She put the chick in the grass and knelt down to wash the trousers. Before she finished that chore, the two children who had no bread came crying for what was due them.

Dropping the half-washed trousers beside the dying chick, Noémi went to the kitchen to cut the last two slices of bread; she was about to spread some jelly on the bread when she heard Lion barking furiously. "That cursed animal returned home instead of helping Elie watch the cows! He's definitely getting old and shirks his work. He isn't worth the food he gets. But why does he bark like that?" she wondered.

Leaving the jar of jelly open on the table, Noémi ran to see what was happening outside. It was just as she thought, some strangers walking by.

To be frank, she knew the lady somewhat, having seen her in Francheville. Of course! She was the Russian from the Hotel Panorama who visited the farms to buy butter. But this man with a black beard – a very handsome black beard – this was the first time that she had seen him. A tourist, no doubt. Maybe a butter merchant?

Reassured, Noémi returned to the kitchen where the children had taken advantage of her absence and had eaten more than half a jar of the jelly. She was about to scold them when the youngest, David, seated in his highchair, started coughing.

"Poor baby!" she exclaimed. "I've forgotten to give you your cough syrup!"

She began looking for the syrup. Where could she have put it? In the cupboard among the dishes, perhaps? She opened the cupboard and inspected its contents. The syrup was not there, but she discovered a questionnaire that she had received in the mail several days ago which offered aid to pregnant women that Mr. Longeaud had helped her fill out. She had even given him three cheeses for that. As long a she was going to the mayor's office, she would take the completed questionnaire with her. But to make it valid, she needed to show her marriage certificate. Where could that be?

She was looking in all her drawers, turning everything topsy-turvy, searching for the hidden paper when Lion barked again. An instant later, she heard two knocks on the open door and saw the tall figure of Tibor Verès in the doorway.

"Excuse me for this intrusion, madam," said the newcomer, ceremoniously. "I hope I'm not disturbing you. Please don't interrupt your household chores."

While still rummaging around in her drawers, Noémi turned to her visitor. "Good morning sir," she said, smiling cheerfully. "You're not disturbing me. Do sit down."

"Allow me to introduce myself before I tell you the object of my visit," Verès began, more embarrassed before this peasant woman than when he went to interview important officials.

"Look," said Noémi, charmed by his politeness. "I know you well. Everyone knows you around here."

"Really?" asked the incredulous Verès, flattered by the popularity.

"Of course! You're Vautier's tenant. The other day, I even met your wife and children on the road. Your children are cute. We know that your girl's name is Zette and the boy's name is Junior. They say that you're a writer," she uttered, all in one breath.

Verès was full of admiration for the excellent information services in the village. In Paris, his next-door neighbour did not know so much about him.

"I see that my life is an open book for Saint-Boniface's inhabitants. But since you're so knowledgeable about us, I hope you also know that we need milk badly."

'I know that very well. I know that Legras's son brings your ration from Francheville, but is it ever enough when you have two small ones?"

"Alas," groaned Verès, "the little bit we get creates conflicts. Shall we give it to the nursing mother? Or to the baby who needs supplemental feedings? Or to Zette who is growing? I won't mention myself," he said, resignedly, "although I'm very fond of this beverage. The doctor even prescribed it for me."

"Is that why you left Marseilles, you poor man?"

Noémi followed Verès's speech with mounting admiration. Here was a man who could speak French like a book! She loved books, especially ones where the dukes and marquises exchanged flowery speeches. Now, unfortunately, she never had time to satisfy this passion. Only when she was recovering from a delivery did she have time to read.

"Of course, we cannot leave you in such sad straits," added Noémi. "I'd like to help you every day, but it's impossible with all my children. Did you bring a bottle? I'll fill it for you. What else can I do for you? Do you like eggs? My hens just laid a few."

Verès could not believe his ears. Eggs? Human solidarity existed and was not a vain word.

"Certainly," he murmured. "We're crazy about them. It's almost a complete food, rich in the principal nutrients. I thank you very much."

"Wait a moment, sir. I want to look in the nests. Don't cough so much, David. I'll find your syrup in a little while."

She had just disappeared into the stable when a man entered the kitchen without knocking. Verès's face lit up. It was Brandouille.

The sudden joy that Tibor Verès felt at seeing Brandouille was for a very good reason. Verès was the founder and only adherent of a new religious sect: mailman worship. He venerated all those people throughout the world whose noble mission was to distribute letters, packages and telegrams. Ever since he had reached the age of reason, he had lived with the expectation of receiving some mysterious mail which would make his life meaningful. This expectation was irrational, yet it is always the faith and privilege of pure souls and young children and seems to be derived from an almost messianic optimism. Exactly what did he expect? Everything and nothing. Any hypothesis, no matter how risky, never seemed too improbable to him.

"Good morning, Mr. Mailman," said Verès, in a voice vibrant with hope. "Do you have something for me? I presume you haven't passed my house yet."

"Which house?" demanded Brandouille, angrily.

He was drunk – his usual state at this hour – and in a bad mood besides.

"The little house near the Grange," stammered Verès.

"That's yours?" said Brandouille, turning toward Verès and exhaling a breath heavily perfumed with red wine, and added, "...and if you want to know the truth, you annoy me."

"Pardon...please..." faltered Verès, choking on his words.

"First of all, you should have stayed where you were," continued Brandouille, with a thick tongue. "Instead, you run around like all the Israelites. Well, I've enough work as it is. Furthermore, you're getting letters and journals all the time. The mayor doesn't receive as many as you. You don't have anything to give a man who's thirsty. Never any refreshments. You don't seem to realize that I make thirty-five kilometres every day to bring you your mail."

Without wincing, Verès endured the thunder of his angry god. He had thought that he was in his good graces, since he had tipped him quite often. And here he was, full of hostility, showing his true face which had been all smiles the other day. *In vino veritas.*

"Well, yes," growled Brandouille, going through the mail. "I've a letter for you, and a registered one at that."

Verès paled with emotion. The message that would bring new meaning to his life had come. From whom? From the Minister of Public Education in Venezuela? From the Nobel Prize Committee? From the Maharajah of Manchipur? From the United States Consulate in Marseilles? Yes, that was probably it! Confirmation of his long awaited visa!

"Will you give it to me?" he asked, breathlessly, extending a trembling hand to the miracle worker.

"Not so fast! Not so fast!" said Brandouille, sardonically. "Registered letters are delivered only at one's home."

"Then I'll go with you," suggested Verès, timidly.

"And then what? I was at your house already, and the house was closed. I marked 'absent' on the envelope. Next time you'd better wait for me."

Wise advice! That was what Verès had been doing religiously every day. Just as Muslims turn to Mecca to pray, so he concentrated all his attention toward the door as this sacred moment approached. Today he had performed the ritual of waiting, and was off without having guessed that his god was delayed some two hours in Tournier's shop having a drink and settling his account.

Meanwhile, Noémi appeared in the doorway with several eggs wrapped in a rag. With trembling hands, Brandouille put the latest issue of

Le Relèvement, a religious paper, on the table and then staggered toward the door.

"You're in quite a hurry to leave today," Noémi hurled at him angrily. "We don't see you very often these days. You don't dare show yourself, eh?"

Brandouille's anger vanished like an extinguished flame. Mumbling some indistinct words, he tottered in the dark kitchen while groping for the doorknob.

"I told you to wait a moment!" shouted Noémi, blocking his retreat. "We've some accounts to settle. It's eight days already, and I'm still waiting for the apron for my little Abel, while Tournier's Angèle is wearing it for the past three days. Now that Mr. Postmaster has eaten my rabbit and the story of the money order is forgotten, you're in no hurry to pay."

Brandouille muttered in patois that his sister's trip prevented him from keeping his promise.

"Tarata! Everyone knows you went to see your sister in Saint-Paul the other Sunday and that you brought back an apron. Only you left it with the wine merchant. And speak French! Then this gentleman will know what kind of wine barrel you are!"

Verès felt deeply mortified at being a witness to this sacrilegious scene. How dare Noémi? So what if the god worshipped Bacchus? It is a normal inclination: the gods are thirsty[26].

"Yes," continued Noémi, "you're only a barrel of wine and, on top of that, not very clever! Didn't you lose a whole box of bicycle tools the other day when you were as drunk as an ass? And a brand-new bicycle pump? You can look for it. You'll find it the day I get my apron. And now, get out! I've seen enough of you."

Like a beaten dog, Brandouille sneaked out. He recalled stopping to adjust his load on the bicycle at the garage at the bottom of the hill before

starting his uphill run to Barbarie last Saturday. He could have left his pump at Mottes. He had consumed quite a lot that day! On the road he muttered some vague threats. "Noémi will pay dearly for this, and so will that Jew who bothered me about his mail."

---

26 *The Gods Are Thirsty* is the title of a French historical novel. (JG)

"But dear madam," said Verès, when he had recovered sufficiently from his emotional shock, "aren't you afraid to offend Mr. Brandouille? What if, in a vindictive mood, he were to forget to bring some letters to you?"

"Big deal!" said Noémi, showing a decided lack of respect for the mailman. "He's forced to bring me the notice for family care because it must be signed for. As for the rest... more or less one warning from the tax collector... Wait, I'll wrap your eggs in an old newspaper. You'll pay me another time. I must go to the town hall. What a life! It's six-thirty! I'm too late again! All because of that cursed Brandouille!"

While Verès paid for the milk and eggs, little Dina Sobrevin burst into the kitchen.

"Mama! Mama! I saw a man with a black beard kissing a lady's hand under the pine trees. Samuel and I had a good laugh."

"Keep quiet, you little tattle-tale," said Noémi, trying to suppress a smile. Then turning to Verès, she added, "I know the lady only slightly. She's a Russian who lives in Francheville. But I'm asking myself, who is the man? I saw them walking on the road a while ago."

Verès knew only one black-bearded man in Saint-Boniface, and that was César Fleury. There was an excellent chance that the gallant man was none other than the musician from Lyons. But that did not matter to Verès! The only thing that preoccupied him now was the registered letter whose contents a capricious god refused to allow him to know today, but tomorrow would change his destiny.

VII

Father Mignart reveals to Amélie Martin that one hand washes the other

Miss Martin, the parochial schoolteacher, stopped to catch her breath before climbing the steep steps leading to Tournier's store. In spite of the warm June afternoon, she felt exceedingly chilly and had wrapped herself in the grey wool cape that permitted the inhabitants to identify her from a distance.

She never parted with the cape nor with the white cotton gloves that she washed each evening before retiring for the night. If she avoided uncovering her hands, it was because her delicate skin showed the traces of housework. Sister Félicie had dismissed the housekeeper and required Miss Martin to do all the household chores. One year ago, her fingernails were well-groomed and her hands were white and delicate, barely showing her blue veins.

When her customer entered the shop, Rosalie Tournier, a tall, strong, florid-complexioned woman with short cropped hair and a double chin, dropped the handful of green peas that she was shelling into a basket.

"Well, it's you, Miss Martin!" she exclaimed. "What news are you bringing today? It seems Sister Félicie went on some errands."

"Yes," replied Amélie , "she went shopping in Francheville. But I want to make a telephone call."

Rosalie Tournier was astonished. This was the first time that Miss Martin had ever wanted to use the telephone. Whom was she calling?

"Do you want to a line to Francheville?" she asked insidiously. "I'll get it for you. What number?"

"Oh no, it's not to Francheville," replied Amélie. "It's to Lyons."

At the mention of that prestigious town, Rosalie stiffened, waiting expectantly. But since the teacher remained silent, Rosalie asked, "Have you friends in Lyons? Or family, perhaps?"

"My brother," said Amélie. "He was operated on this morning for appendicitis. I want to call the hospital to see how he's doing."

Rosalie Tournier noted the important fact that Amélie Martin had a brother who was in the hospital in Lyons. But was he really a brother? She would find out when she heard the conversation.

Amélie moved to the back of the store and asked for the number, only to be told that she would have to wait a little while. The line was busy.

"I'll wait here," said the teacher. "I hope it won't be long."

"As you wish," said Rosalie Tournier, regretfully. She would have preferred to keep the spinster in her shop to entice her to divulge more information.

Rosalie had returned to her green peas when the door opened. Mrs. Hermelin, wearing her mattress-cloth dress, burst into the store.

"It's a long walk to your place," she said reproachfully.

At the sight of the wife of the former tax collector, Rosalie stood up quickly and went to the table to hide the sausages and piece of bread that she had prepared for a snack. One never knew...

"I've come to order a case of mineral water. My guests have nothing to drink, and these first hot days make them terribly thirsty."

She had figured out the night before that by supplying mineral water instead of wine and beer and adding a little surcharge, she could realize a sizable profit at the end of the month. Tilleuls had this in common with certain rich establishments, that is, their bills were always full of extra charges for hot water, breakfast served in the rooms, changing the sheets and towels, and so on.

"Fine," said Rosalie. "My husband will deliver it to you from Francheville tomorrow. What kind of mineral water would you like? Vichy? Pestrin? Vals? Moise?"

"Moise!" said Mrs. Hermelin. This choice was a very natural one in the home of a fervent reader of the Bible. It was also motivated by the low price of this mineral water named after the prophet.

"Sit down until you catch your breath, Mrs. Hermelin. Do you always have enough people then?" asked Rosalie, as she wrote down the order.

"Oh, some leave; others arrive. Mr. and Mrs. Bloch are about to leave us. They're moving to a small farm that they've rented from Mr. du Chesne from Rochefontaine Castle. I'm sorry they're going because they're very fine people. He's a very prominent figure in the Haitian car industry, you know!"

"Really? But tell me, Mrs. Hermelin, did a new guest arrive last Sunday?"

"Yes, a Miss Fleury, a very fine young girl. I didn't expect her until the end of the week, but she was able to take her vacation a bit sooner. Anyway, she left on Tuesday."

"Oh?" said Rosalie, becoming more interested. "And why?"

In the telephone booth, Amélie sat resignedly on her stool. It was a long wait. However, she preferred to wait in this dark booth rather than in the store where the two women sat gossiping.

Mrs. Hermelin assumed a mysterious air, and a brief silence ensued. Rosalie was consumed with curiosity.

Enjoying the tension she provoked, Mrs. Hermelin began playing with the peas in the basket. She picked up a pod, opened it, and tasted the small green seeds, munching them like candy.

"Your peas are delicious...and sweet!" Then returning to her former topic, she continued, "I know why her father made her leave. I just happened to be in the corridor arranging my linen closet while they were discussing this very subject. Believe me, I was quite embarrassed to have to listen to them against my will, but I had to fold the sheets. It seems that the young girl – her name is Solange – has a rich elderly aunt in Tournon who is rather sick at the moment. It would be a shame to neglect her, especially since Miss Fleury has some serious expectations of her. Mr. Fleury had just received a letter from the old lady."

"And did she leave without regret?"

"Think again! She liked it so much at Tilleuls that she had no desire to go, but Mr. Fleury is a very strict father. His daughter is a fine, well-bred young lady, although she has her own mind. Nevertheless, she had to take the bus on Tuesday. She'll be back in a few days when

Mrs. Fleury arrives."

That day, Rosalie had to be content with that meagre bit of information, for Mrs. Hermelin suddenly jumped from her seat as though she had been bitten by a tarantula. Once again she urged Rosalie not to forget her mineral water as she rushed outside just in time to avoid finding herself face to face with Father Mignart, whose sturdy figure appeared in front of the shop and was responsible for her hasty departure. Mrs. Hermelin had no particular reason to bear a grudge against Father Mignart, but the sight of a cassock was more than she could bear.

"I notice I've no chance to see the master of this establishment this time either," said Father Mignart, jovially. He wiped his sweaty neck and sat down heavily.

"He isn't too far away, Father," said Rosalie. "If you wait a moment, I'll call him. He's picking beans in the garden."

"Very well, go fetch your husband. I need him."

In the telephone booth, Miss Martin had recognized the priest's voice and the familiar tapping of his stubby fingers on the table, a sound he often made when he was impatient or in a bad mood. Amélie Martin had discovered a long time ago that, under the priest's jovial mask, there lurked a violent, authoritarian character that she dreaded.

Soon the tapping was drowned out by the clacking of wooden shoes on the floor. Once again, Amélie heard the priest's voice.

"Good morning, my friend. I bring you good news. The Corporation has arranged for you to receive a supply of nails, the second allocation in three months. Other applicants are still waiting for their first order. How do you like that, eh?"

Hippolyte Tournier did not have the priest's perfect diction, hence Miss Martin did not understand a single word he grunted in response.

"Don't thank me," said the priest. "One must do what he can to help his friends. Anyway, I expect more than thanks from you. Deeds, my friend, deeds. First of all, I need the kilo of honey you promised me the other day...and a little coffee. I won't be too demanding this time. Just one pound would be sufficient for now."

Amélie felt a vague uneasiness. How could she leave without being seen? It was impossible. The rear of the store had no exit, and if she passed through the store, her presence would be a disagreeable surprise to Father Mignart.

"You seem less happy now than you were with the nails," joked the priest. "But what do you want? One hand washes the other...and this isn't the end of your troubles. Don't make such a face! I'm not asking for your right arm. I'd be satisfied with one kilo of butter."

"But Father," said Tournier, reproachfully, "I gave you a good piece last Monday."

"That's right, my friend," said the priest, genially, "and I'm thankful to you for that. But the butter I'm asking for today isn't for me, but for friends. I leave at dawn tomorrow for two days. Don't worry, I'll pay you for the butter like the last time, and even more because the tax went up two francs per kilo on Monday. But I want it with a smile, you hear, with a smile. There! That's better."

"But you can't find much butter if you pay the regular price," moaned Tourier.

"Yes, of course! But the nails are even harder to find. You ought to know something about that. Some advice: don't be too greedy. Not only should one know how to receive, but also how to give. The main thing is to be shrewd, to wheel and deal. I've confidence in your good business sense. Everyone knows that iron nails are more difficult to find in our villages. It isn't the butter you'll miss from now on! There'll be enough for me and for those who occasionally come from the city to visit you. Don't assume such a terrified air! I'm not reproaching you for anything. I know life!"

This time, Amélie's uneasiness turned into veritable nausea. She hoped that the telephone would not ring before the priest left.

"And to help you recover from the emotion," continued the priest, "I've more good news for you. The Corporation was advised that the hard-working farmers will receive a supplement of wine. You won't be forgotten; I'm making it my business. It just occurred to me that I need some tobacco for my trip. I'll send Justine to you with a metallic box for the butter. Remember my little commission. Goodbye, my friend, until tonight."

Miss Amélie Martin heard the priest's heavy footsteps, and then the clacking of Tournier's wooden shoes, followed by silence. In her dark telephone booth, Amélie shivered from cold and pushed up her cape collar to her chin, but at the same time, she felt beads of sweat breaking out on her forehead. With the furtive steps of a thief, she sneaked out of the telephone booth, entered the store, and stood in front of the open door to breathe a bit of fresh air. Father Mignart's unctuous voice continued to resound in her ears. She recalled her first conversation with him when she had arrived in Saint-Boniface. In that same unctuous voice, he had given her a long explanation of his concept of education for the peasants' children.

"Our school should form not so much their intelligence as character. Above all, you should make an effort to instill respect for authority and a taste for order in these young souls so alienated in this troubled epoch where they are awakening to life. Our duty is to cultivate their pure consciences so that the high Christian virtues of humility and abnegation can bloom. These alone can save our people from moral decadence... One hand washes the other...what counts is to be shrewd... to wheel and deal...I know life..."

Is this what he means by life? High Christian virtues...pure consciences...humility and abnegation...butter, honey, tobacco, coffee...

"Oh, Miss, didn't you get through to Lyons yet?"

Rudely brought back to reality by Rosalie Tournier's question, Amélie Martin jumped.

"No, not yet. It's taking a long time. I wonder if I ought to place the call again."

"No, it happens from time to time. The other day the mayor had to wait an hour to get through to Valence. I'll leave you alone for a moment now. I must go on an errand for the priest. Each time he takes a trip it's the same story. And lately, he's been travelling a lot," Rosalie added, with a grin. "Priests are like other men. They need a few pleasures. That's why he carries a set of civilian clothes in his valise – his maid told me that – just in case he wants to go to a movie, or somewhere else. I'll be back in fifteen minutes."

Amélie remained alone again. She tried to imagine the priest's hefty waist strapped in a light-coloured suit. Did he wear a bright coloured tie also? She was torn between laughter and disgust.

There was still no call from Lyons. If only the operation were successful!

Someone was walking outdoors. Amélie bent forward slightly and saw a long masculine figure balancing a bag of groceries. It was the stranger from the Grange. He seemed to be absorbed in his own thoughts.

Tibor Verès was coming to Tournier's store to replenish his supply of mixed pickles, that famous preserved hors d'oeuvre. He was their sole consumer in the entire county. His destiny had not been changed by the letter that Brandouille had refused to give him the other day and that he received an hour ago. It was not an invitation to the White House, but simply a notice from his former landlord in Marseilles stating that he had forgotten to pay his gas bill.

"Mrs. Tournier will return very soon," said Amélie, in response to his question. "If you wait a few minutes..."

"Very well," said Verès, sitting down. "Climbing this steep hill made me tired."

Amélie, who had taken off her gloves a while ago, put them on again under her cape. She furtively observed this man for a few minutes. In her present solitude with Sister Félicie on the one hand and the priest on the other, he was the first person in several months who reminded her of the world of distant foreign cities that she recalled with nostalgia. Would she ever have a chance to travel abroad again? Several times she opened her mouth to talk, then shut it.

Suddenly, she asked, "You're Hungarian, aren't you?"

He looked at her, astonished.

"Yes, miss."

"So I was told, but I would have guessed it just from your accent. If I took the liberty to ask that question, it's because I know your beautiful country. I lived there for two years. I was a teacher of French in Budapest from 1923 to 1925."

Tibor regarded her with great interest.

"Really?" he said. "I can hardly believe that this forgotten village may have, among its inhabitants, someone who has seen the waters of the Danube. You live in Saint-Boniface, don't you?"

"Yes," she said, with a slight sigh. "I teach in the parochial school."

"And in Budapest, did you teach in a school?"

"No, I was a governess for a family. Ménesiut...in an elegant neighbourhood with many villas..."

"I'm doubly glad to have an occasion to speak with you," said Verès. "You see, I have a little girl of school age. I almost decided to entrust her to Longeaud, but now that I've met you, I'm starting to change my mind and think perhaps she'll be better off in your hands. There are still several weeks left to the school year, isn't that so?"

Amélie wrung her hands under her grey cape. The accent, the somewhat exaggerated courtesy, the entire behaviour of the stranger evoked old memories: walks during the warm summer evenings at the base of Mount Sas; boating on the Danube; ice skating on Lagymanyos where she took her little pupil and where she met Imré, the young dentist who had courted her for several months. All those memories and his openness created a kind of solidarity toward the other Hungarian. In her mind, she saw Sister Félicie's class where the children were required to spend hours stupidly repeating their lessons or copying solutions to the problems dictated by Sister Félicie who applied the methodology of catechism to every lesson that she taught. Kept in this severe atmosphere of intellectual automatism, the little peasant children were trained to become Father Mignart's docile followers one day.

"I must tell you," she said, a bit embarrassed, "I'll not be teaching your little girl. She'll be in Sister Félicie's class, and..."

"What a pity," said Verès.

"To be frank, the children don't do badly in the public school. They speak well of Longeaud, and his classes are more advanced than ours. I'm telling you this in confidence."

Verès looked a little surprised, sensing that he had touched some intimate conflict.

"It would be a pleasure, believe me, but..."

That sentence, destined not to be finished, was interrupted by the ringing telephone. Miss Martin stood up, excused herself, and ran to close herself in the telephone booth.

"Hello? Herriot Hospital? Information, please..."

Chapter Four

The Hunting Exploits of Police Sergeant Auzance

I

The police sergeant hunts for feathered and furry game

"Hey, Auzance! I've work for you. You're to go to Saint-Boniface this afternoon to see three Jewish families. We must have a close look at them."

Francheville's assistant chief of police was speaking to one of his subordinates, a poker-faced young man with a ruddy complexion, bushy eyebrows, and a cantankerous air.

"This morning," he continued, "I received a circular asking me to get information on all the foreign Jews in the district. Your colleagues will take care of the other towns."

Having been given all the necessary instructions, Sergeant Auzance took his bicycle and was on the road a few minutes later.

This was not an unpleasant job for him. The Jews, how well he knew that tribe since the armistice! He had pushed them back by the hundreds when he had served on the Demarcation Line. That had been some sport, true hunting parties, and the game had been abundant. The Israelites had run en masse from the Occupied Zone. They had succeeded in sneaking through the line in many places, but where Auzance had worked, they had to be very shrewd to get across. Not only had he prevented Jews from escaping, but also suspicious characters and 'political' refugees. One should not scorn the fox while chasing the rabbit.

In Francheville, where he had been stationed for several months, his duties were much less interesting: a few banal fights among drunkards, some burglaries, and infractions of supply regulations. Auzance had shown much initiative and was resolved to distinguish himself. He had the record for issuing more summonses than any other gendarme in the police station.

Stopping in front of the post office, he got off his bicycle. It was almost time for the mail to leave, and many people with packages were still lined up in front of the window. Auzance knew what to think of those packages. In violation of postal regulations, they often contained foodstuffs prohibited to be mailed. The sergeant nurtured serious suspicions against two or three persons, particularly the Prokoff woman who sent several packages a week to the Côte d'Azur and a certain stateless Pinkas who also sent packages regularly. Just as one does not scorn the fox when he chases the rabbit, one should not miss an occasion to shoot some pheasants.

Entering the post office, he scrutinized the long line standing in front of the only window. He did not see the Russian who, for several days, had seemed to neglect her mailings, but Pinkas was there with a big package under his arm. "At least two kilogrammes of butter," Auzance said to himself as he cast an expert eye at the package.

Pinkas, a tall, stooped man with greying hair on his temples and a puppet-like face convulsed by a nervous tic, became agitated at seeing Auzance and threw his package into a huge basket. Evidently, the stateless one had a guilty conscience.

Auzance relished his triumph for several minutes. The pheasant was within easy reach and could not escape. Auzance liked to prolong those delicious moments immediately preceding a victory. His victim's anguish increased his joy.

Suddenly, the aforementioned Pinkas completely lost his head, got out of line, and tried to reach the exit by pushing through the milling crowd of new customers. Certain now that his quarry would vanish, Auzance sprang and caught the man in the doorway.

"What's in the package?" he demanded with a sneer.

"Some...something," stammered Pinkas. "A gift for a friend."

"Just what I thought," said Auzance, ironically. "Let's see this gift! Open it!"

Pinkas sighed deeply, retrieved the package, put it on the counter and, in a bad mood, began to undo the package. He spent a long time trying to untie the knot and then, finally, he cut it. He took the wrapping paper off the package, folded it carefully, and stopped.

"I'll never be able to redo my package," he moaned. "The rope's too short now. I cut it too close to the knot."

"All right! All right! Hurry up!" said the impatient gendarme who had already pulled out his pen to write a summons.

In the meantime, a small crowd gathered around them. It did not bother Auzance; he enjoyed publicity on such occasions.

The package was open at last. One more layer and the contents were in full view. Auzance's jaw dropped. Before him were two rolls of toilet paper and a box of suppositories.

"It's for a friend in Marseilles," mumbled Pinkas, piteously. "He's very unhappy. They've nothing."

The crowd laughed. Even in 1942, the French enjoyed watching Punch and Judy[27] belabour the police.

As for Pinkas, underneath his humble, contrite air he was jubilant. When he had sent the food packages regularly to the big centres, he sensed that Auzance was watching him carefully so he had taken precautions. Now he was having his errand boy, Kleinhandler, send the real packages while he, Pinkas, acted as decoy, sending specially prepared packages through Denières, an auxiliary post office. He had arranged all the details for this scene in advance, hoping that it would provide some respite.

"All right," groaned Auzance. "You can redo your package. It's all right this time, but don't try it again."

Without explaining what he meant by Pinkas's not trying again, Auzance left the post office followed by the sound of the people's stifled laughter. He understood perfectly well that Pinkas mocked him, and he seethed with impotent anger.

This feeling of impotence made the blood rise to his face, giving him red angry eyes, and brought back painful childhood memories. As a ward of Public Assistance, Robert Auzance had been raised in central France by a peasant family who had treated him a little better than a dog, but not as bad as a cat. Slapped and beaten at every occasion, Auzance quickly learned to hate his adoptive family so much that he promised himself that he would take it out on anyone who came within his reach. He had chosen the military police because, deep within himself, he had hoped that this profession would provide ample opportunities. The first few years in the service had frustrated him. Luckily, the armistice had brought him unexpected rewards. Promoted to the rank of sergeant, Auzance had begun to feel important and found intense satisfaction performing his duties. "Oh! How wonderful it is to be a gendarme!..." was a refrain from an old movie that he had heard and liked to sing.

He straddled his bicycle and went toward Denières. He had not left the outskirts of Francheville yet, when he noticed Brandouille. A mailman was often a precious source of information for a gendarme. He called to him.

"Hey, Brandouille! Where are you running?"

Brandouille stopped. Auzance got off his bicycle and attacked.

"Are you the one taking letters to Tilleuls?"

Brandouille nodded.

"Then you know the foreign Jews, Rosenfeld and Bloch. What kind of characters are they?"

---

27 Punch and Judy: a puppet show. (HRG)

"Oh," said Brandouille, "they get quite a lot of letters like all the Jews. They really make me work. But this Bloch isn't at Tilleuls anymore. He's renting a little house and some land near the castle. They say he wants to be a farmer."

"Can you believe that?" asked Auzance, incredulously. "A Jew, a farmer? Can you imagine that?"

"Oh, I don't know," replied Brandouille who had no clear opinion about it. "And the other one, Rose...something or other, also rented some land."

"And the one at the Grange? I bet he did the same thing because it's fashionable," smiled Auzance, ironically.

"No, not that one!" said Brandouille, animatedly. "But he gets many letters, even from foreign countries. Journals, certified mail, and packages! I just brought him one today from Marseilles. It's quite big. I'm lucky I don't have too many customers like him."

"Certified mail? Packages?" asked Auzance, with interest. "Money orders also? Could he be dealing on the black market?"

"That wouldn't surprise me," insinuated Brandouille. "He has a whole office in his house. He even writes on a typewriter."

Auzance appeared impressed.

"And then," continued Brandouille, loquaciously, "he often goes to the farms. The other day I met him at Mottes where I'm almost sure he was buying eggs, milk, and butter. The Jews always find what they're looking for in that house. Naturally, paying the price..."

Brandouille was jubilant to finally have an occasion to play a trick on Noémi who refused to return his bicycle pump while still demanding the apron.

"The next time I'm not on duty we'll have a drink together," said Auzance, generously. Then he said goodbye and patted Brandouille as familiarly as one pats a dog that begs nicely.

The information he obtained dissipated the sergeant's bad humour as he rode resolutely toward Denières. He decided to watch those three individuals closely, especially the one called Verès, and even the woman Sobrevin, that black market supplier. He might have a chance to issue an easy summons.

He was pedaling along joyfully when he noticed a cart approaching the Raillon mill. "No doubt this peasant is going to grind his wheat," reasoned Auzance. "To do that, he's required to have a special permit from the government. Let's see if he has it." When one is after a rabbit, there is no reason to miss a partridge, especially if one has already missed a pheasant.

Auzance dismounted and stopped the driver. It was Lévy Seignos of Serre.

"What's in the sacks?" asked Auzance, severely.

"Which sacks?" asked Seignos, phlegmatically, his pipe in his mouth.

"Those two," demanded Auzance, indicating the cart.

"Ah! Oh, you mean these sacks? It's wheat, of course."

"That's what it looks like to me. Where are you going with them?"

"Where do you think I'm going? To the mill, naturally."

"Very well, show me your papers," said Auzance.

"What papers?" asked Seignos, with an innocent air. "I don't have my papers with me, but I'm known in the community and even in Francheville."

"Stop pretending," said Auzance, with an ominous smile. "Show me your permit to take this grain to the mill and nothing else."

"Well, you should have said that right away," said Seignos, greatly relieved. "I must have that paper somewhere. Wait a minute while I look for it."

Mumbling in his moustache, he turned his pockets inside out one by one and found nothing while the gendarme watched him jeeringly. The shot went off, and the partridge was hit.

Suddenly the peasant exclaimed, "This is something! Where's my head? I put it in my hat. The papers, of course, not my head."

Seignos took off his wide-brimmed, beige, linen hat that was famous in the whole region and pulled out a piece of crumpled paper from under the ribbon.

"Here's your permit! Do I have paper work!" he exclaimed. "So many administrative details, one gets lost in them."

Auzance examined the permit carefully to see if the printed form was properly filled out and had all the required stamps. It read:

"The bearer of this sheet of paper, Seignos, Lévy living at Serre, Township of Saint-Boniface, is authorized to carry 120 (one hundred and twenty) kilos of wheat to the Raillon mill today between three and five o'clock to have them ground for his own family's use."

It seemed as though Seignos was legal, but Auzance still had one last hope. The permit was for one hundred and twenty kilos. The peasants, who always had hidden stores of food, cheated mainly on the weight because it was difficult for them to grind all their wheat at the same time. Control really occurred at the mill.

"It's all right," said Auzance dryly. "Now we'll weigh your sacks."

They entered the mill. The miller immediately weighed the sacks in Auzance's presence. They were exactly 117 kilos, not even the authorized amount.

"I made a mistake," said Seignos, appearing distressed. "Too bad. We'll eat a little less bread. It's quite annoying."

Unable to issue a summons, Auzance hid his vexation, bowed haughtily to Seignos and the miller, and went back to his bicycle.

As soon as the sergeant disappeared, Lévy Seignos and Raillon, winking like two soothsayers, slapped each other on the back and laughed until they hiccupped. They had played a nice trick on Auzance.

To prevent any possible fraud, the permit specified not only the amount of grain, but also the day and hour of delivery to the mill. However, in case of a storm or some other major difficulty, the peasant was required to write down the hour he left his home. Seignos found a way to profit from this rule. That same morning he had written on the sheet "from eight to ten o'clock", and left for the mill with his first two sacks of wheat in his cart. Then, with the approval of the miller, he had taken back the permit and gone home with his flour. There he had erased the original time, which he had marked in pencil, and had written in ink from three to five. In the afternoon, he had loaded his cart with two more sacks and was returning to the mill when he met the sergeant. Auzance would have had to have looked for the little erasure marks, but he saw only the obvious.

Biting his moustache, the sergeant continued to pedal. He passed Denières and came to a "Y" in the road. The main road led to the castle; the other went to Saint-Paul. At the intersection, he met a woman with a big bag of groceries coming from Saint-Paul. Auzance turned left to avoid her, but the woman was so frightened that she moved in his direction. The cyclist had to brake quickly and put his foot on the ground.

"Can't you watch where you're going?" he screamed, angrily.

The woman, pale with fright, became immobile.

"Excuse me," she stammered, in a foreign accent.

Auzance's ears pricked up. This woman pronounced French curiously. Perhaps she was one of those Bohemians living in one of the huts! It wasn't big game, but if you cannot get a partridge, you eat a blackbird.

"Show me your papers!" he ordered.

The woman trembled. She was one of those gaunt creatures with piercing dark eyes who wore her hair in a heavy chignon at the nape of her neck. She pulled out her wallet from the pocket of her blouse and handed him her identity card. "You're a foreigner?" asked Auzance, his face lighting up.

She lifted her head.

"Spanish," said Auzance, examining the white paper closely.

This case was interesting. His orders were to verify the situation of Spaniards with great care. For the most part, they were refugees from the Spanish Civil War and, consequently, very suspect.

"According to this paper, you live in Marseilles. What are you doing here?"

"I'm here with my employers, Mr. and Mrs. Martini," stammered the woman. "They're vacationing in Saint-Paul."

Fear was quite evident on her face. From experience, she knew that verification of her papers could bring her difficulties.

"I asked them to get me a safe-conduct pass so that I could go with them," she added, pulling a pink paper from her wallet and handing it to Auzance.

He leaned his bicycle against a tree and, with a sneer on his face, examined the paper.

"Your safe-conduct pass expired! You're in default!"

"Pardon," said the Spanish woman, in a trembling voice, "Mr. and Mrs. Martini had planned to stay in Saint-Paul only one month, but about fifteen days ago, they decided to stay the whole summer. They filed an extension for me."

Turning the paper over, she showed him where it read: "Request for extension applied for," and had a signature and a stamp.

Auzance's face fell. Ill luck was definitely following him this day. The Spanish woman's papers seemed to be in order. He was about to return the papers to her when his eyes suddenly gleamed. He had finally found a victim!

"Tell me, what are you doing here? Your safe-conduct pass is for Saint-Paul, but you're in Denières, district of Saint-Boniface. A foreigner has no right to change their place of residence."

"Excuse me," said the frightened woman, "but there's no baker in Saint-Paul, and the mistress sent me here to get some bread. It's closer."

"Closer, perhaps, but it's prohibited."

"But it's the neighbouring district," she said, almost in tears. "The master told me I was allowed to go to the next village."

"I'm not interested in what your boss told you," yelled Auzance. "It's I who'll decide whether or not you've the right to come here. It's true that foreigners can travel in their village and neighbouring villages, but they cannot cross a district line. Although Denières is next to Saint-Paul, it isn't in the same district. In other words, you're at fault. I must give you a summons. Why can't you foreigners stay in one place?"

"I assure you, Mr. Officer, I didn't know all that," she stammered.

"Then the bread..."

"You'll have to look for bread in your own district."

"But it's seven kilometres," murmured the Spaniard, in a barely audible voice. "And to return it's fourteen."

"Maybe you want me to deliver the bread to your house? I've no time to lose."

He took out his pen and pad and began writing a summons for Dolores Maria Mendoza, Spanish, maid, married, thirty-five years old, living in Marseilles, staying temporarily in Saint-Paul, carrying an expired safe-conduct pass, guilty of violating the regulation governing the movement of foreigners.

"But I haven't harmed anyone," said Dolores, crying.

Auzance was not a man to be moved by tears. He had seen enough of them at the Demarcation Line. Besides, the Spanish woman must pay for Pinkas and Seignos.

"You probably won't go to prison," he replied. "They'll expel you from the *département*."

"But that's terrible!" groaned Dolores. "It's here that I work."

Auzance shrugged his shoulders. That was none of his business. When one is in a foreign country, one must respect its laws.

Having written the summons, the sergeant made her sign it and left her to despair. Pleased to have met his daily quota of summonses, he mounted his bicycle and pedaled toward Rochefontaine Castle. His day was not lost.

II

Bernard Bloch learns the two meanings of the word *binette*[28]

George Duchêne became du Chesne when he married Miss de Laborderie whose dowry was the ancient Rochefontaine Castle. According to his own definition, he became a landowner in spite of himself. Though he came from a bourgeois family in Lyons, he was a dilettante by vocation who, by an error of nature, was stranded in a century of technicians.

In his youth, George Duchêne had dabbled in a succession of muses during the years when Dada was in its last throes. In small magazines, he had published esoteric poems composed of words or sentences cut haphazardly from daily newspapers and arranged in an

---

28 Binette: hoe or face. (HRG)

ingenious 'montage'. He exhibited statuettes made from bits and pieces of scrap iron, laces, hair, and matches. He even staged an avant-garde presentation with a choir and orchestra where the performance was punctuated alternately by a trolley bell and a car horn. He had also given a non-conformist recital. With a ring in his nose and covered with a poodle skin that had been treated with peroxide, he had been a successful attraction in the 'Bear Dance' which had been set to Bartok's music. He had finally reached the height of his artistic career around 1924 when he had improvised a Punch and Judy act for which he invented the character of 'Kluak' whose scalp had nails instead of hair, whose eyes were miniature folding cameras, and who spoke the Ubu-Roi-1923[29] language. His marriage had finally settled his career.

George Duchêne had met his future wife in a large cabaret in Lyons where the young girl had been taken by one of her daring cousins and who, after reading *La Garçonne*, was ready for any adventure. Captivated by the pure pre-Raphaelian smile of his neighbour at the next table, George Duchêne – who disdained the accepted forms of love as well as art – had intentionally spilled a glass of Chartreuse on the unknown young lady's light-coloured dress. The dry cleaner had removed the stain. Since there had been no way to avoid the marriage, he had resigned himself, especially since the young woman had a very lavish dowry.

At first, Duchêne's friends had imagined that he would exploit his wife's property in a way that was characteristic of his reputation: ripping up the earth like a rhinoceros only to plant mandrakes. Instead, the landowner had quickly shed all of his artistic ambitions. For the first time in his life, du Chesne had become a determined conservationist on the Rochefontaine estate. He had continued to grow the usual grains and vegetables and to improve cultivation techniques. At the same time, he had given up the seven arts – without counting the others – in favour of a new one: the art of heraldry. He gathered documents in preparation for a psychoanalytic study of different symbols on coats of arms. Most of the year he stayed in Lyons or Paris, entrusting the management of his domain to an old servant who was elevated to the rank of steward. Under those conditions, the land that had been neglected for two generations had remained partly arid or produced very little.

The day after the armistice, du Chesne decided to establish himself in the castle and to seriously return to the land because that was the current trend. He even made an effort to become the ideal, up-to-date

---

29 Ubu-Roi-1923: a play by Alfred Jarry first performed in Paris in 1895. (HRG)

gentleman farmer. This was when he conceived the idea to sponsor the return to the soil of a colony of intellectuals, thus reconciling the useful with pleasant pursuits. Whoever said that 'intellectual' must mean 'penniless one'? Thanks to this enterprise, his numerous lands, which had remained desolate until now, would become valuable again and he would have the advantage of surrounding himself with people of his own liking. Since he could not go to Mount Parnassus, Mount Parnassus would come to him.

Thus it was that Bernard Bloch discovered the announcement in *Le Petit Dauphinois* a few days after his arrival in Saint-Boniface.

The Haitian of recent vintage did not fall precisely into the category of persons whom the lord of Rochefontaine had hoped to attract to his phalanstery. Du Chesne had laid down very precise statutes which he had written in a style that was a compromise between the first surrealistic language and the language of heraldry. These statutes contained an admissions test, among others, which required the candidate to answer certain questions: "In which season does one plant carrots? Name several famous cubist still-lifes where these umbelliferous plants appear. Define the following: grasses, perennials, compost, transplant, plastic montage, *binette*. Mimic the mooing of a cow and compare it with the vocal sounds of a goat. Recite any of André Breton's poems that you like. Explain the estrus cycle of a ewe." Then there was this final stickler which was designed to settle any uncertainty in case of a tie among the candidates: "What is the difference between the animals that play among the flora in the *pré de Saint-Germain*[30] and the animals that play in the flora of *Saint-Germain-des-Prés*[31]?

On the examination, Bernard Bloch obtained a score of five out of a possible ten, failing all the artistic questions, but faring splendidly on the others despite the tricky terminology. The friendly reception Bloch received at Rochefontaine's phalanstery was due in part to the first six applicants who were penniless city dwellers. They had expected Mr. du Chesne to be a patron of the arts who would offer them free lodging. Bernard Bloch was a vulgar scrap-iron dealer and a Jew besides, but he was not a parasite. Mr. du Chesne ended up renting him a small house and a field in a corner of the property. The house, which bore the symbolic name *Ripailles*, was furnished with a few old pieces of furniture that he had brought down from the loft in the silo and four or five tools, amongst them a *binette* (of the agricultural variety). He gave Bloch some advice and wished him good luck. Du Chesne was not disappointed by the difficulties he encountered with his phalanstery

---

30 Pré de Saint-Germain: woods or forest of Saint-Germain. (HRG)
31 Saint-Germain-des-Prés: a red light district in Paris. (HRG)

project and decided to place a similar ad in another newspaper.

*****

After some inquiries, Sergeant Auzance finally found *Ripailles*[32] and discovered himself standing in front of a rather dilapidated hut. Knocking on the door energetically and receiving no response, he looked around. A man with his back to him was bent over in the fields. Auzance was sure that this was the Jew. Before going over to him, Auzance inspected the premises.

In front of the house was a little garden that had been tilled and planted recently. The gendarme bent over to examine a tiny green shoot and concluded that green beans were growing there. A little farther away, he noticed some lettuce, cabbage, and tomato plants.

From his pocket he took out the pad he used to describe the facts of his investigations. Using these notes, he later sweated over his reports. The pages contained a rough draft of a report of a couple living out of wedlock in Francheville who were suspected of dealing in the black market. It read as follows:

"Woman: Lelong, Marie Louise, 33 years, born in Puy. Husband dead for two years. Under the circumstances, she considers herself a widow.

Markings: abundant hair on upper lip.

Man: Brely, Ernest Augustin, 38 years, born in Francheville, unemployed mechanic. Although pretending to be destitute, he appears physically well-nourished; his concubine is a good cook. He has a five-year-old girl from a woman now deceased. The above-mentioned seem to be involved in shady affairs; more or less honest."

Auzance pulled out his pen, drew a line under this information, and began writing:

"Bloch, Bernard, Jew. Cultivates a small garden. Planted green beans, cabbages, lettuce, and tomatoes."

When Robert Auzance investigated, he disliked missing anything. One never knew if the detail which at first seemed harmless would not prove to be of great importance later.

At Auzance's approach, the man stood up and came toward him.

"I've been asked to get information from you," said Auzance. "Are you Bernard Bloch? Do you have your papers with you?"

---

32 Ripailles: picnic, feast, or pleasure trip. (HRG)

"Certainly," Bloch replied, holding a big bowl of corn kernels in his hand. He put the bowl down, pulled a large wallet from his pocket, and took out several documents: an ID card, a passport, and a safe-conduct pass. Bloch seemed to know exactly which documents were of interest to his visitor.

Auzance scrupulously copied all the data he found on the papers. One detail puzzled him. In the documents, the Jew was born in Siedlice, Poland. Those same documents indicated that his nationality was Haitian. "No doubt" Auzance said to himself, "the island of Haiti is a Polish colony." However, as a precaution, he noted "Nationality: Polish-Haitian".

These preliminary formalities over, Auzance decided to search for more complete information.

"Is all this land yours?" he asked, mockingly. "How did you manage to work it? Do you have oxen?"

"No," replied Bloch, "but my neighbour lent me a pair."

The day after he had arrived, he had met Nelchet, a very pleasant, helpful young farmer whose land adjoined his. Nelchet graciously allowed Bernard to use his oxen to plough. Bloch wanted to pay him, but Nelchet refused. The few hours that they spent together with the plough had resulted in the Jew and peasant becoming good friends.

Suspecting a black market affair, Auzance pressed on with more questions.

"Now tell me," demanded Auzance, suspiciously, "where did you find the seeds? Did you bring them with you from Haiti?"

Bernard guessed immediately what the gendarme was thinking. To be frank, he got his seeds by bartering. After long, laborious bargaining, Bloch had concluded a deal with Tournier and returned from the grocer-tavern-owner-seed-merchant's store poorer by a pair of new shoes, but richer by a hundred kilos of potato seedlings and a few kilos of green beans and corn. Naturally, Auzance had better not know all those details.

"Mr. Du Chesne gave me some," he said, without batting an eye, "and my neighbours lent me some also. I'll return the seeds after the harvest."

Suddenly from the top of the grassy hill, shrill noises attracted Auzance's attention. Looking up, he saw a goat heading for a plot of cabbages. It was followed by a young, heavy-set brunette with the wind in her hair and a little four-year-old boy brandishing a stick twice as big as he.

"Come, don't go there!" screamed the young woman. Since the goat ignored her calls, she changed her tone and, in a voice soothing enough to charm a bird, she called, *"Kim kozé, Kim...kim!"*

112

The goat understood neither Yiddish nor French, only the dialect of the region and then only when it was in the proper mood. Renée Bloch did not know patois. Only little Jeannot tried to the best of his ability to imitate the strange sounds he had heard in the neighbouring fields.

"*Bedi, bedi... Ano, ano!*" he yelled as loudly as he could. "*Echte, echte... Boulou, boulou!*"

But the goat was too far away, and the child's shrill voice was carried away by the wind.

Excusing himself, Bernard left Auzance and ran up the hill in time to avert a disaster to Nelchet's cabbages. He entrusted the goat to his wife and son and returned to the gendarme, who had taken advantage of the distraction to fill another page in his notebook.

"And this goat," continued Auzance, "is it yours? Where did you buy it and how much did it cost?"

This was another trap to discover whether this Jew acquired the animal legally.

"I bought it from Mr. Chezelas," said Bloch, prudently. "He also let me have chickens and rabbits. I haven't paid him yet because he wanted to find out the price in the market on Thursday."

Another pious lie! The price for this modest husbandry was a magnificent suit and three shirts. This too was none of Auzance's business.

The gendarme grimaced. He could get little out of this Jew. He contented himself by asking to see the Bloch woman's papers and copied a few details on his pad without forgetting little Jeannot, making a special note of his nationality: "Bloch, Jean, 4 years, Jew, nationality: first, French; second, Haitian." Let those fellows in the police department figure it out.

Then, with a sense of accomplishment though regretting having to leave empty-handed – the rabbit was too clever for the hunter – he bowed mockingly to the Jew and left for Tilleuls to find Rosenfeld.

III

Frank Rosenfeld calls his grandfather an old fool

Because of his inexperience and over-confidence in his universal genius, Frank Rosenfeld's initiation into agriculture was very frustrating. He had got it into his head that he could be a successful farmer the very first season. If every half-wit in the region could do it, why couldn't he, Frank

Rosenfeld, do it as well?

He had no intention of being satisfied with growing a few vegetables for his personal consumption, but planned, instead, to reap substantial profits from his land by selling the fruits of his labour to city dwellers. During the growing season he decided that he would work and hoard the produce like an ant. Afterward, he would be busy with the commercial aspect of his enterprise. Dry legumes, cheese, butter, and foods preserved in salt were not too cumbersome and were easy to transport. He planned to apply his marketing principle: the maximum price for the minimum quantity. His fiancée, who would run the business, did not object.

He planted beans, chickpeas, and lentils in abundance. At the same time, he built the chicken coop where the chickens would lay golden eggs. His neighbour, Chazelas, advised him to begin by putting a fence around his garden, but Rosenfeld preferred to build perfect cages to house his rabbits. He negotiated the purchase of several goats, and he ran all over the region looking for a young cow, the cow of his and Mrs. Hermelin's dreams.

Soon Mr. Rosenfeld's blue skies turned cloudy. He had to admit that there were a few things he had to learn. His free-roaming chickens began gorging themselves on the pea and bean seeds he had planted in the garden. Enraged, he killed the best of his chickens and, to Mrs. Hermelin's astonishment, roasted it and garnished it with cherry compote as it was done in his native land.

The goats also caused a number of problems for this pioneer who had returned to the land. First, they ate a jacket that Miss Sten had taken out of mothballs and put out to air. As food, the mothballs may have been quite spicy, but the goats developed a taste for them. What was even worse was that they refused to be milked by the inexperienced Rosenfeld, attacking him with their horns and kicking so much that he became disgusted and rented them out to Chazelas while he took practical lessons in milking. As for the rabbits, fed synthetic food and installed in the modern cages designed by Rosenfeld, they inexplicably began dying in increasing numbers.

When Auzance arrived at Tilleuls, Rosenfeld's sky was decidedly stormy. The thunder erupted when the two equally charged temperaments, Mrs. Hermelin's and Rosenfeld's, collided over nettles.

To save the last of his rabbits, Rosenfeld was advised to cure them with nettles. When Mrs. Hermelin learned that her tenant was pulling up the nettle plants around Tilleuls to feed them to those rodents, the anger that she had nurtured for quite a while erupted. In a torrential flood of words, she reproached him for everything at once: for the suspicious postponement of his marriage, which caused her, the daughter and mother of a minister, to house a couple living in sin; for delaying his conversion; for using her private quarters; and, above all, for the deception he created by postponing the purchase of a cow when she needed the milk so badly! Rosenfeld, whose sweaty nose indicated intense emotion, launched a vigorous counter-attack to this tirade. Even if he were not married yet, the banns were posted in the town hall. Even if he were not converted yet, that concerned only his conscience. Even if he preferred to use Mrs. Hermelin's private quarters, it was because the lodgers' quarters were always occupied by Mr. Hermelin, who spent whole hours there (the unfortunate man's only refuge from conjugal tyranny). As for the cow...

At that moment he spotted Auzance getting off his bicycle and walking toward his house. Rosenfeld quickly swallowed the rest of his speech, murmured something under his breath, left his basket of herbs, and hastily went indoors. He preferred to temporarily abandon the stage at Tilleuls to Mrs. Hermelin, rather than face a gendarme.

This strategic retreat gave him only a short respite. A minute later, the energetic knocking on his door made him understand that the gendarme's visit was meant for him. Rosenfeld trembled; his nose was still sweaty. Quickly regaining his composure, he opened the door.

"Frank Rosenfeld?" asked Auzance, in an official tone. "I must ask you for certain information."

"Completely at your service," said Rosenfeld, amiably but in a somewhat tremulous voice. "Please sit down."

He pushed a chair toward Auzance and dusted it carefully with his handkerchief.

"I'm here to verify your documents," said Auzance, harshly, as he sat down.

Was that all he really wanted? A weight fell from Rosenfeld's chest. What had he not imagined in the space of a few seconds? He had pictured himself being searched, imprisoned, crucified. After that, a simple verification of his documents was a pleasure, a social game.

"Yes, certainly," he said, with a radiant face. "I'm entirely at your service, Mr. Gendarme. Let me express my regrets to you for having you travel here in this heat. If I'd known that you needed me, I'd have been pleased to go down to the police station."

Rosenfeld's attitude clearly indicated that he was aware of the abyss that separated a brave Aryan gendarme from a miserable Jew.

"We must do our duty," grunted Auzance.

"Of course, of course," replied Rosenfeld, trying to get into the gendarme's good graces. "Nevertheless, I'm sorry to be such trouble to you. I know how hard it is to climb this hill on a bicycle. Surely, you must be thirsty, Mr. Gendarme, aren't you? It's inexcusable of me not to think of it sooner. Yes, yes...you've made such an effort, and I've failed to show the most elementary hospitality. Here are my documents. Look at them at your leisure while I look for something to drink."

He quickly disappeared.

Auzance, who knew how to be stoic while on duty, did not have the strength to refuse an offer stated so graciously. While he was examining the Jew's papers with his usual attention to detail, Rosenfeld came up from the cellar with a sealed bottle of white wine under his arm. He had paid a good price to Tournier for this bottle in anticipation of a great occasion. The gendarme's visit was clearly in this category.

"I must ask you to excuse this poor reception," he said, as he took two glasses of faux crystal from the sideboard. "Unfortunately, my fiancée, Miss Sten, went to Francheville. She'll regret having missed you. She'd have served you more ceremoniously."

He uncorked the bottle of Fontecreuse, poured a few drops into his own glass as he had seen others do, then generously filled Auzance's glass, and then his own.

"To your health, Mr. Gendarme, and to the restoration of France!"

How could Auzance refuse a glass of wine after such a toast? He nodded his head as a sign of thanks. Since the wine was agreeably cool, he emptied his glass in one gulp.

"Your visit gives me great pleasure," said Rosenfeld, smiling graciously as he put down his glass. "Alas, at the present time, control and verification measures aren't superfluous. I daresay, they're even indispensable to separate the chaff from the wheat."

Mr. Rosenfeld refrained from being too precise, but he insinuated that he considered himself in the latter category.

While Rosenfeld talked, Auzance made careful notes from the data presented by the named Rosenfeld who willingly submitted the papers one after another, desiring to save the guardian of the law any unnecessary effort. The gendarme noticed that everything was in order: document, stamp, signature.

Meanwhile, Rosenfeld filled Auzance's glass with Fontecreuse. Had Auzance noticed the gesture, he would have refused, but since the wine had been poured, he had to drink it.

"You're an...Israelite?" he asked, making an effort to sound official.

"Yes," replied Rosenfeld with a sigh, sounding as if he were admitting to a shameful malady. "I never made a secret of it." As he spoke, he pulled out another document, and added in his defence, "However, I'm going to marry an Aryan woman in a few days. I'm also a veteran...of two wars."

"What? You were in World War I?" asked the astonished Auzance.

"That's to say, I was in it toward the end, in the National Lithuanian Army, fighting the Bolsheviks. Here are my papers. Please note that detail. The authorities may eventually be interested in it," he added most respectfully.

While Auzance copied the details of Mr. Rosenfeld's military career, Rosenfeld filled his visitor's glass to the brim. Then he pulled out his cigarette case and offered a cigarette to the gendarme. Again Auzance hesitated a moment, but as always, only the first step was difficult. He ended up taking the cigarette. Rosenfeld politely lit Auzance's cigarette. Completely disarmed, Auzance drank his wine in small sips.

"You've surely noticed, Mr. Gendarme, that I had practised as a professional architect. Now unfortunately, France needs bread more than new houses. That's why I decided to switch to farming."

After refilling Auzance's glass, he continued, "If you're interested in the details, I'll tell you my plans. Since the country needs fats and oils, next season I intend to cultivate oil-producing grains on a vast scale. Moreover, I'll raise two pigs; one for the Supply Agency, which needs it badly – the countryside supplies too few – and the other for my family's use. I intend to help my friends, too. Do you like sausages, Mr. Gendarme? I know how to make very good ones, like they're made in my old country. I'd be greatly honoured it you'd taste them when the time comes. Don't protest, sir. I know you object to the restrictions as much as any city dweller. You keep a dignified silence on the subject. It's very commendable of you. Yet, it would be unfortunate if we, the producers, couldn't occasionally show some favours to the people who watch over our safety and guard our property. Another cigarette?"

This time Auzance accepted without hesitation. For a Jew, this Frank Rosenfeld was a well-bred man. As for Auzance being a gendarme, that did not stop him from liking sausages any the less.

"Another drop?" asked Rosenfeld, as he poured another glass for Auzance. "I just mentioned your weighty duties because I want you to know there are still quite a few of us who appreciate your disinterested devotion. I'm among the first to recognize it and also regret that some Israelites cause quite a bit of trouble. As far as I'm concerned, I'm almost at the point of breaking all my ties with my fellow Jews. I won't hide my intention to be converted very soon. This I confide to you as a private citizen, not as a representative of the law."

There was less than a glass of wine left in the bottle. Auzance's mood rose in indirect proportion to the amount of wine in the bottle. "This Mr. Rosenfeld is right. The Jews have given me enough trouble," he thought. However, since he was in a good humour, he saw only the comical side of those experiences. Suddenly, he remembered several incidents that had occurred at the Demarcation Line. They brought a smile to his lips.

"Yes," he said, "I found some difficult characters among the Israelites. For instance, at the Line last winter I arrested a fellow who was hiding in the forest. He tried to camouflage himself with snow when he was about to be caught, but the imbecile hadn't thought of disguising his trail in the snow. All I had to do was to pull him up from his burrow where he was curled up, as the hunters say. He was a sight! All curled up! He was so scared that he writhed with colic. With all that, he never stopped sneezing and farting! Achoo!...prrrt! Again and again! All curled up! That character made me laugh!"

As he recalled the grotesque behavior of the Jew, Auzance's humour improved. He fell out of the chair and laughed his head off until his shirt popped open, and his belly showed. He held his paunch in both hands.

"Ha! Ha! Ha! What diarrhoea! Famous diarrhoea!"

Mr. Rosenfeld listened complacently to this tale. Now he joined in the gendarme's laughter. An instant later, Rosenfeld's laugh cracked. Behind his half-closed eyelids, he saw his grandfather's face. He rarely thought about him.

His grandfather had been an old man with earlocks who had been animated by his ardent Jewish faith. His name for those Jews who failed to show dignity in their relationships with gentiles was *maioufès*. The old man had explained to his grandson that, in times past, some Jews, who were jesters on the estates of Polish nobles, made fun of the liturgical chanting and nasal singing in the synagogue. These harmless fools, who were particularly successful in making the grandees laugh, had received the despised nickname *maioufès*, which is derived from the first words of the *Song of Songs*.

While laughing with the gendarme over the unfortunate Jew sick with fear, Rosenfeld seemed to hear the feeble voice of his grandfather murmuring, *"Maioufès..."* But he quickly chased away this inopportune thought. Instead of telling him those unsuitable bedtime stories, the old fool would have been better off shaving off his earlocks and being converted.

By now, Auzance had all the information for his report. Moreover, the bottle of Fontecreuse was empty. He stood up and shook hands with his host who thanked him warmly for his 'pleasant visit' and offered him another cigarette to smoke on the way.

"Surely," said Auzance to himself as he left, "this is no ordinary hunting party." For the first time whilst running after a rabbit, he had found a fat pig. In the space of half an hour, the Jew Rosenfeld became, in the gendarme's mind, Mr. Frank Rosenfeld.

Under the influence of the wine, Auzance's thoughts were a bit confused as he talked to himself. "He's a Jew. So what? It's I, Robert Auzance, who must decide who amongst the Jews of Saint-Boniface is a gentleman Israelite, or a dirty Jew."

IV

The police sergeant suspects Marquise's assassin to be Hannibal's accomplice in a black market affair

From Tilleuls to the Grange was about twenty minutes by bicycle with a good part of it on foot. Auzance's good humour had dissipated somewhat when he knocked on the door of the chalet around five o'clock in the afternoon. No one came to open it, but he heard a noise behind him. Turning around, he saw Philibert Vautier going home with a shovel on his shoulder.

"Hey, boss! Is anyone in this hut?" shouted Auzance.

Vautier dragged himself over.

"He isn't far away, sir. I just saw him from up there. He's coming from Saint-Boniface. He must have gone to look for groceries."

Vautier turned toward his own place, but the gendarme stopped him.

"Tell me," he said, in a confidential tone, "What's this fellow really like? What's his occupation?

"He's into writing," said Vautier, in a bad mood. "He writes on a typewriter. But then I don't know very much about it," he added prudently.

"We've information that he goes to the farms and deals on the black market," added Auzance, in an official tone.

The sergeant had made a faux pas. One does not talk about a rope in the house of the hanged. Vautier, embarrassed, scratched his head.

"Black market?" he asked, hesitantly. "I know nothing about that."

"But aren't you his closest neighbour?" insisted Auzance.

"Not I, but Bardette. She's closer. Look, there's her house. But they don't get along very well. They had quite an argument this morning."

Auzance smiled. He knew Bardette. He had issued a summons to the old woman the other day because she carried six kilos of bran for her rabbits.

"Did they argue about the black market?" suggested Auzance.

"Oh no! It was over the black cat."

Vautier decided to avoid the touchy subject of the black market.

"Mr. Verès had poisoned Marquise, Bardette's cat. He had put out poison for two or three rats he had in his loft, but the cat had eaten the poison and croaked."

"Ah," said Auzance, disappointed. "But you certainly ought to know if someone brings him things for dealing on the black market, or if he goes to the farms. You must see him passing by."

"Oh, I don't see him too much," said Vautier, evasively. "To get water, he walks over there, close to Bardette's garden, even if the old woman argues with him each time he goes by."

"You said he went shopping?" asked Auzance, refusing to follow Vautier's train of thought. "Does he go often?"

"Yesterday, he went to the drugstore in Francheville to buy poison. He'd have been better off staying at home. He did a good job with his death-to-the-rats poison. And Bardette isn't gentle."

Meanwhile, Verès had appeared at the high point in the path leading from the Grange to the chalet. Vautier, who noticed him first, pointed him out to Auzance and then prudently disappeared. Tibor, plunged in his thoughts, had not noticed the two men, but continued down the path while balancing his sack of groceries.

"Are you Tibor Verès?" asked Auzance, rushing from behind the house. "I'm here to inspect your papers."

Taken aback, Verès opened the chalet door to let the gendarme in. Auzance set to work at once. The status of Mr. Verès, Tibor, Hungarian, thirty-five years old, also his spouse, born Myran, Ellen, twenty-eight, of Norwegian nationality, and of their two children soon filled an entire page. The first difficulty arose when it was time to record Verès's occupation. His ID card specified journalist, man of letters.

This corroborated what Brandouille, the mailman, had said about Verès receiving many newspapers and letters. Nevertheless, in Auzance's eyes, this description was not clear enough.

"All right," he grumbled, "we must know what you're really doing."

"You see," said Verès, with a grand gesture, "in normal times I write articles for newspapers. Naturally, right now..."

"But what are you writing, and for which newspapers? That's what interests us," insisted Auzance.

He did not specify who was meant by 'us'. Was it the plural for majesty, or the police station in Francheville, or the county officials, or the Vichy government?

"Oh, I wrote mainly for foreign newspapers. Some reports, some articles about life in France, and in general whatever was interesting," said Verès.

"So you inform foreigners what's happening here," concluded Auzance.

Startled by such a statement, Verès protested vehemently. "No, no! That's the job of spies. I'm a journalist. Please note: I write articles."

Auzance, always contrary, scribbled some words on his pad.

"Right now, on the eve of our departure for America – I already have a visa" Verès said, animatedly. "I'm writing a history book I'll call *The Paradoxes of History*. It's a series of generally little known facts that I'm presenting in a new light. Take, for instance, Frederick the Great, King of Prussia who's believed..."

His explanation was brutally interrupted by a hoarse scream rather close by.

"The assassin! The assassin!"

Instantly Auzance jumped up demanding, "Who's been killed! Where? Why?" But the confused Verès begged him to remain seated.

"Don't let it bother you. It's nothing! Only a stupid story about a cat. My neighbour is a bit nervous."

"Hey, assassin!" shouted Bardette, who had come out of her den after hearing Verès familiar voice. Hidden in her kitchen behind closed doors, she had not seen Auzance arrive.

"Ah yes," said the sergeant, assuming an air of importance, "we've already been informed of this incident. You've poisoned your neighbour's cat."

Verès jaw dropped. The police in Francheville were admirably alert, almost like Scotland Yard.

Suddenly, a shower of pebbles, thrown through a small window facing Bardette's garden, fell on the kitchen floor.

"Look, sweet peas for the assassin's soup!" yelled Bardette, and she began insulting him in patois.

"Granda borriqua! Viaoux pas ré! Va!"

"I beg you to be quiet, madam. I'm busy," shouted the journalist.

"Caliou! Mesca murlet! Granda rocha! Caliou va!" continued Bardette.

"Enough, enough," said Verès, in a conciliatory manner. "And now madam, it's about time you calmed down."

But much more was needed to appease Bardette's fury. She continued her curses in patois.

"Londzo braïo! Voleur d'aïo! Achachin!"

"That's quite enough, madam," shouted Verès, tired of her screams. "Be quiet! *Favete linguis!* Yes, madam, *favete linguis!*"

Impressed, no doubt, by this learned quotation to quiet down, Bardette stopped speaking patois.

"Poisoner! Water stealer!" screeched the old woman. "Try passing through my garden with a pail! I'll break it over your head! Then I'll look for the police! It will give those lazy bones something to do!"

Hearing those words, Auzance jumped like a jack-in-the-box. Suddenly, Bardette saw the sergeant's cap framed in the kitchen window. Terrified by this supernatural apparition, the old girl fell silent, beat a hasty retreat and, arriving at her home, barricaded herself.

"It's not my fault," stammered Verès, very annoyed. "Our loft's full of rats. I tried everything to get rid of them. I didn't know my neighbour's cat frequently went to my loft. I can't understand why the attic is still so full of rats when it's haunted by a domestic feline."

Auzance returned to his seat. After all, Marquise's assassination was not under his jurisdiction.

"I sympathize with this poor woman's feelings. She was very attached to that animal, but all that isn't very serious. She insults me in patois; I reply in Latin, and so we are even. What I really can't understand is why she hates to have me pass through her garden for..."

"We know that," interrupted Auzance. "You go through her garden to get water, and she objects."

Verès could not believe his ears. This gendarme truly was a Sherlock Holmes! Nevertheless, he found it necessary to be precise.

"Excuse me. In this case, my neighbour is at fault. The water doesn't belong to her."

But Saint-Boniface's Sherlock Holmes was deaf to those explanations. He added to his notes: "a troublemaker".

Trying to continue with the investigation, Auzance said, "Now if I understand you correctly, you're writing a book. At whose request?"

Such ignorance convinced Verès that there was no use explaining. Big detectives were not too erudite.

He finally said, "A Swiss publisher to whom my book was recommended by Professor Ferrero, the eminent Italian historian who's very interested in my work."

All this was secondary to Auzance. He was impatient to get to the purpose of his visit: the black market. He pointed to the sack of provisions Verès had put on a chair.

"But meanwhile," he said with a smile, "you're doing business, aren't you? You're fending for yourself. What's in the bag?"

"Not much," said Verès, who misunderstood his insinuation. "A pocketbook for my girl, a pencil for me, and mixed pickles for all of us."

"Mixed pickles?" asked Auzance, suspiciously.

"Mixed pickles. It's an hors d'oeuvre of various vegetables prepared in an English manner and preserved in a jar. I was very happy to find it in the grocery in Saint-Boniface."

"Hear, hear!" said Auzance feeling deceived when he looked into the bag. "We've been informed that you receive many packages," he continued, suddenly becoming stern, "and that the mailman brought you a big package today. What was in it?"

"Our stove doesn't work well so I ordered a Norwegian pot from Marseilles. It's an isothermic apparatus which prolongs cooking by retaining heat."

Auzance looked at the partly unpacked gadget, and his brow furrowed. He picked up his notebook and, in a moment of inspiration, began writing:

"Suspicious foreigner, Hungarian origin, has a Swiss editor, an Italian professor, and American visa, is interested in the King of Prussia, eats an English hors d'oeuvre, argues in Latin, owns a Norwegian pot..." Then, after reflecting an instant, he added: "...and a wife of the same nationality".

He had a good account of this fellow Verès, but he was anxious to find proof of his black market activities.

"We've been advised," he said, astutely, "that you use a typewriter. What do you type? Your bills? Your accounts? Invoices? For what kind of merchandise?"

Verès's pride was hurt and he remonstrated, "But sir, I just told you I'm writing a book. I'm typing my work on the machine."

He picked up a voluminous file and handed it to Auzance who opened it haphazardly. Suddenly, Auzance noticed a sentence at the bottom of a page:

"Provided with a considerable quantity of foodstuffs, in view of the approaching winter: 550 sacks of flour, 80 containers of oil, 90 tons of vegetables..."

Finally he had proof of black market activity! This imbecile of a Jew made a mistake showing him the file of his affairs. Instead of his famous book which served as a cover-up, he was dealing wholesale. Auzance turned the page and continued reading:

"...the Carthaginian army was approaching the Alps. Even today, historians argue the question of which passes Hannibal took to cross the mountain chain. The author of these lines is personally inclined to believe that it was the Argentières Pass. Whichever it was, when the Consul Publius Scipio, the father of Scipio the African, arrived with his army..."

Disappointed, Auzance closed the file. Since it was a question of supplies for an army, it was not a matter for the police to investigate. Anyway, he had enough evidence against the named Verès.

Apathetically, the sergeant took leave of the Jew. He put his notes in his pocket and started for the door. As for Verès's visits to the farms, Auzance decided not to mention them. He did not want to alert him. The gendarme hoped that he might issue a summons for this activity. Thanks to Brandouille, he knew about the woman who was his main supplier. The trap had been set and the rabbit would certainly fall into it.

V

Auzance hands a summons to a migratory bird

After guiding his bicycle by the handlebars as he went downhill along the small cow path from the Grange to the main road, Auzance's attention was suddenly attracted to the strange figure of a tall, slightly stooped woman wearing beach slacks and, on her head, a turban decorated with a feather. The 'Hindu Mummy' had received a telegram announcing the extension of her visa and was on her way to share the good news with Verès.

When Auzance came abreast of Mrs. Clips, he scrutinized her attentively. Not only could he not recall having seen her before, but never had he ever seen a woman dressed in such a manner and with such a scary face. He was not afraid, not he. Surely, she was a foreigner and only passing small game. He had already caught a blackbird, that Spanish gypsy, and maybe this one would be another. However, this was a white blackbird.

"Your papers, madam," he said, as he barred her way.

From her large leather purse decorated with hieroglyphics around a sphinx, the white blackbird extracted an identity card, a safe-conduct pass, and two papers, one green and the other pink.

Auzance carefully unfolded the green paper from the police precinct and examined it thoroughly. Then he examined the pink paper.

The 'Hindu Mummy' watched him indifferently. She was above all those formalities! She knew that her papers were in perfect order.

But this was not the sergeant's opinion. His expert eye quickly discovered a flaw in the armour.

"Where did you get the stamps for your safe-conduct pass when you arrived in Saint-Boniface?" he demanded.

"It's quite clear. In the mayor's office," she said, aloofly.

She showed him the stamp Mr. Longeaud had affixed above the printed words: "Visa on arrival – mayor's office or police station".

"The stamp isn't valid," Auzance said sharply. "According to the new police decree, all safe-conduct passes must be stamped at the police station and nowhere else."

"Oh, wait a minute, I beg you," she said, irritably. "All those stories about papers make me nervous. I feel as though I'm getting a headache. And my heart isn't very strong, I warn you."

The feather on her turban wavered like the mainsail of a vessel in distress.

"I'm sorry, madam, but your papers aren't in order. You'll have to come to the police station."

"How could I have known about the decree?" the 'Hindu Mummy' protested. "The mayor's office agreed to stamp my paper. Besides, it states clearly on the document: mayor's office or police station."

"I don't care how it's marked. I've a job to do. The mayor's office had no right to stamp your safe-conduct pass. Moreover, I see you came after the 25th of May. After that date, every foreigner who intended to stay more than forty-eight hours had to apply for a permit. I don't see any among your papers."

"But my safe-conduct pass is valid for a month. Isn't that enough?"

"Well, it's not enough for us. You're in violation, and even in double violation. I must give you a summons."

"If it amuses you," said the 'Hindu Mummy' haughtily. "But do it quickly. I warn you, I'm getting a headache. I'm leaving Saint-Boniface at the end of the week," and in a voice meant to impose respect, she added, "I'm leaving for the United States."

His hunch was correct. This was a migratory bird.

"You, too?" he grumbled. "By the way, are you Jewish?"

"Never in my life!" she exclaimed, in the tone of an outraged queen.

Without being a bit upset, Auzance sat on a fallen tree trunk at the edge of the road and wrote: "violation of arrival registration; violation of safe-conduct pass".

"Don't go to too much trouble," said Mrs. Clips, glacially. "I'm leaving at the end of the week. In eight days I'll be out of France. Then..."

"Pardon, madam," interrupted Auzance, "It won't be at the end of the week that you'll leave, but on the date on your expulsion order which will probably be tomorrow."

"But that's impossible!" exclaimed Mrs. Clips. "I just gave all my laundry to be washed. I'll never be ready to leave tomorrow! Oh, my head!"

Auzance shrugged his shoulders. Those details were not his concern.

"You may do as you wish, madam, but if you don't leave on the designated date, I'll be obliged to bring you to the camp."

"This is too much!" said the 'Hindu Mummy', her nostrils quivering. "You're no gentleman! One doesn't treat a lady like that. Oh, my head! I'll remember this."

Auzance appeared not to listen and finished writing the summons.

"Will you sign it?" he asked, holding the paper out to her.

"No sir!" said the 'Hindu Mummy' with a ghostly smile. "I don't give autographs to just anyone."

"Then I'll have to note that you refused to sign. It's a grave offence, very grave."

"Enough, sir! Then I'll sign."

She scribbled some hieroglyphics like those on her purse and haughtily passed the paper back to the gendarme.

"That's all for now, madam," said Auzance, as he arranged his papers. "You may go now."

"I won't speak to you," said Mrs. Clips, with macabre disdain as she lowered her eyelids.

With the majestic step she once used on the screen when she played Cleopatra, she went toward Verès's chalet where her nerves, subjected to this rude treatment, would find solace in a violent, tearful display.

As for Auzance, he regained his good humour. The day that had started so badly had ended with a double triumph. As he pedaled toward Francheville, he instinctively hummed: "Oh! What charm To be a gendarme!"

VI

A disguised painting by Picasso in a display of the French Tobacco Bureau

The sun shining through the Venetian blinds cast stripes on the flowered wallpaper in the room. The same stripes fell on a couch where a turbaned woman lay moaning softly. It was not the green turban of those halcyon days that graced the head of the 'Hindu Mummy', but a white compress of bath towels. On a chair beside the couch was a washbasin filled with water in which pieces of ice melted slowly.

The headache that Mrs. Clips had warned Auzance about yesterday had become a violent migraine. It had reached its climax at eleven o'clock in the morning when a paper from the police station, inviting the 'Hindu Mummy' to "leave the area without delay" had been delivered to Tilleuls.

The abrupt departure of her best client who occupied the most elegant room in the boardinghouse – the room had a Louis XIV style chest of drawers and a closet with mirrors – deeply troubled Mrs. Hermelin. Without knowing it, Mrs. Clips paid ten francs more than the ordinary client, and she ate like a bird. For these reasons, Tilleuls's owner had offered to appeal on her tenant's behalf to the president of Francheville's Legion, who was Joseph's good friend.

With the air of a martyr, Mrs. Clips had refused. She had decided to leave that same evening on the 7.25 train. She only begged Mrs. Hermelin to help soothe her migraine. Since Mrs. Clips's heart condition prevented her from taking tablets, Marguerite, the maid, had stopped all her work for Mrs. Hermelin and hurried to the butcher shop in Francheville for a chunk of ice.

The 'Hindu Mummy' stopped moaning long enough to hear the grandfather clock in the salon downstairs strike one...two...three... With Mrs. Hermelin's help, Mrs. Clips had packed her valises; all that was left was to close them when her laundry arrived. The big question was: would it arrive on time? This doubt exacerbated the 'Hindu Mummy's' headache.

She tried to think of other things. Mr. César Fleury was coming to say goodbye to her. Other visitors would surely follow suit. It was a pity. She would have preferred to have arranged a long private meeting with the seductive musician. Now she regretted not having gone downstairs for breakfast with the others; it would have given her an occasion to say goodbye to everyone.

She propped herself up, picked up the mirror from the night table, and examined her face attentively. Water from the wet towel had trickled down her face, washing away the coating of face powder. Mrs. Clips grimaced, took off the halo of the martyred, and threw it into the washbasin. Then, hiding the washbasin behind the skirt of the dressing table, she stifled her last moan and carefully made up her face again. César Fleury could come; Cleopatra was waiting for him.

Her last moan stifled, she strained to hear. She thought that she heard a noise at the bottom of the stairs. Yes, it was César's Roman sandals. Excited, she closed her eyes. A minute later, she heard a knock on her door, and Mr. Fleury appeared on the threshold.

The 'Hindu Mummy' smiled tenderly and invited him to sit in an armchair beside her couch. Things were proceeding according to her plan.

"Will you excuse me if I don't get up?" she said, in a weak voice. "I'm suffering horribly."

As always, the sight of Fleury's jet black beard and the velvety look in his eyes had an instant effect on her. Today he was even more carefully groomed than usual. He evoked the very picture of virility so reminiscent of the conqueror that Mrs. Clips was filled with sweet yearning.

"I'm distressed at your departure," he said as he sat down. "The punishment you suffered was meant for undesirable foreigners and was unjustified in your case. No discretion was used."

"Alas, but the shock to a defenceless woman is painful nonetheless," said the 'Hindu Mummy'. "I'm leaving tonight, and I must admit, with some regrets," she added, looking tenderly at Fleury through her artificial eyelashes.

"It's unfortunate," said Fleury, compassionately, "but perhaps I can do something for you. I just learned the name of the new governor of this area. I met him several years ago, and we became friends when he was only a minor official. I was often invited to his house where I played chamber music with his wife, who's a distinguished and sensitive violinist. I think it would be enough for me to call him on the telephone, and he'll extend your stay."

At the mention of the sensitive violinist, the 'Hindu Mummy' became jealous and rejected his proposition.

"Thank you, sir, but I've already refused to let Mrs. Hermelin intervene on my behalf. I expect justice from your great country, not favours. I'm leaving with a heavy heart," she said, bitterly.

A short, somewhat embarrassing silence followed.

"The other day you expressed a certain desire," said Fleury. "Perhaps I can comply today."

The 'Hindu Mummy' became animated and rose from the couch. With quivering nostrils, she cast a long, deep look, like that of a languid queen, into her visitor's dark, ardent eyes

"You wished to see the shirt I designed," Fleury added.

"Oh yes, yes," sighed the 'Hindu Mummy', falling back on the couch, her nostrils no longer quivering.

"Unfortunately, most of my laundry is being washed, and I've only the shirt on my back. But then," he said, with false modesty, "this little tailored design may not interest you anymore."

"But yes, yes," murmured the 'Hindu Mummy', animated once again. "I'm very interested."

Fleury checked the knot in his white tie. Then, a bit self-consciously, he said, "You see, my dear madam, I must ask your permission..."

"But I beg you, sir, go ahead. Do it," said the 'Hindu Mummy' while her rouged cheeks turned redder from the emotion.

"...permission to show you only the paper pattern I've drawn."

Then from the inside pocket of his velvet jacket, he pulled out a big yellow envelope and began unfolding the contents.

Just then someone knocked on the door. Mrs. Clips gave Mr. Fleury a final adoring look in which she tried to express all of her feelings that must remain suppressed forever. In a weak voice, she invited the new visitor to enter. The parade of visitors paying homage to the 'Hindu Mummy' had begun. Bernard Bloch and André Murger appeared at the door followed by Mrs. Hermelin. Tilleuls's owner brought good news to her tenant. Her laundry was being ironed. In half an hour, everything would be ready.

"Thank you, madam," said the 'Hindu Mummy' with a sigh of relief. "I'm reassured."

Bloch and Murger deposited their offerings before the 'Hindu Mummy' for her trip: one gave her ten cigarettes he had taken from his own ration and his first piece of goats' cheese as a gift from Renée Bloch; the other left a package of Swiss newspapers he had received from Francheville that same day.

Fleury felt obliged to participate in this generosity.

"Allow me, dear madam, to offer you this pattern as a souvenir," he said, indicating the yellow envelope. "My shirt-maker in Lyons copied it already."

Forgetting her headache completely, Mrs. Clips voluptuously lit a cigarette. She was very touched by this display of sympathy.

There was another knock on the door. It was Verès who had come from Tournier's grocery store where, after a long, difficult bargaining session, he had managed to extract two packages of cigarettes in exchange for his wine ration. On the eve of Mrs. Clip's departure for America, he had wanted to be in her good graces and felt it was even more important to cultivate his relationship with her. Now it was Tibor's turn to deposit his tribute before the 'Hindu Mummy'. For thanks, he got a lugubrious smile that was meant to be gracious.

"Well, madam" said Verès, "it looks as if you've decided to leave."

"I must," said Mrs. Clips, glancing discreetly at Fleury. "I'm a victim of administrative injustice."

"It's regrettable," said Fleury. "However, were I in your place, I wouldn't draw any hasty conclusions. It often happens that, after a military defeat, the power is in the hands of a clumsy administration and is directed by unqualified personnel."

"How true," said Verès, animatedly. "It's even one of the most frightening paradoxes of history. 'Because we have lost the war,' reasoned the army, 'we are the only ones able to win the peace, and the whole nation follows.' See for example, Hannibal[33], MacMahon[34], Hindenburg[35]..."

"But," said Fleury, "those times, when admirals became police chiefs, and cavalry colonels become supply chiefs are coming to an end. We're on the threshold of big changes in all aspects of French life. The corporations, suppressed by a stupid regime and an impotent political machine, are coming to life again. This change represents a huge step forward."

"Now, wait a minute," said Murger, annoyed. "The revival of institutions from the Middle Ages, abandoned precisely because they hindered all technical and social progress, will be a step forward? Rather it's a regression, and what a regression!"

Fleury was about to reply when the arrival of a new visitor created a diversion. Mrs. Hermelin, who during this conversation was making a mental inventory of the room, took advantage of the situation to withdraw.

"Well," said Mr. Rosenfeld, entering the room, "I hear you're getting ready to leave us. What a pity you didn't let me know yesterday. I've just made friends with a police officer from Francheville, a charming young man..."

"You're very lucky," interrupted Mrs. Clips. "The one who stopped me on the road was a brute."

"If I'd had a word with him, maybe he'd have arranged everything."

Frank Rosenfeld liked to play the role of a generous protector. Anyway, he already knew from Mrs. Hermelin that Mrs. Clips had rejected a similar offer.

---

33 Hannibal (249-183 BC). Carthaginian general. (HRG)

34 Marie Edmé Patrice de MacMahon (1808–1903) of Irish descent. Napoleon III named him Duke of Magenta (1859). A monarchist, MacMahon was chosen as the second president of France (1873–1879). Despite a republican victory in the October 1877 elections, MacMahon named a royalist ministry, but was forced to accept a ministry acceptable to the Chamber of Deputies, thus limiting the powers of the president. (HRG)

35 Paul von Hindenburg (1847–1934). German general, last president of German Weimar Republic. (HRG)

"You're very kind, Mr. Rosenfeld, but it's useless. I'm determined to leave Saint-Boniface and France. Alas, gentlemen, France has deceived me. Isn't it deplorable to see how they treat a foreigner today? A foreigner who hasn't taken bread from Frenchmen, but on the contrary, over the past ten years has left a veritable fortune in this country."

This outburst was received with a polite nod of the head.

"A gendarme visited you?" Bloch asked Rosenfeld. "I, too, had that honour. These verifications bode ill."

"I feel the same way," said Verès. "In the end, there's always trouble."

"You're all cowards," blustered Rosenfeld. "As for me, I'm perfectly calm. When one's done his duty and is beyond reproach, he has nothing to fear. Anyway, if you've any problems, I'll protect you."

Stealing a look at his wristwatch, Fleury realized that it was time for him to leave for his date with Génia in Francheville. He excused himself, and ceremoniously kissed Mrs. Clips's trembling hand. She was sorry to see him go.

Fleury's departure was a general signal for the others to leave. Only Verès, who was waiting for his wife and had some requests to make of Mrs. Clips, lingered a while.

A few minutes later, Mrs. Hermelin, thinking that her tenant was alone, appeared, this time with a basket of laundry on her arm, and a sheet of paper and a small cone in her hand.

"I'm bringing your laundry, Mrs. Clips," she said, with a waggish look in her eyes, "also the little note you requested." Noticing Verès, she added, "Don't bother right now. You'll settle it later. I thought of your trip and since it's cherry time, I'm bringing you a few cherries. Our cherry tree isn't too productive right now, but it's a gift from the bottom of my heart."

She added her offering of fifteen or so cherries to the other gifts already on the 'Hindu Mummy's' altar. Then she left.

At the sight of the note, which took the proportions of a diary thanks to some small supplements, Mrs. Clips's face changed colour. She quickly pulled the washbasin from its hiding place – the ice had not entirely melted. Placing the cold compress on her head, she groaned, "Oh, my head! How I suffer!"

Ellen Verès, the last visitor to arrive to wish Mrs. Clips bon voyage, brought her most recent masterpiece, a landscape of Barbarie.

"It's ravishing," said the 'Hindu Mummy' enthusiastically. "Let me kiss you, my dear! Such purity of design and richness of colour! Then she added confidentially, "Your painting, my dear child, will be in good company in my luggage. I'm carrying a small Picasso with me, a true marvel. I got it in Marseilles for a mouthful of bread, eighty thousand francs. Imagine that! I had a specialist cover the signature with a coat of paint so I won't have to pay customs duty. Once I'm in the United States, it will be easy to remove the paint, and I'll get at least four thousand dollars for this canvas. That will pay my fare by 'Clipper' and I'll even be left with a profit. As for your beautiful painting, my dear Ellen, I'll give it a good place in my parlour. It will always remind me of Saint-Boniface where, after having a wonderful time, I received this terrible shock!"

"I hope, though, that we'll meet one another over there," said Verès, adroitly seizing the occasion to join in, "especially if you'd be kind enough to intervene on my behalf as you've so willingly promised. By the way, may I ask you another favour? I'd like you to take the first part of my work with you and mail it in New York to an editor whose name and address I marked on the bottom of the first page. Then, whatever happens, I'll be able say not everything dies. *Non omnis moriar.*"

"I'd be glad to do it," said the 'Hindu Mummy'. "Would you like to put it in my valise yourself? It's behind the couch. I'm too weak to get up."

Then, lighting another cigarette, she turned to Ellen.

"I'm sure you'll be very successful in New York as an artist and as a woman, my little one. You're very well built, do you know that? With those firm breasts like a fifteen-year-old girl's," she said, closing her eyes while her hand caressed the young woman's white forearm to which a slight tan had imparted a honey-like colour. "Don't worry, my dear one. I'll help you... Not that valise, Mr. Verès! The other one, the smaller one," she exclaimed, turning quickly.

It was too late. Verès had already opened the huge pigskin valise. He was petrified to see its contents: a complete display of all the brands of the French Tobacco Bureau, about fifty packs of cigarettes: Balto, Naja, Vizir, Salambo, Gauloise were placed on a red velvet dress like gems in a jewellery box. Just as some millionaires are haunted by the fear of hunger, the 'Hindu Mummy' trembled, fearing a lack of tobacco, so she had amassed a huge supply which she kept as a last resort, preferring to bum cigarettes from her friends and masculine entourage.

VII

Dolores's Punishment

That same afternoon, another traveller was preparing to take the 7.25 train. She, too, was a foreigner, a very tall, skinny, young brunette. All her earthly belongings were in a small wicker basket tied with a string. It held neither cigarettes, nor many gifts, nor paintings of the masters with camouflaged signatures. It contained only a few well-patched shirts and second-hand clothes, and a few photographs of two children and a gaunt-faced man with piercing eyes.

The man was the traveller's husband, José Mendoza, a Spaniard, a miner by profession, a corporal in the Spanish Republican Army, a refugee from that civil war and, at present, in a concentration camp in French Morocco.

As for the two children, the younger was in Mexico, having been taken there by a charitable organization, while the older one, who was all of thirteen, was in a children's home in Creuse waiting for new transport to America. The transport was becoming increasingly dubious. Their mother had not seen them for more than a year.

This traveller – the other blackbird snared by Sergeant Auzance in the course of his hunt – had not come to France with a fortune to spend. No doubt she was considered an undesirable alien because she competed with the French for a position as a maid servant. Nobody came to console her or comfort her during the hours before her departure. Nobody offered to intervene in her behalf. Only her employers could have attempted such a procedure, but they were not inclined to do so.

The Spanish woman was certainly not a bad servant. She was clean and conscientious. One could find no fault with her, except for one thing: she always had a sad face which made a disagreeable impression.

Mrs. Martini, a very sensitive person who liked to surround herself with happy faces, could easily find another servant among the young peasants in Saint-Paul who would be very happy to be in a well-to-do home. The salary paid in the countryside would be much less than what she had to pay Dolores in the city. Why should she insist on keeping this Spaniard when one always had all kinds of trouble with foreigners?

Having learned that their servant was to be expelled from the county, her employers had paid her severance pay equivalent to eight days of work and half the price of her ticket to Marseilles. Was it not enough that they paid for her trip here and barely had time to profit from her services? Truly, she could ask for nothing more. Anyway, they had given her a very nice letter of recommendation.

"With such a recommendation, you'll easily find yourself a good position in the city," said the lady, good-naturedly.

The Spanish woman had thanked her, but she was quite sure that it was untrue. Because of the many refugees, housemaids were plentiful in Marseilles. Moreover, Dolores would not have enough time to look for work. At the first check-point, she would be found unemployed and without resources, and would be sent immediately to a camp, probably Gurs. This was what Dolores feared the most. Of course, she knew that thousands and thousands of people were living in the camps and that one is not killed there. After all, her husband was surviving in such a camp; he had been there for three years. Nevertheless, it would be very hard if she could not help her family by sending them a money order from time to time. Oh yes, it would be very hard indeed!

Dolores was perfectly aware that her chances of escaping from the camp were minimal. As she peeled the vegetables for her masters' soup for the last time, she moaned loudly and swallowed her tears.

Chapter Five

The Cemetery of Ships

I

Delphine compares Fleury to Landru and Latière's dog

After his nap, Fleury removed the net protecting his moustache and carefully brushed his beard. Standing in front of the open closet in his room, he hesitated and then, after an instant's reflection, decided to wear his Roman sandals, choosing them against his better judgement because a storm was brewing and he did not like to get his feet wet. However, he thought that he would have enough time to put on his brown casual shoes before he left for Francheville.

His feet had already received their cosmic ray treatment for that day. As everyone knows, early in the morning the sun's rays are enhanced by the radioactive effect of the dew. Fleury had strolled in the grass in his bare feet for half an hour and completed the treatment by resting on a chaise-longue for an hour with his feet turned to the sun. Having received the desired amount of exposure, Fleury had entered Tilleuls's dining room where he had gulped down the two eggs that he had obtained to supplement his allotted ration. César hoped to prove his virility that same night and wanted to be in peak condition.

As a precautionary measure, he had sprinkled plenty of pepper on his breakfast to have an additional benefit from this spicy aphrodisiac, even though the pepper was indigenous to the area. Upon leaving the table, he returned to his room to expose his entire body to the life-sustaining air emanating from the earth's soil. He undressed completely, even taking off the one-piece suit of underwear of his own design. Then after a nap, a nap that had regenerated his vigor, he felt quite satisfied that he was in possession of all his physical attributes and hopeful that, once evening came, his powers would return.

We must admit that, for the past several days, César was in the throes of sexual passion. He still recoiled from the burning memory of a failure that he had experienced earlier and from which his virile pride still suffered. The fault was entirely that of a young radio employee who, after much fussing, had finally submitted to his advances at a bad time for him. Memories of this event haunted him whenever he had attempted a new conquest, and her stinging words paralysed his ardour and rang in his ears for a long time. As for Mrs. Fleury, he had stopped trying to prove his virility to her.

Ever since the day when the musician had played "Apassionata" in the parlour in Tilleuls for Génia, daily meetings with this charming young Russian had produced a true miracle in him. Being over-cautious, he had delayed the final hour by playing futile but charming games that reminded him of the time when he was twenty. The young woman had submitted ardently to these innocent fantasies. "For her," César had repeated to himself, "my time will also be her time." He, himself, had fixed the hour five days ago: Thursday at 10.30 p.m. It is good to impose discipline on oneself.

However, since it was only 3.30 p.m., Fleury had all the time he wished to make the last minute preparations for this big test. He put on a pair of tennis shorts. From the umbrella stand, he pulled out the whip that the 'Hindu Mummy' forgot to take with her to New York and went for a stroll.

Leaving Tilleuls, he took the road to Barbarie. As he went he whistled a new tune that he had composed to Rimbaud's famous poem,

"Oh seasons, Oh castles!..." After a brisk twenty minute walk, he reached the first house on the outskirts of Barbarie and knocked on the kitchen door, hoping to find a few more eggs to gobble down.

A woman's sweaty, disheveled head appeared at the door. Delphine, who was about to take her cows out to pasture, stared wide-eyed at him. The arrival of this unknown visitor struck panic in her heart.

"Excuse me for bothering you, madam," said Fleury, surprised at having made such an impression on the peasant woman. "Can you sell me some eggs?"

"Some eggs?" she stammered. "Some eggs?..." and said to herself, "What do all these bizarre people want from me? The other day it was a phantom in trousers and now this bearded man in his underwear displaying his hairy legs. These city people have no shame."

Delphine stood on the doorstep blocking the way and said,

"It's that... Eggs at this time... I must look." Meanwhile she thought, "They don't go to old Crouzet who thrusts his pitchfork toward them at the slightest provocation. I must be careful."

Suddenly she noticed the whip in the stranger's hand. "Another one looking for a little horse!" But what impressed Delphine the most was his beard. And what a beard! In all of Saint-Boniface no man had hair on his chin. This spectre looking for eggs must not have shaved for eight weeks. Ever since the Landru affair which Delphine had followed in the newspapers, given to her by the teacher who had preceded

Mr. Longeaud in Saint-Boniface, a beard was a symbol of crime and perversion for her.

"I'm not asking for too many," said Fleury, trying to reassure the peasant woman. "Two or three, for instance..."

Delphine was horrified. "Two or three?" she grumbled. "In this season? You don't realize what you're asking!"

Even as she protested, she thought it was not prudent to incur the wrath of a man with a beard.

"I can't give you that many," she said, embarrassed, "but if you're satisfied with four... They'll be fresh, very fresh."

"Perfect," said Fleury, surprised. Due to his ignorance of the nuances of the regional idiom, Delphine's answer left him wondering.

"I'll look for some," she said.

Against her better judgement, she let the bearded man into her house. A minute later she returned carrying the eggs in her apron.

"How will you carry them?" she asked, becoming upset again. "I've no paper. How awful!"

"Oh, that isn't important," said Fleury, his mood improving at the sight of the eggs. "I'm going to gulp them down immediately, right here."

"But they should be warmed. I'll make a quick fire and boil them for you."

"No, no," said Fleury, smiling. "I like them like that, raw. In the countryside near Lyons, a farmer's wife, who knows me and wants to please me, always keeps freshly laid eggs for me to swallow."

"I also wish to please you," said Delphine, deciding to placate her Landru. "I'll put a piece of lard on the stove, open the eggs, and fry them."

That was not what Fleury wanted. To cook fresh eggs would completely destroy their vital ingredients, those marvellous components that enhance virility, so before Delphine had time to suggest an omelette with herbs, he took the first egg, broke the shell, and gulped down the white and yolk as if it were a ritual.

"It will upset your stomach," mumbled Delphine as she thought to herself, "These city people definitely are savages. The phantom in trousers lapped up the cold milk and this man in his underwear gulps down raw eggs. How abominable!"

"Rest assured, madam," said Fleury, jovially, "I'm used to them this way."

Noticing that there was no way to make her understand his ideas about eggs, he changed the subject.

"What splendid weather! I hope it stays this way. That small cloud over the trees could bring rain."

"I hope so," sighed Delphine. "We need it. What will happen to us? We've had none..."

Fleury, busy with his eggs, had stopped listening. "For us city people," he interrupted, "fresh eggs are a treat. Would you permit me to come back from time to time to have one or two?"

Delphine was annoyed and gave him one of her evasive but diplomatic answers.

"Some eggs?" she groaned. "Of course. For those who like them it's always a pleasure. My daughter in Saint-Etienne wrote to me the other day that they can't find any at all. She'll be coming here soon to bring her father some nails because we're ashamed to ask our customers to bring their own nails when they need a coffin. Tournier, the grocer, has a supply of them, but he wants two kilos of butter for one kilo of nails."

"I'll return on Sunday," Fleury interrupted, impatiently. "Maybe you could put one or two aside for me."

"If I could only close the door to the stable," continued Delphine, "but because of the chickens it's impossible. They must find their nest to lay their eggs, and Latière's dog comes and goes like a windmill..."

"Don't you have a chicken coop?" asked Fleury.

"Chicken coop?" Delphine was taken aback. "But the stable is our chicken coop. The other day, Latière's dog ate all the eggs in the nest. Some people have pets that die of hunger..."

Fleury shrugged his shoulders and took out his change purse. It was stuffy in the kitchen and the conversation with the peasant woman was beginning to annoy him. After satisfying his yearning for his fancy titbit, he paid Delphine generously and left.

Delphine heaved a sigh of relief. What a story! To swallow four raw eggs like Latière's dog! Well, what could you expect from a man who walked around in his undershorts displaying his hairy legs and chin? Moreover, he understood nothing! He did not know that hens laid eggs in the stable and then, without blinking an eye, he wished for good weather when all the streams were dry; the grass was burned; the animals walked around with their tongues hanging out; the cabbage worms were devouring the cabbages; and this good-for-nothing wished it to continue that way. A man who resembled Landru as if he were his brother! Who knew if he might not be?

Terrified and indignant at the same time, Delphine hurried to her husband's shop to share her emotions with him, but Legras barely listened to her. He never stopped planing and sawing his cabinets and coffins even to come to the table, or feed the cows, or watch them for half an hour. During the entire thirty-eight years of their married life,

Delphine was never able to make him understand her hopes, her fears, her desires...

*****

"Those peasants are so queer!" said Fleury to himself as he walked toward Tilleuls. "They don't even know what a chicken coop is. Their minds are peculiar. You talk to them about eggs and they talk about nails, coffins, and dogs. They pretend that they don't have enough eggs to give you two or three, and they give you four. You tell them, 'It would please me to have them served raw.' They reply, 'I'd like to please you, therefore I'll cook them for you.' I think, therefore I am... but what do they think? That is the question."

Actually, it was Fleury who was totally ignorant of how those people thought and what they thought. Perhaps they thought like everyone else, but expressed themselves differently. Maybe, amongst themselves, they displayed common sense and their odd way of talking to strangers was a defence stratagem. The enigma bothered Fleury. All those people were Frenchmen like himself. They spoke the same language and, in addition, patois, yet it was not the same language. Between Fleury and those anti-Cartesian peasants was a thick concrete wall of incomprehensibility. They were the same nation, but belonged to two different species: the bears and the gazelles...

II

A virtuoso of remote diagnosis activates the handle of an automatic cash register three times

When Fleury arrived in front of Francheville's Modern Pharmacy one hour later, it was full of customers and not the right moment to ask the pharmacist for advice on a very delicate matter. He looked with interest at the display of ads for hormonal extracts in a corner of the window: Firm breasts in ten days... Power and vigour with Vigorex... Virilor will restore your virility...

A fifty-year-old woman, wearing a cape on her shoulders and gloves on her hands in spite of the heat, stopped beside him. Since her brother, her only close relative, had died as a result of the operation in Lyons, Amélie Martin's nervousness prevented her from sleeping unless she took a sleeping pill. She approached the entrance to the pharmacy, hesitated, then resolutely went inside.

Fleury was witness to an act of open rebellion. By going to buy medicine in the Modern Pharmacy, Miss Martin had publicly defied Sister Félicie, Father Mignart, and all those who considered it sacrilegious to buy their aspirin tablets or castor oil anywhere else but the White Cross Pharmacy.

Amélie's rebellious act did not escape the attention of Mrs. Hermelin, who had made her purchases in town and was preparing to return to Saint-Boniface. The wife of the former tax collector was shocked to see Amélie enter this disreputable store. The instructor from the girl's parochial school in a shop owned by an atheist! How scandalous! It caused Tilleuls's owner to forget completely about the Jouvence de l'abbé Soury that she had finally decided to buy in the White Cross Pharmacy after overcoming her instinctive distrust of the picture of a priest on each box of tonic, a distrust born out of being the daughter and mother of a minister.

On the other hand, Fleury, ignorant of the controversy over the two pharmacies in Francheville and its environs, changed his mind about entering the Modern Pharmacy and, instead, directed his steps to its competitor. He found only one peasant there, conversing with the white-gowned pharmacist's assistant.

Gregoire Laffont of Saint-Boniface had already bought several products. His large family and he were being treated by the pharmacist's assistant, the learned Mr. Chameix, who could diagnose diseases even at a distance and whose consultations had the advantage of being free. Naturally, the drugs were not free, but at least you got something for your money.

"...give me a box of Préfectoral tablets also, like the other day," said Laffont. "They helped my wife. And then there's my mother-in-law who has been constipated for eight days. Give me a little Ouragan for her."

Mr. Chameix, who not only knew the local dialect but also the peculiar kind of French the peasants spoke in the region, immediately climbed up the ladder to get the medication. Then he activated the handle of the automatic cash register and handed the peasant a slip. Laffont pulled out his wallet, paid for his Ouragan, his Préfectoral tablets and other drugs prescribed by the competent Mr. Chameix, and left.

With a friendly smile, Chameix, a short, keen-eyed young man with a circumflex-shaped moustache to make him look older, turned to Fleury.

"Look," said Fleury, clearing his throat and feeling somewhat embarrassed, "I wonder if you have..."

At this moment, the door opened and a tall, lean man with a long nose and nervous tic entered the store. It was Pinkas, the stateless one, to whom Auzance, in spite of all his efforts, was unable to give a summons.

"...a tube of aspirin," Fleury quickly said.

"We only have boxes of one hundred, but you'll save three francs seventy-five. Anything else, sir?"

Hesitatingly, Fleury said, "Oh, take care of this gentleman. I'm in no hurry."

"What would you like, Mr. Pinkas?" asked Chameix, with a smile as he turned to the new customer.

"Three boxes of suppositories," replied Pinkas, his tic contorting his mime-like face.

"Not those," said Pinkas, shaking his head. "I want the true suppositories, those with glycerine."

"Look, Mr. Pinkas," said the surprised Chameix, "you got some the day before yesterday. We're very limited in these products, you know."

At the customer's insistence, the pharmacist's assistant finally gave in. Pinkas picked up his three boxes, paid, and left the store quite satisfied. One could say that he was relieved.

"You see," said Fleury, "What I want is a kind of tonic...a fortifier... um...a stimulant to be more precise...something like a whiplash...a sexual stimulant. It's for a friend who's a bit tired."

Chameix had guessed some time ago what the customer wanted. This man with the beard belonged to a particularly interesting category of customers.

"Yes, certainly," he said, most understandingly. "Do you prefer Herculine, Vigorex, or Virilor?"

"Well," said Fleury, "perhaps you can help me choose. I need a fast-acting product."

"I see," said the pharmacist's assistant, very seriously. "I'll give you a big box of Virilor. It's a good stimulant with an almost instantaneous effect, but it's necessary to keep up the treatment to avoid a relapse. It contains a product from the colonies called yohimbine[36] which is becoming scarce."

Fleury hesitated. "Which do you think...?" he asked.

The arrival of a new customer stopped him from finishing his question. The man was short, dark-haired, unshaven, and disheveled. His collar was frayed.

"Take care of this man," sighed Fleury.

---

36 Yohimbine: derived from yohimbehoa, a West Indian tree. (HRG)

"Please," said the man, in a very strong foreign accent, "I need a package of twenty-four sup...sup...sup..."

"Pardon?" asked Chameix, patiently.

"Suppositorium!" exclaimed the foreigner, with a supreme effort while spraying droplets of saliva all over as he spoke.

"A box of suppositories," corrected Mr. Chameix, as he discreetly dried his face and handed him a box.

"Not good. I need *glytzérina.*"

"We have no more," said Chameix, emphatically. "A customer bought the last three boxes."

"Good! He bought them already," said the man, more reassured. "Excuse me...I didn't see. Well, thanks. Goodbye sirs – madams," and he left.

"It seems there's a real constipation epidemic in this town," observed Fleury, keenly.

"Especially in certain circles," commented the pharmacist's assistant, thoughtfully. He had his own theory on that subject, but he did not care to discuss it with his customer.

"So you're advising me to take Virilor?" asked Fleury, with an air of complicity. "Is it truly the best you have?"

Chameix's eyes sparkled as he said, "Oh yes! It's a very honest product. Naturally, the formula can be improved. A few days ago, the boss prepared a similar tablet for himself and several of his friends, but with a much stronger dose. I tried them the other day," he said, with an insinuating smile, "and I can tell you from personal experience, it's truly extraordinary. Of course, since it was for the boss, himself, he spared nothing. All this ought to remain between us. I see I can confide in you."

"Naturally," said Fleury. "And do you have any left?"

"Enough for one cure perhaps, but not more. But now that I know the formula, I can make them as needed. Do you want some?"

"Yes, a whole cure," said Fleury.

The pharmacist's assistant disappeared into the back of the shop, took down a big bottle of Virilor from a shelf, opened it, took out the tablets, put them into a box, and returned to the front of the store.

"Take four tablets *before*," he said, as he scribbled on a label and pasted it on the box. "Then follow it with five tablets daily. I repeat, this is a product I sell only to trustworthy customers. I count on your discretion."

Fleury reassured him as best he could and paid one hundred and eighty francs. (Yohimbine was so scarce!) He thanked the sympathetic pharmacist's assistant and since it was almost time to meet Génia, he went toward the Hotel Panorama.

Chameix noted on the sales register: one Virilor, large size, ninety francs. Then he conscientiously pulled the handle of the automatic cash register.

A little ruse, and his daily salary was doubled. The boss, Mr. Astier, was very pleased with the services of his assistant. This one was hired because his predecessor had a habit of not recording the sales on the cash register. Mr. Astier's frequent inventory checks quieted any suspicions he had in the beginning, for they never revealed any irregularities with Phillippe Chameix. Even better, sales had soared thanks to Mr. Chameix's courteous remote diagnostic consultations. Freed from business worries thanks to that, Mr. Astier could devote himself to politics and the administration of the small town where he was the mayor. Mr. Chameix, for his part, did not complain about his boss's absence. One must fend for himself and keep up with the times. Isn't that so?

*****

Reclining lazily in a rattan chair at the rear of the Hotel Panorama's garden, Génia Prokoff closed her book, a history of music which ended with Gounod. It smelled mouldy, like all the books in the Francheville library.

The nervous excitement that usually overcame her whenever she met Fleury had already manifested itself. She did not remember having such a feeling except when she was a young girl, but she did not recall it too well.

Suddenly, Génia heard footsteps on the gravel behind her chair. She stood up quickly and felt the blood rush to her face. No, it was not he, but a hotel guest, a certain Pinkas who had come outside for some fresh air. He settled himself at a table and began arranging many small boxes in a carton.

Génia stretched out on her chair again and her thoughts returned to Paris and a Russian antique shop in the suburbs of Saint-Honoré. She had been unemployed for many months, but finally managed to get a job after having found a small advertisement in the *Intrasigeant*. She liked her job, and the proprietor, Tatiana, soon became her friend. Alexander Prokoff, in the throes of his nihilistic crises, continued to drink and beat his wife, but on the 10th of June 1940, this existence changed radically. Tatiana's friend and supporter, a certain Bernheim whose chauffeur was mobilized into military service, hired Alexander to drive his powerful Auburn to more clement southern skies. Naturally, Génia was included in this trip.

That was how, two days later and after several epic adventures which reminded Génia of her escape from Russia, the foursome had arrived in Francheville.

Several weeks later, Mr. Bernheim was notified that his visa for Brazil had arrived, and he quickly left for Marseilles to arrange all the formalities for his trip. The others, who had no urgent reason to leave the Old World, returned to Paris in the old Auburn that Mr. Bernheim had given to his friend as a consolation.

As soon as they arrived in the capital, the former Russian officer underwent a curious transformation. A strong need for activity overcame him. Who would believe it? – he simply quit drinking. In this new Europe, people of his kind – well-educated, experienced, and above all, a polyglot – were destined to play a role between the victor and the vanquished. At first, Count Prokoff had guided foreigners around Paris, but soon new horizons were open to him. He understood that he did not have to limit himself to showing his clients the day or night curiosities in the capital. He strove to provide them with certain worldly possessions that the new regulations had made impossible to get, thanks to his contacts, his shrewdness and ruses, his lack of scruples and enterprising nature. After one year, Alexander became an important person in the world of illicit affairs.

Somewhat dazzled by his rapid rise to fortune, he established his headquarters in a hotel near the Etoile. He quickly realized that Génia, who was an acceptable companion when they had lived in the sordid Hotel Terrasses, was not enough of a 'woman of the world' and no longer suitable for him in his new role. In a few short months he had several adventures and finally chose Tatiana, Génia's former employer, who was not only beautiful but also an excellent businesswoman.

When Génia understood the situation, she felt only slightly bitter. It was Tatiana whom she hated for her breach of trust. As for Alexander, she had only tolerated him for years, like a chronic, incurable disease that one is unable to treat. Times back, when he was drunk on vodka and covered her with blows, she felt an attachment mixed with pity. However, this new Alexander, self-assured and always elegantly dressed, she thoroughly despised. That is why, when Alexander sent her to Francheville under the pretext of getting a fresh-air cure, she had no desire to return to Paris.

However, all she needed was the arrival of Fleury in her life to make her understand how base her existence had been with Alexander. Finally, she had met a man of higher qualities, an artist at that, with whom she felt more pure, more noble. She was ashamed of her past. She would leave Francheville and its black market so below her dignity, and return to the city with Fleury who had promised to establish her in a music store. It would permit her to earn a living 'in a much less humiliating way', as he had said. Above all, he would teach her to see the world with new eyes, would introduce her to his luminous existence, and would give her his friendship and tenderness so sweet and different from the brutal sensuality of men. Fleury, who was no adolescent, sometimes showed a timidity and freshness that captivated Génia. Maybe this complex feeling that he evoked in her was due in great part to this touching reserve. Sometimes, while his hand caressed her shoulder during their long walks down deserted paths among the trees, she was afraid to see the sudden appearance of the 'beast', but each time she noticed that he withdrew and, instead, tenderly kissed her hand as though asking for forgiveness. After such walks, she returned to her room longing and tormented. She slept badly and impatiently awaited her next rendezvous. In the last few days, she had reached the point where she hoped and wished for what she had feared in the beginning.

Once again the gravel grated at the entrance to the garden. Génia quickly turned around. A smiling, radiant Fleury stood before her. The clock in the town hall struck seven.

III

Mr. Longeaud finds a bottle of Vitamin P in the Sargasso Sea

An old legend cherished by navigators has it that the Sargasso Sea in the North Atlantic is a cemetery for ships. It is there that the wrecks, abandoned by their crews, come to be stranded amid the seaweed and sunken hulks and are dragged along by the current. In Francheville's market place that summer of 1942, the Café de la Marine was like the Sargasso Sea, a veritable cemetery for wrecks.

The most venerable of the wrecks was a battle cruiser or, as the English say, a man-of-war. It was, in effect, that 'man of war' George Richard Fentimore, a retired general who, after a particularly brilliant but short career, had handed in his resignation in order to marry for the second time, this time to a young actress. He had gone to live on the Côte d'Azur where he had cultivated a beautiful little piece of property. Seventy-year-old General Fentimore, built like a colossus, looked fifty. Strong and authoritative, he seemed as unhappy as a child whenever his wife, a charming, frail, pink little person, left him for an instant.

Expelled from the Côte d'Azur with all the other British, the general established his headquarters in the Hotel Farémido in Francheville. However, he often came to the Café de la Marine where the owner had a supply of real Ceylonese tea. Francheville's natives would use the tea only in case of serious illness, but for this prodigal son of Albion, this brew was as indispensable as daily bread. Moreover, the Café de la Marine was the only place where the man of war and his wife, that gracious light sentinel – only as far as tonnage was concerned – could find bridge partners worthy of them.

One of these partners was another conspicuous hulk, a respectable transatlantic wreck stranded in this cemetery of ships who, as a protest against his destiny, had refused to cross the Atlantic when it was still possible. When his compatriots sent for him, Signor Vincente Benedetti, one of the directors of the Italian Socialist Party, had given up his chance to go to America for two reasons. First, the Italian Armistice Commission was opposed to his leaving. He did not wish to go clandestinely under a false name since it would compel him to sacrifice his magnificent, grey patriarchal beard. Then again, as a convinced pacifist proclaiming that the authoritarian regimes should be overthrown from inside those countries, he did not care to take part in the interventionist meeting from which he knew he could not escape once he was in America. Under those conditions, he preferred to wait in France for the inevitable defeat of fascism, even if it meant being exposed to risks. He was soon banished from Marseilles to Valence and from Valence to Francheville where this lost transatlantic came to be stranded in the Café de la Marine. Now and then, Signor Benedetti had heated political arguments with General Fentimore, a convinced conservative, but they always understood each other at the bridge table.

The fourth partner was Safranek, a Czech intellectual, an aesthete whom the war surprised in the National Library. A true lightship in this cemetery of ships, this scholar was the luminary of the café. Very abstemious, eating mainly dry bread that he chewed all day long, Safranek was a short man with prematurely grey hair who had two passions: poetry and chess. He was certainly good at bridge and, as a dedicated volunteer, was a fourth hand, but his heart was not in the game.

His heart was somewhere else. Somewhere else meant with his chess partner, an ill-shaven little Polish Jew who had black hair protruding from his ears and nose and could not speak any language correctly, but who was a genius in front of the chess board. A former sweater manufacturer, this unemployed workboat turned incessantly around the lightship as though blinded by the light. At least one hundred times, Safranek swore to himself that he would not play with Moses

Kleinhandler whose breath smelled badly, who sprayed saliva as he spoke, and who insulted him loudly in a whimsical, broken French where the vowels were easily reversed, accusing the Czech of cheating and calling him a bedbug. Just as certain elite men succumb to vulgar women and are unable to break away from this shameful passion, so Safranek was unable to escape from Kleinhandler and unfailingly fell back to his vice.

But if Kleinhandler exploited his power over Safranek, he was subdued by Jeroboam Pinkas. This last named, even though he was a very mediocre chess player, had enslaved the hairy little man, sending him to pharmacies, to the post office in Francheville or neighbouring communities, and even to the farms to pick up the produce he had ordered. Pinkas, a small fishing trawler in the cemetery of ships, especially liked to fish in troubled waters and personally preferred to avoid the coast guard, the police.

The days when Safranek tried to shake off Kleinhandler's yoke, he chose for his partner Ernst Muller, an Austrian political refugee, a pitifully thin man in fragile health who was often shaken by asthmatic attacks. Muller's pockets always contained quantities of vials, capsules, and tablets so that he would always be prepared to prevent or alleviate his crises. The Austrian was a hospital ship. Very poor, living from day to day on help from meager and irregular sources, he ran from his miserable garret and spent his days in the Café de la Marine where the owner, understanding his situation, did not force him to eat and drink.

Amongst the wrecks in the Café de la Marine, one often saw a tug emitting thick clouds of smoke and pulling a sluggish barge. This tug was a bustling little woman in her thirties who, as the daughter of a minister from the Balkans, had known better days. Having some notions of sewing, this Parisian by adoption quickly built up a clientele among those ladies in Francheville who had pretensions of elegance. She arrived at the café with a small bag that she immediately opened once she was seated at a table and soon covered it with pieces of fabric, ribbons, thread, needles, thimbles, scissors and other sewing accessories. A placid young, blond athlete, a former physical education teacher and a masseur with whom she was infatuated, placed himself beside her.

The minister's daughter was a heavy smoker, but since the introduction of ration cards for tobacco, she was hard-pressed. One day, when the need for tobacco was gnawing at her, she had committed the fatal act that led to her downfall. When she arrived at the Café de la Marine that day, she noticed that General Fentimore's wife, who had just left the café, had abandoned a barely started cigarette in her ashtray. There was enough tobacco to make a thinly rolled cigarette. The temptation was too great. She reached for it. After that first experience, it became a habit. From that day forth, the minister's daughter hunted for cigarette butts that became shorter and shorter and less and less appetizing, putting them into a metallic box. Only the first step is difficult.

Whenever she was in a café, a store, or a movie house and saw a man smoking, she approached him and, in a very mundane tone that she had used especially for her father's diplomatic receptions, she would say, "Would you be so kind not to throw your butt too far?"

The people in Francheville gossiped, but the minister's daughter no longer cared what people thought of her.

The submarine of the Café de la Marine was a Spaniard, Pedro Gonzalez. His status was a bit irregular. Every time an alert was sounded, he would prudently submerge. A sculptor, he had escaped from a concentration camp thanks to a work contract given to him as a favour by a marble dealer. The annoying part of the deal was that the marble dealer was required to pay the administration seven francs a day for his fictional employee, according to the regulations for foreign workers who were supplied to the bosses at advantageous prices. Naturally, it was up to Gonzalez to pay this 'tax', and the sculptor was forced to do all kinds of chores to avoid returning to the camp. Liberty is priceless.

On occasion, there were also ships in transit. Tibor Verès, for example, was a mail packet. Whenever he came to Francheville, he lay in wait for Brandouille. Not only would the mailman give him his own mail, but everyone else's in the neighbourhood to distribute. There also was a dismantled cargo carrier, Daniel Cahen, a former representative of a Parisian textile firm for thirty years who had been fired because of his Jewish origins. Since the day the armistice had been signed, he had been a refugee in Francheville. This dignified, neatly dressed little man waited for the war to end while enduring, with resignation, the shrewish disposition of his wife whose maiden name was Forgeron. In 1940, she had added to her long list of matrimonial complaints: he was a Jew. After twenty-eight years of marriage, she had discovered this peculiarity and harped on it, so that it was more like a monologue. When she said 'Jew' for the third time, Cahen took his hat and walked quietly out the door. Before the tempest, he took refuge in the harbour of the Café de la Marine.

Occasionally, one could find a training ship in the person of Mr. Longeaud. This boat, which was always anchored in port, was attracted to the cosmopolitan company in whose midst he felt as if he were getting a taste of the high seas. There also were modest coastal vessels: several labourers from the sawmills and paper mills. Their features were gaunt; their faces, emaciated. They came to drink a cup of coffee with saccharine or swallow a shot of red wine. For the most part, they were strangers in this region. They dragged their hard knocks and misery with them from place to place. For them, the mills in Francheville were only a stopover, as were the other places where they had worked.

While the coastal vessels navigated close to the counter and prudently discussed politics in muted voices, on the other side of the counter was Marius, the waiter – yet another who was not a native of Francheville – who chopped ice for the more demanding customers seated at the tables. Marius, the ice breaker in the cemetery of ships.

In this summer of 1942, the Café de la Marine was the only place in Francheville where wine and coffee were not rationed. The customers of this establishment were those rare inhabitants of Francheville who, rightly or wrongly, thought that their ration of coffee and even their own fate depended on the outcome of the battles in Russia and Africa. That was why they had a passion for politics and strategy. Naturally, General Fentimore, in his capacity of headquarters officer, was the uncontested authority on military matters. Every day they awaited his arrival to hear his enlightened analysis of such and such an encircling action, or the chances of any fortified city resisting. Puffing big clouds of smoke from his pipe, General Fentimore stated his competent opinion with all that natural reserve so typical of the British and of a member of the Great Secret Society, an opinion that sooner or later events proved false.

Hope enables one to live, and all the customers of the Café de la Marine were optimistic about the war and its consequences for themselves. However, each one was haunted by the same spectre: the concentration camp. Even the general himself was no exception. Ever since the day he had been caught in a police raid while leaving the Gare Saint-Charles in Marseilles and been detained in spite of his titles, his decorations from the French Legion of Honour and all his papers being in order, he still trembled, although he bragged about it.

To ward off the fate that menaced them, the Café de la Marine's customers offered appeasing sacrifices: they collected things for the benefit of the internees in the camp. Each had his protégés: Benedetti his socialists, Muller his communists, Verès his Jews. They gave willingly and from their hearts, and General Fentimore matched their contributions with some five hundred franc notes that, thanks to the devotion of Mrs. Fentimore, were transformed into a pile of food and mailed to the camps.

The last activity of this kind was conducted by Jeroboam Pinkas who, until now, had been somewhat indifferent to the collections and got out of it by contributing ten francs. "But this time," he said, "no

149

one should remain indifferent. A dysentery epidemic is raging in the camp at Drancy. It left the survivors so weakened that they are unable to take care of their physical needs. What misery! In the north, it is impossible to get glycerine suppositories which are the only things that could alleviate their discomfort." Pinkas had obtained this information from a Relief Committee and was very upset about the news. He had offered to find a certain number of boxes of this precious remedy for the hundreds of convalescents. The committee would underwrite all the expenses. "For shame! How revolting!" cried the General who proposed that they write to his friends on the Côte d'Azur to have them send all the suppositories they could find. Everyone else had done the same, and the suppositories had arrived in Francheville in massive numbers. Pinkas had reimbursed the contributors and thanked them wholeheartedly in the name of the committee. Then he retired to the Hotel Panorama's garden to assemble his boxes.

*****

The clock in the town hall struck seven when Longeaud, with unsteady steps, entered the Café de la Marine. Every Thursday at this hour the training school ship, loaded with a full cargo of alcohol, became a tanker. He sat down at a table and looked at his watch; it was 7.04. He was four minutes late. He tapped his foot under the table as he watched the door anxiously. His behaviour resembled that of a man waiting for his lover.

"Marius! A cognac!" he shouted in a husky voice, trying to make himself important.

At exactly 7.07 the door opened. Philippe Chameix, the pharmacist's assistant at the White Cross Pharmacy, entered carrying an object wrapped in newspaper under his arm. Noticing Longeaud, he went to him.

The teacher's heart skipped a beat. He guessed that, in those newspapers, was the object of his desires, a bottle of Pernod that Mr. Chameix had promised to prepare for him eight days ago. To the litre of vodka that Mr. Longeaud had given him, the pharmacist's assistant added dill, anise, and some plant extracts and produced a fairly respectable Pernod.

With the gestures of a conspirator, the schoolteacher slipped the prearranged fee, two packs of cigarettes, under the table. Then he retired to the men's room where he moistened his lips with this much desired drink, and clicked his tongue appreciatively. He reflected for a second, contemplating the blank label glued to the bottle, then seized by a sudden inspiration, he took out his pen and wrote in capital letters:

IRRADIATED EMULSION FOR CHILDREN WITH RICKETS –
VITAMIN P

This precautionary measure was necessary, for it was always possible to meet a tax inspector on the road. The Vichy government was after him!

He rewrapped the bottle in an old newspaper, hiding it in the leather pouch that he had brought for that purpose and re-entered the café. He found Chameix had moved to a table where Pinkas sat talking with Kleinhandler.

Longeaud shook the alchemist's hand warmly, congratulating him for his great masterpiece, paid for his glass of cognac, and left the café to return to Saint-Boniface. It was exactly 7.11 p.m.

The pharmacist's assistant turned to Pinkas saying, "Mr. Pinkas, I must talk with you about a very urgent, strictly confidential matter."

Pinkas glanced imperiously at Kleinhandler who understood what that look meant. With the eyes of a beaten dog, Kleinhandler stood up and turned to join Safranek. Safranek swallowed his crust of bread, closed the volume of Valéry[37] that he was reading and, in the feeble voice of a man resigned to the inevitable, called, "Marius, the chess game!"

"Look," said Chameix, while his eyes scrutinized the restless Pinkas. "I've noticed that, for several days, you've been consuming a huge amount of suppositories. I think I know why."

Pinkas blushed, raised his hand in a gesture of protest, and stammered, "This is... I assure you..."

"No, I've not come to moralize about that. I came to see if I could help you. If you're planning to make soap from the glycerine, I can make you an interesting offer."

"Where did you get such an idea?" protested Pinkas, "Why soap? Well, all right, let's hear your proposition," he added.

"Just in time," said Chameix, "I'm in a hurry. If you want to buy two cases of excellent medicinal tar soap, pre-war quality, tell me at once. The manufacturer is in Francheville today and sold three cases to the Modern Pharmacy. He wanted to sell some to my boss, but Mr. Astier is too old and refused the offer. It certainly is a good business. Look, a bar like this will cost you five francs twenty-five. You can easily sell it for fourteen. I want thirty per cent of the profit. I think that's reasonable. But hurry up! The manufacturer is taking the 7.25 train. We have just enough time to stop him. You understand, he has reasons to sell his entire stock without delay."

---

37 Paul Ambrose Valéry (1871–1945). French poet. (HRG)

Pinkas looked at the sample, smelled it, made a face, spat on it, and rubbed it with his thumb. His grimace turned into an approving smile.

"It's a deal," he said. "I'm running there."

He threw a bill on the table and rushed to the nearby railway station accompanied by Chameix.

The pharmacist's assistant had guessed correctly. Pinkas was not preoccupied with the sluggishness of his own bowels, nor with the dysentery epidemic in Drancy. His project was a small soap factory for which he had already gathered the raw material, enough for a start. No one in the Café de la Marine, nor in Francheville, ever suspected it, not even his errand boy, the hairy Polish Jew. One must fend for himself and keep up with the times, isn't that so?

Meanwhile the world was a bloody magma torn by steel and fire. On the Ukrainian plains and on the Libyan sands, the German High Command, playing the big game, launched its armoured divisions, opening gigantic pincers. The fate of the world was about to be decided. On the battlefields, in the skies, in the depths of the ocean, in the bombarded cities, people were dying by the thousands for a cause that was not their own. In the prisons, in the concentration camps, hundreds of thousands of human beings, reduced to an animal existence, rotted. In the cities, the workers were sliding slowly from deprivation to a famine whose ugly, grimacing face became an obsession.

However in Saint-Boniface and Francheville, life crept along as usual. Delphine Legras's big worry was to find a way to prevent Latière's dog from stealing her eggs. Noémi Sobrevin concerned herself with ways to force Brandouille to bring the apron for her little Abel. For his part, the mailman schemed to force Noémi to return his bicycle pump without having to give her anything in exchange. Vautier was absorbed in a project of the clandestine slaughter of animals for Sarzier from the Hotel Panorama, and Bardette, while mourning for her cat, conceived tenebrous plans for vengeance against the poisoner. Mrs. Hermelin, who was expecting new boarders, was haunted by the problem of supplies and ways to reduce her expenses. Mr. du Chesne was improving his phalanstery project and rewording his new announcement. Miss Amélie Martin, completely disoriented since her brother's death, and persecuted by Sister Félicie, was going through a severe moral crisis aggravated by the uncertainty of her future. André Murger sometimes forgot the drama being played on the battlefields in the east and reflected on Solange Fleury's short stay in Tilleuls for which he had no explanation. Would she ever come back? César Fleury, enchanted at having recovered his virility in Génia's arms, was trying to discover how he could, without awakening his wife's suspicions, dedicate to his mistress all the time that his newly aroused senses required. Génia thought only of her love and the man who personified it. Pinkas, who had succeeded in getting two cases of medicinal soap and whose useful conversation with Philippe Chameix dragged on into the late hours of the night, was revisiting the initial plans for his soap factory; the resourceful, competent pharmacist's assistant would become his partner. In addition to soap, they would produce Pernod for sale at five hundred francs a litre, an excellent business if one considered that Chameix could get pharmaceutical alcohol at one tenth the price. Mr. Astier, the owner of the White Cross Pharmacy would only notice the flame; Chameix would not forget to pull the handle of the automatic cash register. Finally, it was this same Pernod that was the greatest preoccupation of Camille Longeaud who had been the last beneficiary of Chameix's talents.

IV

Whosoever at forty has no haemorrhoids...

This morning even Mr. Longeaud's hair hurt. It was not the kind of hangover of the good old days, but the customary malaise which followed his escapades on Thursday and Sunday: a heavy head, a coated tongue, and foul breath. Having declared that he was suffering pain, he had his wife take over his class which was going on an excursion that day. She was capable of handling it easily. Then, too, this Friday was the 18th of June, Mr. Longeaud's fortieth birthday. How could one avoid being sad the day one awoke and realized that he was forty? He recalled the alexandrine verse in *The Counterfeiters* from the time when he still read books:

"Whosoever at forty has no haemorrhoids..."

Oh well, he had none. Encouraged by this consoling thought, Mr. Longeaud stretched, jumped out of bed, washed his face quickly, went down to the kitchen where the coffee was still hot on the stove, poured himself a big bowlful and drank it. Then he lit his first cigarette of the day. It did not taste too good, but for Friday morning, that was normal. He lacked the patience to finish it and snuffed it out in his butt-filled ashtray.

This foul wartime tobacco! The national tobacco was like the national coffee, the national shoes, the national linen. The other day, when Mr. Longeaud had asked Maurice Gideaux the meaning of the word 'national', the urchin answered, "It's something not as good as before the war." He could not have said it better. Whatever it was, he smoked too much, an average of thirty cigarettes a day. That was not reasonable, especially when he was forty years old. It was a strain on the heart; it clogged the arteries; it warped memory. From now on he would smoke less, ten cigarettes, for example.

At forty, one must realize that his youth was over. What had he accomplished? Not too much he had to admit. For the past twenty years he had prepared several dozen brighter children for graduation, engaged a bit in politics, and got married. The rest of the time did not amount to much. That was not how he had imagined his career would be when he was graduated from Normal School[38]. At that time his profession had appeared to be a vocation: fighting ignorance in the countryside, the lack of hygiene both physical and moral, and the power of the priests. Mr. Longeaud had maintained contact with two or three friends who described the fight that they were waging, but they had been stationed in less remote areas. Mr. Longeaud had also tried to fight. In his first position, he was so zealous about hygiene – head lice, runny noses and no handkerchiefs, dirty ears and nails – that he had antagonized most of the mothers. You see, the children had demanded toothbrushes and tissues for their runny noses! He had also tried to work with the peasants, explaining and showing them that they wasted too much time watching a miserable beast in tiny fields that, very often, were several kilometres from their houses. One herdsman would suffice for the whole village. That was how they did it in the Jura where the grazing land was communal. But the peasants had shrugged their shoulders, the priests had interfered, and it had become such a big argument that, when he had been assigned to a different post, he had sighed with relief. This experience had taught him a lesson. One did not give up his ideas. Instead one renewed subscriptions to such magazines as: *Progress*, *The Light*, and *Crapouillot*. One voted and made others vote for the Left, but one did not meddle in the life of the peasants.

When a man married a woman like his wife, he was lost forever. Lost forever? Well, perhaps not! Mr. Longeaud had not said his last word. He was forty years old but he still had resources: a steady foot, a sharp eye, and no haemorrhoids! The essential thing was to react to prevent the degeneration of the body and mind.

To prevent a fat, flabby body there was nothing better than a cold shower every morning on arising, then fifteen minutes of callisthenics with weight-lifting. One ought to smoke less. Ten cigarettes? Even this was too much. Eight would be enough: three in the morning and five

---

38 Normal School: teacher training college. (HRG)

in the afternoon. On Thursday and Sunday, ten, for after all...

Above all, one must drink less. One should not become drunk. Let us say, one quart with each meal, and Thursdays, an additional drink or two with friends. It would be hard in the beginning, but with willpower one could accomplish it.

So much for the body. As for the mind, that would be a more delicate matter. For some years now, Longeaud had ceased to read. One needed to go back to reading books. One should not allow himself to get rusty. The other day he was unable to reply to the priest who had tried to confuse him by citing the authority of several writers whom Longeaud had never read: "The Leftists," said the priest, "are wishy-washy." One must close certain gaps and then learn a living language. A man who knows a foreign language is worth two. To know English, for instance, is very advantageous and gives you prestige. He still retained some notion of English from his Normal School days. Thanks to the *Assimil Method* that he had bought just before the war, it would be child's play for him. What a relief it was to know what one wanted.

In such circumstances, the most difficult thing was to make a decision. Now that the principal difficulty had been overcome, that deserved something – a small reward, don't you think? Mr. Longeaud took out his pack of Gauloise and lit a cigarette. It was the second one of the day, if you counted the one he had not finished. Then he would take a shower followed by weight-lifting exercises. Longeaud found this cigarette much tastier than the first.

He went to the tap, filled a large watering can with water, and returned to the kitchen where he improvised a shower in a wooden washtub. He was not out of his washtub yet when he noticed, through the transparent curtains, the figure of a neatly dressed man with a briefcase under his arm approaching the entrance. A minute later he was knocking energetically on the door.

In his bathtub, the schoolteacher shivered from cold and fear. Who could this man with the briefcase be? Surely, an inspector or tax collector from the Supply Agency. The Vichy government was after him! Perhaps they had heard about the bottle of Pernod. Someone could have seen him in the café or in the men's room. That was all he needed!

"Wait until I'm dressed!" he called out, in an insecure voice. "I'm in the shower!"

As soon as he had pulled on his trousers and shirt over his wet body, he ran in his bare feet to the dining room to take out three or four old pharmaceutical flasks from a cupboard and placed them in front of the bottle of Vitamin P, like bodyguards in front of the king. Everyone knows that the most visible objects attract the least attention.

Quickly putting on his shoes, he rushed to open the door. Standing before him was Prosper Baudrier, a surveyor and inhabitant of a large town near Francheville. A weight fell from Longeaud's heart.

The surveyor, an expert referee, was a fat, paunchy, well-nourished, short man. He came to consult the land survey register in the town hall in order to evaluate and divide the property of the late Anselme Laffont among his five nephews. Mr. Longeaud took him to the proper office in the town hall which was next to the school. Before leaving him to his work, Mr. Longeaud stayed to gossip a while. As they talked, Longeaud automatically pulled a pack of cigarettes from his pocket and offered one to the surveyor who took it readily. He was used to people offering him things. Longeaud already had a cigarette between his lips when he remembered his resolution. It was his third cigarette, and it was not eleven o'clock yet, but to be polite he could not allow the surveyor to smoke by himself.

Longeaud lit the fourth cigarette one hour later, also quite automatically, after he had done some weight-lifting exercises and had eaten an omelette with bacon that he had prepared over a fire of pine cones. However, this cigarette was on his programme, especially since he had not washed down the meal with a carefully measured quart of wine. Now to work!

Effortless English Assimil Method It does not require perseverance. It is essential to regularly devote at least ten minutes a day.

"All right. Fifteen and even twenty if necessary. One doesn't quibble over a few minutes when it's a question of moral and intellectual rebirth."

Taking into consideration the possibility you will fail to study daily, you will need three to six months to complete the course.

"First, there will be no failures, no failures at all. Finally, let us accept six months. At that rate, one could learn two foreign languages a year. As soon as I finish English, I'll begin Spanish, then German, and even Italian." In two years he would be a polyglot.

First (1st) Lesson (pron: feurst less'n)
My tailor is rich.
Our doctor is good.
Your cigarette is finished.

Yes, the cigarette was finished. What a pity. He worked better while he smoked.

Mr. Longeaud read the first lesson of thirteen sentences aloud several times. He even tried the exercise (egg'zecaiz):

"Our cigarettes are good. Our cigarettes are not good."

"Always these cigarettes! How provoking! Well, to hell with it! Since the author insists so much, I'll light a cigarette. There! I'm entitled to it; it's only the fifth. 'My cigarette is good. My cigarette is not finished'."

The lesson was over; it had taken Mr. Longeaud exactly eighteen minutes. The schoolteacher noticed with satisfaction that he still had timebefore Mrs. Longeaud and the students returned at four o'clock. He thumbed through the *Fables of La Fontaine* and after hesitating several times, he chose "The Oyster and the Lawyers" for his pupils to study. Suddenly he remembered that, for the past three days, he had had papers to correct for that same class. The assignment was to choose a part of the face and describe it.

Mr. Longeaud opened Michel Vautier's notebook. His composition was entitled "The Nose" and was not very long. This boy never applied himself.

The nose is to breathe, to smell and to blow. It can serve to hold eyeglasses, to sneeze and to snore. Maurice Gideaux has some small brown hairs inside his nose that catch the mique-robes. When one has a cold, the nose runs.

Mr. Longeaud underlined the spelling mistakes, crossed out the reference to Maurice Gideaux's nose with the notation "not relevant to the subject", and gave him a passing mark. Then he picked up Dina Sobrevin's notebook. This conscientious little girl had chosen the ears as her subject.

The ears are shaped like a small shell. They serve to hear and to wear earrings. Aunt Rachel bought me a pair and my mother put them away with my dolls and now she cannot find them. When I grow up, I will find them and put them on. You can put cotton in your ears. Deep inside the ear there is a kind of yellow wax. When you pull the ears, they get red.

She had only three spelling mistakes. This was worth A—Good.

The third notebook belonged to Maurice Gideaux. He had a good memory, but oh, so lazy. His composition consisted of two sentences.

The teeth. The teeth look like little soldiers in a line.
The tongue is the captain...

Mr. Longeaud shrugged his shoulders and wrote in the margin: "Why? Justify this comparison."

...I know three kind of teeth: baby teeth, grown-up teeth, false
teeth.

This Gideaux certainly was a dunce. Mr. Longeaud marked his paper
mediocre and thought that was still too good for him.

He had corrected another three or four papers when he began to
sense something was amiss. He was not exactly thirsty, but he had a
bad taste in his mouth. A few drops of alcohol and this bad taste might
disappear. Anyway, it would be interesting to know the true flavor of
Chameix's Pernod when his head was clear.

He emptied his glass, smacked his tongue and remained thoughtful
for a moment, considering whether this Pernod was as good as the one
before the war. It was difficult to judge from one small glass. Pernod
must be tasted in the classical manner. Amateurs have good reason to
drink it in a big glass with very cold water or ice.

While all these thoughts were going through his head, Longeaud
automatically prepared a big glass of Pernod in the classical manner. It
was not until he had drunk it and put his glass down that he realized
the gravity of his act. While he was full of remorse and made plans to
repent, an irresistible urge to smoke seized him. Quickly, so as not to
give himself time to reconsider, he lit the sixth cigarette of the day.

It was only two o'clock in the afternoon. He still had a long day
ahead of him. He began to crave more to drink. This time he was truly
thirsty.

To hell with it! It was only Friday. He would start his new life on
Monday.

V

After a serious border incident, Vautier and Bardette returned to the *status quo ante*

On a radiantly sunny hill among Saint-Boniface's enchanting farms
where milk and honey ran, where bacon and sausages hung from the
ceilings, where the chickens sang from morning to night as they laid
their eggs, their clucking mingling with the noise of the butter churn,
Tibor Verès compared his sufferings to those of Tantalus, a man who
was tortured by a burning thirst while standing in the middle of a river
and striving to drink some water. As soon as his lips almost touched the
water, the water receded. He was also tortured by hunger. Each time he
tried to pull some fruit off the heavily laden branches of a fruit tree at
the water's edge, the branches moved upward, just beyond his reach.

Verès had become tired of a diet of carrots and Jerusalem artichokes which were sold openly in Francheville, and decided to use his time exploring the neighbouring farms. He was naively surprised to discover a very simple fact: he had nothing to offer for the products he desired.

One day he decided to confront the irascible old Crouzet. With his pitchfork planted close to him in a pile of manure, the peasant was sharpening a big kitchen knife. When Verès approached him and told him his needs – that day he needed some butter – the man with the pitchfork passed his hand over the edge of his knife and replied in a sinister voice, "I haven't killed yet this year."

Trembling and terrified, appalled by the icy cynicism of this brute, Verès retreated. The next day, Longeaud explained that this very concise statement meant that old Crouzet had not killed a pig this winter, consequently, he had no bacon and no lard and needed all his butter.

Verès then decided to offer his labour. It was haying time and he offered to help Vautier. Perhaps the old codger would be touched by the generous offer of his tenant, who asked nothing of him, and might consent to sell him some food. Vautier emitted a growl which Verès understood to mean that he accepted the offer. For three days, not a single line was added to *The Paradoxes of History*. Armed alternately with a pitchfork or a rake, the clumsy figure of the former journalist could be seen floundering in the middle of the mowed meadow, climbing up and down the long slopes, and tripping over rocks. The third day, all stiff and bruised, he tumbled down a haystack, scattering the hay that the children had taken two hours to pile. Vautier, with his cryptic way of talking, made him understand that he preferred to dispense with his services. During all the time that he worked, the only recognition Verès received for his kind help was when Vautier offered him two or three glasses of such sour wine that Verès discreetly poured it on the ground. As for provisions, they were out of the question.

To make matters worse, the crisis over water entered a critical phase. Bardette who, since the death of Marquise, had harboured a tenacious hatred of the Verès family, declared one day that she did not want to see them passing through her garden for water. For several days, Verès was obliged to go at night and sneak to the spring like a thief. Finally tired of all this, Verès went to see his landlord and presented his list of complaints: the electricity had not been installed yet; according to Longeaud the furnace chimney needed to be repaired and cleaned because smoke backed up; and lastly, Bardette cut off his water.

The only thing that Vautier would recognize was the problem with Bardette.

"Well," he grumbled, "take your pail and go quietly for water. I'll follow you. We'll see if the old one will stop you on my path."

Tibor Verès ran to his chalet, grabbed a pail and, making sure that Vautier was behind him, crossed the Demarcation Line. As soon as Verès was near the old spinster's house, she emerged menacingly from her cave. She began insulting Verès in patois, but Vautier immediately replied in the same language.

Thirty years of accumulated feuding caused by small chicaneries and vexations exploded into curses from Vautier. Bardette raised her voice, sneered, and spat three times. Then they shouted in chorus: Vautier in a deep baritone; Bardette in a high soprano. Finally out of breath, Vautier picked up the hoe that she had left on his path and threw it at one of her chickens that had had the audacity to venture among his beans.

Choking with anger, Bardette stood open-mouthed. Then with a noise resembling a cat's sneeze, she re-entered her den.

"Now you can go," said the victor, turning to Verès. "She won't bother you for a while."

Verès took advantage of the occasion to fill all his available receptacles. Then he attacked the thirty-first lesson of *English Made Simple* that Mr. Longeaud had lent him and from which he had assimilated five lessons per day.

However, Bardette was not cowed. The next day she went to complain to Father Mignart. The priest was as attentive to this faithful member of his flock as he was to the superb rabbit she had brought for his kitchen. He advised her to submit the argument that she had with Vautier over the spring to a land surveyor, especially since Prosper Baudrier was in town. Father Mignart promised to ask Vautier to accept him as an arbitrator. This would be a friendly arrangement which should not be too expensive and would be borne by the loser.

Mr. Prosper Baudrier, an expert land surveyor, was engaged in the sale of real estate, but his real speciality was litigation over land parcels. In the countryside, his surgical ability in matters of inheritance was more in demand than those of a doctor or veterinarian. The peasant families who would hesitate two or even three times to call the doctor to the bedside of the sick, never hesitated, when the sick died, to bring in the expert surveyor. It was true that Mr. Prosper did not work for nothing, but one had to use his services just as one paid a notary and taxes. It was unfortunate, but it was as inevitable as the frost or hail in April. An inheritance could not be divided like a piece of cheese. One could not divide lands into equal parcels without causing injustices. One must take into consideration the quality, exposure, and irrigation, not to mention the buildings which, in many circumstances, enhanced or diminished the value. In these cases, the intervention of the surveyor was priceless.

That was how it had been in the times of Mr. Prosper's father and grandfather – the Baudriers were a dynasty – and it probably would be the same in his son's time. Such authority passing from one generation to another was infallible. After scores of years it seemed divine, like that of those kings who could only be overthrown by revolution. Saint-Boniface's peasants had never even thought of rebelling against Mr. Prosper's verdicts, nor his fees, nor his ever increasing demands for payment in farm produce ever since rationing had been introduced.

With the prospect of using his services, the arrival of this Solomon in Saint-Boniface was a signal for Vautier and Bardette to start slaughtering their animals surreptitiously. As soon as it was evening, Tibor Verès noticed the feverish preparations of the two litigants. At the Grange, the noise of the butter churn blended with little Michel's monotonous voice as he struggled over "The Oyster and the Lawyers". Mr. Baudrier arrived with an empty valise and a full briefcase. He ate breakfast at Vautier's and, not to make anyone jealous, he dined at Bardette's. Here as there, the surveyor had veritable feasts that produced so much congestion for him that he postponed his work for the next day. He finally decided to consult the land survey records and discovered that the town hall in Saint-Boniface could not furnish all the information he needed. The main piece of evidence was an old will dating back fifty-five years that he had found in the attorney's office in Saint-Paul. The next day he returned there, and twenty-four hours later, after engaging in some mysterious measurements amongst Bardette's peas and Vautier's beans, he finally gave his verdict. It was quite unexpected. The path that Vautier claimed so insistently really belonged to Bardette by virtue of a land division more than fifty years ago. On the other hand, a strip of land about a metre wide in Bardette's pea field belonged to Vautier. Thus the two litigants were both right and wrong at the same time. As a result, each had to share the surveyor's fee.

After that, the surveyor had his last extravagant meal with Vautier and then, contrary to the normal procedure, the partaker of the meal presented a bill. Then Mr. Prosper went to Bardette's to have coffee where he repeated the same formality. He left early the next day. Henri, the oldest of Vautier's seven children, carried the big, bulging valise full of food on the luggage rack of his bicycle.

A common disaster brings enemies together. After bleeding themselves dry to meet the surveyor's fee and appetite, Vautier's and Bardette's animosity melted like butter on the surveyor's hot toast. That same morning, Eugénie Vautier and Bardette, with a new kerchief on her head, had coffee at the Grange. That evening, Eugènie reciprocated

Bardette's visit and, to celebrate the reconciliation, brought her a small sack of bran for her rabbits.

During the course of all those comings and goings, a unanimous decision was made to return to the *status quo ante*, which was that the path leading to the spring would remain Vautier's property and he would give up the strip of land in Bardette's field. Since it is natural for people who suffer a calamity to look for a scapegoat, Bardette and Vautier quickly discovered that all the trouble came from Verès, that good-for-nothing mangy fellow in threadbare clothes who came all the way from Marseilles to sow discord between good neighbours. Verès did not have to attend the discussions to guess the conclusion. Vautier's angry face and Bardette's ferocious, withering glare continued to hound him each time he walked the international boundary to get some water and were enough proof for him.

Feeling quite melancholy as he passed in front of the Grange that evening, Verès heard Michel Vautier studying his lesson. Chanting it like a prayer, he recited "The Oyster and the Lawyers".

"Consider what it costs to sue today
Count what is left for the family,
You will see Perrin takes the money
And leaves only a sack and ninepins for the plaintiffs.
Consider what it costs to sue today
Count what is left..."

VI

A castle in Spain crumbles in a hotel in Francheville

The train that was due to arrive at 9.13 p.m. was two hours late. This ancient snail-paced train, which took nearly three hours to laboriously climb the some forty kilometres of incline that separated Francheville from the Rhône Valley, had derailed once more. Just as old horses become wiser with age and cling to the memories of their youth, so this antiquated train had its caprices and left the rails to fly into space.

It was exactly 11.18 when the slow moving train arrived in the Francheville station that night. About twenty passengers got off. Among them was a petite, middle-aged woman whose grey hair escaped from under her felt hat and whose brow was lined with fine wrinkles. She looked around uneasily, waited until the last passenger disappeared beyond the exit, then resignedly shrugging her shoulders, dragged her valise to the baggage room where she left it. She took only a small bag with toiletry articles.

At that hour of the night, the gentle gusts of wind carried a few raindrops. The passenger, who had just come from the city, feared to get wet. Moreover, she did not know the way. With bitterness, she thought that the person whom she had been expecting should have taken the trouble to meet the train. Disoriented, deceived, and tired, she decided to spend the night in a hotel.

Half an hour later, Mrs. Blanche Fleury settled in room 23 of the Hotel Panorama. She undressed, lay down, and closed her eyes. Alas, a goblin seemed to have crawled under the mattress. He plucked the coils of the bedspring, like one playing the lute, each time she made the slightest move.

Utterly exhausted, she found herself falling asleep when, suddenly, the goblin began playing his instrument. Blanche Fleury was sure that she had not moved. Irritated, she listened carefully. This time she was positive that it was not her mattress that squeaked. There must be another goblin in the next room.

After a while she heard some whispering through the wall. Then a woman's little cry...then a muffled jerky laugh. Blanche raised herself on her elbow. Was it possible that two men could have the same laugh?

She pressed her ear to the wall. Sleep was out of the question. In the other room there was silence again, yet she sensed the presence of two very close human bodies. How strongly her heart beat.

She heard a veiled feminine voice whispering caresses. However, it was the laugh of the man who responded that shook Blanche back to life, and that same male voice adding some indistinct words dispelled any doubt. With clenched teeth and whirling head, she quickly got up, put on her coat over her nightgown and opened her door.

She waited a second in front of the first door on her right and listened again. Then taken by sudden rage, she banged on the door with her fist. It became silent inside. She banged again, hurting her fist.

"Who is it?" asked a musical feminine voice.

"Open the door! Open the door at once, César!"

Inside it was quiet again, followed by muffled cursing. Then slippers slapped on the floor.

"Who are you, madam?" asked the voice behind the door.

"Open immediately, otherwise I'll create a scandal!"

She heard someone moving inside the room. The key turned in the lock.

Panting angrily, Blanche pushed aside the young woman blocking her way and went straight to the bed. The crescent moon coming out from behind a cloud illuminated the room sufficiently so that she could recognize the figure of her husband. With an angry gesture, she flipped the light switch. Choked with fury, incapable of uttering a word, she remained immobile.

Wrapped in a bathrobe, Génia stood close to the door without budging.

César Fleury recovered his wits and wrapped himself in a sheet. He looked at his wife, and, in spite of the ridiculous situation, he felt that he had an advantage over Blanche – he was calm.

"What are you doing here?" he asked, sulkily. "You should have written to me, letting me know when you planned to arrive!"

Blanche felt as if she were suffocating.

"Write to you? But I wrote to you. You should have received my letter this morning. You didn't even come to the station to meet me!"

She bit her lips. Was it this that upset her? It looked as though she was defending herself and César was attacking. The situation was simply grotesque.

Fleury had gained the advantage and exploited it further.

"You calculated badly as usual," he grumbled. "Your letter will probably come tomorrow. I told you a hundred times not to postpone things to the last moment."

If the truth were told, that day César Fleury had left for Francheville before Brandouille came to Tilleuls.

Blanche was mute, stupefied, and indignant. However, her trembling hands showed that she was ready to explode. César realized that he would need to take precautions.

"Look," he said, reproachfully, "you see what kind of state you're in...and then this idea to stop at the hotel!"

As Blanche's angry eyes looked with revulsion from César to Génia and from Génia to César, Fleury understood that he had overstepped the limits. Above all, avoid a scandal! Yes, harass Blanche, but calm her first. The most important thing was to have her admit to a version that would spare her self-esteem and sensibility as a woman.

"Finally, since you were here already," he continued, "you should have waited until morning to ask for explanations instead of entering suddenly as in vaudeville. A little dignity, please!"

"Surely you don't expect me to stand by while you frolic in the next room!"

"Frolic, frolic!" mimicked Fleury, always the master of himself. "Another word from vaudeville! I never thought you'd lack such tact!"

Génia, standing near the door, felt weak. She should have vanished, disappeared, but she did not have the energy. She reached for a chair, sat down heavily, and hid her face in her hands. César seemed to have forgotten her presence.

Resolutely, César quickly got out of bed and pulled on his shirt and trousers. There! Now he was more sure of himself. He thrust a chair toward his wife while he sat on the edge of the bed.

"You talk to me about tact at such a moment," said Blanche, in a trembling voice as tears welled in her eyes. "It's unheard of! You're outrageous! I come here and find you in bed with a woman, and you... You're a monstrous egotist, César!"

She stopped, shaken by sobs. She was cruelly aware that her words were too meek, but she felt paralysed and embarrassed by the presence of the other woman at the other end of the room who only ten minutes before... She should have spoken louder and more forcefully, but she was afraid that her tears would choke her. Perhaps César was right after all. She should not have come into this room. Anyway, it was too late.

"And you?" Fleury counter-attacked. "As for egotism, you aren't without reproach. Have you thought of me for an instant? You know the state of my nerves! Continuous overwork, exhaustion, chronic fatigue, my inspiration completely stunted, and an absolute indifference to emotional life. My poor Blanche, you didn't notice the results of all that. Do you think I would have got this long vacation if my state of health were not serious? Well, for the perfect egotist that I am, I didn't want to worry you."

"I don't understand...what does that have to do with...?" stammered Blanche, while tears rolled down her cheeks.

"But it's so simple!" pursued Fleury. "If you'd only thought a second, you'd have understood it yourself."

"Understood what?"

Near the door, Génia, her cheeks ashen, lifted her head and stared in amazement at Fleury.

"I can't express myself more clearly," said Fleury, impatiently. "You know very well I had to consult a doctor. He recommended not only a fresh-air cure and good fresh food, but, in addition, some sort of psychological treatment, psycho-physical to be more exact. You've heard about shock therapy. Well, this is something like that."

"And this is why you ridicule me in front of this woman?"

César had the smile of a misunderstood man as he said, "What language, my poor Blanche! What a lack of understanding! You know quite well what you mean to me, and you know I'm incapable of betraying you."

As he said that, he glanced at Génia. She was sitting with her chin in her hands, looking at him with glaring eyes. This sentimental little woman was taking the situation too much to heart. One hour ago, he had promised to dedicate a new song to her based on Rimbaud's[39] words: "Oh Seasons, Oh Castles!" She had assured him, in a voice trembling with emotion, that she had only him, that there never had been and that there never would be another man in her life. He, for his part, had replied in an enthusiastic manner. Such nonsense! Those were words said easily in certain circumstances. He would try to repair the damages the next time he had a chance to talk with her. But now he had to calm Blanche. She was his wife, the mother of his child, and then with her little business, she was his security; his own situation at the radio station was at the mercy of events. Were the regime to change... Finally, he abhorred useless complications. He would not upset his life for a passing fancy!

"I'm completely incapable of betraying you," he repeated.

"Yes, you just proved it to me," retorted Blanche.

"I beg you, stop being mean," said César, his voice reflecting some agitation. Then he continued in a more conciliatory and understanding tone, "Do you think this will change anything between us? A foolish coincidence brought you here to witness this episode that's not important to me for reasons I've explained to you. I understand your pain and it saddens me greatly, but nothing can affect the tenderness I feel for you. You know that!"

"You're lying, César," sobbed Blanche. "You're lying shamelessly! Perhaps you're beginning to regret what you did, but it's too late."

"I see you don't understand," said Fleury, with the air of a martyr.

Then throwing a furtive look at Génia who did not react, he made another attempt. "My health, my equilibrium, my art, all this means nothing to you? Then I must speak bluntly to you. The fact is I need a whipping to straighten me out...for my nerves...for my senses...an escape, a refreshing escape for me, and in the final analysis, for you too."

"That's impossible," groaned Blanche obstinately. "I don't understand what you're saying. Furthermore, I don't want to understand."

"But it's quite simple, madam," said Génia, getting up quickly. "Your husband's nerves were in bad shape and he needed a little adventure. He needed a woman. Do you understand? It so happened that I could be of service to him. That's all."

Fleury did not recognize her. Her eyes were shining, her cheeks were on fire, her whole body was trembling, and her voice was high-pitched.

---

39 Arthur Rimbaud (1854–1891). French poet; one of the promoters of symbolism. (HRG)

"Look, madam," said Fleury, feeling his self-assurance waning, "don't get into such a state!"

This appeal to calmness only made Génia lose all self-control. The world was whirling around her. Her temples throbbed. Under her bathrobe, her heaving chest was ready to burst from the pressure.

"Leave me alone!" she shouted. "I'm not talking to you."

Turning to Blanche, she continued, "Don't be afraid, madam. I mean nothing to your husband, and he means nothing to me. It's a little adventure without a future, on doctor's advice, nothing more. You can believe me. You're a housewife, madam, and you may not know there are lonely women without support who need to make a living. Well, I'm one of them."

She fell silent for a minute, then added in a changed voice, "I'm no better or worse than you. I simply had less of a chance. And now... please leave me alone. I'm in my room and I need my rest."

This time Génia felt that she had snapped the constriction around her chest. That feeling of tightness had been atrocious, but now she was relieved. She felt like a sick person who, in order to relieve an intolerable, lancing pain, digs her fingernails into her skin until they draw blood. Only later is relief quickly followed by sensations of anguish and dizziness. Then, little by little, the pain returns.

An abashed Fleury regarded her intently. She certainly was clever, perhaps a little too clever. He had not expected her to help him calm Blanche. What an excellent idea to make herself appear to be a prostitute! Yet, why the devil did she view this whole incident so tragically? One should always be suspicious of these sentimental little women. She was capable of tormenting herself with the words he would have to use to calm Blanche. Oh well...it must end sooner or later.

Blanche stood up.

"Come César," she murmured. "You're right, madam. This conversation has lasted much too long."

Blanche had already taken one step toward the door when she suddenly hesitated, seeming to reflect for a second, and then went over to her husband. He was hastily putting on his shoes. His jacket was still hanging on the back of the chair. Blanche took his wallet from inside jacket pocket, pulled out a bill and, with a dignified gesture, put it on the night table. Then, resolutely, she went to the door followed by César. Passing by Génia, Fleury gave her one last look. The young woman's face became impenetrable again; her eyes were riveted on the floor. Too bad...

Left alone, Génia remained transfixed a moment. Then she mechanically seized the bill, turned it over in her hand, crumpled it and, with a dry laugh, smoothed it out. She looked at the design. The background was a castle...a fairy castle...one of those marvellous castles that exist only in dreams... O seasons, O castles!...

*****

The next day at seven o'clock in the morning, Suzanne, the chamber maid in the Hotel Panorama, was surprised to see the guest in room 23, who had arrived so late last night, leaving with the handsome bearded gentleman who had dined with Mrs. Prokoff, and afterwards she had seen them go up to room 24 together. These men were all the same!

VII

Two of God's ministers come to argue over Frank Rosenfeld's soul

André Murger wanted to write an important letter, but the noisy conversation in the garden under his window annoyed him. He got up to close the window. Since his return from captivity, he had been 'contacted' by a friend, another former prisoner of war who had escaped from Germany and had put him in touch with a resistance organization. André had received orders to paste paper butterflies on walls and in public urinals, spending four or five nights doing this very important job. Now he was expecting other orders, but his chief seemed to have forgotten him.

With the month of June approaching, André followed his doctor's orders and left for the country to complete his convalescence. After more than two months of silence, he received a letter asking if he were ready to resume his work. Ready? He was more than ready. But would they give him something other than pasting paper butterflies in the public urinals?

At this time of the solstice, the atmosphere inside a room quickly becomes stuffy, but even with the window closed the noises continued to filter in from outside. Murger stooped to glance at the people who, at this torrid hour of the day, had gathered in the shade of a large linden tree behind the house.

Just a while ago, André had thought that he recognized Solange's step on the stairs. However, among the voices that came to him, he had not heard the young girl's voice although she was there, sitting in a rattan armchair next to her mother's chaise-longue. André could not see her face which was hidden behind an open magazine, but he saw her white dress with the blue polka dots that she had worn at breakfast. She remained silent while her father talked as usual.

César Fleury, who was torn between the desire to seduce and to scandalize, expounded his theories for every newcomer to Tilleuls. During breakfast, he could not give the matter his full attention because he was catering to Mrs. Fleury, anticipating her smallest desire. Finally, his hour of triumph came. Neither Mr. nor Mrs. Létourneau, the new boarders, nor Joseph Hermelin could escape his harangue.

Mrs. Hermelin had informed the other guests that Mr. and Mrs. Létourneau were high-class guests. It was understood that he was in the 'silk' business in Lyons. Mr. Létourneau was, indeed, part of a silk manufacturing house, but as its chief accountant.

Distracted, André went back to his letter, but the white sheet seemed to be full of blue polka dots. For a moment he fought against the desire to go downstairs. He knew that he was incapable of listening to Fleury's discourse without getting angry and resolved not to participate. He finished his letter, but as soon as he had put it into the envelope blue polka dots began to dance in front of his eyes. He brushed his disorderly hair, snatched a book from the table, and went out.

Mrs. Hermelin, who had just finished arranging the work schedule for her husband and the maid, sat in an armchair with her hand embroidery. It was a large square of linen on which she was embroidering a sentence that at first intrigued André, "Come to me, all you tired and burdened". Was it an advertisement for her boardinghouse? Not at all. Passing behind his landlady's armchair, he read the reference: (Matthew 2:26). So it was a verse from the Bible. He should have guessed it sooner. Now he knew why the wife of the former tax collector hid her work each time the engaged couple appeared on the horizon. The wedding was to be held the next day. No doubt this must be her wedding gift. Evidently, the verse alluded to Mr. Rosenfeld's conversion which Mrs. Hermelin considered imminent, as did the surprise that she had announced so mysteriously to her lodgers.

Since there was no chair available, André sat on the ground a few paces from Solange. Fleury continued talking.

"This so-called progress we've elevated to a religion is nothing more than a deplorable step backwards. The few inventions that have increased our comfort, we've paid for in physical degeneration. With each generation we forget, little by little, how to use our arms. Why bother? We've machines! Our legs are becoming superfluous appendages. We've trains, subways, automobiles, and planes to move us. We don't know how to go up or down stairs; we use lifts. Our eyes and ears? We already have machines that listen and see for us. Soon we'll have machines to make children! It will be less tiring!"

Blanche Fleury looked indulgently at her husband. Mrs. Létourneau, a red-haired, little woman with the eyes of a surprised child, blushed violently. Solange, hidden behind her magazine, shrugged her shoulders. Only Mrs. Hermelin protested vehemently.

"Oh! No, Mr. Fleury! Never! It's written: 'You shall give birth with pain'."

"In short," concluded Fleury, "it's about time we understood that, in order to advance, we must take a few steps backwards. Only today, when all order is breaking down, do we begin to appreciate the benefits of authority. The great minds of the Middle Ages understood, long before we did, that man is bad. Humanity is a pack of wolves that devour each other without a healthy fear of a whip or revolver."

"Isn't that because the regime is bad?" observed Murger. No one paid any attention to him.

The usually calm expression on Mr. Létourneau's round face registered his astonishment. Since France's defeat, the brave man never knew which saint he should honour. Fleury's theories plunged him into disarray.

"In any case," interrupted Joseph, "what was good in the Middle Ages was that the Jews were kept separated from society."

"Long live the ghetto!" murmured Murger to himself.

"Why not?" attacked Fleury. "The solution was elegant and reasonable. It allowed the Jews to be eliminated from society and let those who belonged to that cursed race, which poisons and degrades everything it touches, to live amongst themselves."

"According to you," said André, forgetting his wise resolution, "if a Jew makes bread, the bread is inevitably bad."

"Certainly. I maintain that bread made by a Jew is intrinsically bad even if it doesn't give you colic immediately after it's eaten. I say that conditionally. Do you know any Jewish bakers? I don't. That's the crux of the problem. Productive work is repugnant to Jews. They prefer to play the role of the middleman and parasites. If by chance they do produce something, whether it's a house or a book, usually the work is bad."

"Yet they say that the Jews are intelligent," risked Létourneau.

"Alas," interposed Joseph, "the more intelligent they are, the more harmful they are."

Mrs. Hermelin's younger son, who seemed quite fit for his thirty years, sweated profusely in the dark vest that he never considered proper to remove no matter how hot it became. He was of medium height with plastered-down black hair and a dull face sporting a Charlie Chaplin-like moustache.

"That's not the point," protested Fleury. "According to you, the intelligence of Jews is formidable. I'm not afraid of it – I despise it.

This intelligence is directed toward destruction. In practice it's geared to very big business deals and trickery. Their keen brainpower isn't counterbalanced by the good sense and equilibrium of sane people. Without roots, the Jews have nothing to replace the old ancestral wisdom, the fruit of many centuries of tradition inherited by the most humble Frenchmen and which, alone, provides true strength."

"Yet the Jewish people with their long history and their tradition can't lack ancestral wisdom, to use your expression," insinuated André.

Fleury smiled contemptuously.

"It was lost many centuries ago," he replied. "A piece of meat that was excellent yesterday will smell bad tomorrow and will be completely rotten the day after tomorrow. The offence of the Jewish people is to have prolonged its existence uselessly and to have become an agent of putrefaction. When you scratch deep enough, you'll find that a Jew is the cause of all our evils. This war, for example..."

"The Freemasons of the Elders of Zion," interrupted Joseph, "are aiming to conquer the world. There's the danger. Then there's something clammy and sticky about a Jew that exasperates me personally. Whenever I'm in the presence of a Jew, this feeling of repugnance and irritation is invariably aroused. It's never failed me. It's enough for me to be in the company of a man for five minutes to know if he's Jewish. I believe there must be a definite reason for that."

"Of course," said Mrs. Hermelin. "They haven't turned to Christ yet."

"If I understand you correctly, Mr. Fleury," said André, "it's the Jews who are responsible for this war." (He made an effort to keep calm because that physical repugnance of which Joseph spoke, he felt for this musician.) "For people so gifted with good business sense, they end up in very bad situations. Here they are trapped and persecuted more than ever."

"A miscalculation," replied Fleury.

"Come now!" said André. "It's easy to make the Jews scapegoats for all those evils. It's so convenient that, if the Jews didn't exist, you'd have to invent them. When this war is over, humanity will blush at this collective madness, that is, hatred of Jews. Nevermore will we see the return of pogroms and massacres of Jews. Anti-Semitism will disappear when Hitler's regime does."

Mr. Létourneau, who by instinct looked for a compromise for difficult problems, tried to round off and smooth the edges.

"Basically, gentlemen, we're in accord. There are many things that aren't right. Our country must change!" he said.

"Yes," said Mrs. Hermelin, folding her work, "it must change, and it will change the day when men will return to the Saviour. Mr.

Rosenfeld understood that and is changing his religion. We're sincerely happy about it. That's why I prepared a big surprise in honour of his marriage."

That said, she stood up, put her hands up to shade her eyes and scrutinized the horizon for quite a while. Perceiving nothing, she seemed impatient.

"Excuse me," she said, mysteriously, "I must see if the surprise is here."

When she returned, she seemed somewhat upset and went into the kitchen at once. The Létourneaus had already gone to their room, and Joseph was gone. Mrs. Fleury stood by her chaise-longue talking to her husband.

"I'm going to change, and then, shall we go for a little walk, César?"

He kissed her hand ceremoniously.

"That's fine, my dear, I'll wait for you in the parlour," said Fleury and kissed her hand ceremoniously

Fleury's tenderness toward his wife was even greater than the previous day when he had tried in vain to talk to Génia. Suzanne, the chambermaid, had told him that for the past twenty-four hours Mrs. Prokoff had not left her room, that she was 'tired', and that she had barely touched her food. Fleury had begged Suzanne to insist that he be received, but she had returned shaking her head.

"Mrs. Prokoff doesn't want to see anyone," she said, "and as soon as she feels better, she'll take a trip."

It was a pity, but after all César could do nothing.

In the shade of the linden tree, Solange continued to turn the pages of the magazine. A few steps from her, Murger pretended to read, but in reality he contemplated all he could see of Solange, that is to say, her bare arm, the hem of her skirt, and her long tanned legs. Did she know that he was there? Did she think like her father? Did she think at all? What was she thinking right now? André was tempted to ask her point-blank, but he remembered, just in time, the surprised cold look she had given him at their first encounter when he had offered to carry her luggage to the house. What was she hiding behind this inscrutable air of a distant princess? Perhaps nothing, perhaps very much. Fleury's daughter, what could she be like?

Without taking his eyes off the paper behind which Solange hid, André got up from the grass and sat down in an armchair. If only she would accord him one look. He would like to see her smile to see if she had dimples.

Meanwhile, in Tilleuls's parlour, Fleury played several chords on the piano. Then he began the "Second Fugue" from Bach's *Well Tempered*

Clavichord. Each time that Solange's father was at the piano, André bore indulgent feelings toward him.

"Are you a musician, too?" he asked her, trying to engage her in conversation. "You ought to give us a little concert one of these days."

It was one of those platitudes of a travelling salesman, but he had to say something.

Solange's face appeared from behind the lowered magazine and – oh miracle of miracles! – two charming dimples appeared in her cheeks, transforming the distant princess into an enraptured child.

"Oh no! My father never wanted me to learn music. I don't even know the scale."

There was a certain subtle regret and even some anger in her voice, but the smile still lingered on her lips.

"Curious!" murmured André. "Such an ardent musician... He certainly has some original ideas," he added.

"His ideas can be shocking," she said sharply, while her face became stern, "but he compensates for it with his music. Not everyone can do as much."

She stood up, and without looking at André, went toward the house.

He was very annoyed with Solange and was about to resume his reading when he saw Mrs. Hermelin leave the kitchen. She headed for an armchair, but instead of sitting, she climbed on it and cupped her hand over her eyes like a visor to scan the short-cut between Francheville and Tilleuls.

"It's the surprise," she confided to André.

Suddenly, she swayed, groaned, and would have fallen backward if the young man's arm had not supported her.

"Fancy that!" she muttered, pointing to the path.

André looked and noticed two people walking among the chestnut trees toward Tilleuls.

"I can't understand it," sputtered Mrs. Hermelin. "I recognize my son Jeremy, the minister, but he isn't alone...and this other one... No! It's impossible!"

André squinted to see the apparition that had so upset the owner of Tilleuls. It was a man dressed in black like his companion, but instead of a minister's vest, he had a cassock

"A priest! And it isn't Father Mignart," said Mrs. Hermelin, in a broken voice. "I'm stupid! Maybe he isn't coming here," she added, with a surge of hope.

She would be dismayed. It was to Tilleuls that the two servants of the Saviour were coming, each bent on winning the still hesitant soul of Mr. Frank Rosenfeld.

Chapter Six

Trips into the Unknown

I

Lion gets old

For three days Lion, the Sobrevin's dog, wandered through the countryside looking for Mottes, his farmhouse home.

He was terribly skinny. His fur, normally so lustrous, was now a dirty grey with patches of dried mud here and there. Where his collar had rubbed on his neck, he had lost his fur. On one of his flanks, he had a round sore that penetrated deep into his flesh, a souvenir from a peasant woman who had thrown some scalding water at him when he prowled around her kitchen. With his tail between his legs, his ears flattened, his eyes red, his muzzle close to the ground, Lion continued to wander and search.

Three days of running through the woods and valleys, and in meadows scorched by drought, briars skinning him and thistles sticking to his fur, three days without shelter, food or master, chased everywhere with sticks and attacked by dogs, the most respectable dog becomes a tramp.

Lion did not understand. He sensed vaguely that a dreadful catastrophe had befallen him and robbed him of everything that had been his life. He was terribly unhappy, but he had no wish to revolt, only a feeling of immense, almost human distress, and an aching nostalgia for a lost paradise: the large house full of children, the barn, the big red pot that smelled of lard, the lawns, the cows, the goats. He had been rudely snatched from all that the day Elie Sobrevin, his master, had put him into a basket where he spent two long hours of incessant shaking in his darkened prison into which smells of woods and meadows alternately penetrated. Finally, on being pulled out of the basket, he found himself with his master in a strange house, face to face with an old woman who had sometimes visited Mottes. Then his master tied him under a strange barn and disappeared. Lion's misfortune was complete.

The most frightening disaster, whose horror is beyond our understanding, sometimes has a simple explanation. What had happened to Lion was a common, daily event.

Lion was ten years old. That is to say, he was not an old dog yet, but, like a fifty-year-old worker, he had reached the age when faculties diminish and reflexes are slower, joints stiffen and physical misery was ready to pounce upon him. Sometimes he was caught napping, and he was not as eager and as fast to tend the cows and goats that ventured into the neighbours' pastures as he once was. In other words, he was getting old.

For several months, Elie Sobrevin had been dissatisfied with his service. In a neighbour's house, Elie had just found a young bitch, Friquette, he started to train. Having a bitch had its advantages. It was more faithful than a male. It ran around less among the neighbouring farms and was less of a hindrance. Of course they had litters, but the stream was not too far away. Anyway in a few months, a year perhaps, he would have a replacement for Lion who would be good for nothing by then.

Lion's presence did not help him train Friquette. As soon as Elie gave her an order, Lion, jealous of his prerogatives, jumped first, barked at his rival and, in his fits of unaccustomed rage, even bit the cows. In short, he was full of zeal. But this intermittent eagerness to work did not fool his master. Elie noticed that, after those moments of frenetic agitation, Lion had long intervals of apathy and his strength declined. To make matters worse, he did not get along with Friquette. He barked furiously at her in the meadow and at the feeding dish. He had unreasonable fits of anger and sometimes even used his fangs. Lion was jealous and made Friquette's life difficult. Such a state of affairs could not continue. Elie could have tied Lion up in the shed while he trained his successor and, to avoid vexing incidents at feeding time, he could have fed them separately, but one did not bother to feed a mouth that had become useless.

It was Elie who, in an incisive tone, had first announced everyone's secret thought: we must get rid of Lion. But one cannot dismiss a dog by giving him eight days' severance pay. Try to explain to him that you did not need him anymore, that his place had been filled by another, and that he must go. Dogs may be intelligent, but some things are beyond their comprehension.

It so happened that Elie's mother, who lived in an isolated house just beyond the limits of a hamlet some thirty kilometres from Mottes, had just lost her dog. The old woman, no longer too agile anymore, needed a dog not only to guard her little flock of three goats and two kids, but also to keep her company. Perhaps she would understand Lion since both of them were old. Elie had removed Lion's collar with Mottes's name and address and, as a sign of change, had put it on Friquette. Then he took off on his bicycle with Lion.

175

For three days, Lion wandered through the countryside. Several times he believed that he found the way to Mottes, but each time the scents were mixed, confusing him; the tracks were entangled. Each time he found himself in an unfamiliar landscape with strange dogs and unknown people who threatened him with sticks and threw stones at him.

Twice the tracks led him to the banks of a swift, turbulent river. He stopped and barked at his reflection in the middle of a twinkling, sunny pool at the river's edge. He could not swim across the river. His master had warned him. All along the twenty kilometre stretch of water, there was only one bridge. To find it, he had to make detours because the river made a wide bend.

Elie thought that only a miracle would enable the dog to find his way back. This miracle happened. On the afternoon of the fourth day, Lion, a muddy shadow of his former self with fur unkempt and tongue hanging out, appeared at Mottes like a hungry wolf. When he realized that he was on the right road, the desperate rage that had urged him on for the past four days dissipated. As he approached Mottes, he became timid. He would have liked to break into a fast run to re-enter his lost paradise, but his limbs behaved as though they were paralysed. Did he have a premonition that, by returning, he was defying his master's will?

When he reached the vine-encircled well some thirty metres from the house, he stopped. This was where he came each time his mistress scolded him. No one seemed to be at home. The familiar smell of soup wafted from the kitchen. Lion curled up in his corner, happy, but exhausted by hunger, fatigue, and fear.

Suddenly his ears pricked up. From the top of the hill, he heard the sound of a metal-tipped cane striking the stones in the road. Lion knew that sound for he had heard it daily for many years. That sound automatically caused him to bark. Lion dreaded Brandouille and the wine smell that preceded and followed him, and especially the metal-tipped cane the mailman thrust into his face to taunt him. One day, Brandouille had driven the sharp point into Lion's flank, and Lion had bitten the man with the mailbag. After that, each time Lion saw him he felt like biting him.

But today, Lion was tired and too troubled by all that had happened to him. He did not bark at Brandouille, but watched silently as his enemy with the metal-tipped cane approached.

The mailman stopped several paces from the shed. Elie Sobrevin kept his tools in there. Suddenly, Brandouille stopped, fascinated. Through the half-open door he saw his bicycle pump that Noémi had kept as security to force him to bring the apron he owed her. It was a unique opportunity for him to recover his property.

Lion did not know Brandouille's motives. All he saw was the enemy trying to enter a part of his paradise in the absence of his masters. Suddenly, his conscience as a watchdog, his professional conscience, overcame everything: fear, remorse, hunger, weariness. Barking furiously, his fangs ready to bite, Lion sprang toward Brandouille. Brandouille brandished his cane, but just then Noémi appeared in the kitchen doorway. The mailman handed her a letter without looking at her and hastily went away mumbling threats. He would find a way to get his pump without giving her the apron. As for the rabbit, he had paid the price for it, and that should be enough!

"Look! It's Lion!" exclaimed Noémi, very surprised but also quite moved. "This Lion! How did he do it?"

It is well known that dogs will travel great distances to return, but after all those precautions: closed in a basket on a bicycle rack, transported a distance of thirty kilometres, and a bridge so difficult to find! Yet he had found his way.

For ten years, Lion had been part of the household. Noémi had received him as a gift from a cousin shortly after her wedding. It was she who had trained him. When he was little, she had made him sleep in the kitchen and had covered him with straw because he shook from the cold. When he had been wormy, she had given him pills in a ball of bread, and when he had the usual dogs' illnesses, she had treated him with black coffee. She had saved his life, just as she was sure that she had saved her son Abel from diphtheria when she had painted his throat with paraffin while he was choking. Lion was almost like one of her children, the eldest of eight. He had seen all the others being born. This brave old Lion!

Singing loudly, the children arrived from school. Seeing him, they threw themselves on him, caressing him, hugging and squeezing him. They climbed on his back, pulled his tail and ears; he never got angry at them. Lion licked one after another, yapping happily. What happiness it was to be with the family again!

"I told you so," said little Abel, triumphantly. "Now we won't let them take him away."

"Look how skinny he is," said Noémi. "It's unbelievable, in four days. He has nothing in his stomach, the poor thing!"

She threw him a big piece of bread which Lion caught in midair and swallowed with gusto. His legs trembled with joy, fatigue, and emotion. What a pitiful sight! Noémi brought him a full dish of buttermilk and put it before him.

"Come drink, my poor Lion. You've earned it."

"We must get rid of him. We can't feed him for long," declared Elie,

177

arriving for lunch a few minutes later.

It was an exaggeration to say that Lion was a big eater. He was not choosy. Only in books is it written that dogs are carnivores. Saint-Boniface's dogs were vegetarians, vegetarians and scavengers. They were satisfied with a bit of soup and some leftovers from the pots. As for meat, they did not know the taste, only from the scraped bones and the entrails of a rabbit during the holidays.

Elie Sobrevin was very annoyed. This dog had given him trouble for quite some time. He did not want to feed him for doing nothing while he waited for him to die. Dogs could live to be sixteen. Too bad for him, he should have stayed with the old woman.

"I'd better finish him off right away," said Elie.

He went to the cellar to look for an old sack.

Noémi felt ill at ease. This poor Lion! Elie was in a rush. Yet, after all, one day sooner or later... She cut another slice of bread and threw it to the dog. He always liked bread and only ate it on special occasions. She poured him a little coffee made from rye that she had toasted in an old pot – the last meal of the condemned.

Elie returned from the cellar with the sack and whistled to Lion as he used to do in the meadow. The little Sobrevins were excited and joyful at the thought of the spectacle that they were about to behold. It was entertainment for them.

Only Abel remained in the kitchen with his mother. He never liked to look for small birds in their nests, or pin butterflies to sheets of paper. He did not like to see goats or rabbits killed, or how one bled the chickens. He was different from the others.

Dina returned and called to him from the doorway, "Come Abel, let's see Lion drown!"

Abel turned his back to her. He did not want to see anything. He was sad.

"Go now, you foolish fellow," his mother said to him. "You don't have to make such a face over a dog. What is a dog, especially today when so many people die from bombs!"

"Yes," said Abel, thoughtfully, "but I don't know them. Lion I know."

Elie Sobrevin reached the stream in the lower meadow. Lion followed him happily. He had stopped trembling. The master was not angry. He had called to him like in the good old days. That entire terrible catastrophe had only been a nightmare.

Elie stopped at the edge of the stream, picked up a heavy stone and put it into the sack. He whistled again and Lion came close, wagging his tail confidently.

Then something incomprehensible happened, incomprehensible and terrifying. The master seized Lion as he had done the day he put him into the basket. He pushed Lion into the sack. Once again it was a very dark night. Lion barked desperately. Would he be taken back to the old woman? Would he be able to return?

Elie tied the bag to the end of a long cord. The children surrounded him; their eyes shone brilliantly. The spectacle had begun.

"Tell us, Daddy, are you going to leave the sack in the water?"

Elie shrugged his shoulders. The children were having a good time! Leave the sack in the water? It could be used again. Why not order a coffin while one was about it!

Slowly, he lifted the sack in which Lion barked hoarsely and fought furiously. He grasped the other end of the cord and plunged the sack into the water. The weight of the big stone dragged it to the bottom. Lion was silenced. This time he would not find his way back.

A few minutes passed. Finally, Elie pulled out the sack with the animal's body. It was heavy. The children were already preparing a great funeral for Lion. It was odd. Even in death, Lion amused them. For them, the spectacle continued. For Lion, all was finished. Ten years of loyal service, joys and suffering. The life of a dog.

II

Meditations on turnips in brine

"It's a long way to Tipperary
It's a long way..."

Joseph stopped quickly, realizing that he was singing an English marching song. After Mer-el-Kébir and Syria! However, since he liked to walk to a definite rhythm and since he could think of nothing better, he began humming:

"Maréchal, here we are!
You've restored our hope!"

Doubled over under the weight of an enormous Tyrolean pack, he was leaving the outskirts of Francheville and was on his way to Saint-Boniface. The civil servant was on vacation for several days and his mother had already found a reason to send him to Francheville on all sorts of errands.

The former lieutenant had found a position as chief of supply services in a small town in the county about fifty kilometres from Francheville. He had accepted it while he waited for something better. "It isn't a position with a future," he had thought, believing that the war would end in a few months.

While he climbed the steep hill, he smiled as he recalled his apprehensions. Since then two years had passed and his position seemed more secure than when he first began.

What bothered Joseph more now was the moral and ideological aspect of things. Of course, once France was finally rid of the leading Freemasons and Jewish vermin, it would regain its former place even if it were meant to be in servitude. The new discipline was preferable to the disorder of freedom. Yet something was wrong.

First, one must consider the general order. Of course those bastards were checkmated, but they were continuing to increase, presenting a passive resistance to all efforts to suppress them. They were very stubborn. They would perish the day when a new Europe would be built after the Germans were victorious in the east. But was a German victory that certain? The victor, who after each triumph seemed to take a bow and wait for applause, gave the world a spectacle of strength, but it now appeared exhausted, sweating profusely after each act and, at the end, sponging its forehead as it stood on wobbly legs. Doubt slyly instilled itself in Joseph's soul.

Then there was the matter of obeying the rules and regulations. However, in practice, it was not always easy. In his speciality, for example, Joseph remembered the story of turnips in brine. In normal times, only a fool could conceive of such a grotesque idea to put such hardy vegetables into brine when the crop did not spoil from one harvest to another. But this was not a fool's invention. All vegetables in their natural state were rigorously taxed while the fancier preparations could escape taxation and be sold at exorbitant prices. That is why, in March of 1942, the merchants in the city preferred to sell turnips in brine rather than in their natural state. One merchant in the city, an influential member of the Legion of Fighters who had had nothing but annoyances under the Republic, had imported five or six barrels of this new kind of delicacy from Algeria. Since the public did not accept this article, which was terribly expensive and had very little flavour, the turnips began to spoil. Instead of resigning himself to his loss, the merchant had preferred to bring a lawsuit against the shipper. Joseph seemed to think that the Supply Agency should have had the right to force the merchant to sell the turnips at a more reasonable price, instead of letting them rot. Vegetables were very scarce that season! Now the turnips were a foul-smelling mash, and the salt, a bad preservative, had caused the wooden casks to rot.

Leaving the county highway, Joseph took the road to Barbarie. Delphine Legras had promised to give a dozen eggs to Mrs. Hermelin, who had asked her son to pick them up on his way back from Francheville.

Approaching Mottes, Joseph smelled the strong odour of burning grains. The kitchen door was wide open and, in spite of the darkness, he saw Noémi shaking a smoking pot. It was evident that she was changing rye into coffee. This modern process of alchemy was strictly prohibited by the Supply Agency, and Joseph even remembered the specific number of the decree. However, nobody ever tried to enforce this regulation in the countryside. Had not Mrs. Hermelin, herself, served coffee prepared from burnt barley for breakfast this very morning?

With a shrug of his shoulders, Joseph went around the house. Behind the house, Elie Sobrevin was on the threshing floor with a flail in his hand. The peasant greeted him calmly and continued flailing the wheat. All of Barbarie's wheat was supposed to have been flailed mechanically the preceding week. Elie Sobrevin was certainly not the only one to hide several sacks and beat the wheat clandestinely. This, too, was prohibited. But Joseph was on vacation in Saint-Boniface, not on duty.

Engrossed in his reflections on the selfishness and lack of discipline amongst the peasants, Joseph followed a path through the pine forest and came to the first house in Barbarie. From a distance, he had heard the typical sound of a butter churn. Delphine Legras was making butter even though an individual was prohibited from owning a churn if the farm supplied milk to the Supply Agency.

Joseph knocked energetically on the door. The noise inside stopped, then Delphine's disheveled head appeared in the half-open doorway. Seeing Joseph, her eyes opened wide in fright. She came out of the house, closing the door carefully behind her. When she heard what had brought Mrs. Hermelin's son to her house, she calmed down a bit, went into the stable, and returned with a small basket padded with hay. A minute later the eggs, protected by the hay, were in Joseph's sack. "Your mother will pay me another day," she said when Joseph offered to pay her. Thus, he was unable to ascertain by how much the price control regulation on eggs was being violated. As law-abiding as his mother was, she surely overpaid.

Continuing on his way, Joseph passed old Crouzet's garden. In a large plot he noticed some green plants with characteristic leaves – tobacco plants, at least sixty square feet of them. The tobacco had been planted despite a regulation strictly prohibiting it. Almost all the peasants in Saint-Boniface were doing the same thing.

"Ti! Chicks, ti! Ti! Ti!" Félicie Latière, holding an old pot in her hand, called her chickens. She must be tossing wheat to them. Have all the inhabitants conspired to give him a demonstration of the disdain in which they held the regime's decrees?

Passing in front of Laffont's house, he saw the butcher from Francheville leaving. He regularly supplied Tilleuls. The man mounted his bicycle and quickly pedaled to the city. No doubt the butcher had come to the farmer to arrange for a clandestine slaughtering.

Clandestine slaughtering, there was the enemy. In a meadow behind Seignos's stable three piglets romped in the grass. Unless he delivered them to the Supply Agency, Serre's owner did not have the right to raise more than one per year. In the whole town, in the entire county, no one delivered pigs to the Supply Agency. No one raised pigs anymore. In the market place, one could only see piglets which were exempt from price control and were being sold on the hoof at a price per kilo five times higher than that of a slaughtered pig. Under these conditions, one had to be insane to deliver pigs fattened on tons of potatoes, cabbages, and bran.

Yes, it was a vicious circle. The more one taxed commodities, the more they disappeared from circulation. But, the National Revolution's economic machine could only function with the active support of citizens who were willing to make sacrifices. In principle, this was not impossible. There could be no revolution without the citizens committing some acts that seem contrary to their immediate interests. They would throw themselves in front of machine guns, or in a fit of rage they'd give up their privileges like those brainless ones on the night of the 4th of August[40]. But Joseph did not know a single person who would give up one privilege under the National Revolution.

He adjusted his Tyrolean pack and continued on his way; now the road took him past Chirolles's farm. An enticing aroma of warm dough wafted from the oven and tickled his nostrils. Old Chirolles was baking bread. At this particular time, all bread-making by a family was temporarily prohibited in the entire county. "White bread on the farm is black misery in the city!" clamoured the radio and newspapers. Evidently, the peasants did not care, just as with the other rules.

Taking a shortcut, Joseph passed in front of Vautier's house. On a heap of garbage of all sorts was a discarded streamer, faded by the rain but still legible: "Saint-Boniface 1937…Work, Family, Country!", the slogan of the local chapter of the Cross of Fire which had become the motto of the National Revolution. At that time, Vautier had been

---

40 4th August, 1790, when the Constitutional Assembly abolished feudal privileges. (HRG)

a sworn enemy of the Front Populaire and a convinced member of the Cross of Fire. Now he was a rather indifferent legionnaire.

Joseph sighed. All in all, the National Revolution looked much better under the republic!

III

Frank Rosenfeld tries to assure himself maximum salvation with a minimum of prayer

Whilst Mrs. Hermelin had prepared a wedding surprise for Mr. Rosenfeld by inviting her son Jeremy the minister, her tenant had prepared one for her by inviting Father Paroli to spend a few days in Saint-Boniface. They had met in town, and Rosenfeld had considered him a valuable acquaintance.

When Father Paroli had come to where the county road crossed the chestnut-tree-lined road to Tilleuls, he had got out of his car because the way was too narrow for automobiles. The first person he had met was the minister Jeremy Hermelin, who had arrived in Francheville on the midday train. The result of this fortuitous coincidence had caused Mrs. Hermelin to experience one of the greatest emotional upsets of her entire life. The one thousand five hundred metres that they had walked together permitted the clergymen to strike up as good a relationship as was possible between the rival churches.

Minister Hermelin and Father Paroli were unaware that, besides the general rivalry between the two churches, there would be another, more personal conflict that would divide them during their short stay in Saint-Boniface. The object of this conflict was the salvation of the soul of the still hesitant Frank Rosenfeld. In each of her letters to her son, Mrs. Hermelin had assured him that, thanks to the influence she had exerted over her tenant, his conversion was virtually a fact except for the final blessing which, in her mind, would take place during the ceremony. Since Miss Sten was already a Protestant, the couple could be united after the ceremony in the town hall, according to the rites of the Reformed Church. On the other hand, Father Paroli had reasons to assume that he could count Mr. Rosenfeld amongst his flock; he even hoped to bring Rosenfeld's fiancée into his fold. As for his scheme, this simultaneous attack on two fronts was rather risky.

Mr. Rosenfeld was still not entirely sure which ceremony would save his soul. For some time, he was inclined to think that he would find the haven and security he sought in the bosom of the apostolic

Roman Church. The protection of Catholics in France seemed to promise greater guarantees than the Protestants. To all appearances, the Protestants seemed a weak minority in the margins of the regime, while the Catholics were everywhere, from the lower echelons of the administration to the cabinet of the chief of state. Mr. Rosenfeld was terrified of the Red International; he felt disdain for the Pink International, which sought refuge in London; he was quite knowledgeable about the fame of the Yellow International, the Jews; he found that he had a definite fascination, even to the point of exaggeration, for the Black International, the priests.

He was annoyed by the dilemma he faced. Nevertheless, he was flattered, and his self-esteem soared. In these times when Jews without means were in a worse situation than the Untouchables in India, two Aryan notables as eminent as the minister and the priest were seeking his allegiance. In all sincerity, he would have liked to opt for both religions at the same time and to be agreeable to everyone.

He even had a third alternative. His neighbour, Chazelas, was a fervent member of the Salvation Army and had already dragged him to two Sunday meetings. Captain Chaudeval, who presided, received the newcomer eagerly. At one time even the Salvation Army had attracted Frank Rosenfeld, who wanted to assure himself maximum salvation with a minimum of prayers. General Booth's Army represented a force in the Anglo-Saxon world. Unfortunately, they had very little influence in France. Three religions wooed for the favour of Mr. Rosenfeld who, atop the peaceful hill known as Tilleuls, felt like Paris on Mount Ida, invited by three goddesses to choose the prettiest among them.

Words vanish; scriptures endure. To enlighten the soul of her protégé, Mrs. Hermelin had offered him her whole library which contained a sizable number of holy books. One day, Mr. Rosenfeld had found a magnificent Bible on his night table and had shrugged his shoulders, thinking that it was from his fiancée, Miss Sten. In reality, this surprise had been the work of the person who wished to be his godmother. One day while her tenants were out, Mrs. Hermelin had entered their home through an open window. It was not the first time that she had done it. However, this day she had not been content to inspect his cupboard and pantry – where did Mr. Rosenfeld get all those goats' cheeses? Instead she had delicately deposited a set of the Holy Scriptures on the night table.

Father Paroli had also used his form of religious persuasion. He had sent Mr. Rosenfeld several appropriate papers, among them a small book entitled, *Beautiful Conversions*. The former architect had read this one with interest. The conversion of Henry IV, in particular, had made him think, and had convinced him that it is always best to temporize.

The result was that even on his wedding day Frank Rosenfeld had not made a final decision.

The ceremony took place in the mayor's office in Saint-Boniface the day after the two clergymen arrived. In accordance with the wishes of the bride, it was performed in the strictest privacy. In addition to the mayor, Mr. Longeaud and the two young people, there were the witnesses: Mrs. Hermelin for the bride and Ferdinand Gideaux, a wealthy peasant from Saint-Boniface and president of the local chapter of the Legion, for the groom. Even whilst maintaining the strictest privacy, the former architect liked to be surrounded by influential people.

There was no religious ceremony – neither Catholic, nor Protestant, nor Salvation Army...not even a Jewish one. On the eve of the wedding, Bloch had suggested a Jewish ceremony. He advised it so strongly that he even offered to recruit a *minyan*, a group of ten Jewish male witnesses, for Rosenfeld and to improvise a *chupah*, a wedding canopy, with Mrs. Hermelin's old blanket – the two things needed to fulfill the requirements for a ceremony according to the Laws of Moses. Bloch was so set on this idea that he even proposed to act as a rabbi. He was distressed when Rosenfeld indignantly rejected his suggestion.

*****

This solemn day for which Mrs. Hermelin had prepared herself for the past several weeks brought her only annoyances and deceptions. The first one was the arrival of Father Paroli. Mrs. Hermelin had never received a man in a cassock in her house. Moreover, her son Jeremy, the minister, had insisted that the priest not be lodged in a room in the annex where Mr. Rosenfeld lived, but in one of the most comfortable rooms in the boardinghouse, thus forcing Mrs. Hermelin to tolerate the presence of the man in black under her own roof. What was even worse, she could not avoid having him at her table and having him taste the magnificent wedding cake for which she had not skimped on eggs or sugar because, in her mind, she was also celebrating the happy conversion. According to Mrs. Hermelin, all these annoying deceptions were the work of the cursed priest who came specially to accomplish the diabolical work of bewitching the soul.

If she had been told that Father Paroli was the devil himself, she could not have been more surprised. What was more, Mr. Rosenfeld had told her that Father Paroli was the head, not of a parish like Father Mignart, but of certain institutions of the greatest importance. What kinds of institutions could he be directing? The works of Satan, certainly. There was even something diabolical in the insidious way in which he advocated camping and athletics; he even praised dancing highly.

"Apart from sports," said the priest whose modern attitudes horrified Mrs. Hermelin, "there's a certain exercise that should be encouraged among the young. I have in mind dancing."

"Really?" asked Mrs. Hermelin, indignantly.

"Is there a more appropriate way to satisfy the senses and, at the same time, use all the energy that could be expended in a worse way?" continued the priest. "Oh, I don't mean the plastic poses of an Isadora Duncan, or even the Shimmy or the Lambeth Walk, or any similar horrors that originated in the basest sensuality."

"You don't need to say it, Father," said Mrs. Hermelin, venomously.

"I allude," replied the priest, "to those popular, primitive dances one performs without having contact with the other sex – a very important point – the Haute-Auvergne jig for example and also the jitterbug. The new regime has revived so many beautiful traditions. What a comforting spectacle it would be if, in the main square of our villages, we could see the adolescents and the elderly, children together with their parents, enjoying esthetic, healthy amusements on a Sunday!"

The priest's arguments were quite clever, but it would take much more to convince Mrs. Hermelin. In spite of all the precautions he took and all the subtleties he employed, the sinner did not stop apologizing for that work of the devil, dancing. Mrs. Hermelin had understood it at once. She had proof of it when, exhausted from all the emotional upheavals, she withdrew after dinner to the now deserted dining room where she liked to stretch out on the sofa for a nap. She had an incoherent, bizarre dream. She was in the White Cross Pharmacy asking Mr. Chameix for a bottle of Jouvence de l'abbé Soury. While she examined the bottle, she looked at the portrait on the label. The portrait came alive, winked an eye at her, and suddenly seemed to resemble Father Paroli. With a penetrating look from his grey eyes into hers, he carried her off in a wild dance that must have been the jitterbug or the Charleston because, in executing the complicated steps, the two sexes had occasion to touch one another.

Suddenly, there was a terrible noise of broken glass. Fluttering in the arms of her befrocked cavalier, she had just destroyed all the bottles of Jouvance displayed on the shelves. Startled awake, she saw Mr. Hermelin looking sadly at the pieces of a broken faux crystal dessert bowl that he had just placed on the buffet after he had finished washing the dishes. As soon as she recovered from her fright, and after severely reprimanding her husband, Mrs. Hermelin remembered her dream and shook with horror. That she had abandoned herself, and not without pleasure, to her dancing partner's embrace instead of experiencing revulsion for him, proved to her the devilish nature of the priest's propaganda.

IV

Moses Kleinhandler remembers a prayer and a psalm

Shut in his hotel room behind double-locked doors, Moses Kleinhandler sat *shiva*, but he was not sitting shoeless on a low bench as his religion prescribed while he mourned for his father and mother, his two sons and a daughter. Emotionally overwrought at their loss, he imposed a penance on himself.

On the table among the remnants of his unfinished meal and greasy papers accumulated over several days, and next to a chess board with overturned chessmen, lay the card sent from Poland to Paris and then forwarded to him: "Your parents and children have died in a hospital from a contagious disease. Condolences. Benjamin"

The sender's name and address were obviously fictitious. No doubt it was either a friend or relative who knew Kleinhandler's address in Paris.

Tired of pacing the long narrow room that looked more like a corridor and where he tripped at every step over a big box and rolls of paper that were part of Pinkas's trafficking business, Kleinhandler, in complete despair, threw himself on the unmade bed. The sheets had not been changed for several weeks and smelled of sweat; the quilt was torn here and there, exposing the wool filling which adhered to a dirty sock lost in the bedding. Suddenly feeling very bitter, Kleinhandler seized the sock and threw it on the cover of the chamber pot. He stretched out on his back and stared vacantly at the ceiling where some spider webs, undisturbed by a broom, were being spun.

*****

In 1931, when the Colonial Exposition was in progress, Kleinhandler had taken advantage of the occasion to get a visa to go to France. A tourist in spite of himself, instead of visiting the Temple of Angkor, he had visited the Tiled Temple and the little synagogues in that quarter of the city, not to pray to God, but to make some useful acquaintances. In a few days, the textile worker from Lodz, unemployed for several long months, had managed to be hired by a knitting factory near Rosiers

Street. His boss, another Polish Jew, had come to Paris in 1925 on a tourist visa when the Decorative Exhibition was in progress.

If the employer had not been too strict as far as a work permit was concerned, the police were. It had taken them fourteen months to discover that Kleinhandler had been working without an official permit. This fact established, the boss had been compelled to pay a fine, and Kleinhandler had been invited to leave France without delay.

However, the undesirable had not wasted his fourteen months in Paris. He had managed to save a few thousand francs, and, even if he had not learned the language too well, he had acquired practical experience. He knew that the multi-coloured document with which the police department bombarded people in his predicament was not definite and irrevocable, except for the poor people who were caught before they could earn some money. Thanks to the one thousand francs he had given a *macher*, an intermediary, who had contacts in the police department, he had managed to get a postponement which he had used to his advantage by having himself hired by his former boss's competitor, and, all the while shaking at the thought of being caught a second time, he had brought his wife and two-year-old son Maurice from Poland. One year later, thanks to a more substantial payment, the *macher* had provided him with a regular work permit.

Then came the years of plenty. He evoked those times of splendour as he lay on the moist sheets and torn quilt. The man that he had been then seemed a stranger to him now. What had he not been capable of doing in those days to earn a living, a piece of bread! He had worked very hard, struggling relentlessly, fighting and clawing with bare nails. He had left his boss, opened his own small shop, bought some machines on credit, and hired two Polish Jewish workers, the second of whom had come for Expo '37. He had gained clients and enlarged his family by two new Kleinhandlers. As he strove to prosper, the musty smell of misery had continued to hover over this magnificence. The children, with bare bottoms, had screeched in a room adjoining the shop because their mother repaired the knitting defects from the machine all day long, and could not find the time to care for them. The living quarters were full of dust from the wool and bits of thread that had come from the shop. It had not been important when they ate, nor how they ate. Mealtimes depended on the schedule for orders and deliveries. They had led a feverish and yet numbing existence. Ah, those had been the good old days! The endless chess parties on Sundays in the dark rear of a café in a sector near the Temple would cause Kleinhandler to forget about dinner and earned him the tears and reproaches of his wife. All that was happiness, of which the weekly family events had formed an integral part.

Then one day everything collapsed. Sarah Kleinhandler, who had to strain her eyes to repair the stitches and was seeing less and less, had been crushed by a truck one morning while shopping. She had died in the hospital two hours later. What could one do with three children, two of whom were very young? The simplest solution would be to send them to Poland to their grandparents. Helped by a neighbour, Kleinhandler had filled two battered valises with clothes and some toys from Uniprix, a well-known department store in Paris. He had tied everything with twine reinforced with straps and safety pins, and had taken the baggage and children to the Gare du Nord.

The day he had sent his children to Poland, he had sentenced them to death. He had already had a premonition during the first year of the war. Now his crime was complete. The children had died in a hospital from a contagious disease... Contagious or hereditary?...

Moses Kleinhandler was shaken. He paced up and down in the room in which the sun never shone. Even with the window wide open, it was stifling and smelled stuffy. This odour permeated everything.

Seized by nausea, he put on his shoes and tattered jacket, and left. If one sat *shiva*, what was the difference if he paced the room or dragged himself through the streets of Francheville? Kleinhandler had ceased to practise his religion for the past twenty-five years. Yet now, he mechanically murmured the words of the *Kaddish*, the prayer the oldest son must say for the peace of his father's soul, which came to him from the depths of his memory. It was stupid, but it was stronger than he. *Yisgadal ve'yiskadash sh'mey rabo...* He felt ridiculous with tears rolling down his cheeks. Through misty eyes, he saw the urchins laughing and pointing their fingers at him. Let them laugh, those *shkootzim*[41] and all the *goyim*[42] with them! Let them try to be Jews for a while, and they would see how easy it is!

Yisgadal veyiskadash sh'mey rabo... The words came to his lips by themselves. It was curious that he had not forgotten this prayer. When he, Moses Kleinhandler, would be no more, there would be no one to say *Kaddish* for him. His two sons had died in a hospital, victims of an epidemic.

He walked by the Modern Pharmacy. It was as full as ever. The narrow mirror framing the shop window reflected his image. What could have made the urchins laugh at him a while ago? His big hairy ears? The three-day-old beard on his cheeks? His rumpled trousers bulging at the fly? His grease-stained jacket was ragged at the cuffs and torn under the arm allowing the lining to show. His shoulders

---

41 Shkootzim: non-Jewish boys. (Author)
42 Goyim, plural of goy: gentiles. (Author)

were covered with dandruff and his lapel, with ashes. So what? Ashes and torn clothes, were they not a sign of mourning?

On the plantain-tree-lined Railway Avenue, Kleinhandler sat down on a bench with his back to the Hotel Farémido. Suddenly feeling tired and defeated, he had no strength to struggle, not even to walk. Anyway, how could he fight? With what? His choice was very limited. In Marseilles, where he had to renew his registration as a foreigner, the authorities had taken away the card that identified him as a skilled knitter and given him a new one for the unemployed with the notation: "no profession". With that he had no chance of finding a job. His only recourse was the black market. It could be said that the laws were made expressly to drive Kleinhandler to become a black marketeer. But that was not his profession. With every two tries, he missed three. A true *schlimmazel*, that was what he had become. One needed to be shrewd to deal on the black market, and have stamina and nerve like Pinkas. So he preferred to run errands and receive a tip. From time to time, Pinkas slipped him ten or twenty francs for looking for suppositories in the pharmacies, or for butter from the usual suppliers in the countryside. This little salary and the meager, irregular help he received from the Jewish Welfare Agency were his principal sources of income. What good would it do to struggle? It was not worthwhile, except in chess. Chess, what a marvellous thing! Seated in front of a chessboard, Kleinhandler became a different man. Reality faded and vanished; he was formidable, magnificent. He sensed the spectators' mounting admiration for him. He captured queens, knocked down castles, removed bishops, and won battles. In chess, he sometimes had fits of audacity, insolence, and contempt that amazed even him, all the while ridiculing and insulting his opponents. Yet those were the same people before whom he bowed in real life. For him, chess was poetry, a dream, escape.

It was three years since he had given up his children. Maurice had been a big boy when he returned to Poland. He had not been very good-looking; his big ears stuck out like his father's, his nose had been a bit crooked, and he had many freckles and red hair, somewhat like his mother's, the poor woman. He had not been dumb. Not at all! At the age of seven he could play a game of chess to the very end. And how funny he had been! A *yiddishe keppele*! A good little Jewish brain! For many months, Kleinhandler had felt his heart constrict when he thought that the Germans could take his little Maurice and make him an SS man – a rumour to explain why they picked up Jewish children – or perhaps turn him into Maurice Scharf who would accuse his own father of ritual crimes. Maybe it was better he had died in the hospital after all. As for the other two, Kleinhandler had hardly known them.

What did it mean "hospital"? Had they really died from a contagious disease? Typhoid? Dysentery? Typhus? Those words could also indicate the ghetto or a concentration camp. Pinkas said that, according to London, the Germans exterminated the Jews, big and small. That must be propaganda! One did not kill children like that, even if they were Jewish. Maurice, Aron, and Rachel had probably died in an accident with their grandparents – a bomb, no doubt. One thing was certain, little Maurice would never be a chess champion.

Behind Kleinhandler, a conversation was in progress in the Hotel Farémido's garden. Three people were sipping tea around a rattan table. All Kleinhandler had to do was to turn around and look through the sparse hedge. He knew two of the guests, Mr. and Mrs. Wolff, Jews from Alsace. As for the man in the grey suit who was with them, he had never seen him before. The Wolffs were held in high esteem in Francheville. They had money, jewels, and fine clothes. Before the war, they had also been in the knitting business. Kleinhandler had knitted only fine, made-to-order clothes, while they had mass-produced, which was more profitable.

"But, madam," said the man in the grey suit, "no one would intentionally think of confusing you, French citizens for generations, with those foreign, unassimilated elements."

"Alas," answered Mr. Wolff, in an aggrieved tone, "we suffer because of their presence. It is we who must pay for their lack of scruples, their bad manners, and their greedy business deals."

"In any case, I was officially assured that only they are affected by the new measures being prepared by the police."

The next moment, a big truck made much noise as it left the garage next to the hotel. The conversation behind the hedge continued, but Kleinhandler could not hear it.

New measures in preparation? What could that mean? In the last several months, and even in the last few weeks, new regulations had been issued. "Prohibited to reside in large cities... Prohibited to move to another county other than the one that accepted you... Prohibited to work in a trade other than the one specified on the identity card..." If one heeded all of those prohibitions, there would be no end to it. If Kleinhandler had obeyed all the regulations in the past, he would never have been able to stay in France.

Evidently, none of this applied to Mr. Wolff, even if he was of the same faith. Yes, the same faith, but not a brother. He, a brother, this big, fat well-cared-for gentleman with the signet ring on his finger and his French manners? Mr. Wolff was not a Jew; he was an Israelite. Yes, Kleinhandler was certainly no brother of Mr. Wolff's, maybe a distant cousin or poor relative if they should meet in a synagogue saying the same prayer. A ridiculous thought! When he was in Paris, Mr. Wolff must surely have gone to the big synagogue on Victoire Street, while he, Kleinhandler, would have gone to some ill-smelling *shul* on Rosiers Street. But years had passed since Kleinhandler had set foot in a temple.

The truck disappeared on the road to Saint-Paul. The voices were audible again.

"The police will round them up tomorrow morning and send them back to their native countries. But, I repeat, you've no reason to worry. You're at home in France."

This was said in an indifferent tone, like one would use in ordinary conversation. Even the meaning of those words was trivial and banal.

On the bench, the little hairy man had not budged, and under his furrowed brow, thoughts and words whirled, colliding like the pieces in a devilish chess game: Police...roundup...the big sweep...the Last Judgement...

The epidemic was spreading to Francheville.

The three voices continued to reverberate in his ears, changing in tone, intensity, and pitch. To Kleinhandler, it was no longer a meaningless noise that he hardly noticed, like background music in a movie.

"Each to his own country!" What a joke! Nobody would believe it, not even the stranger in the grey suit. Once caught in the gears, one was finished. One was thrown in with a group of Jews where one may not die at once, but one always caught a contagious disease. A new Egypt where one built pyramids under a whip, only these pyramids were in the salt mines or fetid swamps. There was no Moses this time. As if surging from a timeless abyss, the words of the prophet sprang into Kleinhandler's mind:

"Run, children of Benjamin, from the midst of Jerusalem,
For one sees misfortune coming from the north
And what a disaster it is!"

The psalmist's voice broke. Kleinhandler did not remember the rest. He had never been a brilliant Bible scholar. He made an effort to remember, but he was unable to recall the scattered fragments from his memory. He was only aware of the cry of alarm that was the refrain of his distant youth in Poland: *Oy vey, Yiden, oy vey!*

What was he still doing on the bench? Quick, quick! The pogrom is tomorrow! Well, the pogrom would not take place. He, Kleinhandler, was chosen by fate to cancel it.

*****

At two o'clock in the morning, when he returned to his hotel room that smelled from smoke and the overpowering stench of bedbugs, his flat feet ached, his shirt was soaked with sweat, his empty stomach was growling, and he had a nasty taste of gall in his mouth. Still he was happy! A profound peace pervaded his being. He had warned all the Jews in the area about the looming danger and had beseeched them to flee. He had seen Pinkas, Verés, Bloch and three other families, one of whom lived in Manvin, twelve kilometres away in the mountains. He had arrived panting, announced the news, asked if there were other Jews in the region and, without even sitting down, had left to take up his mission as the herald of doom. He had not noticed that, very often, he was not taken seriously. The Ehrlichs in Manvin almost threw him out of the house.

"There are people who amuse themselves by creating panic," said the wife as soon as he had turned his back.

But Kleinhandler was not aware of this attitude. He was doing his duty, and nothing could turn him back, nothing except the police. All along the way, he trembled at the thought that Auzance, or one of his colleagues, might spring out at some corner and ask him where he was running.

Now the disorder in the room shocked him. He must straighten up this mess. Pick up the strewn papers. Empty the basin where he had washed the day before. Make the bed and prepare his little pack. They would certainly not wait for him. It would be good to remove the spider webs. When one went away, his place must be neat. How simple it was! Why prolong this hopeless life? The others were safe. He was just good to be the *kapore*, the offering to redeem the Jews of Saint-Boniface.

When, about seven o'clock in the morning, the police sergeant, followed by a young trainee, knocked on the door of the Hotel Michel and went up to room seven to pick up the Jew, he found Kleinhandler somewhat pale, his eyes swollen from lack of sleep, but perfectly calm. His pack containing some laundry and a chess game was on a chair.

For the first time in his life, Kleinhandler was not afraid.

*****

That same morning, the morning after Mr. Rosenfeld's wedding, two uniformed cyclists arrived at Tilleuls. The former architect was awakened by an energetic knocking on his door and a loud shout, "Open in the name of the law!". When he ran to the door in his nightshirt, he found himself face to face with Auzance in the company of a young colleague. So sure of immunity was he – since he could count Auzance among his friends – that he had laughed when Bloch brought him the announcement the night before. Bloch, who was sent to him by Kleinhandler, had advised him to disappear for several days until the storm was over. That was what Bloch himself intended to do. Nelchet had put an old shack in the middle of the forest at his disposal.

"It might be right for you to hide," Rosenfeld had answered, "but as far as I'm concerned, I've nothing to fear."

This time friend Auzance was on strictly official business. He had orders to take the Jew Rosenfeld, Frank, to Francheville. From there, a truck would take him and some other Jews to the Venissieux concentration camp. This was neither the time nor the occasion for Mr. Rosenfeld to show his hospitality or display his gifts as a diplomat.

Four other Jews from the county were in the same cart, the ones who had not taken Kleinhandler's alarm seriously. Neither Verès nor Bloch were in the category of Jews to be deported; both had children born in France. Pinkas should have come, but at the police station, they had forgotten to put his name on the list, while the unfortunate Muller, the hospital boat of the Café de la Marine, though not Jewish and could even prove it, was shipped out in spite of his vehement objections.

V

Bloch refuses to supply Marseilles with soap of Marseilles[43]

Three days after he had left Nelchet's shack where he had hidden during the roundup, Bernard Bloch returned from hoeing potatoes to find two letters at his house. They had been addressed to his former home in Cassis and were forwarded to him from there. The letterhead of one was Bouches-du-Rhône Police Department and the other, Social Services of the Quakers of Marseilles.

Heeding his premonition, Bloch opened the letter from the police department. It was a form letter with his name filled in, inviting him, with administrative severity, to come "without delay" to pick up an exit visa from France.

Bloch burst out laughing. He had asked for the visa six months ago when he had still hoped to go to Haiti. Now that the Vichy offices

---

43 Marseilles is known for its excellent soap. (JG)

had finally decided to grant it, he could no longer do anything with it.

The letter from the Quakers advised him that two valises with personal effects, sent by some friends in Paris through the good services of the Quakers in the capital, had arrived in Marseilles. He was asked to come to verify the contents and to pick them up.

"Darn it!" shouted Bloch. "I'll have to pick them up and those asses in the police station are liable to refuse to issue me a safe-conduct pass under the pretext that I'm here on forced residence."

"Look here," said Renée, "you're asked to go without delay to the police station in Marseilles. What more do you need? The police don't know we can't leave for Haiti."

Around ten o'clock in the morning, Bloch went to Francheville ready to take the train to Marseilles in case he received the safe-conduct pass on the spot. Not too far from the fountain halfway between Francheville and Saint-Boniface, he noticed a woman sitting on the embankment alongside the road. Although she did not face the road, he recognized her cape and knew it was Amélie Martin, the teacher from the parochial school. He had seen her several times in the village, and she had always seemed peculiar to him, and more so lately.

The old girl must have heard his steps for she suddenly turned around and stood up. In greeting her, Bloch was struck by the expression on her face. She looked absent-minded, with the sunken eyes of a sick person. Bloch could not say why, but he had always pitied this lonely woman. Absurdly, she had always reminded him of Kleinhandler.

At the police station, he explained his request to the police officer, who looked at Bloch scoffingly and wanted to send him away under the pretext that foreigners who wanted to go to the Bouches-du-Rhône Police Department had to obtain permission from that police department. However, confronted with the document requesting Bloch to appear at that very office, and in addition "without delay", he scratched his head. After consulting with his sergeant in the next office, he re-entered the room, searched among the papers in the filing cabinet, pulled out a pink paper and announced in the tone of a good fairy who is satisfying the whim of a child, "You're getting the 8ter. It's a special safe-conduct pass. Return for it in three hours."

After the roundup, only a few people were in the Café de la Marine. There was no news of Rosenfeld, Muller, or Kleinhandler. Near the window, Daniel Cahen was reading a newspaper, a mug of beer in front of him. His wife was probably not in a good mood that day. Sad and lonesome like a widower, a book of poetry open in front of him, Safranek glanced idly about the room. If only he could play another game of chess with the little Jew! His opponent would certainly call him "cheat" or "bedbug" and he would have loved it!

Being in this cemetery of the ravaged fleet made Bloch melancholy. After exchanging a few words with Safranek, he left to pick up a few Swiss newspapers in preparation for his trip, and then headed for the Hotel Panorama.

It was eleven-thirty. In the dining room of the hotel, several people were waiting for the meal to be served. At a few tables, the napkins were open a bit, indicating that the places were reserved for guests. Bloch was careful to choose a table that seemed free, judging from the immaculate napkin and a vase of flowers. He sat down, opened the *Journal de Genève*, put the other paper on the windowsill, and began reading René Payot's article.

Suddenly, a short-legged man with an enormous mop of red hair, a face full of freckles, and a napkin over his arm appeared before him. It was the owner of the establishment.

"Excuse me, sir," said Sarzier, politely but firmly, "this table is reserved."

Bloch was ready to stand up when a man appeared behind the restaurateur. He was tall, good-looking and very elegant, and seemed to be about forty years old. His face was freshly shaven and lightly powdered. His whole appearance and manner indicated that he was a man of distinction.

"Please, Mr. Sarzier," he said, "don't disturb the gentleman. This table is big enough for two."

He spoke French with a slight foreign accent.

"As you wish," said Sarzier, obsequiously. "I was only concerned for your comfort."

The hotel owner left after bowing several times.

"I'm going to have lunch in the company of some prince," thought Bloch, intrigued.

After the hotel owner had served an aperitif to his distinguished client, the guest turned to Bloch, indicated the paper on the windowsill, and asked, "Would you permit me to glance at your newspaper?"

"With pleasure," said Bloch, handing the paper to his neighbour.

He leafed through the paper, glanced absentmindedly at the headlines, and became absorbed with the financial news on the last page. From behind his newspaper, Bloch did not miss a single gesture of his. "This man must certainly be a financier," he said to himself. "He's studying the Zurich Stock Market."

After having looked rapidly at certain figures, the financier returned the paper to Bloch with a friendly smile and began drinking his port. Sarzier reappeared with a wine list, and the man asked him for a train schedule.

"At your service, Mr. Beer," said Sarzier, pirouetting.

Mr. Beer's request was granted very quickly. He immediately began studying the complicated timetable like an expert. "This financier is also a great traveller," noted Bloch.

Mr. Beer seemed only interested in the main lines, examining the connections with the Spanish border with particular interest. He opened to the page on international lines to verify some information.

"How lucky for him!" said Bloch, to himself. "No doubt he's preparing to go to Spain, and from there to leave Europe."

The stranger was about to return the timetable to Sarzier when Bloch stopped him with a gesture. "If you'll permit me," he said, indicating the timetable, "I'm leaving for Marseilles in a little while..."

"You're leaving for Marseilles?" his neighbour asked with surprise as he handed him the schedule.

That was how the conversation that would change the course of Bloch's existence began. After a few minutes, the stranger knew about the former junk car dealer's return to the soil – for which he congratulated him – and why he was going to Marseilles. For his part, Bloch had the satisfaction of seeing that his idea about his table companion was right. Mr. Beer of Czech origin, was a banker and was preparing to leave Europe to go to some South American republic. He was resting in Francheville, waiting for his ship to leave.

Since I'm ready and have my visas in my pocket, I wanted to go directly to the Spanish border from Francheville, instead of going through Marseilles, a city I detest. Unfortunately, HICEM, to whom I had entrusted my travel arrangements, informs me that my tickets cannot be delivered to me or my representative except in their offices. I just telephoned them to send the tickets to me by mail, but it seems that's not possible either. What bureaucracy!"

Bloch timidly suggested that he could do the errand for him, if he trusted him.

"Of course!" said the banker, smiling. "I see who I'm dealing with. As you've so kindly proposed to do it for me, I accept gladly. This afternoon the agency will be notified of your arrival."

At this moment, the waitress brought Bernard Bloch his first course, a meager salad of cucumbers and tomatoes, and for Mr. Beer, a big dish of various hors d'oeuvres.

The meal that Bloch partook that day was, in many ways, in contradiction to the austerity regulations of the minister of the Supply Agency and was, without doubt, the best one Bloch had had since the war. He could not hide his surprise from Mr. Beer, but that gentleman only pouted.

"Mediocre cuisine!" Mr. Beer announced with the air of a connoisseur. "The menu would be better if it were less copious and more carefully prepared. In the French provinces, the restaurants are either very good or decidedly mediocre."

Bloch was tempted to protest, but decided to say nothing. This man was an habitué of the Ritzes and Savoys which he, Bernard Bloch, had never been able to enter, and naturally found mediocre all that appeared absolutely extraordinary to him.

"Evidently," continued the banker, "I should have stayed at the Hotel Farémido whose cuisine is excellent, but the day I arrived, there was no room available. If I were to change now, I'd offend this nice man, Sarzier, whom I recognize is making a big effort to satisfy me. Anyway..." he said with a resigned gesture, and poured his guest a glass of burgundy.

During the meal he disclosed a few more confidences.

"I had a choice between North America and South America. Even with all its formalities, the United States presented some advantages for me since my family is associated with the Morganthaus. Our banking firm in Prague has represented their interests in Bohemia for several generations. But I opted for a completely new country."

Bloch's admiration for his host was growing. Mr. Beer was not just any financier, but a sort of patrician, the head of an old Jewish banking family like the Rothschilds. He was right to have taken him for an aristocrat. What was more, his ancestors had acquired their position among the nobility in the world of finance.

A young brunette with almond-shaped eyes, accompanied by a well-dressed man, came in and sat at the next table. Although he was very interested in what the banker had to say, Bloch could not help looking at her. Where had he met her? At Tilleuls, of course! He had walked by her once at the entrance to the boardinghouse, and later he saw her with Fleury! She seemed to enjoy the company of her gallant friend very much, laughing often in a provocative manner.

"But frankly speaking," continued the financier, while the coffee was being served, "I'd like to ask you another favour, but I don't want to abuse your kindness."

"Not at all," protested Bloch. "What is it?"

"You see," said Mr. Beer, offering his guest a cigar, "I've a certain amount of francs that I'd like to get rid of before I leave. Oh, not a huge sum, merely one million. My assets have already been transferred. For the trip, however, I'd prefer to have this amount in dollars. I thought of having an agent come here for this transaction, but I'd like to avoid explaining the thing to him in a letter because of the censorship. I don't deal with him regularly, and we don't have a correspondence code. If you have a free moment in Marseilles, maybe you could look him up and explain what I want. He knows me by my reputation, and I'm sure he'd be willing to come."

Bloch assured the financier that it would be a pleasure to do this little errand, and Mr. Beer pulled two cards from his wallet, one for the travel agent and the other for the business agent. Scribbling some words on them, he put them into small envelopes and gave them to his guest.

With an anxious expression, the restaurateur approached the table and asked the banker if he were satisfied with the meal.

"Thanks, very much so," said Mr. Beer, affably. "By the way, Mr. Sarzier, I just saw that Rio Tinto[44] lost another three points on the Zurich Stock Exchange. I think I predicted it the other day."

"Indeed you did," said Sarzier, admiringly. "That's what it means to really know!"

"Oh," said the banker, "it wasn't difficult to foresee with all those events. After all, it's a business like any other."

In his tone was a veiled hint that only a few are allowed to share the secrets of the gods. With that, the banker stood up and shook hands with Bloch, nodded benevolently to Mr. Sarzier who bowed several times, and then went to his suite.

Bloch left the restaurant with the feeling that the world seemed marvellously beautiful, and all the pressing problems easily solved. Was that not the euphoria after a good meal? Certainly not! Now he had contact with this elite man whom money did not corrupt but, on the contrary, caused to be refined. Since childhood, Bloch, the son of a taxi driver, had felt a sort of admiration mixed with envy for the children of the rich who had their own rooms with beautiful carpets, mechanical toys and governesses who taught them French. He still felt the same way. Those who had this kind of childhood could very easily become men like Mr. Beer: self-assured, mannerly, very distinguished. Bloch was enchanted by the turn of events that had given him the occasion to have this flattering relationship.

It was too soon to return to the police station. Automatically, Bloch directed his steps to the Café de la Marine. The establishment was almost empty at this hour. This time he found only Jeroboam Pinkas who had also left his hideout, reassured when the police did not come to look for him. With his nervous tic more noticeable than ever, he made columns of figures in his notebook. With a friendly sign, he invited Bloch to sit at his table.

---

44 Rio Tinto: a multi-national mining company. (HRG)

"Just a little while ago, Mr. Safranek told me that you're going to Marseilles. Would you like to earn your fare?"

Bloch sat down next to Pinkas and looked questioningly at him.

"You can take a small amount of excellent soap of Marseilles with you," said Pinkas, in a confidential tone. "Soap of such quality isn't made anymore. You can easily sell it at a fifty per cent profit."

From his pouch, he took a piece of soap that was still soft and fresh, and proudly showed it to Bloch.

"No thank you," Bloch replied smiling. "I've promised myself not to engage in commercial ventures. I want to remain a peasant, if only until the end of the war. Tell me instead, do you have any news from Kleinhandler or any of the others?"

"Well," said Pinkas, "it looks as though they'll be taken to Drancy. From there, who knows... But," he insisted, "as far as the soap is concerned, is it a definite no? You're missing a good business deal without any risk."

Bloch shook his head, stood up, said goodbye to the soap merchant, and left the café. After having spent an hour in the company of that aristocrat of finance, Mr. Beer, this little black market dealer appeared ridiculous and pitiable. However, Pinkas's proposition did not lack appeal. To supply Marseilles with soap of Marseilles! The world is upside down. Even business is reversed. There are probably some shrewd fellows who 'export' silk to Lyons, Bordeaux wine to Bordeaux, and who knows, perhaps cigars to Havana.

VI

The second appearance of the seven Isadores and a Marseilles fairy tale

When Renée Bloch entered Ripailles with her son and the goat, she found a big yellow envelope under the door. The address was written in an unfamiliar feminine hand. This envelope contained two regular sized sealed envelopes, each one bearing her name written by Bernard Bloch and, in the corner, the hastily scrawled notations: "Letter #1" and "Letter #2". "To be opened in that order!"

Intrigued, Renée put Letter #2 aside and opened the first one. The letter was written in Yiddish, the only language which Bernard wrote fluently. Translated, it read as follows:

"Marseilles, 18th of August, 1942

My dear wife,

I'm taking advantage of an opportunity to write this note to you without the risk of having it censored on the way. A refugee, a certain Mrs. Prokoff of Francheville whom I just met here, was kind enough to mail it for me upon her return to Francheville.

I'd like to tell you at once that this letter contains no good news. On the contrary! Cursed be the moment when I decided to leave for Marseilles. It would have been better if I had broken a leg on my way from Saint-Boniface to the station.

My thoughts are in such disorder that I don't know how to start. You know, when a brick suddenly falls on your head...

I've told you, in my preceding letter, how I had got acquainted with Mr. Beer, that rich banker who entrusted me to do some errands for him. I must mention it so that you will understand what I'm going to tell you.

After spending the night in Cassis in our old hotel on Avenue Victor Hugo, I took the bus at six in the morning and, as you might expect, arrived in Marseilles too early to see the Quakers. So, as in other times, I entered the Café Noailles to swallow something hot. It was there that my misfortune started.

Around eight-thirty I saw Jacob Schlesinger entering the café. Do you remember that leather goods dealer from Roquette Street whom I knew in Poland, and whom we met once in Marseilles near the stock exchange? He sat at my table and started to complain as usual.

'*Oy, oy,* listen to the misfortune that's befallen me!' he said. 'Imagine, my cousin in New York sent me a visa for my family and me.'

'Is that what you call misfortune? I wish such a misfortune would happen to me!' I exclaimed.

'You don't understand,' he said. 'I've all my visas in my pocket. I've reserved a ticket for the boat and I can't leave. All I own is a gold ingot that I can't expect to pass through three different customs inspections. I have to change it into dollars. Unfortunately, there was a big roundup of all currency traffickers in Marseilles last week, and they're in hiding. Now here I am with my gold! What a disaster, *oy, oy*! What a disaster!'

I already know what you're going to say, that I didn't have any business occupying myself with Schlesinger's affairs. Once again

201

I've become a *kochleffel*[45], and I assure you that I'm still biting my fingers.

'Well,' I said, 'I can put you in contact with a businessman who hands out dollars with a shovel!'

After that I took him, all excited, to the Hotel Splendid to meet a dealer, a certain Mr. Angelotti, whom I was supposed to have seen on Mr. Beer's behalf.

This Mr. Angelotti, a Corsican, was very friendly after I showed him Mr. Beer's card, and was ready to help Schlesinger. They didn't bargain for more than five minutes, and agreed to exchange at a price advantageous to Schlesinger. I was pleased for him and said to myself, 'Maybe he'll invite me to a Jewish restaurant on Belzunce Court where they're supposed to serve excellent gefilte fish.' This would have been a change from the horrible bouillabaisse with salted sardines that they served at the railway station in Marseilles. But wait, and you'll see!

Angelotti counted out the dollars to Schlesinger who handed over his gold.

After that, Schlesinger went to the window to examine the dollar bills while the other appraised the gold ingot and struck it like a tuning fork. I had the impression there was little confidence between them. Since I wanted the business to be concluded to the satisfaction of both parties, I proposed to have the merchandise be seen by an expert.

Angelotti accepted the suggestion at once. He just asked for time to set up an appointment, and he'd be at our disposal. He spoke on the telephone and exchanged a few words in Corsican, and we were on our way.

We followed the Canabière to submit the gold ingot to the expert who was in the Quatre-Chemins sector when, suddenly, in front of the Church of the Reformation, two individuals grabbed the Corsican and said, 'Police!' They showed their badges. Angelotti protested and put up a fight, but the policemen pushed him into a car and gave the driver this reassuring address: Security Police.

All this took only a few seconds. Schlesinger, who had hidden in a doorway, came out pale and shaking with fear.

'What an adventure!' he groaned. 'I just escaped in time. Poor Mr. Angelotti! I regret having taken him for two thousand francs. He didn't know that the dollar went up three points since last night.'

---

45 kochleffel: Yiddish word. Literal translation: gravy spoon; figurative: busybody. (Author)

He began to laugh between two groans. But fifteen minutes later, at the American Express office, he stopped laughing. The cashier told him that all his dollar bills were counterfeit, absolutely counterfeit. At that point, Schlesinger had enough to lament and, believe me, he outdid himself.

'I'm finished,' he repeated, pulling his hair. 'We're nothing more than beggars. What will I do in the States without a penny and three children on my hands? I'll never dare tell my wife the truth.'

I felt somewhat responsible for this misadventure. But Schlesinger was in such a state that he even forgot to reproach me. No matter how used I was to his complaining, I truly pitied him. We both ran after Angelotti without too much hope of finding him. A middleman, who had contacts with the police, assured us that no one by that name had been brought to the station that morning. I am convinced now that Angelotti was a crook who planned his arrest in order to escape with the gold. In our presence, he had arranged it all over the telephone. Like two imbeciles, we had allowed ourselves to be cheated. I thought that I was clever, but I certainly am not able to handle those gangsters in Marseilles. The most annoying thing was, it was impossible to lodge a complaint in such an illicit affair where there is a question of gold ingots and dollars. Anyway, this misfortune was good for something: Angelotti could not count Mr. Beer amongst his victims. I'm pleased!

In any case, do not expect me in Saint-Boniface tomorrow or the day after. I'll do everything possible to find this Corsican bandit. If I don't succeed, I ask myself: how will I ever manage to repay this poor Schlesinger? Believe me, it's a peculiar feeling having contributed to the ruin of a man to whom I wished no harm. And when I think of all the reproaches you'll heap on me when I return, I lose the little bit of courage I have left.

Your unfortunate Bernard"

The second letter read as follows:

"Marseilles, 19th of August, 1942

My dear wife,

I'm certainly a very lucky man. First, let me tell you I saw Mrs. Prokoff in the Café du Mont Ventoux. She had postponed her trip until this evening and could take this letter as well as the first, so you'll be reassured right away.

You might consider me crazy to speak of luck after what I told you in Letter #1. The fact is that we have had an extraordinary, unheard of bit of luck. It's so extraordinary that I still cannot believe it; I'm compelled to touch my pocket every few minutes and to even open my wallet to convince myself that I'm not dreaming. The sixty bills of five thousand francs are in there, and are not counterfeit, and are the only things that dispel my doubts. Since this morning, I'm the owner of three hundred thousand francs, and on top of that, I've a formal promise of a visa. If everything goes well, we'll be able to leave for South America shortly. What do you say to that? Now I must tell you everything in an orderly fashion.

After spending a sleepless night in Cassis, because of this unfortunate affair with counterfeit dollars, I got up this morning at five o'clock to take the bus to Marseilles. Yesterday, I had obtained an appointment over the telephone to settle the problem of Mr. Beer's boat ticket. At nine o'clock I went to the HICEM office on Paradise Street. No longer were there crowds waiting to emigrate like last year, but there were about forty people in the waiting room. After fifteen minutes, the receptionist called, 'Mr. Bloch!' Two of us stood up – there are Blochs everywhere, especially when everyone runs to the emigration office – so he said very precisely, 'Mr. Bloch from Cassis.' At that moment, a man jumped up from his chair and ran toward me. He was very excited and said that he must talk with me and would wait for me near the office door. I wondered what he wanted from me. I was sure I had never met him before.

Beer's affair was settled in two minutes. The tickets were ready, and since the employee was notified that I would be coming instead of the interested party, he gave me the tickets as soon as I showed him the card.

The excited man was waiting for me on the bench in the waiting room. He dragged me outside and, with a mysterious air, asked me if I really was Mr. Bloch from Cassis. More and more astonished, I asked him why he was interested in me.

'You'll see,' said the gentleman. 'But first, you must tell me your exact address in Cassis.'

'Twenty-seven *bis* Avenue Victor Hugo,' I replied.

'Now I understand what happened!' he exclaimed. 'I'll explain everything to you, but to be absolutely certain, I must ask you once again to prove your identity.'

Since I paid for the hotel room by the day, I showed him the hotel receipt the hotel owner had given me yesterday and, on top of that, I showed him the police notice. All that convinced him. Then, looking into my eyes, he asked, 'Don't you expect money from somewhere?'

It was then that it suddenly dawned on me. No doubt this man had money for me. And who else could be sending it to me but my Uncle Isadore? One of the seven letters I had sent to New York had finally reached him!

'I was expecting some from my uncle in New York,' I told him. 'But it's taken such a long time for this money to come that I'd given up hope.'

'Aren't you foolish!' said the other, shrugging his shoulders. 'Do you think it's easy to send money from New York to Marseilles today? You're lucky your uncle found a way to do it. I've three hundred thousand francs to give to you.'

I was baffled and had to ask him to repeat the sum to be sure I'd heard correctly. Then he explained the circumstances by which he became my banker. Before leaving for New York, he had had a relative send him a list of people who wanted to send money to France. He disbursed the money from his own pocket for a receipt and was reimbursed in dollars on his arrival there. This is a widely used system of clearing these days. All he had to do now was to give me the money Uncle Isadore had sent. He had been looking for me in Cassis and Marseilles for the past five days, but would never have found me except for this extraordinary coincidence. Also, the telegram was badly transmitted and full of errors. There was no first name and the address was inexact: 7 Victorugo Street, instead of 27 Avenue Victor Hugo, etc. Luckily, the sum was clearly specified.

You told me a hundred times we'd never have an answer from Uncle Isadore. Now I have one. Family is not a vain word. I only regret not knowing to which of the seven Isadore Blochs I should send my thanks.

The messenger made me sign for the three hundred thousand francs. The receipt, which had been drawn up beforehand, read: "Kisses for Cecile. Signed: Bernard Bloch". Since it was the third letter of the alphabet, it signified three hundred thousand francs. This made sense, once you thought about it. Then he walked away with a sprightly step.

When I left the HICEM office, I felt a bit drunk. It wasn't the money so much that made my head whirl, but the possibility I saw to get out of Europe. After the arrest of Rosenfeld, Kleinhandler, and the others, I felt inclined to leave this Old World where it isn't good to be a Jew.

Wait, I'm not finished! I returned to the Café Noailles where I had to meet Schlesinger. He hadn't arrived yet, but I met José Vagaria, you know that Spanish middleman who, thanks to his contacts, was able to send many people to South America. I told him I'd received some money from my family and was anxious to see what was happening on the other side of the ocean. He replied that it was practically impossible because they weren't issuing any visas.

'How is it they don't give visas!' I exclaimed. 'I've a friend's ticket in my pocket. He received a visa for four hundred thousand francs!'

Mr. Beer didn't tell me the price he'd paid. Vagaria didn't believe me at first, but when I showed him the ticket to convince him, he got red in his face. He claimed he could never make a deal with the consulate that gave Mr. Beer a visa, and pretended to be incorruptible, while it turned out he was very expensive.

'Wait for me here,' he said. 'I'll return in a little while.'

As a matter of fact, he returned in an hour, even redder than before and very excited.

'I saw the consul and we had a little discussion. You're profiting from an exceptional opportunity. I got you a visa for a song...one hundred thousand francs for you, your wife, and the little one. I told the consul you were a farmer; that's why you can get it so cheaply. It seems the country needs agricultural technicians.'

If you want to know what I really think, my dear Renée, I suspect that Vagaria used a little persuasion, not to use the word blackmail. The visa he secured didn't cost Vagaria more than three hundred seventy-five francs, the price of the tax. He's very shrewd, this Spaniard. Whatever he is, he took me to the visa office right away where I was very well received. They promised to have all the papers ready tomorrow.

As my grandfather used to say, 'when it rains, it pours'. Things are going well; we're going to have our tickets tomorrow. After I left the consulate, I quickly ran to HICEM to ask when we'll be able to leave. You know that one must usually wait several months. Well, even in this case, our luck didn't abandon us. On the boat leaving Europe for South America at the end of the month, two seats have become available because a candidate for emigration gave birth to a child while she waited. Her doctor recommended she postpone her trip until later and her husband is staying with her. One's misfortune...

To get back to poor Schlesinger, he spent the whole day with the police inspector, looking for the Corsican bandit. Thanks to the generosity of our Uncle Isadore, we'll be left with a nice tidy sum after paying for everything. I intend to indemnify Schlesinger as much as I can. When I told him I'm inclined to take part of his loss, he threw his arms around me and kissed me – he could have saved himself that trouble because he has halitosis. He continued to lament as usual as he filled my pockets with his counterfeit dollars to get rid of them.

Tomorrow, I'll try to complete all the final formalities and shall pay Vagaria his commission. He seems to be in a hurry. There's a man who always gets whatever he goes after. You'll see me returning with visas, tickets, and the rest of the money. I'm in a hurry to get out of Marseilles with its consulates, crooks, shady middlemen, ersatz bouillabaisse, and its thin ratatouilles, which are almost the only things served in the legal restaurants.

I hope Jeannot is helping you take care of the goat and that you've made some good cheese. Did you think to water the tomato plants a little?

Tenderly, your Bernard

P.S. Just think, I owe this marvellous adventure to the Quakers. If they hadn't occupied themselves with my luggage, I never would have had the idea to go to Marseilles, nor would I have met Uncle Isadore's messenger."

VII

During a scandal, Mrs. Hermelin is called a procuress

André Murger lengthened his stride. The rain that had surprised him as he passed the last houses in Francheville began to soak through his clothes. He was in a hurry to change.

This time the die was cast. At noon tomorrow, he would take the train to Lyons as he had told a friend in a telegram. It was simple. Yet this morning, he had been unable to decide. To extend his stay here was senseless, but to leave while she was still here, was that not even more foolish? Those were his thoughts before he had received the letter that settled the question. They needed him. This time it was not to decorate the public lavatories in Lyons with slogans against the government.

The rain falling through the foliage of the chestnut trees along the road became heavier. Another ten minutes to Tilleuls...he had already reached the corner with the old abandoned shack where Mrs. Hermelin's farmer sometimes left his harvest.

Pelted by the rain, André ran toward the shanty for shelter. Once inside, he had the feeling that someone else was there. He trembled, then steadied himself as he held his breath and tried to get used to the darkness.

"My word! One might say I scare you," said a voice in the back of the structure.

Solange, seated on a block of wood, looked at him mockingly. Murger mumbled something, and with one hand straightened his hair, causing several raindrops to roll off.

"But you're drenched," she said, feigning solicitude. Since he continued brushing himself without replying and behaving as if he were annoyed, she went on laughingly, "You look like a weeping willow...and even more if that's possible!"

Irritated, André approached Solange and seized her arm.

"Ouch!" she cried. "You're hurting me..."

"Each of us has his turn. You hurt me enough these past few days. You never miss an occasion to hurt me. And even when you say nothing to me, you make it apparent you're ignoring me."

He was sure that those half-confessions made him ridiculous in Solange's eyes. Too bad! He was leaving the next day.

"I don't understand you," she said, "and I even suspect you don't understand what you're saying."

She stood up and, turning her back to the young man, went to the door.

"It's stopped raining," she said. *"Au revoir!"*

Soon she was on the road, walking rapidly toward Tilleuls.

Suddenly, Murger felt his anger melt. Would he ever know the thoughts of this distant, impenetrable young woman walking away so quickly? He was in love with an enigma. Solange Fleury! What a funny girl!

In a few long steps he rejoined her.

"Please excuse me for being so abrupt," he said, in a husky voice. "I didn't mean to make you angry, believe me. It's only that I'm leaving tomorrow, and there may never be a chance for us to talk with each other."

"So what?" asked Solange, without turning her head.

"So what?" repeated André, like an echo. "You're right. I'm leaving tomorrow and that's all. Tell me *adieu* instead of *au revoir*. I'd like to tell you so many things," he added, in a low voice.

She pretended not to have heard his last words.

"If that's what you want, *adieu!*" and without looking at him, she quickly went upstairs.

"My poor Mr. Murger!" exclaimed Mrs. Hermelin, coming out of the kitchen with a small basket of peaches in her hand. "You're soaked! You'll catch cold! I'm going to fix you a cup of herb tea."

"Thank you, madam. Please don't bother. I'm going to change. If it isn't too much trouble, send my dinner up to my room in a little while. I must pack my valises. I'm tired."

He had decided not to see Solange again, not even at the table.

"With pleasure, Mr. Murger. I'll send up Marguerite with a good dish of nettle soup. You're in luck; it's the last one of the season. The nettles are getting coarse. I'll also send up an egg." Then, assuming an expectant air, she added, "and a peach from my garden. Our peach tree isn't very generous this season, but then again, you shouldn't abuse the first peaches. Health before everything else, isn't that so?"

At ten-thirty that night, André was busy transferring the contents of the chest of drawers to his open valise on the table when an energetic knock on his door made him straighten up.

"Enter!" he said mechanically.

Solange stood before him in the doorway. She wore a bathrobe that reached to her ankles and made her look taller than usual. The look on her face was strange, and her lips trembled. André had the impression that he was seeing her for the first time.

"You'll let me come in, won't you?" she asked, with false assurance and, without waiting for a reply, closed the door behind her. "It seems you've something to tell me. Well, I'm listening."

As André, with a pile of laundry in his arms, remained mute, she approached the window saying, "You don't close the shutters at night? It's true there are no neighbours nearby, but I don't like to be awakened by the sun in the morning."

André thought that he had heard wrong. Solange Fleury, 'the distant princess!' Was this how she talked?

"Are you speechless?" she asked, and then continued in an insecure voice, "You told me you'd like to talk with me. Have you changed your mind?"

As she spoke, her lips trembled like those of a child ready to cry. She tried to force a smile.

"Don't you understand yet? I want to spend the night here...in your room...with you. Do you understand now?"

Murger put down his laundry, took a step toward Solange, took her hand in his and, looking straight into her eyes, said emphatically, "I understand nothing, absolutely nothing... I hope you'll be kind enough to explain all this tomorrow. Right now, you seem very fatigued. Go back to your room and go to bed."

She instilled in him a feeling very close to pity. She seemed to be at her wits end and spoke in a voice that was not hers. What could have happened to her in those few hours? In spite of her long robe that made her look taller, she now appeared very distressed and unhappy, like a beaten child.

"Don't send me away!" she cried, in a voice strangled with tears. "I've a right to stay here if I want...and if you want me. Today I'm twenty-one years old; I'm an adult."

"That's no reason to throw a temper tantrum. Look, calm down and think a little," he said softly when he saw that she was shaking with muffled sobs.

"This isn't a temper tantrum. It's all thought through very carefully. I'm an adult," she repeated, stubbornly. "I guessed what you wanted to tell me. And, as for me...I'm attracted to you too. I thought..."

André took her by the arm and guided her to the armchair.

"There...sit down and we'll talk like friends." He brought over a chair, sat down, took Solange's hands in his, and said, "You've had some trying times and need to confide in someone. You may consider me your friend. It's a very banal phrase, but believe me, it's sincere. The first day I met you with *War and Peace* in your pocket, I immediately felt friendship for you...and perhaps somewhat more," he added in a low voice.

Solange relaxed, leaned her head against the back of the armchair, and closed her eyes. Her lips had stopped trembling.

"I, also," she said. "I'm sorry to have been so mean to you. It's stronger than I. It's this terrible spirit of contradiction! I get it from my father. There are other things, too. If you only knew how afraid I am to be like him! Tell me frankly, am I like him?"

"Not at all," said André, with conviction.

"You don't know how terrible he can be. There are times when I hate him. I've had enough! I've waited for this day for years...to end this slavery in an instant! Not to live according to his theories!...his inhuman principles...his tyranny...his 'discipline'... What a nightmare! It's over! He's told me often enough that I'll be free when I reach my majority! Well, it has come! I'm twenty-one years old. You said you were leaving tomorrow. Do you mind taking me with you? I assure you, I won't be a burden to you; you'll have no obligation to me. I've a little money and it's mine, all mine. Please say you'll take me."

"Are you sure you haven't lost your mind?" he murmured.

The situation was unreal and left him baffled. Only a few minutes ago, he could have sworn that he would never get a smile or sign of interest from Solange, and he was desperate. Now she was here, ready to throw herself into his arms, begging him to accept her, and he was the one who was moralizing like an old uncle. It was a thankless role, but he felt that he had no right to take advantage of the young woman's confusion. His premonition had not deceived him. There truly was a puzzle in Solange's life, a puzzle to which he now had the key.

"Lost my mind?" repeated Solange, thoughtfully. "Perhaps. Anyway, I've decided."

She stood up and stared hard at André. Now she really looked like her father.

"If you refuse to take me with you, I'll go by myself. In any case, I will leave."

"Solange, my dear," he said, making her sit down, "We'll create an appallingly dismaying and unnecessary scandal. What will your parents say?"

"Oh, my parents! You already know what I think of my father. My mother is a brave woman, but she sees the world only through his eyes. I don't count for her. I'm alone in the world. As for the scandal, I'd be more than happy to see it happen. After that, they won't be able to stop me from leaving."

André hesitated. He did not dare to look at Solange for fear of losing his ability to think clearly. He felt that the moralizing uncle would disappear into thin air any second.

"If you've truly thought through everything you are doing... But to be frank with you, I also have a confession to make to you. When I leave tomorrow, my life won't be my own. There are moments when one must take sides. As for me, I've made my choice."

She looked at him without saying a word and then said, "I know your ideas. I know there are situations where personal considerations become secondary. I accept your conditions."

"Good," said André, gravely.

He took her in his arms and kissed her for a long time.

"And now," he said, making an effort to regain his poise, "you're going to sleep. I'll prepare the bed for you. As for me, I'll spend the night in this armchair and use the other one as an extension. I'll be comfortable."

She took his hand and pressed it against her cheek.

"Thank you. You're a fine gentleman." Then changing her tone quickly, she added, "But I still want a scandal. It will avoid explanations. I want to show my independence once and for all."

Quickly removing her sandals, she grabbed André's shoes that were near his valise, opened the door, and put the two pairs of shoes in the corridor, one beside the other.

*****

The scandal in Tilleuls evolved as planned. At seven o'clock in the morning, Mr. Hermelin, as he did every day, picked up all the shoes that the guests had left in the hall outside their rooms. Half an hour later, after giving them a trembling treatment, he put them back in place. Mrs. Hermelin, seeing him put Solange's sandals at Murger's door, angrily reproached her poor husband.

"You're out of your mind! Where are you putting Miss Fleury's shoes? Her room's over there!"

The old tax collector protested as energetically as he could. He was certain that he had picked up the white shoes in front of this door. During this exchange of words, André Murger's door opened and Solange, in men's pajamas, appeared on the threshold.

Mrs. Hermelin felt faint and stopped breathing. To have this happen to her! Under her roof! This was too much! Who would believe that Mr. Murger, with his innocent airs, was a perverted, brutal, lascivious seducer...and Solange, a vulgar prostitute? The devil was everywhere!

Solange, smiling and unembarrassed, picked up the two pairs of shoes, thanked Mr. Hermelin kindly, and closed the door.

Mrs. Hermelin was mortified. She was still looking at the panelled door behind which the orgies of perdition took place when Mr. Fleury, with disheveled beard, eyebrows drawn together, and dressed in underwear of his own design with a toga improvised from a sheet, came out of Solange's room.

"What is going on?" he demanded, turning to Mrs. Hermelin. "My daughter isn't in her room, and her bed is undisturbed. Do you know where she can be?"

With the dramatic gesture of an avenging archangel, a speechless Mrs. Hermelin indicated Mr. Murger's room.

It was at that moment that the true scandal erupted, unleashing an unprecedented storm in Tilleuls and upsetting life in the boardinghouse. There was a succession of violent scenes: César Fleury's angry storms and accusations, his wife's tearful crises, Mrs. Hermelin's lamentations. Nevertheless, they were faced with a *fait accompli*. Solange and André took the 11.45 train.

In the course of the afternoon, the storm resumed with a new violence. Mrs. Hermelin, having dared to make a transparent allusion to the effects of an education without God, caused César Fleury, in a paroxysm of anger, to accuse her of having encouraged his daughter's temper tantrum and to call the owner of Tilleuls a procuress. Mrs. Hermelin did not know the exact meaning of the word, but in her mind, she associated it with a vision of debauchery and apocalyptic lewdness. Procuress! After having obeyed all the Lord's commandments for sixty-one years and then be insulted like that! The injustice seemed so monstrous to her that she could not find the strength to answer. Instead, she limited herself to notifying Fleury that, without delay, he was to leave the house that his family had dishonoured. César did not have to be told twice. Leading his wife, he took the train that same evening.

However, it was Joseph who had the last word.

"Do you want me to tell you the truth? This Fleury really ought to be called Blum," he declared to his mother. "I knew at once that he had something of a Jew in him. His vanity and his double-dealing are the signs that never deceive me. This ignoble individual thought it was enough to change his name to a French one and to rant against other Jews, thinking I'd be taken in!"

Joseph's world was peopled with Jewish phantoms...

Chapter Seven

The Potato Revolution

I

In the roaring lion's lair, they deal in sausages, soap, and dollars

Great turmoil reigned in the Hotel Panorama's kitchen. It was ten o'clock in the morning on market day. Sarzier and his personnel were overworked. On the top of the kitchen range in the rear huge pots boiled, and around the table all the servants were peeling vegetables.

Sarzier, who had not had the time to cover his flaming "roaring lion" locks with his high chef's hat, was standing near the window conversing with Tournier and paying him for the latest delivery of sardines, sugar, and coffee that he had ordered from the stocks of the grocer-bureaucrat who somehow avoided his obligation to the Supply Agency.

Through the open door, Sarzier suddenly saw Vautier, turning his cap in his hand and waiting. The restaurateur cut the formalities short and said goodbye to the grocer. Was the owner of the Grange bringing the rabbits and sausages he had ordered? The food was essential to feed his clients, especially every Thursday when the dining room was filled with the regular hotel guests plus a few market day vendors, three travelling salesmen, in addition to Chameix, Longeaud, and their friends, who would be behind closed doors.

No sooner had Vautier's merchandise been delivered and the account paid – not without a serious argument over the price of the sausages – when Sarzier noticed a big car stopping at the entrance. This was a rare sight, having become rarer over the past two years. Sarzier left the kitchen to run to the client, who was closing the car door. The hotel owner was incredulous. Was it possible? Mr. Prokoff, Mrs. Génia's husband in person!

There was no doubt about it. It certainly was Mr. Prokoff. But what a change! At the time that Sarzier had known him in June 1940, he had been barely respectable. He had driven the car for the elegant lady who was returning to Paris at the same time as the Prokoffs. Now Prokoff was a gentleman! In a very elegant grey suit, a gabardine topcoat that was no longer being made, and most of all, he was driving this beautiful car! And with all this, he behaved with the assurance of a man whose wallet was full. People like that Sarzier recognized immediately. For dinner, he would bring a bottle of Ermitage from the wine cellar, and there would be liqueurs to serve. That was where the profit was.

On learning that his wife was on a trip, Alexander was annoyed. He had not anticipated a situation that would force him to treat the affair by mail. He would have liked to have dealt with it face to face. However, since he was tired from his trip, he decided to take a bath, to shave and to rest in the Hotel Panorama until evening before returning. Sarzier considered Génia's room available and quickly prepared it. The young woman, who had become less reserved lately, had left with a salesman from Marseilles for a week. Sarzier supervised the transfer of all of Génia's belongings to the storeroom. He left nothing to chance. "With all her airs of innocence, she was as fiery as anyone else," thought the hotel owner, hiding a particularly compromising object.

At a quarter after ten, Mr. Beer came to the dining room for his breakfast. Sarzier rushed to serve him personally. He knew how to take care of good clients. He brought him real coffee (Tournier), some milk (Vautier), some butter and honey (Laffont). It wasn't that Sarzier particularly liked the Jews. On the contrary. He bore a grudge against them because they patronized the Hotel Farémido. Mr. Beer, in spite of his being a multi-millionaire, had no airs. And it was a real pleasure to hear him talk about the stock market.

Sarzier's admiration for Mr. Beer was not without a reason. He had some money to invest and counted on Mr. Beer to give him a good tip.

While the banker was having his breakfast, the hotel owner decided to ask him for advice. Mr. Beer listened attentively and regarded him with a worried expression on his face.

"At the present time," he said, "with the stock market paralysed, I see only one safe investment, the dollar. What is even better, at the moment its present price is slightly undervalued. A rise in value can be expected. On the other hand, at a time of hidden devaluation as we are experiencing now, only stable investments, like the dollar or the Swiss franc, offer reliable guarantees."

Sarzier soaked up these words with delight. He would have liked to have investigated the matter more thoroughly, but since a new arrival approached the banker's table, Sarzier left, much to his displeasure.

Bernard Bloch, harassed and tired after spending the night standing in the aisle of a crowded train, shook hands with Mr. Beer and dropped into the chair the other had designated.

"Well, what's new in Marseilles?" asked the banker, pushing his cup of coffee aside. "Were you able to complete my errands?"

Bloch handed him the envelope with the tickets and, before telling him his complicated adventures, sighed deeply. To illustrate his story, he pulled from his pocket a handful of counterfeit dollars that the Corsican had given his friend Schlesinger.

Mr. Beer was first horrified, then indignant. What a crook! What mores! Was it not lamentable that businessmen were at the mercy of such thieves? But he was pleased that everything ended well and congratulated Bloch for his idea to offer to compensate the crook's victim.

"That was an honorable gesture, but you must permit me to reimburse you. I consider myself somewhat responsible for this affair because it was I who gave you the middleman's address. I should have obtained more precise information. I can't forgive myself."

And in spite of Bloch's protests, he handed Bloch a check for fifty thousand francs.

"At this time, my friend, your means don't permit you the luxury of such generosity," he said, cordially. "And as for the Corsican crook, leave it to me. I haven't said the last word yet. If the police are unable to catch him, I'll find him. I'll keep those grossly counterfeit, valueless bills. They'll be proof of his guilt."

Bloch's admiration for the banker reached its peak. Not only was Mr. Beer a man of distinction and great means, but he also had a heart. And to think there were people who pretended that Jews were incapable of a magnificent gesture when it came to money! A Jew like Mr. Beer compensated for such chicaneries.

Thanking him effusively, Bloch said goodbye to the financier and went to the post office. In his briefcase he had seven thank-you letters, addressed to the seven Isadore Blochs in New York that he had not had time to mail in Marseilles. He felt that six of them would never understand this display of gratitude, but the seventh one would know that his nephew Bernard was not ungrateful.

Bloch never suspected that not even one of the Isadore Blochs in New York would understand a word of his letter because the money that had fallen from heaven in the HICEM offices had not come from his uncle and had not even been meant for him. Blochs were not rare in New York, nor anywhere else. It had been a fortuitous coincidence that the Polish Haitian had a namesake among the refugees on Avenue Victor Hugo in Cassis. He, too, had been a candidate for emigration and had had greater luck with his family in America. But, on the other hand, he had had the misfortune of being arrested by the police in Marseilles before the money for his trip arrived. Ignorant of all those details and, in addition, deceived by the error in the street number, the stranger in HICEM had given Bernard Bloch the sum agreed upon by letter and cashed in America. Bernard Bloch would never know that his salvation came, not from the generosity of an uncle, but through the mix-up and unfortunate disappearance of one of his brothers of misfortune.

*****

Half an hour later, Alexander Prokoff, freshly shaved, installed himself on the terrace of the Hotel Panorama and ordered a cocktail. From the time when he had been a simple guide, Alexander had now become a business man, operating successfully in European economic affairs, and had decided to get rid of Génia. A man who had made it in life rarely kept the wife of his struggles. Alexander thought that the moment had come to officially replace his wife for Tatiana, her former boss. Why in the devil did Génia have to take a trip just now? By surprising her in her retreat in Francheville, Alexander had hoped to settle the affair under advantageous conditions. She had never been too bright.

"Well, Mr. Prokoff, did you have a good bath?" asked Sarzier, as he personally served a cocktail to his illustrious guest. 'I left you some soap. Did you notice how good it is?"

"Excellent," said Alexander. "All my compliments. It's impossible to find soap of that quality in the stores anymore."

"If you'd like to take a few cakes with you, it's very easy. A young man, one of my clients, makes them. Naturally, I tell you this in the strictest confidence."

This was why, toward the end of breakfast, Sarzier brought Chameix to Alexander's table. They drank coffee together and spoke about one thing or another. Alexander, who had developed business sense, was continually on the alert lately for new prospects and asked the pharmacist's assistant about his little industry. Flattered and accepting all the compliments which were in part due to Pinkas, Chameix explained his entire commercial concept. Alexander became increasingly interested. He wanted to know the price of raw materials. Were the suppositories available in sufficient quantities? How much did they cost? Surely butter was very easy to find in Francheville, although a bit expensive. Alexander was immersed in his thoughts.

"We're going to do a little estimating," he said.

He ordered two Armagnacs and took his notebook from his pocket.

Half an hour later, when they said goodbye to one another, they had already reached a certain accord in principle. The Chameix and

Pinkas's factory would produce soap from butter, thus increasing production tenfold. Alexander Prokoff would furnish the necessary capital and also handle the distribution of the merchandise. Once a week, the soap from Francheville would be sent to Marseilles in a truck of the Armistice Commission, where Alexander had some good friends. You must keep up with the times, isn't that so?

IIAmélie Martin knocks on Mr. Longeaud's door and finds herself face to face with Father Bournisien

Longeaud put down his pen and looked at the grandfather clock. It was 9.20 p.m. With satisfaction, he read the lines he had written in his big notebook on whose cover he had printed "My Readings" in blue and red.

"25th August. Flaubert 'Madam Bovary – Mores of a Province'.

A masterful, powerful work rich in dramatic situations. The part where the author has us witness the heroine's visit to Father Bournisien (Part II, Chapter 6) is particularly well introduced. Emma, in the throes of a deep, internal conflict, comes to seek comfort from the priest who is preoccupied only with trivial worries and is quite absorbed by the problems of material life. He lets the visitor leave without suspecting that he has failed in his duty as a ' doctor of the soul'. Two thoughts compel attention:

First: the need for confession at crucial moments in life is inherent in human nature. The Church has always exploited this tendency to increase its power. For instance, the role of Jesuit confessors for the reigning families.

Second: the need to replace those professional exploiters of the human soul with lay confessors who will be true guides for the conscience."

This was the second day of Mr. Longeaud's new work schedule. It consisted of studying literature, history, and sociology from works by Durkheim[46], Marx[47], Seignobos[48], and Mathiez[49] as well as a series of

---

46 Emile Durkheim (1858–1917). French sociologist and philosopher. (HRG)
47 Karl Heinrich Marx (1818–1833). German philosopher, economist, and socialist leader. (HRG)
48 Charles Seignobos (1854–1924)--French historian. (HRG)
49 Albert Mathiez (1874–1932). French historian, student of the French Revolution.

novels from Flaubert[50] to Proust[51]. The details of this programme were planned carefully and written in pencils of three colours: red, blue, and green.

Saint-Boniface's teacher had stopped studying English. He had decided that knowing a second language was secondary and contributed little to enrich the spirit. On the other hand, history and literature were full of precious teachings.

According to his timetable, at 9.30 p.m. he ought to switch to reading Durkheim. He still had another ten minutes before he should begin, enough time to smoke a cigarette and drink a glass of wine.

He finally opened the book, but barking dogs in the village diverted his attention. He went to the door, opened it, and looked outside. Not seeing anything unusual, he returned to his book. Durkheim was a rather dry author. Although the dogs had stopped barking, Longeaud thought that he heard a noise in the yard. He stood up, went to the window, and peeked out.

For half an hour, Amélie Martin had been wandering near the school. First, she had heard Mrs. Longeaud leave; then when she was a certain distance she had decided to wait a little longer. She wanted to count to a thousand. When that time was up she had approached the door, but at the moment that she was about to ring the doorbell, she had hesitated again. She had retreated as far as the electric transformer on the road, and then ten minutes later, she had returned to the school. She might not even have had the courage to make up her mind this time if she had not had the impression that she had seen Mr. Longeaud standing near the window and thought that he had noticed her. It was impossible to go back. She must go in at once. Anyway, if she did not talk to him tonight, she would never have the strength to do so again.

Pleased at the prospect of stopping work, Mr. Longeaud eagerly invited her to come in.

Awkward and timid, the old girl entered the room and slowly slipped off her cape.

"Sit down, miss," said the teacher, almost cordially. "What a day we've had! This hot spell is enough to make you melt. One is pleased to breathe a bit in the evening. Have you come to see Mrs. Longeaud?"

Amélie did not reply. She took off her gloves and then nervously put them on again.

---

50 Charles Flaubert (1821–1881). French writer and novelist. (HRG)
51 Marcel Proust (1871–1922). French novelist. (HRG)

"She just left to visit Noémi Sobrevin who has had her baby. Lately Mrs. Longeaud is always going to see babies. It amuses her. What can I do?"

Mr. Longeaud felt the pleasure of this unexpected visit give way to annoyance.

"No, I haven't come to see Mrs. Longeaud," said Amélie, with an effort. "But I'm disturbing you. I see you're working," she added, pointing with her gloved hand to the open book on the table.

"She doesn't seem to want to leave," Longeaud thought. He would need to make some kind of conversation.

"Oh yes, my life is all work. I think it's necessary to cultivate and enrich one's spirit, so I undertook a small literary project." With an affected detachment, he continued, "There's nothing like literature to open new horizons."

He was quiet for a while. Amélie, her eyes downcast, was also silent.

"But truly," he began again, "it seems you're going to leave us soon. Just between us, they've not been very correct with you, waiting until August to tell you that they'll not renew your contract. But go look for correct behaviour in parochial education! As soon as they no longer need you, they show you the door without further ado. Your only solution is to look for another school!"

"Oh, that isn't important! There are other changes."

"Oh yes, if you must leave the countryside for the city, you'll notice a big difference. These days the restrictions are harsher in the big centres."

"Restrictions," she murmured. "If only that was all there was to it! Life has even harder challenges in store for us."

"Oh, excuse me! Don't underestimate food restrictions. Marx proved to what degree material factors can determine our existence. Speaking of that, I should try to get Lyons on the radio at ten o'clock. They ought to be announcing a supplementary distribution of wine to grape pickers. It interests me because I've a little idea in the back of my mind. One of my friends is a wine grower not far from Tain. I'm planning to see him and to register as a grape picker. His mayor's secretary is a friend of mine from Normal School. I'm turning on the radio right now so I won't miss the announcement. Fifty litres of wine is quite a considerable amount, don't you think?"

Turning on the set provoked an explosion of jazz music. He quickly turned down the volume.

Amélie waited patiently while Longeaud tuned the set. It was evident that he could not suspect what she wanted to tell him. But she would tell him anyway. It all depended on how she expressed herself.

This was her last attempt to reconcile herself with the world.

"That they weren't correct with me isn't important," she said rather calmly, but without conviction. "To be forced to leave the countryside for the city is a bit annoying. But ever since I returned to France, I can't find a place where I can feel at home. France and I are strangers. When I was abroad, I represented something. Here, I'm less than nothing. In coming to Saint-Boniface, I renounced many things," she continued, as she looked at her now ungloved hands with their rough skin and broken nails, "but I had hoped to find in this countryside a rustic refuge...a little warmth...some purity...some spiritual heightening which, for me, was always associated with the Church. I have a hard time expressing what I want to say. But there's so much vileness and compromise among those whose duty it is to communicate a moral force. And to think so many people have confidence in them!"

"Oh, they aren't as numerous as that!" said Longeaud, eyeing his radio. "How many students do you have? Thirty, not more. Isn't that so? How do you expect them to keep you with conditions the way they are? Especially since Sister Thérèse whom you replaced is returning now that she's cured. If only our students would come to class regularly! But it's not I who will tell you that half of them are always missing. Look, even we, my wife and I, have a difficult time justifying a double position in this forlorn hole. I've been obliged to carry six city children on my register. They'd been placed on farms during their vacation. Since the inspector comes once a year and they aren't present, they're considered absent. This is between us, do you understand? This is my little system to see me through. You may know this trick as practised under Louis XIV very well – they carried imaginary soldiers on the books to inflate the numbers."

He laughed maliciously, very satisfied with himself.

A short silence followed.

"If you only knew what I have to endure," Amélie began again. "To be the servant of that mean, imbecilic woman, Sister Félicie! As for Father Mignart, who professes such high moral principles..."

"Father Mignart is a priest like any other," said Longeaud, being prudent and evasive while thinking, no, this old girl would not drag him into Church quarrels. He continued aloud, "It's about time those exploiters of human weakness be replaced with lay confessors who would be true directors of conscience."

Amélie's face lit up.

"You're right, Mr. Longeaud," she said, enthusiastically. "I, who am a believer, have asked myself if it wouldn't be better to go to minds more understanding, more generous, and free from all religious doctrines to whom one could come in case of doubt..." and lowering her voice, added, "...and when one has lost all faith in life..."

"Certainly, certainly," said Longeaud, tapping his fingers on the table. "Priests aren't too bright! Excuse me, I think the broadcast is starting."

He ran to the set and turned up the volume. From the speaker came a voice that filled the room.

"From Berlin. The Führer's headquarters announce the battle in the region around Stalingrad has begun again with increased intensity..."

"No, that isn't what we're interested in. You were saying...oh, the priests. You know..."

"It's they who are supposed to be the intermediaries between God and the Christian conscience. Don't they sometimes assume a role beyond their capacity?"

Despairingly, Amélie felt that her words were getting farther and farther from her thoughts and, like clumsy little toads, were falling into a deep, murky swamp.

"Certainly they're usurping and how!" Longeaud said, emphatically. "Father Mignart doesn't hesitate to pull the blanket to his side. Since he's the secretary of the Corporation, he takes advantage of his position to force Delphine Legras to bring him two dozen eggs each week. She's obliging even though she isn't Catholic. And it's I who suffers because Mother Legras used to keep the eggs for me. But it's already ten after ten and this damn communique isn't over!"

He turned the knob and looked anxiously at the set.

"In spite of the terrorist bombardment, production in the German munitions factories is increasing..."

"No it isn't over. Now if you want to see Mrs. Longeaud," he said, tapping his fingers on the table again, "you'll have to wait a while. She isn't ready to return. A birth in Saint-Boniface is a big event."

"Oh yes, births...and deaths," murmured Amélie. "Although the death of some..."

"If you must see her tonight, you can always go to the Sobrevins. It won't take you more than fifteen minutes...and the moon will come out at any moment.

"Ah, here's the local news. Let's see what they have to say. It's a mistake to think that wine is a luxury. It's a food of utmost importance. Since there's a scarcity of wine, I haven't stopped losing weight. Five kilos add up."

Amélie stood up. Her empty look expressed nothing of her inner turmoil. She wanted to say something, but the words stuck in her constricted throat. Longeaud also stood up, intending to escort her to the door, but he was so absorbed by the information on the radio that he did not notice that his visitor went to the door by herself. Amélie did not turn around. She opened the door and went into the darkness. The moon still had not risen.

Longeaud waited until the speaker finished, then seeing that it was 10.25, he decided that it was definitely too late to go back to work that night. He closed Durkheim's book. Tomorrow would be the first day of food ration card distribution, and he would have too little time. Too bad! His study programme would be delayed a day or two. His new life would start on Monday. He poured himself a glass of wine. He no longer needed to deprive himself because he would soon get an additional fifty litres.

III

In twenty-four hours, Francheville becomes the scene of an embezzlement, a suicide, and a mysterious disappearance

Noémi Sobrevin was finally enjoying everything with delight and complete abandonment. She had given birth the day before and was resting between fresh sheets on her bed, in a deep alcove which was separated from the kitchen by a drape that was pulled open. To her heart's content, she could observe all the comings and goings in the house. The baby – another boy! – carefully swaddled by a neighbour, slept against the wall.

For at least three days Noémi would be on vacation and able to read. On a pillow close to her was a popular novel with a colourful cover and the latest issue of her newspaper, *Le Relévement*, a Protestant publication. She was having a well-earned reward.

At four o'clock the previous day, when she knew that she only had one or two hours – Noémi was never mistaken in her timing – she had told the smaller ones to join Abel and Dina in the meadow where they were guarding the cows. Left alone with David, who was asleep, she had washed her feet and gone to bed. Soon Elie returned from Tournier's where he had gone to telephone the midwife. He could not count on the midwife; she had a delivery in town and did not have enough gas to get to Mottes. After all, Noémi was no apprentice.

Between two pains, she remembered that she needed a pair of scissors and told Elie to look for them in the drawers. Since he could not find them, she sent him to Delphine's or Latière's for a pair. When he returned, it was all over and just in time for the scissors.

Noémi stretched voluptuously and picked up her newspaper. In the stable, the calf bellowed plaintively. He had not suckled since morning. Too bad! He would have to wait until Elie returned from the fields. She also heard a chicken cackling in the nest in the stable. She should look for the egg, but let it cackle. Noémi decided not to let herself be disturbed. Today was a holiday!

There was a knock on the door. Tibor Verès stood in the doorway.

"Come in, Mr. Verès, come in! Come see my newest one. He's cute, isn't he? Just like my little Abel when he was born. When Mrs. Longeaud came to see me yesterday, she found him very strong."

"Permit me, madam, to express my most cordial congratulations on the occasion of the birth of this robust fellow and also my wishes for a quick recovery for you."

Noémi blushed from confusion and pleasure. This was the ninth child that she had brought into the world, but never before had she ever received such a well-turned compliment.

"You must be coming to pick up your litre of milk," she said, trying to express her appreciation. "Only my husband isn't here to fill it for you."

"Oh! No," replied the journalist, "don't disturb yourself today.

I wouldn't have come to interrupt your rest if you hadn't asked me..."

"Oh dear! It's true!" she exclaimed, just remembering that she had asked him to come. "Now what was it? Since yesterday I've lost my head. Of course! Am I dumb! I must give you something. You can imagine how I felt when I found a letter addressed to you in my newspaper. It's the fault of that imbecile Brandouille who delivered it by mistake. He must have had one glass too many that day. Excuse me for having troubled you for such a little thing, but I wanted to explain it to you myself. Your letter's been here for the past two or three days. I don't have time to read except when I've had a baby. When I opened my newspaper this morning, I found it."

At the sight of the return address, the journalist blanched, felt faint, and sat down. He had been expecting this letter for months. The envelope bore the magic words: "Consulate of the United States of America, Marseilles".

With a wildly beating heart and trembling fingers, he tore open the letter. The contents read as follows:

"Sir, your visa has arrived and you are *urgently* invited to present yourself at the Consulate, Place Saint-Ferréol in Marseilles. Signed: illegible"

Feverishly, Verès looked at the date at the top of the letter: 17th of July, 1942. It was now the 25th of August. But for two days, Verès had known that he needed to give up the idea of emigrating, even if his visa had arrived. On the 21st of August, the offices of the Committee for Help to Intellectuals, which had agreed to finance the trip for the Verès family, had closed, and the most beautiful visa in the world could only give him what he had, that is, the right to enter the United States, but not the boat tickets. Tibor Verès's personal finances would only permit him to transport himself and his family to the frontier, the first stage of their voyage.

"As I said," continued Noémi, "Mrs. Longeaud came yesterday. It was very nice of her. I took advantage of her being here to have her fill out the questionnaire for assistance to pregnant women that I didn't have time to take to the mayor's office."

While she talked, Tibor Verès made some calculations. The letter had arrived in Francheville on the 19th of July; Brandouille must have brought it to Saint-Boniface on the 20th. If this notice had reached him on time, the 25th of July at the latest, he would have been in Marseilles with his family. He would have had the time to take care of all the formalities before the Committee's doors were closed. Right now, he could have been in the United States. The fervent admirer of mailmen felt his faith crumbling.

Tibor was unaware of the epic quarrel over the rabbit, the apron, and the bicycle pump that had closed the doors to the New World to him. Several days after Lion's death, Brandouille had arrived at Mottes, determined to recover his pump. The ugly dog was no longer there to alert that witch Noémi as he had done before. Resolutely, he had sneaked up to the shed and had already opened the door when he suddenly heard a noise. What a disaster! It was Noémi coming out of the house. Brandouille lost his head. In one hand he was holding the mail for Saint-Boniface that he still had to deliver: a newspaper for Noémi and a letter for that Jew who never failed to have mail. In his fright, he had slid one into the other and thrown *Le Relévement* through the open window at Mottes. It had landed on a heap of dirty laundry.

It was not until the day after her delivery that Noémi had had an occasion to read. Thus for six weeks, the notice from the consulate came to be between two pages of an edifying letter on the Scriptures while laying on the sideboard in Mottes's kitchen.

*****

For an instant, Bernard Bloch laid down his sprayer in the middle of the cornfield. He was dead tired. He had worked the whole day with sweat running down his face. In the morning, he had repaired the disintegrating roof on the stable and carried all the manure out into the field to clean the place better; in the afternoon, he was spreading sulphur with a sprayer he had borrowed from Nelchet. It would not be him who would reap the harvest, but that was unimportant. Bernard Bloch was proud of his potatoes. He had fought the drought that ravaged Saint-Boniface. Convinced that one ploughing was worth three waterings, he ploughed often and his effort was not in vain.

Renée reproached him all day for wasting his time on the stable and in the field instead of helping with the luggage because they were leaving the day after tomorrow. But Bernard did not want to hear about it. When one does a job, he does it thoroughly, especially if he likes it. To work the soil was truly another, better way of living than turning broken-down old jalopies into scrap iron. While he was still in Poland attending the agricultural school for one year, he had understood how much he loved the soil. But one cannot always do what one likes in life, especially if you are Jewish. Once upon a time he would have liked to have gone to Palestine to become a farmer on a kibbutz, but they would not let him into the country. In a sense, he was being forced to emigrate twice, wasn't he? It was decidedly better not to attach oneself to the soil. If now, for example, he insisted on remaining in Saint-Boniface and foregoing emigration, sooner or later the police would force him to emigrate to a concentration camp. It is hard for a Jew to play the farmer, even with hands like his. Even if everything were going well, he must be ready to liquidate all his possessions.

Bernard Bloch could repeat all those truths to himself, and yet it hurt him to leave his fields of potatoes, his garden, his animals. He also regretted leaving this beautiful, rugged country with its wild hills; its peaks bristling with gorse resembling tousled heads; its mysterious ravines and innumerable streams that cut through the meadows in all directions; its forests of pine and chestnut that already smelled of Boletus mushrooms; its zigzagging roads that encircled the hills. He even regretted leaving these taciturn peasants – Nelchet, Seignos, Chazelas – amongst whom, for the first time in his life, he was able to forget that he was a Jew. Was it, as Verès said, because these peasants were not yet "socially evolved enough" to become anti-Semitic?

He was immersed in his thoughts when he noticed Verès panting as he climbed the hill with a bundle of newspapers in his hand.

"Finally I found you!" the journalist called to him. "Have you heard the news?" And when he had joined him, Verès continued, "If you only knew what a commotion this is causing in the village! Everyone is talking about it."

Bloch looked surprised. No sensational news had reached as far as Ripailles.

Instead of an explanation, Verès shoved the most recent issue of a Swiss newspaper under his nose. In the column for short notes on the last page, he saw encircled with a blue pencil:

"A CROOK WANTED TO EMIGRATE TO AMERICA

Barcelona, 31st of August. From our special correspondent. (INS)

Spanish police have arrested a daring crook who was about to board a boat leaving for Argentina. He is a certain Svoboda, a Czechoslovakian national who posed as a very rich banker under the name of Beer and who left numerous victims in the Unoccupied Zone of France, especially in Marseilles.

The arrest had taken place at the request of the French authorities with whom numerous complaints had been lodged about him.

To inspire confidence in his victims, many of whom were Israelites, Svoboda pretended to be Jewish, and as such, he could profit from easy terms for emigration. (INS)"

"A client in the Hotel Panorama noticed this article in the newspaper," added Verès. "Sarzier immediately ran to the bank to have a wad of dollar bills that Beer had sold him examined. Naturally, they were all counterfeit."

"I thought they would be," said Bloch, recovering from the shock. "They were the ones I brought from Marseilles myself. What a gangster!"

What a blow! And he had taken Beer for a big aristocrat in finance, an artist in business! Imbecile that he was, it was he who had run the errand for the crook in Marseilles, where the false banker was probably already known and did not want to go himself! It was useless to even cash his cheque. It certainly was not worth more than his counterfeit dollars.

What Bernard Bloch could not forgive himself for was to have considered Beer a Jew. It was true that he could recognize, at first glance, the Jews from Poland and Russia, but he often lacked that flair when it came to his co-religionists from central Europe: Czechs, Hungarians, Austrians, Romanians. They did not have the typical way of talking nor behaving, and very often they did not even have the Jewish look which he knew. In short, this one had taken him for a

227

fool. Poor Bernard, you should have noticed, though, that there was something not very Catholic in this affair, or better yet, there was not enough Jew in it. This little lesson cost you fifty thousand francs, and it could have cost you more!

They spoke for a long time about this affair and then about Bloch's departure.

"You seem very happy, my old pal," said the former journalist, hiding his envy. "When I think I could have left before you!..."

"Yes, fate is blind," said Bloch, philosophically. "I must confess that I regret leaving. Just between us, it isn't too bad here. I'll have a nice harvest, you know," he added, dejectedly. "I had thought of leaving it all to you, if you have the courage to continue."

"Oh! I..." said Verès, shrugging his shoulders. "Agriculture has never been my strong point. I'm not made for the plough. Because I'm Jewish I don't know a thing about it."

"Think it over," said Bloch, dreamily. "Whether one is a Jew or not, either one likes the soil or doesn't like it. However, to come back to my harvest, I'll ask Nelchet to do the work and share it with you. Now for some advice from me. Even if you don't want to do any farming, you should try a little gardening at least. You'll have to be registered at once with the Syndicate to get seeds in the spring. Anybody can garden. It's so easy and gives so much satisfaction, not to mention that it will help you with food supplies!"

"I'll see," said Verès, indecisively. "In the country the big problem is the food supply. I don't know how you managed, but I could get nothing from them. The other day I had an idea. I asked my wife to try to establish some useful contacts by painting some portraits. Not with oil paints, we lack the fats, only some pastels. At Delphine's in Barbarie, there's often some butter. My wife went there to make a little portrait, nothing modern, naturally, for that would scare her, but just to Delphine's taste."

"And then?" asked Bloch, amused.

"It wasn't very successful. Delphine and her husband thought the photographer in Francheville made better pictures and people didn't have to pose for half an hour without moving. As for pay, my wife got six eggs and that was all."

"And they still think they're doing you a favour," observed Bloch. "If I were you, I wouldn't try to do any art work here and would speak in a simpler way to the peasants. You speak such good French that nobody can understand you. I speak it badly, but no one notices my mistakes."

"Perhaps you're right," said Verès, somewhat disconsolately. "I can't ask these people to follow my complicated thoughts. However, I don't regret staying here with them. Who knows, perhaps it was providence that wanted me to remain in Europe? I'll witness many events that will give me material for my *Paradoxes of History*."

*****

Ever since Francheville was Francheville, never was it the scene of so many sensational events in twenty-four hours. No sooner had the people calmed down after the news of the false banker's arrest than other dramatic events shook the inhabitants' humdrum routine. That same evening, news came of the disappearance of Mrs. Rosenfeld whom everyone had continued to call Miss Sten. In the afternoon, a strange man with unusual features, and a big leather briefcase, came to visit her at Tilleuls. He spoke with her for a long time. In the evening, Miss Sten, who was very nervous, packed her valises and was taken to the station by Chazelas. When she left, she promised Mrs. Hermelin that she would hear from her.

All kinds of rumours circulated in Saint-Boniface, and even in Francheville, about the sudden departure that resembled an escape. Joseph Hermelin formulated a hypothesis that was generally accepted. During and before the war, Miss Sten, although a foreigner, was spying for France throughout the world. Her visitor had been a messenger from the French Secret Service who came to warn her that the Germans were on her trail. To escape from them, she, no doubt, had hidden in the countryside and agreed to become Mrs. Rosenfeld, hoping that her new status would serve as a disguise.

Finally, the third drama. Very early the next day, someone discovered Miss Amélie Martin's mutilated body on the railway tracks between Denières and Saint-Boniface. She had thrown herself in front of the ridiculously small county train that could kill just as well as an express. Several hypotheses were formulated on the subject of her suicide, but none of them were generally accepted. Even those who thought they knew Amélie could not explain this desperate act: neither Sister Félicie, nor Rosalie Tournier, and not even Mr. Longeaud. Father Mignart, of course, refused to give her a Christian burial.

IV

In spite of his stye, Officer Auzance tries to see clearly

For several days, Chameix felt himself becoming anti-Semitic. Before the war, he had seldom met Jews and did not have a well-formed opinion about them. Since then he had met a few, but knew only Pinkas. For Chameix, Pinkas became the symbol of the Jew. The pharmacist's assistant liked his shrewd, puppet-like face less and less.

Chameix asked himself if he still needed this Jew. Since Chameix had met Alexander Prokoff, the situation had changed completely. The Pernod and soap maker had found steady suppliers of butter in the region and a butcher in town who delivered beef fat regularly. The business had grown considerably; it almost became a factory, at least in Chameix's eyes.

Around the courtyard of the house where he lived in Francheville, there were only unoccupied rooms and no immediate neighbours. Helped by his fiancée and her brother, Chameix could engage in his alchemy under the pretext of making pharmaceutical preparations. Mr. Astier, the drugstore's owner and Francheville's mayor, was absorbed in municipal affairs and had blind confidence in his assistant, leaving the management of the White Cross Pharmacy to Chameix. Since the business was growing constantly, Mr. Astier had no complaints. The idea to check on his employee never entered his mind.

According to their agreement, Prokoff had furnished the capital and had completely taken over the transportation and delivery of the merchandise. Once a week the Armistice Commission's truck, which commuted between Lyons and Marseilles, came to Francheville to pick up the week's production and went on its way. Mr. Chameix knew all the necessary precautions to disguise the product for delivery. Once the goods were on the official vehicle, there was no fear of control.

Mr. Prokoff reaped fifty per cent of the profits. That was right. However, what was intolerable was the way the other fifty per cent was divided, giving twenty per cent to Chameix and thirty per cent to Pinkas, the same proportion as in the beginning. What was Pinkas really doing to earn it? It almost amounted to a pension for Pinkas! Chameix had once read in the *Signal* that all the Jews were parasites. How true that was! Pinkas was the best example, and he gave himself the big airs of a boss under the pretext that it was all his idea. Chameix was fed up with all of this.

The pharmacist's assistant was pondering these strong feelings of resentment as he arranged the bottles on the shelves when the doorbell rang. It was the gendarme, Auzance.

"Tell me, Mr. Chameix, can you give me something for this nasty thing growing on my eye? It annoys me!"

The policeman had a stye. Quickly, Chameix concocted an eyewash and handed him the bottle with very detailed instructions.

The handle of the cash register was turning and Auzance was getting ready to leave when he suddenly had an idea.

"Mr. Chameix, I think you can also give me some information while I'm here. What is this Pinkas doing? I saw you together once or twice."

For several weeks, Pinkas was not among the people sending out packages and that intrigued Auzance. "He certainly must be trafficking, but in what and how can I catch him?" This time Auzance had decided to collar him for good.

"Pinkas?" asked Chameix, troubled. "What's he doing? I've no idea."

"What sort of character is he?" insisted Auzance.

"How should I know? He's a Jew."

"Of course he's a Jew. I'm surprised he wasn't on the police list the other day when we had the roundup. In such cases we only execute orders. I wonder if he isn't dealing on the black market."

Chameix felt ill at ease. "To be frank, maybe yes, maybe no. How would I know?"

If Auzance continued to be interested in Pinkas, he was capable of smelling a rat, and it probably would be he, Chameix, who would be caught hobnobbing. That would be the pinnacle of injustice! He ought to make that parasite pay! No doubt it was a good time to get rid of Pinkas. The sooner, the better.

"If you really want to know what I think, I'll tell you. I don't think Pinkas deals on the black market. As for what he's doing," he said in a mysterious tone, "I wouldn't put my hand in the fire."

Auzance's ears pricked up.

"Aha! I see! He's in politics," he said slyly.

"In politics, maybe that's too big a word," said Chameix. "However he does talk and talk. He tells what he hears on the radio. He listens to London all day, like all the Jews. And, as you know, they discuss the news amongst themselves. Listen, they're as thick as thieves. He has his cronies."

"Truly? Do you know his cronies, too?" asked Auzance.

Chameix realized that he had talked too much. Since the deportation of Kleinhandler and the other foreign Jews, he did not know Pinkas's regular friends. But he could not escape. He recalled that one day he had seen Pinkas in the Café de la Marine sitting at the same table as the old Jew from Paris whose wife was so noisy.

"Pals? He has many, especially Cahen, the one with a little grey moustache."

"Very good...very good," said the policeman, thoughtfully. "So I must wash my eye twice a day?"

Stye or not, Auzance was on his guard. The daily summons was being readied.

*****

Daniel Cahen shrugged his shoulders wearily.

"And lastly, I don't know what you want from me. I hardly know this Pinkas. For the past three weeks we haven't exchanged a word."

For a quarter of an hour, Auzance, with all the shrewdness he possessed, had grilled the old Parisian business representative, who was a refugee in Francheville. He had surprised Cahen at the dinner table in a small apartment he occupied not far from the mayor's office. Auzance wanted to make a big impression on this little man, who proved to be particularly tough.

"He was exposing you to anti-French propaganda," insisted Auzance. "Admit it!"

Cahen shook his head obstinately.

"And you listened to him carefully instead of reacting like a good Frenchman."

"Don't give me any lessons, please," said Cahen.

Since Mrs. Cahen had left on a trip two days before after an extremely violent scene, he had been able to enjoy a little rest. Now this idiot in uniform had to come to poison the 'vacation' that his Xanthippe had accorded him. It was even more stupid since he barely knew this refugee about whom the policeman spoke. He decided to let him know at once.

"Cut it out, mister. If that's all you came here for, I think we've exhausted the subject," he said to Auzance.

Auzance took this rebuke badly and was displeased at being put in his place. In his investigations, he never allowed the interrogated to take the initiative. It was he who talked; the other had to limit himself to answers.

"I want you to know, you're treating me disrespectfully. It could cost you dearly. You better pay attention."

"And I tell you, shit," replied Cahen, as he pulled a cigarette from his pocket.

Auzance's face turned bright red.

"If this is the way you're going to talk," he hissed, "we'll see. Your case is simple: offence to an agent. But I'll give you one last chance. Confess and I'll ignore what you said. If you refuse, I can issue a summons, and I can even take you to the police station."

"At your disposal," said Cahen, smoking. "Just go ahead. I hope we'll find the police adjutant there. The more fools there are, the merrier."

"You're beginning again!" shouted Auzance. "Now you're calling me a fool!"

Auzance's loud voice was meant to hide his embarrassment. This Jew took him at his word. He had no intention of taking him to the police station. He had begun this inquiry on his own initiative. It was amateurish and he was not sure if his superior would approve. He was afraid of the whole business.

Cahen had already put on his jacket. He took his wallet from the chest of drawers, pulled some bills from it and put them into the drawer. He made sure that he had all his papers and calmly prepared to leave. Then, on second thought, he picked up a little metal box.

"And now I'm ready," he said.

Auzance's curiosity was aroused. What was the object that the Jew was carrying so surreptitiously? An explosive, perhaps? No doubt. They were made in all dimensions now, even very small ones. Some pens filled with explosive material were capable of tremendous destructive power. The more he thought about it, the more plausible it seemed that Pinkas and Cahen were producing infernal machines for an anti-French purpose.

"What's that?" he demanded, severely.

"Oh, it's personal. A small souvenir."

"Aha! A souvenir? Open that box immediately if you dare!"

"Oh no! Not here! You'll see it in the police station."

"We won't look at anything there. You'll go to the cell with your souvenir."

"Excuse me, not with my souvenir. I'd like to see you imprison it."

"Enough babbling!" shouted Auzance. "Give me your trinket at once, otherwise..."

If only he could discover an explosive device and bring it to his supervisor, perhaps he would be eligible for promotion. Meanwhile, there was no risk. The mechanism was not wound up. He reached out to grab it, but Cahen pulled it back and, in a sudden rage, threw the object through the open window.

Auzance threw himself face down. He remained immobile several seconds, waiting for the explosion. Slowly, he raised his head. Cahen was flabbergasted as he watched him, and then began laughing. In one swift movement, the gendarme stood up, went to the window, and jumped out.

The box was in the grass in front of him. It appeared very innocent. "No," he thought, "it cannot be an explosive."

Auzance picked up the box and opened it. His chin dropped in astonishment. The box contained a decoration. This was something! This rat had the Military Medal!

That scoundrel was right when he said that you could put this 'souvenir' in a prison cell. Auzance knew the regulation and thus was aware that in no case whatsoever could the Military Medal ever be taken into a prison cell. If its owner must ever be imprisoned, this decoration, the most precious of all, must be prevented from being dishonoured and must remain pinned outside the door of the cell.

*****

By 9.15 p.m. Auzance, who had finally given up questioning Cahen and had not even taken him to the police station, stood in front of Pinkas's door in the company of a colleague. This time he wanted to do everything according to the rules.

He put his ear to the door, listened for a second and then, all of a sudden, his face lit up. The signal from London, three beeps and then a fourth, resounded through the panelled door. The speaker's voice got louder in spite of the jamming. "This is London. Listen to some personal messages."

And while some Frenchmen told other Frenchmen that the doorman had a black eye, Auzance turned the key in the lock, opened the door, entered, and immediately arrested Pinkas for being guilty of listening to a prohibited station.

In vain Pinkas protested, arguing that everyone in Francheville listened to London. Auzance would not listen to reason. It was strictly forbidden to listen to the Allied broadcasts and he was doing his duty. The Jew, caught red-handed, was taken immediately to the police station.

The next day, Pinkas was transferred to Lyons. Several months later, when mail service was restored between the two zones, Chameix received a letter signed by Pinkas asking for food. The stateless one was interred in the Drancy concentration camp and was suffering from severe dysentery. He begged Chameix to put a box of glycerine suppositories in the package.

V

Mr. Longeaud, the Machiavelli of Saint-Boniface, unleashes a revolution

At 12.45 p.m. Mr. Longeaud left Vichy and switched to Sottens. The manoeuver did not take more than a few seconds and he was at once in neutral territory. The nasal voice of the Swiss speaker announced the recent Anglo-American landing in Africa. It was the 10th of November. For the past two days, Mr. Longeaud had followed the events with greater interest than usual. In the yard, the children were very noisy. Mrs. Longeaud had gone to shop at Tournier's grocery immediately after breakfast.

While he listened to the radio, someone knocked on the door. Mr. Longeaud jumped to the set and quickly turned back to Vichy. He never listened to a foreign station without carefully locking the door to prevent being surprised. But one never knew; agents and stool-pigeons were everywhere. In a firm voice he called, "Come in!"

The visitor opened the door slowly. It was Philibert Vautier. He stood in the doorway visibly embarrassed, turning his cap in his hand, and shaking his head.

"It's this report about potatoes," he began, taking a step forward.

Longeaud pointed to a chair. Of course, the owner of the Grange was a rascal, but he killed two or three pigs each year whether or not it was a good year. His bacon and sausages deserved some respect. From Vautier's confused account, Longeaud extracted the following facts:

In spite of a disastrous potato harvest, the result of an unusual drought, this crop was heavily taxed in Saint-Boniface. The tax was so heavy that even the producers found it impossible to deliver the quantity demanded by the Supply Agency.

Longeaud was paid to know whether the peasants complained out of habit as they usually did, but even he had a difficult time scraping together the four hundred kilos of this tuber that he needed for his own household this year.

According to the Supply Agency's demands, the growers were required to have made the first delivery last week. With only a few exceptions, they had delivered nothing, hoping to get a considerable reduction in their quotas thanks to the intervention of the Corporation. But the newly-named chief of the Supply Agency in Francheville favoured more severe methods than his predecessor. That day, Brandouille had brought notices to five farmers, informing them that each had three days to pay a heavy fine and to deliver their entire quota under threat of severe sanctions.

Vautier was excusing himself profusely. He was distressed to have disturbed Mr. Longeaud, especially at this hour, but he had decided to make an immediate appeal and did not know how to proceed. It was urgent, and the priest was away.

If Mr. Longeaud had not known that Father Mignart was away, he would have guessed it, after hearing the names of the peasants affected by this new measure. Of the five, four were members of the Legion, and three of the legionnaires were fervent Catholics. The new chief, who did not know the people, their opinions and habits, had just struck out blindly.

"We could lodge a complaint," said Longeaud, scratching his head. "Unfortunately, it may not amount to much."

Vautier paled.

"It's horrible," he groaned. "If I deliver what they demand, we won't even have enough for the winter. What will I feed my pigs? What will I use for seed next spring if they take everything away? The other four are in the same boat as I."

Longeaud assumed a worried expression, although deep down he was delighted. To have the regime beat these rascals at their own game was perfect. He was pleased to see Vautier hanging onto his every word, like a sick person anxiously awaiting the doctor's verdict. Suddenly, he had an idea.

"Well, as long as all five of you are in the same predicament," he said, "you'll have to act together. In unity there's strength."

"That's what they say," said Vautier. "But how do we do it?"

With measured gestures, Longeaud lit a cigarette as he observed the peasant's face, where big drops of sweat formed as he alternated between hope and discouragement.

"Maybe there's a way," Longeaud said finally. "Last summer the Supply Agency demanded too many eggs and too much milk from Manvin's inhabitants. Since they didn't deliver the eggs and milk, the Supply Agency did to them what it has done to you – it imposed heavy fines to scare them. Only they met and agreed not to deliver anything until the demands had been revised. The police and tax accountants came to issue summonses, and they discovered that the Agency had demanded eggs from farmers who had no chickens and milk from farmers who had nursing calves. It was quite a scandal. The chief of supplies had problems with the police authorities and was finally forced to revise the demands. You could try it."

Mr. Longeaud's story was true. If it were tried in this case and succeeded, it would provide an excellent occasion to enrage the priest and play a nice trick on the tax authorities.

Vautier's eyes opened wide. "Then we don't have to pay the fine?"

Longeaud made a vague gesture that seemed to say, "Yes, indeed," but he did not press the point.

"I can't give you any advice. It will be too delicate for me in my position. You'll have to decide amongst yourselves. I just told you how others got out of a similar situation. They got together and said, 'Today it's our turn; tomorrow it will be yours.' Now if you don't want to do the same thing, I can always write a letter for you."

This time Vautier understood. He, Philibert Vautier, realized that the best way to avoid paying the fine and to obtain a reduction in his quota was for him to bring the others together. He would have to explain to them what Mr. Longeaud had made him understand, namely, "Today it's my turn; tomorrow it will be yours."

"The folks from Manvin," continued Longeaud, "got together in the mayor's office. All of them, including the Legion's president, signed a collective protest to be presented to the administration."

"Maybe we could do the same thing," said Vautier, regaining his confidence. "I'm going to see the other four at once and we'll go to all the farms. I'll try to call a meeting in the town hall tomorrow, and the Legion's president should attend. Thank you very much, Mr. Longeaud, for your good advice."

Longeaud protested. "Wait a minute! I didn't advise you. It's your decision. Remember, don't tell anyone you spoke to me about this."

"I understand," said Vautier, with a shrewd smile. "You can count on me." He put his hand into his pocket, pulled out a pack of cigarettes, and put it on the table. "I thought you might like these."

"You're very brave," said Longeaud, accepting the gift as homage to his sagacity.

When Vautier left, Longeaud rubbed his hands together and congratulated himself. Was it not a stroke of genius to put Vautier in the forefront of such an enterprise? A peasant to the Left of even a Protestant, would have no chance of succeeding. But Vautier...

The schoolteacher felt that he was the very soul of Machiavelli. By acting prudently behind the scenes, it was he who pulled the political strings in Saint-Boniface, and, who knows, even in the county. Things could go far. Every revolution had its origin in the history of potatoes. Mr. Longeaud was forty years old, just the age when statesmen begin their careers. This was real action, not the sterile study of English and literature.

He noticed that it was time to return to his class. He had missed the broadcast from London. Too bad! If he had not been listening, at least he was still at his post.

*****

News that a meeting would take place in the town hall the next day spread throughout the community, even to the most remote farms. Vautier and his companions in misfortune ran around the countryside, arguing with the farmers while they sipped the proffered glass of thin sour wine or a bitter country one. Wherever Vautier went, he repeated, "In unity there's strength! Today it's my turn; tomorrow it will be yours!" The indignant peasants approved.

Toward the end of the afternoon, when Verès was nearing the crossroad to Barbarie and the village to pick up the milk, he found three farmers engaged in a heated discussion. The peasants rarely wasted time arguing in the middle of the day, especially with such passion. Verès already knew about the potato affair, and recognized Ferdinand Blache, the town clerk, in the group and, without any difficulty, understood the subject of the argument.

Ferdinand Blache, who came from Francheville, was being violently taken to task by Jean Nelchet and Lévy Seignos.

"You idiot!" Nelchet screamed at the clerk. "You shouldn't have joined the plot!"

"And since you were dumb enough to be pushed into it, you should have resigned as soon as you noticed what kind of work they gave you," added Seignos.

Excitedly, the clerk tried to defend his point of view. He was an old socialist who had been recruited for an office in the local section of the Corporation where, solidly flanked by the secretary, Father Mignart, and his cronies, he was soon reduced to impotence.

"Resign?" he groaned. "That would have helped a lot!"

"And how does that help us if you stay in office?" retorted Nelchet. "Both you and the priest drew up the list of quotas. You've stuck me with a delivery of one thousand, two hundred kilos of potatoes when you know I haven't any."

"That's right," protested the clerk. "Do you think I can deliver the quota they set all by myself? There was another way. They assigned so much for the entire community. All I had to do was to divide it in an equitable fashion. The amounts are proportional and just. If I'd let the priest and his gang have their way a few big shots would give less and the small fry would give much more. As for you, you'd have had to deliver two thousand kilos. The choice was simple: either I'd please the priest's friends or I'd remain at my post to save all that I could. I chose the lesser evil."

"That was clever!" said Seignos.

"The community has no other recourse than to protest and ask for a revision," replied Blache. "I agree with that wholeheartedly. Meanwhile, I've got a formal promise that we'll get the quantity of seed potatoes we asked for. Were you in my place, I wonder how much better you'd have handled it."

Noticing Verès pacing up and down some twenty metres away, Blache used him as a diversion.

"Hey, Mr. Verès!" he called. "I've put you on the list for seeds. They'll give you fifty kilos for your garden."

"Thank you. Mr. Blache," Verès called, as he approached the group. "You're very kind. Is it true there'll be a meeting in the town hall on the subject of potatoes?"

"Oh yes, at nine o'clock in the morning," said Nelchet.

"So then, are all of you going to defend Mr. Vautier? He's very annoyed."

"Vautier isn't the question," said the clerk. "He's made enough money on the black market to pay a fine. He's right when he says, 'Today it's my turn; tomorrow it will be yours'. Everyone will defend himself."

"*Hodie mihi...*" began Verès, but, remembering Bloch's advice, he bit his lips.

"In fact," said the clerk, "now that you're a member of the Corporation, you may come to the meeting if you wish."

Blache could not imagine how happy this invitation made Verès feel. The natives would finally let him in on their secrets! This reminded him of his duties as a journalist. What an original article he could write on such a subject!

The clerk, taking advantage of the interruption, ended the discussion and left, leaving Verès with the other two.

"So," said Seignos, with a smile, "are you going to do some farming?"

Verès had never met Serre's owner before, but the man with the beige linen hat seemed sympathetic. He had a frank smile and a direct look.

"Not precisely," replied the journalist. "My ambitions don't go that far. A little gardening, and that's all. You see, after this war is over, should anyone ask me what I did during that time, I'd like to reply, 'I subsisted'. Once upon a time a great politician said that, after he survived an agitated period like ours."

"Ah yes, Sieyès," said Seignos.

"You know Father Sieyès?" asked Verès, his eyes opening wide.

"Of course," said Seignos, pulling on his pipe. "The fellow said, 'What is the Third Estate? Everything'."

The journalist stood open-mouthed. He did not know that Seignos's hobby was reading about the French Revolution, even to the point of fanaticism. Serre's owner kept a dozen books devoted to this era in his

239

house and had read them so often that he knew them by heart.

Long after he left the peasants, Verès continued to shake his head. "Those peasants are something! Some cannot pronounce electricity and others can cite Sieyès. It's a hard thing to understand." Verès could not get over it.

VI

After having triumphed over the Girondist[52] opposition, the mountain of Saint-Boniface gives birth to a mouse

Around nine o'clock the next morning, Verès left his chalet to go to the town hall. Passing in front of Chirolles's farm, where he sometimes went to listen to the radio, he noticed the owner's wife.

"Anything new?" asked the journalist, as usual.

"You know the news," said Mother Chirolles. "All the men are in the town hall discussing the potato quotas. My husband is there as well. He should have prepared his onion sets for next year, but he left everything. As it is, he's waited too long. They should have been taken care of more than a month ago, but with all the chestnuts, you understand."

"Was there any interesting news on the radio?" interrupted Verès.

"It's always the same," said the peasant woman. "Some advance; others retreat. There's almost no battle in Algeria anymore it seems. And the Germans are everywhere."

"What do you mean 'everywhere'? asked Verès, worried.

"Well, in Vichy, Lyons, Marseilles, everywhere. They've occupied the Free Zone."

Tibor Verès was shaken. This was some news! The war was entering a new phase. And not only the war...

"This won't settle our potato problem," said Mother Chirolles. "We have to pay a three thousand franc fine. What a disaster!"

Verès, very upset about what he had just learned, left her. Mother Chirolles was ridiculous. To think only of her potatoes and seedlings at such a moment! After a little reflection, he said to himself, "In one sense she's right. No matter how grave the general situation is, one must take care of his onions, and the same goes for the potatoes."

---

52 Girondist: ruling party of moderate French republicans in 1792, overthrown in 1793. Many of its leaders came from Gironde département. (HRG)

When he arrived at Saint-Boniface's town hall, the meeting had not started. The big room was crowded. Some peasants sat on benches and chairs. Others leaned against a wall covered with administrative announcements. "There certainly is a quorum," thought Tibor who, once upon a time, had covered many sessions in the Palais Bourbon[53]. Behind a table that served as a desk at the end of the hall, he noticed Longeaud flanked by three municipal councilmen. Next to them were some empty seats. The entrance of the former journalist went unnoticed. Only Nelchet saw him enter and, with a friendly gesture, signalled him to take a seat next to him.

Suddenly, a door opened behind Longeaud's table. The mayor, accompanied by the priest and two municipal councilmen, entered and took their seats amid the general confusion.

"The government," said Verès, wittily, as he inclined his head toward his neighbour.

Then the clerk came in. A murmur of disapproval greeted him, and even some boos. The question of potatoes seemed to have seriously shaken the popularity of the minister of agriculture.

The mayor, a tense, intelligent-looking fifty-year-old peasant who never became involved in the arguments of his administrators, invited Vautier to explain his point of view.

The owner of the Grange did not wait to be begged. He immediately began talking at length in patois. Verès grimaced; he understood nothing. He could not help noticing that, while Vautier sometimes had trouble speaking French, he talked easily in patois, and everyone listened to him. He embellished his statement with some French words and ended it quite competently with two sentences in French: "In unity there's strength! Today it's my turn; tomorrow it will be yours!"

A murmur of approval greeted his words. Longeaud appeared indifferent, but inwardly he was jubilant.

The president of the local section of the Legion, Ferdinand Gideaux, took the floor. A strong, square-shouldered man with the shaggy, pendulous moustache worn by the warriors of old Gaul, Gideaux was an eloquent public speaker. As he spoke, he turned to the priest who, after having listened impatiently to Vautier, approved of this speaker.

"The situation that Vautier described to you is certainly unfortunate," began Gideaux. "The potato quotas are too high. Even I have difficulty delivering the first part, and I'm ready to deliver the rest. The times are past when one could dispute the orders of the authorities. Our duty is

---

53 Palais Bourbon: where the Chamber of Deputies, France's legislative body, meets in Paris. (HRG)

to show that we're ready and worthy of the confidence that the leaders of the country accord us.

"What is the problem? They ask us for potatoes for the hungry population in the cities. Some of us would prefer to keep the potatoes to feed their pigs. I can understand that. It's hard to raise animals today. However, to understand does not mean to approve. Thinking it over, here's how the problem appears: to feed the pigs or to feed the unfortunate children. Who is the Frenchman who can hesitate when faced with such a choice? As for our pigs, we will feed them peelings and chestnuts."

"You could add bran. You've enough of it," shouted Nelchet. "But that isn't so for everyone."

This interruption provoked general hilarity. However, without referring to this personal allusion, the speaker continued.

"It would be foolhardy to stand up against the administration before whom we're helpless. What will we do if, as a counter-measure, they refuse to distribute our ration cards, especially the ones for bread? Or if they should requisition our animals? As for the potatoes, in a few months we will be very content to receive seedlings at the regulated price. Let us deliver the required amounts; it will be a loan to be repaid. Let us do our duty. We've been vanquished; everyone must make sacrifices."

Several peasants grouped around Gideaux approved unenthusiastically. However, the majority of the audience kept a glacial silence. In Nelchet's corner there were even protests. The mayor finally had to raise his hand to establish order. Verès noticed that, like all meetings, the peasants of Saint-Boniface had their Right and Left. It seemed to him to be a natural law.

It was Blache himself who pointed out the contradiction. He spoke in patois, and Verès could only follow his speech through Nelchet's résumé. In essence he said:

"It wasn't a question of a choice between pigs and children in the cities. The cities have potatoes this year since the harvest was generally good, especially in the north, but the region around Francheville, in particular, was at a disadvantage.

"The potato quotas are unfair, and we ask for justice. We have few resources! It would be foolish to squander them. We ought to address a protest to the administration explaining the situation and ask for another survey. They may come to inspect our cellars; we have nothing to hide!"

Tournier, the grocer, was restless on his bench. This last suggestion did not seem to please him.

In conclusion, the clerk read a draft of a collective protest that he had drawn up ahead of time with Longeaud and asked that, after voting, all present sign it.

Blache spoke so forcefully that he dissipated all the doubt that had greeted him at first, and was applauded. With a beaming face, Longeaud followed the audience's reaction. The priest was worried, the president of the Legion was so angry that his face was red. Mr. du Chesne, the lord of Rochefontaine, who sat next to Gideaux, shook his head sceptically. This whole affair did not concern him personally for he had fine, well-irrigated lands and could, without any trouble, satisfy the authorities' demands. He would not have bothered to come to the meeting if it had not been for the priest's special invitation.

The success of Blache's plan seemed assured when Lévy Seignos raised his hand to ask for silence. Drowning the murmurs with his harsh voice, he began to speak at first in patois, then, after saying one sentence in French, he continued in French.

"It's to act that we've come here and not to sign some letter. Send a letter of protest to the administration? That's fine! But does the trouble originate with the local administration? Not at all! It comes from Francheville, from the chief of the Supply Agency. This gentleman wanted to show his zeal, to earn a promotion. He doesn't give a damn about us because he thinks anything is permitted. Well, we must show him he's mistaken. We're not asses. (A storm of applause greeted his words.) Let's not be afraid to raise our voices. It's the only thing these gentlemen understand. It's too bad for the chief of the Supply Agency in Francheville if this should cause him to be vexed."

"Get it out! What do you want?" shouted old Crouzet, violent as always. He was one of the five hit with a fine and, for this reason, was more irascible than ever.

"Well, here it is. Tomorrow's market day in Francheville. We'll all go there at the same time with our carts. We'll block all the roads, tying up traffic. Then we'll all go in a group to the chief of the Supply Agency to demand the immediate cancellation of all the fines and a reduction of the quotas. If he objects too much, we'll step on his toes. He's mocked us enough by sending us those papers, and it will be our turn to laugh."

The enthusiasm was widespread. This Seignos! No one else knew how to play a trick on those who put obstacles in his path. Go down with the carts, block all the streets, stop traffic! What a fine idea! That gentleman would get jaundice.

The temperature in the room was mounting. "The Hour of the Mountain," said Verès to himself. These Girondists, the schoolteacher and the clerk – repairing the injustices within the legal framework – already seemed overthrown.

When the hubbub had quietened a little, Mr. du Chesne turned to Seignos and said ironically, "Oh yes, gentlemen, go down in your carts. Why not? But while you're at it, why not make it somewhat unusual?"

The crowd was somewhat restless, but Mr. du Chesne continued.

"I suggest the procession be preceded by schoolchildren waving rattles. We'll lead our cows, decorated with chrysanthemum wreaths, to the flourish of Salvation Army trumpets. This should be effective. Finally, why not hoist a bull on the roof of the town hall and make him come down in a parachute? We shouldn't do things halfway."

Mr. du Chesne's cold irony, tainted by his past surrealist inclinations, failed to cover his irritation. Although he was an atheist, he entirely shared the opinion of the priest who was listening to everything he said with an indulgent smile. On certain questions, the castle and the altar were in accord.

Seignos stood up.

"That's a carnival, Mr. du Chesne," he said. "We want to make our demands known. This won't be the first demonstration in this region. There were times when things even got out of hand. You ought to know, since from your window you can see the ruins of Beauregard Castle which the peasants burned during the Revolution. They said that the lords wanted to mock the peasants."

"Is this a threat?" asked du Chesne, stung to the quick.

"I would never dare," replied Seignos. "It's just a little reminder from history."

Father Mignart was very annoyed and tried to re-establish order. It seemed that he only had to be away for twenty-four hours for the people to become embroiled in such a mad scheme. If only he could have spoken with Vautier yesterday, nothing would have happened. One could never watch his flock enough.

"Be calm my friends," he said. "Let's reason a bit. Do you think the gendarmes will let you do that? Surely Mr. Seignos didn't mean it seriously! Everyone knows he has a sense of humour. Let's laugh at that, but let us not forget our duty. Vanity is a bad advisor. It's not with an insurrection against the powers that you can expect to alleviate the burden that is crushing you. It has been said, 'Render unto Caesar what is Caesar's.' You must give the authorities what is theirs. Pay your fines, deliver the first shipment of potatoes even if it is too burdensome, and then respectfully ask for a revision of all your quotas. This is the right way, believe me."

In the middle of this tumult, Nelchet raised his powerful voice.

"'Render unto Caesar what is Caesar's,' eh, Mr. Priest? That's what we learned in catechism. Well, we must give the chief of the Supply Agency what is due him, and that is a good kick in the ass. Not only won't we deliver our potatoes, but we'll suspend the delivery of all other products: milk, cheese, and all the rest. What do we have to fear? Francheville has only five policemen. We'll be one hundred and fifty without counting the cows."

"We'll go down with our pitchforks!" yelled Crouzet.

"Our numbers will be greater," continued Nelchet. "Peasants in other villages in the county are in the same situation as we. They, too, have fines to pay. So much the better! The greater our numbers the less vulnerable we'll be. Therefore, I propose that we alert the other communities. As Vautier says, 'In unity there's strength!' Tomorrow we'll go to Francheville with our carts. The entire county will march with us."

When Nelchet had finished, everyone in the room was stamping his feet.

"He's the leader," said Verès to himself, as he looked at his neighbour admiringly. The opposition had been swept aside. The priest raised his arms to heaven. Ferdinand Gideaux's face turned purple. Longeaud and the clerk exchanged signs of distress. The movement that they had initiated now took over completely. The schoolmaster seemed to be sitting on a fire. A huge peasant demonstration that had planned incidents! It might develop into political unrest again. After a while, Vautier became imprudent and told about his conversation with the schoolmaster; thus Longeaud was made the principal agitator. He mopped his brow. After exchanging a few words with the priest, Longeaud left his place on the platform, went into the arena, plunged into the unruly crowd in the room, and tried to reason with the high-spirited group.

Verès, who had noticed this turn of events, thought that it was only proper, as in all revolutions, that the early leaders be replaced by new ones. These, once the violence was released, were incapable of stopping events and most often ended up by being overthrown in their turn. Saturn devours his own children, a truism of history.

No one listened to the schoolteacher's objections. One had ears and eyes only for the promoters of direct action: Nelchet and Seignos. With much difficulty, they managed to calm old Crouzet who, completely enraged, proposed that they descend on Francheville at once with carts, pitchforks, and scythes. "You must strike while the iron is hot," he repeated, obstinately. Finally, after a short discussion, the Nelchet-Seignos plan was unanimously adopted with only a few abstentions. Crouzet's amendment was rejected by the great majority. "In unity there's strength!" screamed Vautier who, believing that he was the hero of the day, had let his success go to his head. All of them, flushed with emotion, appeared intoxicated. The spirit of the Jacquerie[54] dominated the hall.

*****

The revolution did not take place. Early in the afternoon, Father Mignart went looking for Vautier and talked with him for a long time. A father of seven children and a good Catholic to top it off, how could he commit such foolishness? The retaliation would be terrible: his house and herds would be sold; he would go to prison; what's more, he would endanger the salvation of his soul. The sin of pride, the spirit of revolt to which was added the evil advice of an infidel, could only furnish a very poor excuse. Fortunately, it was not too late; Vautier could repent and atone. In this case, and only in this case, Father Mignart would personally intervene when his case was reviewed.

Saint-Boniface's priest rarely spoke in vain. Contrite and repentant, Vautier hastened to lay all the responsibility on Mr. Longeaud. The priest had a shrewd smile, for he already knew what to think, and hastily left for Francheville to cancel Vautier's fine. Three highly esteemed farmers, who had been slapped with fines and had been lectured in turn by Father Mignart, had followed suit. The only one who remained recalcitrant was old Crouzet. But one swallow, even if armed with a pitchfork, cannot bring spring.

News of a break in the united front spread quickly throughout the community. The next morning, most of the carts going to Francheville's market carried potatoes for the Supply Agency.

The mountain of Saint-Boniface had given birth to a mouse.

VII

The potato cycle closes again

Mrs. Hermelin stopped, pulled a man's handkerchief from her purse, cleaned her pince-nez, and blew her nose vigorously.

It was the 15th of November and on the cracked face of the sundial on Rochefontaine Castle the hand showed three o'clock in the afternoon, but all the other clocks in the community read five o'clock.

---

54 Jacquerie: a peasant uprising against the nobles in 1357. (HRG)

Tilleuls's owner was coming from Delphine Legras's home after having spent the afternoon visiting the principal farms in Saint-Boniface. Once again it was a question of potatoes, however, this time Mrs. Hermelin was not looking to buy, but to sell. She had found herself the owner of sixteen sacks of potatoes taken from Frank Rosenfeld's fields. She had inherited the crop without a proper will because, since his arrest on his wedding night, Rosenfeld had never sent any word to her. His wife, in spite of her promise, had not written to Mrs. Hermelin either. When she left so suddenly after the mysterious stranger's visit, her rent had been paid until the end of the month, but Tilleuls's owner considered that she was entitled to at least three month's notice.

She wondered what had happened to Mr. Rosenfeld. He was a bit hot-headed, but he was not a bad fellow. His not getting a cow had dashed all of Mrs. Hermelin's hopes. As for the cabinets he had not built, he was not entirely beyond reproach. Mrs. Hermelin hoped, however, that nothing had happened to him. Perhaps he had been sent back to his country of origin as Joseph had told her. Mrs. Hermelin prayed to God to protect him despite his being a little slow to convert. Like a good Christian, she wished him well, but if he were to suddenly return to Saint-Boniface she would have been very annoyed because of the chickens and rabbits he left, and even more so because of the potatoes. He had planted too many and his harvest was not too bad in spite of the drought. Once the potatoes were sold or bartered, Mr. Rosenfeld would have no good reason to reclaim his harvest, especially since the official price was cheap compared to a few extras he owed her and to which she had to add the cost of harvesting them.

In short, Tilleuls's owner had definitely decided to get rid of sixteen sacks of potatoes, but it was not easy to bargain with Saint-Boniface's farmers. When she went to Noémi, that poor woman thought that Mrs. Hermelin wanted to give her a charitable gift. With Vautier, it was impossible to know if it was a yes or no. He could have made her wait for weeks. Seignos was ready to buy the entire harvest, but at the official price, while Mrs. Hermelin wanted to receive a supplement of lard and sausages. From Delphine she would have liked regular deliveries of milk and butter, but her butter was already promised to her daughter in Saint-Etienne for several months ahead.

By the time Mrs. Hermelin had left the road to Barbarie and was on the main road, she had resolved that tomorrow morning she would go to Francheville and make an offer to Sarzier, even though she found it repugnant to deal with this anti-Christ with the red mane, but life had its demands. On the same occasion, she would go to the White Cross Pharmacy to finally buy a bottle of Jouvence de l'abbé Soury.

Suddenly she stopped, frowned, and looked around. She was about to crouch when, rounding the turn in the road, she saw a tall man pushing a wheelbarrow. It was Verès followed by Zette and his wife pushing a baby carriage. In the wheelbarrow were several valises with an easel and a Norwegian pot on top.

"Oh, Mr. Verès, are you moving?" she asked intrigued.

Verès stopped and dried his forehead.

"How do you do, madam?" he said, bowing ceremoniously. "Yes, we're moving. We're going to live at Ripailles, Mr. Bloch's old house."

"Will you be better off there?" asked Mrs. Hermelin.

"Certainly, although we'll be a little farther from town and especially the post office," said the journalist. "Anyway, Mr. Vautier is anxious to repossess the chalet."

Vautier, having discovered that the Verès family was getting poorer and poorer, showed less and less interest in them. Then again, the quarrel with Bardette had cost Vautier the expenses of an expert which amounted to almost one year's rent for the chalet. He blamed it on his tenant. After taking everything into consideration, he had finally determined that he would be better off to use the chalet to house the male goat that he had raised during the summer. In this way, the shed would revert to its original use. With the general rise in prices, he would ask ten francs to mate each female goat. What was even more interesting, he could add a second story to the shed where he would install a hand mill that he had just bought and could grind his own wheat secretly. He could even grind his neighbours' wheat. In exchange for this service, he would keep part of the flour and all of the bran. Since both mills in Francheville were very strictly controlled, he had no doubt that he would find many customers. Thanks to this combination, he could feed two pigs without having to pay for feed, and at the price of lard...

"At Ripailles," said Verès, "we'll be close to the forest and can pick up all the dead wood quite easily. In winter, this represents an appreciable economy. And Mr. du Chesne is a very polite and wise gentleman. I've decided that, from now on, I'll do some gardening. It's easy and provides so much satisfaction. It will amount to my walking in Candide's footsteps."

"On the condition that they'll let you," said Ellen, discouraged. "I'm afraid you're too optimistic again."

"One day I'll visit you in your garden," said Mrs. Hermelin, with a smirk. "I must leave now. I'm already late."

She continued on her walk, her bunch of keys jangling at her side. Suddenly she heard a motorcycle approaching, and the electric company's new metre reader whizzed by. He wore a leather jacket, a detail that allowed her to identify him.

The motorcyclist disappeared in the distance and Mrs. Hermelin glanced all around. No one was to be seen on the horizon. A hundred paces from her, the road turned, but she was sure that she had time!

She was beginning to pull up her clothes when the underbrush in the ditch snapped. She jumped. An instant later, Mr. Longeaud, his hair disheveled, cheeks scratched by the branches, and clothes half-drenched, emerged from the ditch.

After looking around uneasily, he pointed to the disappearing motorcyclist and asked in a hoarse voice, "Who was that?"

He was so upset that he forgot to greet the wife of the former tax collector.

"The new man who reads the electric metres. Don't you know him?"

"Ah, good! Then it wasn't him" said the teacher, relieved but somewhat ashamed of his fear.

While he was lecturing his class on the dangers of alcoholism, he had heard the noise of the approaching motorcycle. Glancing through the window, he had noticed a man in a leather jacket. This attire was very unusual in Francheville. Who could it be but the special police inspector from Vichy? No doubt he was coming to arrest him. This would be his punishment for his involvement in the potato affair!

In the middle of a sentence and in front of his bewildered pupils, he had immediately jumped through the window that opened onto the garden, then ran into the bushes as if he were being chased by the devil and rolled down the embankment into the ditch.

When he stopped rolling, he felt a bit out of breath. Soon the noise of the motorcycle made him think that the danger was not over. The man, not finding him in school, was probably pursuing him down the road. That was why he was still hiding in the ditch hoping to escape from him.

Mr. Longeaud had never seen this new employee of the Vercors Company before.

"Well," he said, changing the subject, "now that it's several months later, are you still looking for potatoes for your boardinghouse?"

"Oh no," said Mrs. Hermelin. "There are no boarders in my house anymore. The last one left some fifteen days ago, and I'm glad. I tried so hard, and what ingratitude I reaped!"

"Surely you weren't displeased with your boarders, like Mr. Fleury?"

"Oh, I beg you, I don't want to hear his name. I prefer to deal with Jews. They're not as bad as people say. One thing I can't understand is that they're never quite settled. This is so curious! In the end, all's well that ends well. Now each is in his new home and it will be better for everyone. There's only one foreigner left in Saint-Boniface and that's poor Mr. Verès who will live close to Mr. du Chesne. It's somewhat far from here, and we won't see him very often. We can finally say we're amongst our own!"

In the distance, the sound of motors could be heard coming from Francheville. The noise intensified rapidly. A few minutes later, two open trucks full of German soldiers rushed by Mrs. Hermelin and the schoolteacher.

They were racing full speed toward Saint-Boniface's town hall.

THE END

Translator's Note

Dear Reader,

As I worked on the translation, it became apparent to me that the names of the characters provided a clue to their attributes and added to the humour in the story. For those who know little or no French, I have prepared this list.

Name	Derivation	Translation
Auzance	aux; ancre	to fix firmly
Barbarie	barbare	barbaric, rude, savage
Bardette	barder	things are going to get hot
Baudrier	baudre	piece of skin
Blanche	blanche	white
Boniface	----------	a pope, a saint, an innkeeper
Brandouille	bran; douille	bran, excrement; socket, hose, pipe
Buttes	butte	mound, hillock
Cadet	cadet	second son
Chameix	chameau	camel
Chazelas	la chasse	the chase
Delphine	delphi	oracle
Dolores	dolor (Sp)	sad
Félicie	félicité	happiness, bliss
Fleuri	fleuri	flowery
Forgeron	forger	to forge, contrive, make up
Fricou	frocpter	to get a good thing illicitly
Grandjean	grand; jean	large, big; jeans
Grange	grange	farm
Hermelin	hermine	ermine (a weasel whose winter coat is white)
Jeroboam	Biblical name	may he increase
Laffont	la font the;	fount, font, fountain

Name	Derivation	Translation
Landru	Landri	an assassinated mayor of Neustrie
Leborgne	le borgne	the; one-eyed
Longeaud	longer	to go, to walk along
Martin	martien	martyr
Mignart	mignard	sweet, cute, mincing, two-faced
Mottes	motte	lump, clod of earth
Murger	mur	wall, mature
Paroli	parole	word
Pilon	pilon	pestle
Pinkas	Biblical name	zealot
Prosper	prospère	prosperity
Rimbeaud	--------------	an action type character
Ripailles	ripaille	picnic, feast, a chateau where the Duke of Savoy retired after he abdicated
Sarzier	sarcier	to weed
Seignos	seigneur	lord
Serre	serre	greenhouse
Solange	lange	nappy
Sten	steno	stenographer
Tilleuls	tilleul	linden tree, lime tree
Tournier	turner	to turn
Vautier	vautour	vulture
Verès	ver	worm
Vergnon	vergogne	shamelessly